"Evans and Jameson follow their bestselling debut with an ecothriller with an even more imaginative premise. Readers will race right along with the novel's good guys as they feverishly strive to save the world."

—*Publishers Weekly* on *Frozen Fire*

"All the women are beautiful and sexy, while all the men are handsome and hard-bodied. But the science makes sense, the gore factor is off the chart, and the villains are high-end despicable, so count on this one for a no-calorie summer snack—perfect for lazing on the beach or passing time in the airport."

—*Booklist* on *Frozen Fire*

Praise for the *New York Times* bestseller
Category 7

"A great read!"

—Sam Champion,
Good Morning America weather anchor
and ABC News weather editor

"A superb thriller of a disaster untold until now. Suspenseful and shocking."

—Clive Cussler,
New York Times bestselling author

"A fast-paced action-adventure that promises a rousing finale and delivers it."

—*Booklist*

**BOOKS BY
BILL EVANS AND MARIANNA JAMESON
FROM TOM DOHERTY ASSOCIATES**

Category 7

Frozen Fire

FROZEN FIRE

BILL EVANS

AND

MARIANNA JAMESON

TOR®

A TOM DOHERTY ASSOCIATES BOOK
NEW YORK

This is a work of fiction. All of the characters, organizations, and events portrayed in this novel are either products of the authors' imaginations or are used fictitiously.

FROZEN FIRE

Copyright © 2009 by William H. Evans and Marianna Jameson

A Tor Book
Published by Tom Doherty Associates, LLC
175 Fifth Avenue
New York, NY 10010

www.tor-forge.com

Tor® is a registered trademark of Tom Doherty Associates, LLC.

ISBN 978-0-7653-5974-2

First Edition: June 2009
First Mass Market Edition: August 2010

Printed in the United States of America

0 9 8 7 6 5 4 3 2 1

We met on a blind date on Halloween. She didn't own a television, so she had no idea who I was or what I did for a living. We stayed out all night on that first date, and I walked her home to the Lower East Side. She called me the next day and said, "Let's go for a walk, I know a great Thai restaurant in the Village." She called again the day after that. "What are you doing?"

"Nothing," I said.

"Let's go for a walk and get some ice cream."

"Okay," I said. This went on for months. Nice long walks and lots of talking. She wasn't pushy. She certainly wasn't a stalker, and she definitely wasn't desperate. She's smart and beautiful. So what in the world did she see in me?

I believe that God has a way of putting people in your life for a reason.

On that blind date I mentioned I would love to have four children. Years later when she was pregnant with our third child she said, "I know you wanted four, but this is the worst-feeling pregnancy ever, so maybe you should pray that number three is twins."

Not long after that, I was driving home on I-95 when the phone rang.

"Hello?"

"I'm at the doctor's office, and I have only one word for you . . . *twins*!"

Indeed she was pregnant with twins. I am so grateful to her because she gave up her Wall Street career to raise our four kids.

She's the ultimate in tough love. Sometimes she can push all my buttons in one easy stroke. But at the same time, she is the greatest companion. That's how you know there is divine intervention. I couldn't make it without her.

So what does she see in me? I'm not great looking, and I don't have lots of money, but I make her laugh, and that's what she loves about me.

When I wrote *Category 7* with Marianna Jameson, I said to my wife, "Maybe I could speak to your book club." She said, "Honey, they read *literature*." I love her sense of humor. We both love to laugh, and we share the same sense of acerbic, or what might be described as sick, humor. That's our biggest bond, along with our four beautiful children.

Dana, thanks for your love and support all these years. God put us together so you can enjoy this great work of literature.

—BILL H. EVANS

ACKNOWLEDGMENTS

Holy Mother of Research! It all started with a little line in one of Clive Cussler's books about this gas in an ice form called "methane hydrate." I was intrigued, and once I started researching, it took just minutes to realize that with the astronomical cost of oil and gasoline, this could be an alternative fuel of tremendous interest.

My findings were tremendous. Until I scoured the U.S. Department of Energy's Web site, I had no idea that millions of dollars had been poured into research on methane hydrate and that for years countries like Russia had been mining the stuff in the permafrost of Siberia. Methane hydrate is the world's largest fossil fuel, eclipsing oil and natural gas by trillions of metric tons. You can heat your home with it, use it to propel your car, cook your dinner, fuel industry, and it burns completely cleanly without harming the environment. Wow! What a find!

You can find methane hydrate just about anywhere below the ocean floor and in the Alaskan and Siberian permafrost, but only minuscule amounts are readily available or have been mined. Mining methane hydrate is very tricky and expensive, plus there is one big inherent danger. Released in its natural state, methane hydrate is a greenhouse gas multiplier by a force of ten!

I got a tremendous amount of help from many people, but there are three folks in particular whom I would like to thank. First, Professor David Archer, who is a computational ocean chemist in the Geophysics Department at the University of Chicago. He was a fantastic resource on methane hydrate as well as global warming. He has written *Global Warming: Understanding the Forecast,* which is a great book on how global warming works. David also turned me on to John Barnes's wonderful science fiction thriller, *Mother of Storms,* which is about a giant methane release that's hell-bent on destroying the Earth. *Mother of Storms* is also published by Tor/Forge, which obviously has a great affinity for projects such as these!

My third resource came in the form of the sweetest, kindest, and most brilliant person when it comes to geophysics. Dr. Arnold Stancell has spent his career in the oil and gas business. He is currently a professor of geophysics at Georgia Tech University. He helped me to understand how methane hydrate would have to be mined, the danger, and the costs. As an alternative fuel, methane hydrate's potential is unlimited, but getting it is very tricky and it could pose a tremendous danger to the planet if disturbed on a grand scale.

Words cannot express my thanks to the wonderful people at Tor/Forge for their confidence and vision in my work. I cannot understand why they have such confidence in me, but they obviously see something I don't and I really appreciate it! I want to thank Tom Doherty for taking me on as a rookie with *Category 7* and giving me another great opportunity with this book. He had the guts to introduce me to the big leagues with such backing that it would be impossible to fail. I owe a big thank-you to Linda Quinton for her undying support and trust. The two have been so supportive that it makes me want to go to the ends of the Earth to sign and sell books. To the greatest editor in the world, Melissa Ann Singer, I owe you more than I could ever repay. You are such a talented editor who knows how to tell a story. Your editing on this work was phenomenal. You have quite a gift. Thank you for sharing your gift of writing with me. I have learned so much from you.

Finally, I want to thank my coauthor, Marianna Jameson. You have done such a great job on this work! You are a great partner and a great writer. The sky is not the limit for you! Thank you for sharing your wonderful talent with me!

—BILL H. EVANS

In the course of writing *Frozen Fire,* I received the help and support of many and would like to thank them now.

First thanks must go to my coauthor, Bill Evans, for his great ideas, unflagging enthusiasm, upbeat outlook, and boundless energy and, of course, for his fascinating contacts in the scientific community. The many talented and wonderful people at Tor/Forge have my deepest thanks for their hard work and immense talent.

Thanks to Scott and Ellen Jones, who were very generous with their time and knowledge and taught me about chemistry and microbiology, respectively. Michael Rowan, CDR, USN, retired, helped immeasurably with everything naval and/or underwater, and did so with much laughter and gusto. (I hope you realize this means you'll be hearing from me again.) My favorite cop, Mike Hutson, was, as always, extremely helpful—this time with his knowledge and insight regarding weaponry and "riding the lightning." My favorite former spook, Joanna Novins, was again invaluable for her willingness to share some insights into the world of capital-I intelligence. Richard Smith provided his usual stellar technical support and expert advice on all matters electronic and/or digital. Thanks, too, to Kappy Revels for letting me see what the world looks like through night-vision goggles. Now I know what to put on my Christmas list.

Despite all the generous help from all of the subject-matter experts mentioned above, I know there will be errors. All mistakes are my own.

A little closer to home, I have to thank my usual peeps: my writing posse, Jody Novins, Karen Kendall, Deirdre Martin, Alisa Kwitney, and Liz Maverick, who are always available for a daily dilemma or odd question, and whose biting wit and infinite wisdom make writing a much less solitary, much less serious endeavor. Deb Dufel, Thea Devine, Sharon Sobel, Jenna Kernan, and Mary Beth Bass, writers all, who unquestioningly share with me whatever they have and whatever I need. Nancy Mitchell and Carol Smith, who pick up the pieces and always have and hopefully always will. New members of the crew deserve a mention for their much-appreciated support: Debbie Marsh, Vicki Rowan, Pam Taeckens, and Francene Venesky.

Special thanks to Elaine English for her expertise and assistance. Most especially, this book would not be what it is without the talent, insight, and deeply appreciated patience of Melissa Ann Singer, editor extraordinaire and all-around fabulous woman. Thank you times a million.

Last on the list but first in my heart are my husband and children, for whom I am very, very, very thankful.

—MARIANNA JAMESON

FROZEN
FIRE

PROLOGUE

The equally high-risk parallels of probable success and possible failure sent twin feeds of adrenaline streaming into Micki Crenshaw's veins as she watched her shadow gradually stretch less and less far across the gently pitching deck of the research ship and submersible tender *Wangari Maathai*. The sun had crept above the horizon and around the low swell of Taino's lone volcanic peak. That small tip of light was gilding the waters of the eastern Caribbean and expanding the roseate glow that hung low in the sky. The soft hum of the engine throbbed beneath her feet. The slap of small waves against the hull and the screams of the seabirds overhead broke the early subtropical stillness. The flag identifying the ship as part of the fleet of The Paradise of Taino—her home and her target—flapped randomly in the cool, quiet air.

It was a beautiful morning in paradise.

A morning more beautiful than this paradise deserves.

Micki glanced over her shoulder at the ship's captain, who she knew was only pretending to be absorbed by the contents of the clipboard in his hands. He was young, handsome, ex–Royal Navy, and nobody's fool, and he'd been gently flirting with her for the last few weeks. There was little else to do on such a small island and, although the difference in their rank made it a bad idea, she'd allowed it. Actually, Micki had encouraged it. She'd never had any qualms about using anything in her repertoire if it would help the cause. And being on Captain Simon Broadhurst's good side, and having him think he was on hers, could help.

"Captain Broadhurst, the sun is up. Can we get under way?" she asked quietly, even though there wasn't a crew member within earshot.

"*I'm English, Micki. The proprieties must be observed,*" he'd said earlier, giving her that smile. She'd wanted to roll her eyes but had stopped herself.

"In a few more minutes. I'm still reviewing your dive plan."

She turned to face him full on with a mildly amused expression on her face and one slim eyebrow cocked. Deploying her silkiest Alabama drawl, she answered him. "I know it's unorthodox, Captain. But, as we've discussed, that unorthodoxy is necessary. Vital."

"You ought to have briefed me *before* we left port," he replied.

Tradition and the law of the sea gave him absolute authority on his ship. However, both Micki and the captain knew that, as the second in command of Taino's security forces, she outranked him on land, and that's what she was leveraging out here in the soft predawn light. And that's why the censure in his tone was more mild than it would have been had she been anyone else.

"Your dive plan flouts protocol, and may thereby endanger yourself and my crew," he continued in his starchiest, high-street voice. "You're not to dive alone without tracking capabilities. I shouldn't allow it."

Micki looked down and made her lips twitch as though they were concealing laughter, then looked him in the eyes as she let loose a smile that left him a bit dazzled, as intended.

"But you will allow it, Captain, despite its unorthodoxy, won't you?" she said softly. "This is a high-priority mission and one that will be over quickly. I've tried to make it clear that we have to place this equipment this morning."

Simon let a silent moment slide by, then folded his arms across his broad, uniformed chest, all the while maintaining eye contact. "I'm not certain you understand the risks, Ms. Crenshaw. They're substantial."

"Oh, I understand them, Captain. I also understand, to a degree that you can't, that the risk faced by *not* executing this mission is one that will be felt by everyone connected with Taino. I thought I'd made it clear that the placement and purpose of this equipment is top secret, and that's why I have to do the dive alone and without you tracking my movements." She let her voice fumble, stopping short of overdoing the emotion. "The accountability for undertaking this mission is mine and mine alone, Captain, and I willingly accept that."

"Ms. Crenshaw—"

"Captain Broadhurst—Simon—please don't make me get all official on you," she said, interrupting him with a near-whisper. "Darlin', this little dive of mine is a national security issue and your failure to assist me with it would be a grave violation of the oath you took when you became an officer of the Taino Security Force. As a senior official, I wouldn't be able to overlook something like that." She paused and gave him a sad smile. "You really only have two options, Simon. You can help me execute this mission, or you can refuse to help."

Her quiet words hung in the air, as did the words she didn't have to say. Under Taino's laws, if he didn't help her, she could relieve him of his command and have him secured to his quarters. Then she'd carry out the mission anyway.

Clearly displeased at having his options so neatly delineated, however softly Micki might have done it, the captain gave clipped orders to his crew, his now-cool gaze never leaving Micki's face. She acknowledged his surrender with a nod that held a convincing hint of feminine contrition, but inside triumph reigned. Then she turned her attention to the approaching crew member who would help her into the one-atmosphere diving tube. She was going down. That's all that mattered now.

In one easy movement, she pulled off the wind pants she wore over her swimming suit, then slid the matching anorak over her head. She reveled for a moment in the cool breeze that brushed her bare flesh and pretended not to notice the surreptitious looks Simon and the small, all-male crew were giving her almost-naked body.

A few feet way, the crew was doing their final checkout on the dive tube they'd christened *Flipper*. It was sleek, gray, and highly maneuverable underwater, but that's where the resemblance to everyone's favorite dolphin ended. It was just another useful high-tech toy, as far as Micki was concerned. She'd trained in it, as all the security personnel had trained in this and all the other high-tech dive equipment her commander in chief, Dennis Cavendish, kept acquiring. Despite never having actually used the tube for any purpose other than training, Micki was confident that she could carry out her duty and be topside before anyone could learn that the entire mission was a fabrication.

This dive was an extremely daring act, but it was a necessary part of the plan. It was a heady feeling to know that the years she'd put into gaining her boss's trust and into learning everything there was to know about the nation of Taino—and the reality behind its clever façade—would soon pay off. All the condescension she'd endured at Dennis's hands was a small price to pay to ensure that the money and energy Dennis and his minions had put into achieving his megalomaniacal dream of controlling the world's next-generation energy source would be wasted. The world would be shown once again, vividly, that greed and arrogance led inevitably to incalculable damage to the Earth and all Her inhabitants.

Yes, Dennis, in a few days, you will have changed the world forever. For the worse.

Fully ensconced in the one-person diving tube, Micki mentally counted the clicks and hisses as the crew secured the seals that would keep her separate from the sea and safe from its frigid pressures. As she waited for the dive master to speak to her through the headphones, she kept her eyes trained on the small black boxes she'd carefully secured to the platform at the front of the tiny vessel.

When she'd approached Simon about this unscheduled trip, Micki had told him the twin units were a pair of new, state-of-the-art surveillance devices made by a boutique firm in Switzerland. With a deprecating roll of her eyes, she'd added that they were being deployed as a favor to the company's owner, a business associate of Dennis's. The boxes were beta units and Dennis had agreed to let Taino be their first real-world test bed because he believed the technology held promise and would provide them with useful data if it worked as planned. Micki had added, as offhand as ever, that even she wasn't entirely sure what the devices were meant to do; she had been told only that she was to place them in specific secure locations without her movements being tracked.

Everything she'd said was a lie, of course. The units were highly sophisticated bombs, the brainchild of Garner Blaylock, Earth activist, unsung genius, and Dennis Cavendish's worst nightmare. When activated remotely by Micki, the black boxes would exploit the one vulnerability that Victoria Clark, Taino's white-hat paranoiac secretary of national security and Micki's immediate boss, hadn't taken into account in all of her continual brainstorming about terrorism: sabotage. The kind that could be carried out by an insider, a member of Victoria's trusted, handpicked inner circle. All those endless hours of security audits and exhaustive tabletop exercises would have been for nothing.

Micki couldn't wait to see the look on Victoria's face when she realized it.

Talk about a blind spot.

Working side by side with Victoria for the last few years and overseeing the ubiquitous background checks, covert surveillance, network trolling, and physical searches on the employees, it had become apparent to an incredulous Micki that Victoria hadn't taken any precautions against the most obvious option. She'd never considered that someone she trusted implicitly—and had investigated so thoroughly—could set a bomb and destroy everything Victoria was meant to protect. This ludicrous arrogance was a rather alarming character flaw in Victoria, who prided herself on her emotionless perfectionism. In a moment of supreme and deliberate irony, Micki had even suggested the notion of a mole, an insider with malicious intent.

Victoria had considered it carefully, of course. She considered everything carefully. But then she dismissed insider cooperation as a viable threat. For such a plan to be carried out would require there to be too many gaps in her heavily fortified, overtly redundant security perimeter. Micki had listened in awe as Victoria, one of the most highly respected security experts in the world, told her that—on Taino, on *her* turf—such a threat fell into the category identified by security experts as having extremely high impact but extremely low probability. Micki had even argued with her, pointing out that that was the same category into which the notion of people flying airliners into tall office buildings had once been placed. But Victoria was adamant. Not on Taino. Not with *her* security parameters in place.

It was a significant source of amusement to Micki that Victoria had never considered that the very person responsible for maintaining those parameters could be the black hat Victoria never stopped looking for. And it was a source of tremendous pride to Micki that she was able to create those vital, improbable gaps, leaving Taino's computer and security networks riddled with hidden virtual tunnels.

And today, in less than an hour, she would place the matched set of small explosives into critical fissures in the cliff walls that loomed above *Atlantis*, the top secret, deep-sea habitat and methane-hydrate mining operation on which Dennis Cavendish was staking the world's future.

Later, Micki would detonate the devices, triggering a submarine landslide that would destroy the entire installation. All of Dennis's proprietary technological advances would be lost and his minions would be sacrificed—horrible but necessary deaths. Dennis

Cavendish, the man who'd crowned himself a king and wanted to be a god, would be hated and reviled, his name cursed, his legacy ruined, his dreams literally crushed.

The plan was so simple, so clean, so elegant that it had made Micki want to laugh out loud each time she'd thought about it over the past few months. When Garner had told her to get inside Dennis's organization eight years ago, neither she nor Garner had had any idea that such an opportunity would present itself. All she was meant to do was simply spy on the organization: observe, dig around when and where she could, and report back. That she was hired to be in charge of so much internal security had been beyond either of their most ambitious fantasies. All they had hoped to do was discover what Dennis Cavendish and his Climate Research Institute were doing, and use that information against him. It had worked in small ways over the years by stopping some of his pet projects, but being able to disrupt not just Dennis's machinations, but to impact the world's future so dramatically was a gift from the gods, a mandate from Earth. Micki would not, could not, fail. That she'd come up with the plan to sabotage *Atlantis* herself, and that Garner had seized on it as viable, just added to the buzz in her bloodstream.

"All set, Ms. Crenshaw?" The dive master's voice came through the headphones clearly and Micki fought back a smile at the rush of excitement.

"I'm ready when you are," she replied, briefly nodding at the beautiful and still-furious Simon Broadhurst through the porthole in front of her.

The dive master issued a command and Micki felt a low vibration begin as the ship's winch was brought to life. Seconds later, the pod encasing her was lifted from the tender ship's dive platform. The deck disappeared from her view as the dive tube swung slowly away from the ship to hang in midair above the surface of the calm early-dawn sea. She felt a brief shudder as the winch's gear shifted and then the sensation of falling in slow motion took over.

The splashdown was easy and controlled, and the dive tube's motors started flawlessly when she initiated the ignition sequence. Less than ten minutes after she'd been given the captain's grudging clearance to dive, she heard the loud metallic clunk as the tether released her and retracted, leaving her free to maneuver the sleek unit to her destination two thousand feet below the surface, and two thousand feet above the most daring mining operation ever undertaken.

Pointing the nose down, Micki left the surface world. The first thing she did was switch off the communications link to the *Wangari*. With the faint radio static gone, the only noises she could hear were the muted hum of the pod's motor and the sparkling rush of bubbles past the porthole. The sounds soothed her as she aimed the vessel away from the well-lit surface and toward the dark, dramatic cliff created by a tectonic shift thousands of years ago. Time seemed suspended as she moved quickly and effortlessly through the water.

As she neared the shallow, twilit floor of the continental shelf, she cut her speed so she could enjoy what would be her last trip to this pristine undersea paradise. She felt no regret about what she was intending to do. She'd been granted an opportunity to right some of humanity's wrongs, and the vista before her was her early reward.

Coral and anemones and brightly colored fish, doing what they'd done for millennia, displayed no curiosity toward the noisy monster that moved past them in the watery dusk. Micki slowed further, gliding just above the smooth seafloor.

Octopi slithered away. Eels and their clueless prey watched her from their crevices among the rocks and maddening human debris that littered the bottom. Curiosity got the best of a pair of shy hammerhead sharks and they swam toward her, arcing up and away seconds before they would have made impact. Moving at a speed that barely registered, Micki steered the submersible to the stark, jagged line where the seafloor gave way to the abyss and hovered there, pointing downward, for a few seconds.

Then, with an abrupt burst of acceleration, she sent the dive tube surging forward past the edge. The deepest dark appeared beneath her, replacing the half-light reflected by the pale, sandy bottom now behind her. Her body braced itself against the sensation of falling that her intuition insisted was taking place, though the tube was stable in the water.

Embraced by the primordial darkness of the abyss, Micki closed her eyes as something close to an orgasmic rush tightened every muscle, electrified every nerve. Her gasp echoed in the tight space and it took more than a moment for her to catch her breath, to bring her mind back to the task at hand.

Hands shaking from both excitement and a sliver of fear, she set the controls to pick up speed as she resumed her dark descent, moving past the craggy outcropping of the abyssal walls. Turning on the external floodlights was an option that she refused to exercise. Part of the thrill, part of the delicious risk was slicing through the silent, lethal, dimensionless darkness guided only by the ghostly glow of the head-up display in front of her.

As she approached a depth of eighteen hundred feet, the small sonar screen at the left of her field of view showed her first destination coming into range. Now she flipped on the vessel's powerful outside lights and the stark, forbidding face wall became clearly visible as she continued to descend parallel to it.

Moments later, she brought the vehicle to a stop opposite a small cave two thousand vertical feet above the habitat and approximately two hundred feet north of it. Setting the auto station keeping thrusters to stabilize her position and maintain pitch and attitude, Micki began initiating the sequences needed to extend the small robotic arm from its sheltered tube at the front of the pod.

Carefully, she maneuvered the arm to allow one of its pincers to open and slide beneath the handle at the top of the first ceramic box. The pincer firmly locked in place, Micki released the clamps that had held the box secure for the descent, and delicately negotiated the box out of its "nest" on the platform. Once the box was clear of the diving unit's structure, she gently rotated the arm holding the deadly, precious cargo and extended its reach deep into the stygian depths beyond the cave's narrow opening.

Her gaze glued to the real-time video playing on the other small screen on the dashboard, Micki worked as hard at keeping her breathing even and her hands dry and steady on the controls as she did at maneuvering the bomb past the random outcroppings and occasional creatures in the cave. She was operating practically blind. Her only guidance came from the small but powerful light mounted on the end of the arm and the live video feed from the even smaller camera next to it. She moved the box forward at a painstakingly slow pace.

Fully extended, the mechanical arm had a range of twelve feet. When it had reached that distance into the cave, Micki set the ceramic box carefully onto a clear space on the floor, released it from the pincers, and began retracting the arm as slowly and carefully as she'd inserted it. Its placement so far into the cave would preclude the box from being seen by anyone who might be sent to these coordinates to investigate her actions—which would only happen if Simon disobeyed her orders and began tracking her movements. Not that it really mattered. Even if Simon could convince Victoria to send an investigative team to find out what she'd been doing, it would be too late. Investigators would not be facing an abyssal wall. They would be facing a blank expanse of ocean, still turbid with the debris of a catastrophic submarine landslide.

The arm fully retracted, Micki moved forward three hundred feet along the wall and repeated the procedure with the second box. Her mission accomplished, she aimed the pod upward and moved in a slow arc back toward the tender ship. When she broke the surface, Micki reactivated the communications channel and announced to the dive master that she was ready to be retrieved.

It wasn't easy keeping the triumph out of her voice.

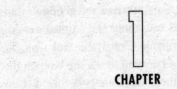

CHAPTER 1

4:30 A.M., Saturday, October 25, Miami, Florida

Dennis Cavendish became aware that he was drifting toward consciousness and forced himself to open his eyes, demanded his brain kick into high gear. Too much was going to happen today for him to allow himself the luxury of a slow awakening, or even another round with the pair of warm, lush redheads flanking him. He pulled himself to a sitting position, then gave the woman on his left a light slap on her well-shaped behind.

"Time to go."

He shook the other woman's shoulder, and both began to make small murmurs, indicating that waking them would not be an easy task. He climbed over one of them, took a moment to stretch his pleasantly aching muscles, then ripped the covers off both women. The chill in the air-conditioned room sent them into fetal crouches.

He flipped on one of the lamps next to the bed. "I said it's time to go."

One of the women pushed herself upright on one elbow, brushing hair out of her eyes with her other hand. "Is something wrong? What time is it?" She looked at him blearily, her eye makeup smudged.

"It's four-thirty and you have to go. I've got work to do," Dennis lied smoothly. "Get your friend to wake up. You have to be out of here in five minutes. There will be a car waiting for you when you get downstairs."

Still confused and squinting, the woman nevertheless pushed her companion until she woke up. With barely a word spoken between them, the women threw on most of their clothes, and Dennis escorted them to the elevator door in the living room of his condo. They departed with wary, friendly waves. The moment the door slid shut, Dennis went to the shower to brace himself for the day ahead.

Forty-five minutes later Dennis was airborne, the engines of his Lear jet screaming as his pilot executed a steep takeoff from Miami International Airport. He would be on the ground on his island, Taino, in twenty minutes. Not long after that he would be in a small submarine headed four thousand feet to the bottom of his slice of the Caribbean. It wouldn't be a joy ride; it would be the last trip to see the dream of his lifetime while it still belonged just to him: *Atlantis*, the first fully staffed habitat ever built at that depth—and the operations center for the newest and best means of changing the way the world worked.

In a few hours, *Atlantis* would begin to retrieve methane hydrate crystals from beneath the seafloor and introduce the world to the next, arguably the only, clean fuel that the planet had to offer.

From entertaining the first glimmer of a thought to watching the last beams being sunk into place, Dennis had known that this was what life was about. This was the brass ring, the golden goose; attaining this kind of power was what every hackneyed cliché referred to, what every fairy tale was about, what every emperor and despot had ever dreamed of—the power to make the world change at one person's command. He was that person.

He picked up his phone and punched a single number. Less than a minute later, he heard a sleepy female voice, that of Victoria Clark, his secretary of national security and chief paranoiac. The woman whose job it was to keep him safe and happy.

"Hi, Dennis."

"Hi, Vic. I'm on my way to the island. Meet me at my office in half an hour."

"Is something wrong? Is everyone with you?"

The thought of dragging the senior executives of some of the world's major corporations out of bed and onto a plane before dawn made him smile. "No, I'm alone. I want to get the day going. It's going to be unforgettable, Vic. Let's get 'em, tiger. See you in thirty."

"Wait. Don't hang up."

Dennis could tell by the soft noises in the background that she was pushing herself to sitting position, getting focused. It rarely took Vic this long to focus on anything, but then, he didn't usually get her up in the middle of the night.

Vic was his workhorse, his closest confidante, and the person who knew more of his secrets than anyone. She was the person he trusted the most—at least that's what he told people. The reality was that Dennis trusted no one but himself.

He had to let people into his circle, but he knew the closer he let them get, the more they had on him, the more he was worth to them. The market price of betrayal was something that never lost value, and Vic was the one person who could command the highest fee for betraying him.

Betrayal was a lesson he'd learned the hard way and, as such lessons do, it had altered his thinking in an instant. Since the first time Dennis had been stabbed in the back by someone he trusted, the degree of closeness and his level of real trust in a person had moved along opposing axes. As one went up, the other went down. Treating betrayal as a "when" rather than an "if" made life much easier.

It was his only gospel, and it worked.

"Dennis, you need to fly with your guests. You need to be there with them—"

"I've been with them for two days nonstop. I'll see them when they get in, in a few hours. Look, I want to go straight down to the habitat when I get there, okay? With you."

"I—"

"Not interested in all the many reasons you can't or won't go there, Vic," he interrupted. "You're going."

Dennis disconnected before she could reply and sat back to sip his coffee.

In less than twenty-four hours, the world would be a different place. Victoria Clark was one of the few people who knew just how different it would be, and she was going to be at his side today. All day. Today of all days the risk was inordinately high.

4:30 A.M., Saturday, October 25, Miami, Florida

Lieutenant Colonel Wendy Watson lay naked on the rough sheets, staring at the shifting patterns of light playing on the cheap popcorn ceiling of an apartment that wasn't hers. Being there, next to a man she'd only met three months ago, a man who had changed her life and its purpose, was an atypical move for her. And that was a word she'd rarely—make that never—known to be applied to herself. If there was one word that she'd heard used to describe her more than any other, despite all the obstacles she'd overcome in her life, despite everything she'd accomplished, that word was "typical."

It wasn't a fair description nor was it an accurate one. That didn't matter to the many people who had uttered it, under their breath derisively or more loudly with intimations of expectations met, upon hearing what Wendy Watson had done, was doing, or was intending to do. She'd heard it when she'd graduated at the top of her class from the most prestigious public high school in Connecticut. When she'd graduated at the top of her class from the United States Air Force Academy. When she'd been selected to train for the elite Combat Search and Rescue force. When it was announced she'd received enough commendations to make her the most highly decorated female air force officer serving in Afghanistan.

She *hadn't* heard it when she refused the offer to become a flight instructor in favor of resigning from the military. But the hated word had quickly resumed its place as a staple in her life when she became the chief pilot for the Climate Research Institute.

The institute was a small, quiet, privately funded think tank and the plaything of the occasionally flamboyant and perpetually eccentric Dennis Cavendish, a telecommunications wunderkind who had retired at forty to take on the challenges of climate change. In his spare time, he served as president for life of The Paradise of Taino, his own private tropical nation-state snugly situated between the Florida Keys and the Bahamas.

Wendy loved her job; it paid well, provided her with lots of perks, and allowed her to have her say in what sort of planes Dennis bought. That had been enough when she'd been hired and for the four years that had passed since then. It had been enough until she'd met Garner Blaylock, a beautiful, earthy man who was lit from within with passions and understanding Wendy could only marvel at. He'd swept her into a world she'd never known existed and had reframed her life, banishing from it forever the association with anything remotely "typical."

And in a few hours from now, to cement her commitment to Garner, to her new way of thinking, to the cause he had introduced her to and which they now shared, Wendy would do something that was anything but typical by anyone's standards. The event was going to be spectacular and meaningful; if her actions were ever to become public knowledge, they would be called crazy by many, but adjudged heroic by the people she cared about most. By the person she cared about most. By Garner.

"What are you thinking about?"

Wendy rolled over and looked into the deep brown, soulful eyes of her lover, her mentor, the man for whom she was about to make the biggest sacrifice in her life.

She reached up and smoothed his tousled golden curls, threaded her fingers through them. "What do you think I'm thinking about?"

He cupped her cheek as he eased his thumb along her bottom lip. "Well, I hope you're thinking about how we spent the last few hours, but I imagine you're thinking of what you'll be doing in the next few." His deep, cultured British voice was husky with sleep and sex.

She didn't allow herself to respond with anything other than a smile.

"Are you afraid?" he asked gently.

"Yes."

Garner watched her, peering into her soul with eyes that were soft and loving. "Were you afraid every time you flew into a battle zone? Or is it just this task that has you worried?" he asked, his voice low.

She hesitated, not wanting him to mistake her fear for doubt. "I was afraid every time, every mission. We all were. The fear helped us keep our edge. If you weren't scared, you weren't focused. But you had to subdue the fear by keeping foremost in your mind the knowledge that you'd be coming back." She paused. "This time, that knowledge, that assurance isn't there, Garner. It's an odd feeling to know I won't be coming back."

"When you flew for them—" He never uttered the name of any of the groups he fought, so deep was his loathing of all things political.

"When you flew for them, you would have died for them, wouldn't you? It's what they expected you to do, if necessary. Am I right?"

"Yes, but—"

He drew his thumb across her lips again, silencing her. "The oath you lived by then was an oath to a political body, Wendy, a myopic, human-centric organization that survives by cannibalizing its allies if they don't support its warped economic ideals." His hand slid to hers, brought her palm to his lips. "You're different now, darling. You operate at a different level of understanding, at a different harmonic frequency as it were. You've learned how badly the Earth needs us. It's left to us—to you—to send the rest of humanity a wake-up call. There's no other way to save Her and all Her creatures from senseless destruction at the hands of shortsighted, parasitic mercenaries." His grip tightened slightly as his voice became more intense. "You're no longer bound to the empty words they made you believe in, Wendy, nor to the desperate actions they made you carry out. You're bound to the true reality now, my love. To the tangible. To the eternal." He looked into her eyes with a passion that stopped just short of ferocity.

The energy radiating from him made her light-headed.

She took in a shaky breath, her eyes never leaving his beautiful face.

"My darling Wendy, the war we're fighting is bigger than all of us. It's so, so much greater. It's the battle for ultimate justice and you, my love, you're our warrior. Our lovely golden warrior," he whispered, trailing his fingers down the front of her body.

She caught her breath as a rush of cool air followed the warmth of his hand, leaving her skin tingling with the cold burn of sparks and desire.

"Only you can do this for me, for us, Wendy. It's your destiny and your debt. Tell me again that you won't fail us. Let me know the depth of your commitment, my love."

Wendy closed her eyes against the tears welling in them. With every pulse of life beating inside her, she knew that what she was going to do today was the right thing, a necessary and noble action undertaken for the good of the Earth. She'd known it since the day three months ago when she'd met Garner purely by chance and had fallen in love with him as if guided by Fate. It never failed to astonish her that he'd felt the same passion for her before that first week's end.

The heady rush of desire she'd felt when she met him was one she'd never expected to feel, and therefore undeserved—until he convinced her otherwise. And when he'd asked her to help him a few weeks later, she hadn't hesitated. She'd known before he'd told her that she was the only person in the entire organization who could execute his plan.

And she would. She had never failed at anything and she would not fail now. It was not in her to fail.

Wendy slid her arms around his hard, muscular body and reveled in his heat and power.

"You don't have to persuade me, Garner," she said in a voice as strong as she could muster, her gaze unwavering as she looked into his endless eyes. "I've made my decision. I accepted the assignment and I'll complete the mission. But there is a part of me—"

"No 'buts,' Wendy," he whispered, his lips warm and soft against hers. "There is no weakness in you. You are my fearless warrior princess and for the rest of my life, if ever I falter, it will be you who will inspire me to continue the fight for justice. Let's stop talking, love. Let me live within you in this moment, and forever."

As he finished speaking, he moved on top of her. His hands, his mouth offered an escape she seized without hesitation. But even his lovemaking, so sure, so tender, could not alter her reality, could not obliterate the knowledge humming in her brain.

In six hours, she was going to die. Horribly.

5:30 A.M., Saturday, October 25, Gainesville, Florida

Sam Briscoe smiled as he made the transition from sleep to wakefulness with a little help from a pair of warm, feminine lips pressed against the back of his neck. He smiled into the pillow and a moment later lifted his head. Slowly, so as not to dislodge the lips.

"I'm leaving." Cynthia's voice was soft, barely a whisper against his skin.

He rolled over as he blinked his way to a clear focus on her face, fully made up and ready to meet the day. Even though day hadn't broken yet.

"It's five-thirty," he mumbled, coherency coming slowly. "What in God's name are you doin'?"

She smiled. "If I'd told you last night what time I had to get up, you wouldn't have let me stay. And I didn't want to miss out on that goodbye . . ." Her voice trailed off, bringing a bigger smile to his face and greater clarity to his brain.

"You wouldn't have anyway," he replied, returning her smile although his voice was still hoarse with sleep. "I thought your flight was at nine."

"I lied. We fly out of here at seven and I still have to pick up Stephanie and Grace." She placed a small kiss on the end of his nose.

"Here" was Gainesville, Florida, a vibrant, bustling town when the University of Florida was in session, and a hot, humid, laid-back town when it wasn't. Right now, the university was bracing for a day of football, which should have meant that Professor Briscoe could sleep in for a few more hours before deciding whether to put on his blue and orange fanwear and head into the madness on campus. But today his long-term girlfriend was heading off for a week-long Caribbean sailing cruise with some girlfriends, and that required wakefulness, at least until her car was backing down the driveway.

Sam didn't bother to stifle a yawn. "Shoot, Cyn, you can get to the airport in fifteen minutes. Come back to bed for a spell." He backed up his offer with a grin.

"I can't get there that fast when I have to pick up Stephanie and Grace," she repeated, pulling away and straightening up just as some of his more primitive mechanical parts were waking up. "You know how disorganized they are."

"I'll make it worth your while," he drawled as he led the hand he held toward the newly erected tent of sheets.

"I'll take a rain check." She stood up with a laugh and stepped away from the bed, slipping her hand out of his grip. Then she reached over and brushed some hair out of his eyes. Like a mother would.

Annoyance flickered within him. They were going to be apart for seven days. No way should picking up her girlfriends take precedence over some last-minute grab-and-tickle.

"So why did you get me up?" he asked mildly, not betraying the shift in his mood. Much.

"To say goodbye."

"Bye."

She cocked her head at him with a look that should have been accompanied by her hands thumping onto her hips. But that might wrinkle the pants she was wearing. He knew that too well. Backwater Georgia boys, even ones with Ph.D.s, learned a lot of new things when they dated princesses from Washington, D.C.

"Don't do this. I want to enjoy myself, Sam. Don't try to send me off all guiltified. It won't work and it'll just piss me off."

"Is that a word? Guiltified?"

"You stick to the weather and let me worry about syntax." She blew him a kiss—letting him know in her own princessy way just how well he'd succeeded in infuriating her—and turned toward the bedroom door.

Well, damn. He pushed himself from elbow to upright and ran a hand over his face. "Hey, Cyn?"

She turned and glanced at him over her shoulder. "Yes?"

"How about you bring that fine body and gorgeous face of yours back over here so we can start this good-bye again?"

The hint of a smile twitched at the corner of her lips. "Apology accepted. I really have to go, Sam. I don't want to be late."

He grinned at her and raised an eyebrow slowly. It was an expression that rarely failed to get him what he wanted. "I won't make you late, darlin'."

"Sam—"

"Don't give me any of that whinin', woman. Just get over here and give me a kiss that doesn't make me think you're channeling Grandmother Briscoe."

The way she hesitated let him know it was just for show, and the way she walked back to the bed made him know that her expectations were high.

"That's my girl," he murmured as she sank onto the bed next to him and ran a cool hand over his chest.

"I'm going to miss you, Sam," she whispered as he brought his face to hers.

"Damned right you will," he growled against her mouth.

They sank into each other with a warmth that had nothing to do with the weather. She pushed him away gently after not nearly enough time. "I really have to go, Sammy."

"I know." Her neck was soft and sweet and too damned close to his mouth for him to think straight.

"We should have planned to go together. All those stars and the sea air . . ." Her words drifted into a contrite smile.

He lifted his head to meet her dark eyes and let his hand trail down her warm, silky arm. "Next time you suggest taking a cruise with those girlfriends of yours,

I'm going to remind you that you said that. Gotta be a big boat, though. Not one of them pissant little things. They turn this big dog into a pup."

She laughed and pushed herself off the bed, sliding out of his grasp. "Okay, Sam. A big boat."

"Hey, just a sec. There's something I forgot to ask you last night," he said, feigning a yawn as she turned to walk to the bedroom door.

"What's that?" she replied, her all-business persona slipping back into place.

He reached into the shallow drawer of the nightstand next to his bed, grabbed the small velvet box in it, and casually tossed it to her.

She caught it with both hands and he watched her eyes widen as she realized what it was. After a long, silent look, she snapped it open. A moment later she looked back to him, even more wide-eyed and pleasingly slack-jawed.

"Yeah, I meant to bring it up last night, but a certain gorgeous wildcat sorta pushed it clear out of my head," he said with an easy shrug. "But think about it, darlin'. I'm kinda crazy about you. And I was wonderin' if you'd let me continue to be for—" He shrugged again. "Well, forever, I guess."

"Sam." It came out as a whisper, with a hoarse edge to it.

"Yes, ma'am?" There was no point in trying to hide his grin.

Without saying anything more, she walked back to the bed and kissed him again, softly this time, and un-hurriedly.

"Is that a 'yes'?"

She smiled. "It's a 'yes.' But can I leave this here with you? I don't want to put it on and then disappear for a week. I want to wear it around you at first, not the girls." She paused and looked down at the diamond solitaire nestled against blue velvet. "It's beautiful, Sam. I love it."

Trying not to frown at her logic, he nodded his reluctant assent, and was rewarded with another kiss.

"Thank you, Sam. I love you." And then she straightened up and left the room, leaving the ring in its box in his hand.

Well, damn.

He felt a little stunned and a little lost, and not at all like a man who'd just gotten engaged.

6:45 A.M., Saturday, October 25, the White House, Washington, D.C.

Lucy Denton, a former CIA case officer and the current director of national intelligence, walked into the anteroom of the Oval Office and nodded a greeting at the president's secretary.

"He's expecting you, Director Denton. Please go in," the woman said with a polite smile, which Lucy returned before continuing to the door and walking through it.

President Winslow Benson was standing at one of the windows, with his back to the room. He was dressed casually, presumably in anticipation of heading out to a golf course shortly, but he still managed to look imposing and almost regal.

The Sterling Fox.

It was what she'd always privately called him, even before he was her commander in chief. Winslow Benson was highly polished, beautiful to look at, and worth a lot of money. But other than the fact that he was dangerous if you crossed him, there wasn't a lot of substance beneath his gleaming exterior.

He glanced at her over his left shoulder and gave a short nod. "Lucy."

"Good morning, Mr. President," she replied, and then glanced around the room, nodding her greetings to the rest of the people gathered there.

It was the usual Saturday-morning crowd: a few national security advisors, the secretaries of state and defense, two of the Joint Chiefs of Staff, the secretary of homeland security, and the president's campaign manager. Everyone was in a suit. No one was smiling. They never did during these "informal and off-the-record" chats about the state of the world, as the president liked to call them.

Lucy was the newest member of the team, everyone else having served with the president throughout his not-yet-complete first term in office. She'd been named DNI less than a year ago, shortly after her predecessor had suffered a catastrophic health failure. She hadn't known the man personally, but he'd seemed to be a pretty fit man. Lucy had found it somewhat odd that a fifty-five-year-old triathlete had suffered such a massive stroke, but then, he had just been blamed for the intelligence failure that had allowed Hurricane Simone and Carter Thompson to terrorize the Eastern seaboard. It wasn't the first time she'd heard of something like that happening and it likely wouldn't be the last, but she didn't like coincidences like that and preferred not to dwell on them. She just did her job and took the necessary hits.

It was a dubious honor to be part of what the president considered his inner circle, much like it had been an honor to be grilled in class by the toughest professor when she'd been in law school. She was certain that the only reason she was part of this group was because of what the president's team had called her "stellar performance" during the confirmation hearings. She'd been the dark horse, the nominee no one had ever heard of. There was no reason they should have—her personal history was classified at the highest level. What had been released to the press and carefully placed into the wild as "confirmable" had been an artful and charming work of fiction. It was just another part of the game, and one she was well used to.

She'd been a hell of a good case officer, spending her entire career on the dark side taking calculated risks, facing occasionally terrifying odds, and receiving accolades she could never publicly acknowledge. But that part of her track record was not what had made the powers that be bring her in from the cold and set her into the heat of the spotlight.

Lucy had been made the president's DNI because she had a cool head, a steady hand, and a flexible morality, and she was known not to flinch. Ever.

If she took aim, she took the shot.

And her shots always hit their mark.

Lucy walked farther into the room and came to a stop in front of one of the two empty chairs opposite the one President Benson usually chose as his own. She could have sat closer to the president, but that would have meant she would have had to sit next to Katy Wirth, the secretary of defense, and that was something she always tried to avoid doing. Their paths had crossed in law school, and later in their training at the Farm. Katy had failed to make the cut into the Agency, though, and they hadn't met again until Lucy had been brought into this office for an interview eleven months ago. By then, they'd hated each other too long to even pretend to get along.

The room was quiet except for the muted clink of silver against china as the occupants served themselves coffee.

"All right. I'm teeing off in an hour. Let's get this show on the road," the president said abruptly, turning from the window and crossing the room. His trademark stride had always struck Lucy as an odd combination of Ronald Reagan's macho Marlboro Man walk and the fluid movement of a trained dancer. It brought to mind both elegance and restrained power, as it was no doubt supposed to, and it fit perfectly with Winslow Benson's aristocratic bearing and silvered good looks.

But something about that walk had never seemed to blend in completely with the rest of the package. That's how Lucy had always perceived the president, even before he'd taken office: a carefully crafted package put forth for public consumption. But she knew there was a flaw in that package and, though she couldn't identify it, the imperfection made it impossible for her to trust him.

The rest of the group seated themselves after the president had lowered himself into his favorite wing chair. Before the last of them was settled, he began to bark out the names of regions, countries, corporations, and their leaders, and the others in the room responded with information relevant to business, the economy, and any real or perceived threats to America's stability. It was like a high-stakes pop quiz where no one person knew all the answers, but everyone was delighted to torch you for missing a nuance.

"Okay, not a whole lot of surprises," the president said at last. The tension in the room dissipated as he rose to his feet.

"It's not a big surprise, sir, but I do have something

I'd like to mention," Lucy interjected quietly. All eyes turned to her. Most of the hostility in them was subtle. Grandstanding was not appreciated among this crowd.

"What's that, Lucy?" The president stopped moving, and didn't sit back down. The message was unmistakable. *Make this quick.*

"Dennis Cavendish is hosting some sort of small conference on—"

"Oh, for Christ's sake, Lucy. That's hardly—" Ken Proust, the president's campaign manager and part-time minion of Satan, rolled his eyes.

Not for the first time Lucy thought how nice it would be to Taser Ken's testicles, just to find out if he'd enjoy the sensation.

"Ken." The president didn't have to say anything more and Ken retreated, glowering.

Lucy continued. "We've confirmed that six heads of major corporations are flying to Taino later today. There may be more. He's been wining and dining a bunch of them in Miami for the past two days. We're still attempting to learn why, but we're fairly certain that it has to do with his underwater drilling project."

"Who's heading there?"

"Kobiashi Nakamura, head of Takayashi International; Muriel Gastenau, CEO of PetroPharmacol; Dave Coopersmith, CEO of Austral Petroleum, and Fritz Dierbaum, his CFO; Tim Flannery, CEO of BGC Industries; and Peggy Lester, COO of Flint Agrochemical."

The president narrowed his eyes as he looked at her. "That's an impressive lineup." He looked at one of the national security advisors. "What do you make of it?"

The woman, a former Wall Street wunderkind, smiled. "As a group, those companies represent highly diversified holdings, and each has a little problem with too much cash on hand right now. They're primed to make some serious capital investment."

President Benson turned his gaze back to Lucy. "And you think there are more heading down there? What's Cavendish drilling for?"

"Yes, sir. As far as the drilling project, we're fairly certain it's for methane hydrate. There has been speculation for years that there is a huge deposit beneath the eastern Caribbean."

"No proof, though?" He looked from Lucy to the security advisor.

The other woman cleared her throat. "I don't mean to be flippant, sir, but that's very deep water. Designing a rig for experimentation is a high-risk, extremely expensive proposition. No company wants to undertake it alone. There are several consortia considering it now but their plans are still only on paper."

"But you think Dennis the Menace is doing it?" the president asked, more than a hint of sarcasm in his voice.

Lucy didn't smile. "Yes, we do, sir. We haven't been able to penetrate security on the island, but we've been tracking purchases and shipping manifests for years, and monitoring everything we can via satellite. If he's not already drilling, he's preparing to drill for something that's not oil or natural gas. We're sure of that."

"How the hell can we not know what he's doing?" The president turned to the chief of naval operations, who was seated to his right. "You people keep telling me and Congress and everyone else who will listen that we have state-of-the-art equipment that can identify anything that moves underwater. Why the hell don't we know what that bastard is doing fifty miles off our coast? And I don't want to hear that his equipment is better than ours."

To his credit, the admiral didn't visibly react to the president's anger. "It's not just about the equipment and technology, sir, although those are certainly significant to the situation. President Cavendish—"

"*Don't call him that.* That island is all of, what, four square miles?" the president snapped. "I don't give a shit if he wears a crown and calls himself emperor of the dolphins. It's a fucking banana republic with a constituency of one."

No one in the room so much as let out a breath, although Lucy was hard-pressed not to laugh.

"Taino is a very small island, sir, about thirty-two square miles, but it's well secured," the admiral replied evenly. "Taino's security forces are relatively small but very highly trained, from what we know. He's picked from among the best, sir. SEALs, Delta Force, Mossad, the Royal Navy. They guard a relatively small area and they use technology that we're still trying to deploy. Cavendish has been able to establish an extremely high level of situational awareness. His entire outfit is tight and fluid, sir, just like a SEAL team. It can adapt to meet threats almost as they occur. And we're his biggest threat."

"If I can add to what the admiral said, sir," Lucy interjected, "we've been monitoring him as heavily as we can. He knows it, too, and has taken a lot of steps to deflect our interest and obscure what he's doing. It doesn't hurt that his secretary of national security is extremely clever."

"So is everyone in this room, Lucy, and everyone in our intelligence services," the president replied with no small amount of acid. "Your people can tell me what

Putin ate for breakfast and what time Chavez got out of bed, so I find it damned hard to believe they can't tell me what Dennis Cavendish is drilling for on the seabed *fifty God-damned miles off Marathon Key*. What is he doing that we can't fucking find out what he's up to?" He pulled in a hard breath. "That prick has been a serious pain in this country's ass for fifteen years. I want to know what the hell he's up to."

Lucy met the president's angry eyes. "I understand that, sir. Part of the difficulty in determining what he's doing is that for more than ten years now he's had a heavy security net set up just inside the boundaries of his territorial waters—"

"A net? What the hell does that mean? Like some giant fishing net?"

"In some respects, yes, sir. It's along the lines of the antisubmarine nets used to secure strategic ports during World War II. In those situations, the nets were raised and lowered, or moved on booms to allow transit. Cavendish has a permanently secured mesh of electronic sensors. In some places it's a physical mesh, almost like a flexible chain-link fence. In most areas it's just a series of huge sensor arrays. They can identify whatever passes near them—similar to the instruments we've been putting on our ships for the last few years. They use sonar, radar, temperature differentials, water displacement, 3-D mapping, electronic frequency and wavelength signatures—the full gamut of identification technologies. He's deployed them around the entire circumference of the island's territorial waters."

The president stared at her in silence for a moment, as did everyone else in the room.

"Lucy, you've got to be fucking kidding me," he said eventually.

"I assure you, sir, I'm not."

"He's built an underwater fence around his entire island? How deep is it?"

"A fence is a reasonable analogy, but it's actually primarily an extensive sensor array. And from what we've been able to determine, it does encircle the island from close to the sea surface to the seafloor," she said, explaining as if she hadn't just said the same thing seconds before.

Another brief silence filled the room.

"Lucy, Taino is a volcanic island on the edge of a Caribbean abyss. The water around that island is thousands of feet deep—" Katy Wirth began.

Lucy refused to react to the patronizing tone. "Yes, Madam Secretary, you're right. The island does sit at the edge of an abyss. The deepest part that's been mapped sits at approximately four thousand feet." She shifted her attention back to the president, who didn't seem convinced. "This barrier is extraordinary in the extreme, sir. The arrays took years, perhaps a decade, to build and deploy, and the project was probably under development long before the U.S. became interested in what Dennis Cavendish was doing on his little island. For years after he bought that island and declared sovereignty, he was written off as another eccentric billionaire with some eco-issues. There have been enough of them." She shrugged. "Even when he built a deepwater port and began bringing in people and equipment, our services took note of it but never bothered to do the math, so to speak."

"Why can't we get in there? We've got people everywhere else on the planet. Why not there?" President Benson demanded.

"Because his secretary of national security, Victoria

Clark, is damned close to a genius when it comes to security, sir, if you'll pardon my language. While we haven't been able to penetrate the organization, we've been able to determine who he has working for him on the island and at his embassy here in Washington. We've collected background data on them and tried to piece it together with the satellite and environmental data we've collected to figure out what he's up to. The personnel list of Cavendish's Climate Research Institute reads like a Who's Who of academic and industrial brain power. Marine architects, engineers from every discipline, informatics and computer geeks, physicists, hydrogeologists, marine biologists—you name it. Stanford, MIT, CalTech, Oxford. They're from everywhere. It's an international brain trust." Lucy paused and looked the president straight in the eyes. "They're also all single, and nearly every one of them fits the clinical definition of having Asperger's syndrome."

The president frowned at her. "What's that?"

Lucy let the faintest hint of a smile appear on her face. "Generally speaking, it's a variation of autism that's broadly characterized by low emotional involvement, poor social skills, rigid, repetitive behaviors, and a propensity to develop an intense, narrow focus on specific subjects. It's a pretty good set of traits to have in a group of geniuses whom you want to work nonstop for a few years on a small island where there's nothing much to do but work. It presents an extra challenge for us, though. We'll eventually infiltrate Cavendish's organization, but these individuals will be difficult to turn. What we consider social norms aren't typically normal for them. They operate on different wavelengths, so to speak, and each person's wavelength will be different from the next."

The silence in the room was only broken by the

gradually louder noise of *Marine One*'s rotors slicing the air as it came to a rest on the lawn beyond the walls of the White House.

"Okay, we're done," the president announced and stood up, causing everyone else in the room to get to their feet. "See you next week."

Lucy blinked as she watched the president walk through the doors and wondered if she was the only person in the room who thought what she'd just said was important.

2

CHAPTER

8:00 A.M., Saturday, October 25, Miami, Florida
Garner Blaylock watched Wendy walk down the concrete steps leading to the trash-strewn parking lot of the slummy apartment complex. It wasn't her knife-creased pilot's uniform that made her look so out of place, it was just her. She was one of those people who had never and would never fit in anywhere.

Lucky, that.

He watched her cross the lot, musing not for the first time that her stride was the farthest thing from feminine, from natural, that he'd ever witnessed. And her posture so erect one could easily infer she had a steel rod running from her flat, boyish ass to her socially calcified brain.

She didn't turn around to see if he was there, which was a good sign. She only glanced up briefly after she had opened her car door. Her grim, tight smile told him everything he needed to know.

She was going to follow through.

He returned her look with a warm, encouraging smile buttressed with an abbreviated nod, and watched her start the car. When she had driven out of sight, his smile disappeared and was replaced with a cold sneer.

What a clueless, miserable whore.

Closing the door, Garner narrowly avoided stepping on a two-inch-long palmetto bug that skittered across his path. He waited until the creature was safely out of his way before he headed to the cheap apartment's puny bathroom, stripping off his worn T-shirt and shorts as he walked.

Killing helpless creatures, even those despised by most people, was something he avoided. Those creatures simply lived and each in its own way kept the world working as smoothly, as elegantly as it should. They ate what Nature intended them to eat, functioned the way Nature intended them to function, and met their fate with grace.

Garner had realized long ago that the dominance of the so-called highest-order species was evidence that evolution had exceeded its utility. Humans had the most evolved cognitive abilities, but wasted them on pursuits that ranged from stupid to criminal, and which extended in scope to the outer edges of horror. Only humans chose to use their so-called intelligence to thwart Nature or harm the helpless; only humans killed in cold blood. Only humans needed weapons; only humans started wars; only humans could destroy the Earth.

Those were just a few reasons Garner held his species

in such low regard. Certain groups, such as politicians, financiers, industrialists—and people like Lieutenant Colonel Wendy Watson, who was a willing stand-in for all of them—deserved even greater scorn. Wendy was a child of disgusting privilege who had no imagination; a hard-bodied, androgynous athlete with no curves and no body fat; an uptight, emotionless, military automaton masquerading as woman. Her flawed veneer of conscience had developed too late. Spending the last twelve hours trying to fuck her boneless had nearly killed him. He needed a shower.

No, I need a bloody vacation.

Stalking into the grimy bathroom, he didn't bother to flick the switch for the overhead lights. The dim sunlight beyond the filthy window provided enough dim illumination. He stepped into the scum-slicked shower and wrenched the tap, bracing himself for the barrage of icy bullets.

Sleeping with the enemy, or doing anything else to the enemy, had never caused Garner a second's guilt or regret. He'd known since the first bright flame of cognition lit his brain that the Earth and Her creatures were to be honored, that following Her dictates and serving Her needs was the most important thing he could do.

His earliest memory was of the soft tickle of roaches scuttling over his skin as he lay still and silent in his crowded cot. The stinking bodies of the other children curled around him in the bed were what kept him warm during those early, harsh Bucharest winters, but providing warmth was all the other children had been good for. None of them had been as fascinating as the other creatures living in the orphanage. He'd spent every day studying the huge and thriving colonies of roaches that swarmed in the broken walls, marveling at the tenacity of the lice that clung to fragile strands of everyone's hair, enjoying every gleeful leap of the fleas across the stained, rotting mattresses. And he remembered how right it had felt to finally punish one of the older boys who delighted in trapping and torturing helpless creatures, including Garner. The boy had always made a point of displaying his cruelty to any interested parties.

One night—he couldn't have been more than five—Garner climbed on top of the bully as he slept, much as the boy had done to him so many times. But Garner hadn't done the horrible, painful things the other boy always did to him. Instead, he'd simply pressed the boy's face into the foul mattress, had sat on his head, gripping the heavy iron bedframe with his hands until the muffled screams and the writhing stopped. The other boys in the bed had watched blankly, making no move to help the bully, no move to stop Garner. They just watched as Garner sat there, his arse and thighs clamped around the bigger boy's ragged, greasy head. After a long time, Garner had climbed off him and dragged the limp body from the cot. He placed it along the wall knowing that it would provide sustenance for many creatures infinitely more deserving of life. The other boys ignored him, too busy staking their claims to the empty, still-warm space on the bed.

The next morning, the matrons found a few dozen mildly curious children gathered around the stiff body, and Garner sitting next to its head. Rats had discovered the corpse during the night, as had the flies and roaches, and they all carried on as Nature directed with sublime disregard for their audience. One of the matrons sent the children scattering with a few heavy, indiscriminate, backhanded slaps; another pulled a sheet from the nearest bed and covered the remains. Late in the day, what was left of the body was taken away.

That necessary removal of such a worthless human from Garner's existence was his first triumph and the first moment in his life that had ever held any meaning for him.

There were other significant moments subsequently, especially the few quiet victories after his "rescue" by the English couple who adopted him the following year. The Blaylocks were what others called "good people." They had unequivocally adored Garner and privately congratulated themselves on having had their noble gesture of saving a Romanian orphan validated by getting a boy who'd turned out to be so "English."

Named Garner after some missionary relative of theirs, he'd accepted his new life with no fuss. He was quiet, stoic, and respectful. He did well in school, did what he was told at home. The Blaylocks and his teachers were certain that his exemplary behavior was rooted in deep-seated gratitude. It never occurred to them that he simply didn't care what he wore, what he was fed, what he was told to do.

But Garner did care about what the people around him did. He watched with mute hatred as the Blaylocks and their friends gathered to hunt foxes, letting the frenzied pack of hounds rip the terrified creatures to pieces after the horses were exhausted and the humans had had their fill of adventure. He said nothing as they set traps baited with poison all around their home and farm to kill insects, rodents, and certain birds that annoyed them. As they castrated their bulls and dogs, as they slaughtered and ate hens and rabbits and weeks-old piglets.

The Blaylocks gave him their name, an education

that led to a degree from Oxford, and, eventually, their entire estate. Their deaths and those of his nominal siblings had been as necessary as the bully's had been as Garner sought to restore balance, and achieve his financial goals. The deaths of his English "family" had required much more planning and forethought than the death of the bully, but he'd gotten away with them just as easily.

When the Blaylocks' biological son and daughter—twins—became teenagers, they also became so-called health nuts. Lacing a few of their herbal supplements with the poison their parents used on the mice in the barn hadn't been difficult. The calamity had resulted in a large financial settlement by the American conglomerate that made the pills, and afterward the grieving Blaylocks had directed all their energy and attention to Garner, their remaining heir, who gave every appearance of caring.

That's why everyone said it was such a tragedy when, mere days after his graduation from university, the valve on his parents' home's ancient heating unit failed. The house had filled with fumes that eventually ignited. The only blessing, people said, was that they'd likely died of asphyxiation some time before the place exploded.

Garner had returned from his barely begun European holiday to attend the funeral. He sold the farm as soon as he was able to. The neighbors were quoted in the local papers as saying it was for the best—the site of so much tragedy was likely too much for the quiet young man who'd always been such a good and devoted son. The statement was one of the few things in life that had ever made Garner laugh out loud.

Despite his success in evading any hint of suspicion in either case, the Blaylocks' deaths hadn't been nearly as rewarding or enlightening as his first eradication. When he'd transformed the bully into a corpse, he'd transformed something evil into something good. As he'd watched Nature reclaim that body, it had become startlingly clear to him that the Earth and all of the innocent life-forms She supported were more important than humans. The last link on evolution's chain—humankind and all the filth and means of destruction it had created and continued to wield with such oblivious abandon—came a distant second to all that preceded it.

Over the intervening years, that epiphany had remained excruciatingly simple. Which instrument of evil a person represented—agroindustry, energy, banking, paper, the media—mattered little. They were all cogs in the ubiquitous, pan-national, military-political-industrial complex that had set the world's population on a course of happy, deluded self-destruction over the last centuries. Prior to that, all living creatures had been of the Earth. Now, humans, and humans alone, were against the Earth. Everyone who lived a modern life, everyone who saw themselves as occupying some hallowed place above the one that Nature had preordained, supported the goals of domination rather than alliance.

And they would pay the highest price for their greed while the Earth, injured, polluted, raped, would survive and thrive again. Garner and his organization, GAIA, would see to it.

Even the overly analytical Wendy Watson was one of the hated, whether or not she wanted to believe it. With remarkable ease, Garner had pried open her tightly closed, middle-class mind and convinced her that she'd evolved beyond mainstream groupthink. In the pursuit of GAIA's goals, nothing had been left to chance. Even while he'd been away, imprisoned for those years for defending the Earth against the rape of industry, GAIA's work had continued, subdued but uninterrupted.

His people, Micki especially, had done well. The selection of Wendy Watson as the first catalyst of GAIA's new dawn had been the result of long, tedious study, and rigorous psychological profiling. She'd risen to the top of their short list as if the Earth Herself had ordained her the perfect candidate.

Wendy had grown disillusioned with her life and its hollow triumphs, its soulless exultation of materialism. Her epiphany, as she liked to call it, had been little more than a nudge.

Shaking his head, Garner began to smile as he remembered their first meeting. She'd been so fucking *hungry* for a new reality, so clearheaded and yet utterly pathetic in her willingness to conform to a vision so radically different from the one she'd adhered to for her entire life. She'd been overripe, and so ready to fall in line with his plans for her that it was a bit of a letdown, really. No challenge at all.

He'd played to her strengths and insecurities without ever betraying that he considered her just another bit of self-serving scum, one of the walking, breathing pustules who deserved whatever karmic retribution they received. The fool never copped to the fact that her conversion had been staged, as had her seduction. And now she was going to carry out the first big action GAIA had undertaken in a long time. Garner was honored to know that he would have a hand in helping the Earth regain Her equilibrium.

The frigid burn of water pelting his flesh was becoming less enjoyable as the moments passed. Scrubbed clean of every trace of her, he shut off the water with an abrupt twist of his wrist, hating the liquid's faintly sulfurous smell and the presence of the murderous chlorine that he knew suffused every drop. He stepped onto the damp tile floor and shook himself like a dog before reaching for the towel. There had never been the need for chemicals to purify water until humans discovered how convenient it was to defile it. It was just one more thing that he would make them pay for in blood.

But first, he needed Wendy to follow through and get the world's attention.

CHAPTER

9:30 A.M., Saturday, October 25, off the coast of Taino

Though she was nearly a foot shorter than him, Victoria Clark matched the even pace of her boss, Dennis Cavendish, as they walked along the smooth bamboo floors of the quiet, softly lit hallway. Stunning photographs of undersea life, ocean sunsets, and submerged icebergs lined the grass-cloth-covered walls. The air was warm and humid enough to be comfortable, and held subtle aromatic hints of coconuts and green leaves, of sunlight and seawater, in its invisible and barely felt breeze. Sounds of the surf were just audible, as though heard from a distance.

The ambience was exactly what one would expect in

a professional building on a Caribbean island. This structure, however, was not on an island. It was adjacent to one. And below it by four thousand feet, give or take a few.

Coming to a stop at the end of the short hallway, Victoria and Dennis in turn each pressed a thumb against the small dark red glass pad to the left of the heavy airlock door. When prompted, first he and then she punched in the alphanumeric codes that appeared on the LED screens of the random code generators that hung from lanyards around their necks.

"Eighteen characters?" Dennis's voice held more amusement than annoyance. "Aren't you getting a bit overzealous?"

"I'd have thought that was a quality to be desired in your secretary of national security," Victoria replied lightly.

"At the topside offices, sure, but we're four thousand feet below sea level, in a facility you can't get to except from a submersible launched from an island that's inaccessible without an invitation from me," he replied, pulling open the titanium door as soon as the cipher lock released.

Victoria stepped into the airlock. "All of which is nothing more than a challenge to persons of a malicious persuasion."

"You know damned well we're not concerned about 'persons.' It's *countries* with malicious intent—and the technology to exploit it—that keep you hopping."

"Excuse me. I don't hop," she said, trying to keep the smile off her face. "We call it 'layering.'"

"And how many layers do we have in place so far?"

"That's classified."

Dennis started laughing and, acknowledging his

amusement with an answering smile, Victoria glanced up at him, taking in his tanned, sailor's complexion and dark hair bleached to gold in some places and to silver in others. His blue eyes held a level of devilment not often found in a CEO or a head of state. These were the eyes of a renegade; the eyes of a man who had repeatedly turned a penchant for risk into fortunes that kept him hovering at the top of the world's earners.

"You can trust me, Vic. I promise. You run security checks on everyone, all the time. Probably even me." He looked down at her with one eyebrow cocked.

She shrugged. "You pay me to be thorough."

"And you are, to an extraordinary degree. That's why no one would have a chance to—"

"With all due respect, sir, 'the chance always exists. All that's ever lacking is someone to decide to move on it.'"

A single note of surprised laughter from him punctuated her quiet statement. "You're quoting me back to me? That's cheeky, Vic. And don't call me 'sir' unless we're in bed."

"For God's sake, Dennis, shut up. You know everything we say is being recorded," she said under her breath even as she bit back a laugh. The heavy door slid shut behind them with a soft hiss and the keypad to the left of the next door lit up.

He lifted a shoulder in unconcern. "It'll give your boys something to think about."

"Like they, and everyone else, haven't already thought that, thanks to you?" she muttered.

"Well, yeah. I'm a man, you're a woman. Obviously everyone thinks you slept your way into the job. People always think good-looking women sleep their way into jobs. If you want to convince them otherwise, you have to quit acting like you give a damn, Vic. You've built a God-damned fortress around this habitat and the island. Only a moron would think you did that while flat on your back with your legs in the air."

She pulled in a deep breath and counted silently to ten while glaring at his smirking face. "Gee, thanks, Dennis. Will you put that in a letter of recommendation for me?"

"Thinking of leaving?" he asked with a grin as he finished punching in the code for the next airlock.

"As a matter of fact—"

"Well, don't even think about it or I *will* tell the world you slept with me to get the job. One blog post is all it would take for everyone to know. And I'll be sure to mention that rising-sun tattoo on your ass," he replied casually as he let her enter the corridor ahead of him. Laughing quietly, he tilted his head toward the small speaker flush-mounted in the ceiling of the hallway. "Hear that, fellas?"

Her mouth dropped open as his comment registered on several levels. "I don't have a rising-sun tattoo anywhere. I don't have *any* tattoos," she protested, and smacked him on the arm none too gently as they began walking. "Certainly not that one."

"I wouldn't know, but putting it out there would sure cloud the old employment issue for you, wouldn't it? Especially with Western firms looking for a security wizard. Think of it. A little Japanese girl with a—"

"I'm not a girl, and I'm not Japanese. I haven't been for thirty-two years," she snapped. "My looks stem from my DNA but cultural identity isn't genetic. I'm a Tainoan and an American, in that order."

"Thank you for giving me priority, sweetheart, but

I'm just pointing out that it's better that you stay here and keep me and Taino safe from all those malicious persons you dream about at night."

They proceeded in silence for a few moments as she regained her composure, then she stopped in front of the next airlock and looked up at him. "Tell you what, Dennis, let's talk business for a while."

"I don't know. Why don't we talk dirty, instead?"

She let out a sigh that was half amusement and half exasperation. "You know, sometimes I really have to wonder how you ever got to be—"

"I got where I am because my shareholders always loved me," he said, interrupting her easily. "I made them a lot of money, I had fun doing it, and I pissed off the old guard at the same time. Even among my peers in the dot-com universe, I was the poster boy for the 'Old enough to know better and young enough not to care' mind-set. And I indulged in a behavior generally considered to be terminal in any industry: I always told the truth. A novel concept, unfortunately. But one that, as I recall, is what finally convinced you that leaving those tight-assed, white-bread old farts on Wall Street for the good life on Taino was a good idea. And it *was* a good idea. You were wasting your talents keeping all their secrets secret. Here on Taino, you're making history. You're helping to change the world. Hell, Vic, to be perfectly candid, I don't even know what the hell you're doing half the time, but I know that this baby"—he waved his hand toward the walls of the corridor—"this baby wouldn't be here if you weren't doing a good job. Make that a great job."

"Thank you, Dennis. I—" she began.

"And that," he continued, as if she hadn't said anything, "is why, as soon as we get topside, I'm going to draft a letter describing that tattoo and how I found it, and put that letter somewhere safe."

Her hands rose slowly in surrender as, laughing, the two of them came to a halt in front of the door that was the last stop on their itinerary.

Operations Control was a dimly lit but comfortable room from which the world's finest mining engineers, marine geologists, and underwater excavation experts ran the brains of *Atlantis,* the underwater habitat that Dennis Cavendish was counting on to change the way the world worked.

Marie LaSalle, the installation's chief science officer, glanced over her shoulder at them without bothering to straighten up from where she leaned casually against a long console covered with a neat bank of flat-screen computer monitors. She held up her hand to stop them from talking and returned her eyes to the screen she'd been watching. Dennis nodded and looked around the room, which was quietly humming with myriad live computers and the low voices of the fifteen people responsible for monitoring them.

A moment later, Victoria saw his eyes widen and quickly realized why. On the screen that held Marie's rapt attention, Victoria watched the real-time, three-dimensional animation that showed the titanium-toothed pipe burrow through the last few meters of cold, hard rock. It stopped abruptly as its sensors made contact with a pale substance that gave way without the slightest resistance. A burst of jubilation from the crew broke the atmosphere of heavy concentration.

Marie stood up and smiled at them with a look of quiet triumph. "*Bonjour, mon president.* Welcome back to *Atlantis.* You were just in time to watch the largest deposit of methane hydrate in the Northern Hemisphere being breached. We've confirmed seismic stability, the tanks of dennisium are in place, and we are about to begin injecting it into the cache to stabilize the first pocket. To start, only twenty-two metric tons in situ," she said in her lilting, flirtatious accent, lifting a shoulder with Gallic nonchalance.

As if making history were all in a day's work and halving the danger of a catastrophic underwater explosion was but a trifling task.

Victoria kept her polite smile in place and unclenched her teeth. The Frenchwoman might be a complete bitch on land, but she was the undisputed queen of the seafloor. There was no one on the staff more talented or more driven than Marie, and if Dennis's grand experiment of mining methane hydrate from an unmapped abyss on the floor of the Caribbean Sea was going to work, it would be because of her. Marie made things happen.

"By tonight we should have test bed preparations complete and water flowing in," she continued. "Then we will begin a test run of the full procedure. We'll extract only a few tons the first time. You are going to return for it? It promises to be a good show." She gestured to the large, unlit screen covering one wall.

"I'll be watching from above with some friends."

"So be it. Just make sure you send down the Champagne chilled and on time," Marie said nonchalantly before turning back to the monitors.

Victoria waited near the door while Dennis moved through the small space, greeting each person by name and congratulating them. While he believed in getting to know his employees personally, Victoria rarely interacted with any of them. She knew them all too intimately and too impersonally from having studied their personnel files and the frequently updated surveillance reports on each one of them, and needed to keep her distance in the event of a problem.

Keeping herself disengaged from the rest of the staff didn't bother her—childhood had provided lots of practice—but it meant the only one of her coworkers she really had a friendly relationship with was Dennis, and that had its benefits and drawbacks.

"Hey, Vic, come over here and see what—"

She sent Dennis a closed-mouth smile and remained where she was. He shook his head and rolled his eyes and returned his attention to the monitor he'd been studying a moment ago.

Fascinated though she was with what Dennis envisioned and what he had accomplished by building a comfortable habitat and functional mining operation four thousand feet below the surface of the sea, her occasional visits to the habitat were trips Victoria would have preferred to miss. She knew it was a state-of-the-art structure designed by the finest marine architects in the world and that everyone on the design team had been required to spend time living in it before the mining operations began. None of that mattered to her. The few times she'd been down here, it took all of her mental energy *not* to focus on the fact that she was in a man-made edifice that had been placed in an environment as alien and unforgiving to humans as outer space. It wasn't a simple thing to dismiss.

She wished Dennis would get on point and do what he came here to do. Not that he couldn't have done it on land. He could have. It just wouldn't have been as much fun. For him.

"Ready?" he asked, coming up to her and rubbing his hands together as if he were about to sit down to a long-anticipated feast.

"Whenever you are," she replied, and followed Dennis

to the corner of the control room that was set up for videoconferencing. The small table and chairs that were usually there had been pushed to the side and a narrow green screen had been lowered from its recessed home in the ceiling.

He came to a stop in front of the screen and turned to face the tripod-mounted camera and its operator. Victoria stopped just out of camera range. As the person who knew more about Dennis Cavendish and his secrets than anyone else alive, she avoided cameras and any other technology that might be used to publicize her existence.

"What background do you want to show, sir?" the young man beside the camera asked.

"External footage of the pods. Give me a count-down." Dennis cleared his throat and stared into the camera.

After a few taps on the keyboard, the young man looked up and nodded. "We're ready on one, sir. Four. Three. Two." He pointed a finger at Dennis, who smiled on cue.

"My friends, you know by now that I was unable to join you today on your flight to my Paradise of Taino, but I am delighted that you've accepted my invitation to join us for the weekend. That invitation was not issued casually. Your visit is not merely a social occasion, nor is it entirely a business event." He paused. "You have been invited to be the first outside witnesses to what is certainly the most significant achievement in my life and, I am no less certain, one of the greatest achievements in the course of human events.

"Ladies and gentlemen, what you see on the screen behind me is *Atlantis*, the world's first deep-sea habitat and fully operational underwater methane-hydrate mining operation. I am speaking to you from the command and control center, which is part of a habitat that houses a permanent staff of twenty-two and a dozen others who rotate through. *Atlantis* rests on the abyssal seafloor at a depth of four thousand feet off the western coast of Taino, less than fifty miles from the eastern shore of the Florida Keys. This combined structure is situated above one of the largest deposits of methane hydrate ever discovered." He paused again and his smile widened. "Three gigatons, my friends. That is our estimate of the first deposit."

His enthusiasm was infectious and, watching him, Victoria felt a zing of excitement.

I'm watching history being made.

Not one to underplay when he had a captive audience, Dennis placed his hands on his hips, stretching the white golf shirt that accentuated both the deepness of his tan and the breadth of his well-toned chest. "I count every one of you as both a personal friend and worthy colleague, and that's why I want you be the first people outside my organization to learn about this venture. You also represent nine of the largest, most diversified conglomerates in the world. You don't need me to tell you that the combination of the size of this deposit and the first safe, economically feasible means of extracting methane hydrate is much more than just another business opportunity. This isn't just another step forward for technological evolution, my friends; this is the dawn of the world's second Industrial Revolution. That means *jobs*. Real jobs, and lots of them. Not just for the boys on Wall Street, not just for the accountants. But for steelworkers and pipe fitters, civil engineers and administrative assistants. There will be jobs at transfer stations, offices, and billing centers. Web sites will need to be built, prospectuses written—this is 'trickle *up*' economics, and there is no doubt in my mind that it will truly take our economy to the top of the world. There's a new Golden Age waiting just ahead, and you, *we,* will be the people who introduce the world to it."

He stopped and stared intently into· the camera. "What we've accomplished here means that the balance of the world's power is about to undergo a civilization-altering shift. It means we in the West can finally achieve independence from petroleum-based fuels without ir-radiating the planet to do it. The success of *Atlantis* means affordable clean power, a surge in the development of new technologies, and the revitalization of stag-nating national economies." He leaned forward from the waist, as if he were talking to a· group standing in front of him instead of a group who would be watching him on a screen.

"I know what some of you might be thinking right now. You're thinking about all the bad things you've heard about methane, how it's the nasty cousin of car-bon dioxide, that its presence in the atmosphere would speed up climate change. That a large release would be catastrophic. Well, we know all about it. We know more about it than anyone does, and that's because we have more to lose than anyone does if something goes wrong, catastrophic or not." He flared his hands in front of him with a half-shrug. "If you need to hear me say something negative about the project, I'll admit that what scientists say about methane is true. Pulling it out of the seafloor could be a double-edged sword—if we have an accident. But there won't be any accidents. Ev-erything we've done has met standards set far beyond the most stringent safety regulations. We've looked into the probability of earthquakes, tsunamis, even terrorist activity. We rewrote the actuarial tables using Dooms-day as our starting point." He grinned and gave another shrug. "Nothing is going to go wrong."

"We have been operational for four months. *Four months.* We've had technical and scientific teams living in the habitat in rotations, making sure it is completely safe, comfortable, and functional. We've had hydrogeologists and seismologists and mining experts down here. We've had everyone down here. And it works." He straightened up and folded his arms across his chest, almost as if he were defiant. "My friends, tomorrow we go live. We will conduct the inaugural excavation exercise and you will be topside on Taino with me, watching it in real time. And then we'll talk about the roles you can play in this new dawn. Until then." He gave his customary half-salute and remained in that pose until the camera's red light went out.

"Thanks. When that's cleaned up, upload it to Micki and tell her to send it to the plane," he said to the technician, then walked to where Victoria stood. "Well?"

Dennis was as renowned for being overbearing and cocky as he was for being a brilliant businessman, and both reputations were fully deserved. But sometimes he just seemed like a kid with more energy than he could contain. Like right now, standing before her bouncing lightly on the balls of his feet, clearly delighted with himself.

She shook her head with a grin. "You did well, Dennis, as you know." She glanced at her watch. "The plane should be taking off from Miami soon. We should probably head up. Was there anything else you wanted to do while we're down here?"

His mood changed perceptibly as he shook his head and let out a deep, annoyed breath.

"You're transparent as hell, Vic," he murmured as they moved toward the door that would lead them out of the operations center. "And you're raining on my damned parade."

They departed the structure less than ten minutes later. Moving back through the same series of airlocks and comforting corridors that bisected the large modular units, they eventually arrived at the docking area where they'd left the small deep-sea submersible *Rachel Carson*. Four other, larger subs remained strategically docked at the habitat and ready at all times in case an emergency evacuation was required.

Fighting the sickening waves of claustrophobia that licked at the edges of her composure, Victoria kept her mind focused strictly on the task of the moment as she strapped herself into one of the *Rachel*'s two passenger seats. Dennis sat comfortably in the pilot's seat and, as always, Victoria kept her eyes on his hands as they moved in a purposeful ballet across the controls that surrounded him on all sides.

Minutes later, the bulbous craft detached itself from the docking pod with a loud clunk and a soft hiss, and Victoria braced herself for the split-second sensation of falling. They weren't actually falling, and she knew it, but that instant when they were no longer attached to something earthbound always caused a burst of adrenaline to spike her bloodstream and terrorize her stomach.

"You still with me?" Dennis asked quietly as he began maneuvering the submersible away from the modular bathyscaphic structure that shone ghostly white in the path of the sub's lights.

"Where else would I be?" she asked, forcing an easiness into her voice. Ease was the last thing she was actually feeling.

She watched his shoulders move as he shrugged without looking back at her.

"I don't know. I thought maybe you'd be unconscious, or immersed in one of those guided visualizations. A rose-covered cottage or something. I know this isn't your favorite place to be, even though I'll never understand that. For someone who swears she's not claustrophobic, you do a hell of a good imitation of someone who is."

"I'm fine. Living in the present," she said tightly, and swallowed against the mild nausea that was, for her, another routine component of these trips. It wasn't so much the motion that bothered her, because there wasn't much of a sensation of moving, and it wasn't the sound. Supposedly this vehicle was quieter than most. The hum of the battery-driven motor was discernible but not obnoxious. What got to her was the sense of isolation, of containment. She'd been punished too many times as a child by being locked in a dark cabinet and told to think hard about the wages of sin and the horrors of Hell.

In those days, she'd never considered that Hell could be underwater, but now, if she still believed in Hell, she'd be willing to consider it.

Partially to conserve energy but mostly as an attempt to placate her nerves, Dennis turned off the lights as soon as they were clear of the habitat structure. The muted blue-white glow of the control panel didn't do much to offset the view from the huge convex window next to her, which revealed a darkness unrivaled by anything she'd ever experienced above sea level.

These trips, the time spent shuttling to the seafloor and back, were what Victoria least enjoyed about her job. Traversing a black, cold, deadly void in a small sphere with only a few layers of titanium, graphite composites, and ceramics between her and a psi greater than one hundred and twenty times the air pressure at sea level was a thrill she would prefer to do without. She usually kept her eyes open but averted from the window despite the darkness on the other side of it. The bizarre bioluminescent creatures that floated by only served to remind her of where she was and that it would be more than half an hour before the slightest glimmer of sunlight would be visible, and an additional fifteen minutes or so beyond that until she would be on dry land again.

Dennis, however, came away from his every trip to *Atlantis*—which were far more frequent than hers—in a state close to euphoria. And why not, she thought wryly, willing her stomach into quiescence. He'd defied logic, reason, and fiscal sanity by insisting on building a habitat and mining operation on the seafloor and, in doing so, he'd pushed science and engineering to new heights, or more accurately, new depths. Eight hundred new patents had been registered to the institute since he'd begun this project, and the world's governments and most major corporations were waging a ferocious competition for his time, his people, his results. And the application of scruples was apparently optional, which is why Victoria figured so importantly into the mix.

A mostly self-taught, shoot-from-the-hip security expert, she had deliberately turned years of careful, subtle observation of how people operated into something that other people didn't want to mess with. Her appearance fed into it. Not the fact that she was rather short and small-boned. That made her fairly ordinary at first glance. But the genetic misfire that had given her, a full-blooded Japanese woman, a pair of blue eyes had always startled people.

Throughout the history of civilization, ridiculous superstitions had been attached to children with obvious differences, and her case was no different. Because of her eyes, a lot of people had assumed she had extra abilities at her disposal. She'd never done anything to ease their minds, because in at least one way, their assumptions were correct.

It was her eyes that had led to her abandonment as an infant in a remote and poverty-stricken village on one of Japan's outer islands, and her adoption by an American missionary couple. Her heritage and her disconcerting eyes had also been what had gotten her placed into an out-of-the-way orphanage when those adoptive parents had died in an accident soon after returning to the United States. None of her adoptive parents' blond, blue-eyed, God-fearing Minnesotan relatives had wanted to take her in, lest an outsider think her presence in the family bespoke a loss of morals rather than an act of charity.

That being exotic had its benefits as well as its downfalls had been an early lesson. By the time she was six, she'd learned that the deliberate application of exquisitely patient silence was all that was usually required to unnerve even the most stoic people. Whether it was cultural heredity or the experience of having grown up as the only Asian in a sea of Teutons, the only dark-haired child among one hundred orphaned blondes, Victoria knew that her patience was her greatest asset. Things always revealed themselves to those who remained calm, who waited—and who watched. Most people, even Dennis, were too busy to do any of those.

"A million for your thoughts." His voice was teasing

but when Victoria turned to face him in the small space, Dennis's eyes were serious.

"Who ever said inflation was a bad thing?" she replied lightly. "Unfortunately, what I'm thinking isn't worth half as much."

He reached up to flip the switch that stopped their conversation from being recorded. "You're clenched."

"Only my hands. And you should be watching the controls, not me."

"Not just your hands. Your whole body. And I don't have to look at you to know it. What's wrong?"

"I'm thirty-seven hundred feet beneath the sea surface inside a small, hard ball. Need I say more?"

"That's not it."

"Well, that's not *all* of it." She paused. "You know that we shouldn't be here together."

"That's what you were thinking?"

"No. But it needs pointing out. You know it's against policy."

Bold and brash, Dennis Cavendish had been a favored target for crime long before Victoria had started working for him. His personal history was littered with attempted kidnappings and attempted extortion. More recently, his companies and even the island—once—had been targeted by terrorists. While he took his own personal safety very seriously, he was a fiend when it came to protecting his people and his companies.

"Relax, Vic. This was an unplanned trip. Only a few people—trusted people—know we're here."

"There are no trusted people, Dennis. Besides, who knows we're here hardly matters. You are the CEO of the company and the president of the country, and I'm your security chief, and here we sit in a battery-operated bowling ball that's moving slowly through four thousand vertical feet of water, with a few miles of horizontal motion in the equation, and will be doing so for nearly an hour. We're throwing off dozens of frequencies in every direction, and we're making a lot of noise. Anyone out there with sonar can pick us up. We're the epitome of a—"

"Sitting duck?"

"Fish in a barrel," she finished with a raised eyebrow.

He sat back as best he could in the contoured chair and put one hand on his hip. The other was wrapped around the joystick. He leveled a hard look at her. "Who don't you trust?"

"Who *do* I trust is the finer point."

"And?"

"The answer is no one, as you well know."

"Not me?"

"No, not you. You trust me, which is required to maintain the dynamic. But I mustn't trust anyone, or the game is over and we've lost."

"Then who do you suspect, and of what?"

She folded her arms and returned his look. "Dennis, it's not a matter of suspecting someone of something, it's a matter of suspecting everyone of anything."

"You do realize that sounds a bit crazy."

"Yes, I do, thank you," she said tightly.

"What is it you want to do?"

"I'd like to send some people to the mainland. Business trip. I don't know. Some excuse."

"Who and why?"

"Micki and a few key managers," she said without hesitation.

"Oh, hell. That's the damned continuity plan, isn't it? You want to put that in play. Well, the answer is no. They've all been working as hard as you and me and they deserve to be here for the test. And the test is what's got you all nervous. That and the guests. Well, quit it. I need you sharp, not muddled, so don't go all woo-woo on me. That may work on some people, but not on me. As you know."

"I'm not woo-woo, but I trust my instinct. The test is huge, Dennis, it's what we've been working toward for years and something about it has my intuition on high alert."

He smiled. "Vic, you've done your thing. We're secure. Our people are safe. Maybe *you* need a break. Why don't you go somewhere for a few days?"

Victoria was momentarily speechless.

"I can't leave now," she sputtered.

"Good. That's settled then. You should relax and enjoy the show."

"Hogwash. The guests you have arriving in"—she checked her watch—"one hour will provide a bigger target for the malefactors of the world than if you were hosting the G8."

"No one knows they're coming here."

She rolled her eyes at his deliberate provocation. "You don't really believe that, do you? You've just been wining and dining them all over Miami for the last few days. And they've all got their crackberries going twenty-four/ seven. If anyone sees them get on that plane, *everyone* will know they're coming here."

"Big deal. No one will know why they're coming. And this is the most secure location in the world. You've made it that. Everything is going to be fine," he said in a patronizing tone that they both knew would infuriate her.

It worked. She took a slow breath. "Dennis—"

"Get over it, Vic," he said flatly. "We've got it covered. You've got it covered. Bring it up again and I'll think you're obsessing."

"Obsessing is part of my job description," she said coolly. "And this is hardly—"

"This conversation is over," he said, and switched on the powerful underwater lights so he could watch the bizarre creatures they were passing by. Victoria closed her eyes.

CHAPTER

9:30 A.M., Saturday, October 25, Miami, Florida
Finishing her walk around the sleek, one-hundred-foot-long Bombardier Global Express that bore The Paradise of Taino ornate purple and gold crest on its tail, Wendy ran her hand over the name painted below the cockpit windshield. As the plane's first pilot, she'd had the privilege of naming it. She'd chosen *Gaia* as a salute to Garner, although she'd never told him. He'd find out when he heard the news that she'd completed her flight plan.

With a tight smile, she climbed the steps into the cabin. It still smelled new, but the mingled aromas of soft leather, rare tropical woods, and fresh coffee were incongruous against the airport's acrid signature scent of hot asphalt and jet fuel.

Lieutenant Colonel Watson made her way to the

state-of-the-art cockpit of the $40 million jet, smiling tightly at the crew milling around the pristine, streamlined, but fully equipped commercial kitchen that masqueraded as the plane's galley. Each member of the crew smiled back as they greeted her. Wendy stopped herself from wondering if her crew—the three flight attendants, her first officer, and the chef—needed to die. The answer was yes, unequivocally yes. They were as much a part of the problem as anyone else.

The flight attendants were more than just beautiful to look at. Each one had completed rigorous security and antiterrorist training, and each was qualified to handle the most serious medical emergencies that could transpire aboard an aircraft. Because of Dennis Cavendish's unerring ability to seriously infuriate the leaders of the world's larger nations, each flight he took was like a military exercise with regard to the security measures taken, but the food was better and the surroundings more luxurious.

Entering the cockpit, Wendy slid into her seat. She automatically scanned the bank of controls in front of her and began her preflight checks.

Everything was in order, as she knew it would be. Even the weather was cooperating. All she needed now were the passengers.

A shadow moved across her instrument panel and she glanced up to see the senior flight attendant appear in the doorway of the cockpit. The woman leaned into Wendy's space gracefully, her Jean Paul Gaultier–designed uniform showing to advantage the assets that had won her a Miss Something-or-Other crown several years earlier. A small diamond tiara displaying the Taino crest was nestled into an artfully tousled swath of honey-and-butter-blond hair.

The entire cabin crew, even the men, resembled the woman in the cockpit doorway: polished, glamorous, pampered. And lethal, if necessary.

"They're going to be late," the attendant—Wendy had never bothered to learn any of their names—purred in cool, cultured British tones that were alluringly underlain with unfettered Brazilian sexiness. "The helicopters are on their way now. Their ETA is twenty minutes."

"Thank you," Wendy replied tonelessly, looking away from the practiced smile, the flawless makeup, the endlessly long legs.

It wasn't the crew members' beauty that annoyed her, nor their overtly sexual languor. It wasn't even their studied vapidity. What annoyed her, when she bothered to think of it, was their lack of purpose. They were drones with no drive and no goals, squandering their utility. It was wasteful, and in direct contradiction to her own life.

Wendy had been born to parents who had worked hard to pull themselves out of their lower-middle-class background and into the cloistered cocoon of Darien, Connecticut, where expectations were high and wealth was assumed. They had no idea that their aspirations and pretensions had isolated their only child from her schoolmates, no idea how difficult it had been for her to assimilate. They had wanted a better life for her, and had raised her against the backdrop of the town's burgeoning wealth and blatant ostentation. Wendy had been indoctrinated every day of her life with the importance of reaching ever higher. Bettering themselves in the eyes of others was her parents' mission in life; for them, to stop moving upward was to stop living.

It was a philosophy she'd never accepted or understood.

Now, after decades of searching for meaning in her life, she had found direction. She would repay the generous sacrifices of past generations of the Earth's creatures with a gift to all future generations. Garner Blaylock had entrusted *her* with the honor of laying the cornerstone of a new world order in which all creatures would have equal worth and be granted equal esteem.

Her time had finally arrived.

"Is there anything I can do for you, Colonel?"

Wendy picked up a clipboard that rested on the still-empty seat beside her. As usual, her first officer considered flirting more important than doing his job.

"Yes, there is something you can do for me. Arrange for me to have some solitude, if you can manage it," Wendy replied bluntly, her flat, American intonation a stark contrast to the sensual tones of the other woman.

A minuscule pause was followed by the soft rustle of fabric. "Certainly, Colonel. I'll inform the crew you are not to be disturbed. Please press the call button if you wish for any attention."

The cockpit door closed with the softest of clicks and Wendy continued running through her preflight checks without giving the crew another thought.

A burst of muffled conversation a short while later was followed by laughter and the sound of the passengers embarking. Fifteen minutes later, after the commotion had quieted, Jason Randall, her first officer, entered the cockpit and strapped himself in.

"Is everyone aboard?" Wendy asked, not looking up from what she was doing.

"All aboard who's going aboard," he replied breezily. "Strapped in nice and tight with their *Wall Street Journals* in one hand and their Cristal mimosas in the other."

Wendy rolled her eyes and said nothing as she stood up and slipped into her jacket. She emerged from the cockpit with her impeccably tailored uniform in perfect order, the traditional, military-style officer's cap placed at a precise angle on her head, and moved through the cabin to personally greet the CEOs of nine of the world's largest corporations. Looking each one in the eyes, she shook hands and smiled and forced herself to make small talk.

They represented so much money, so much power. So much devastation.

It would be a pleasure to kill them.

Dennis wasn't in evidence, but the door to his private cabin at the rear of the plane was closed. It wasn't unusual for him to retreat there to take phone calls, so Wendy didn't think twice about it. The senior flight attendant assured her the head count was complete. As the crew continued its well-rehearsed program of making everyone comfortable, Wendy excused herself to return to the cockpit. She contacted the tower for a departure time for what everyone expected would be a quick trip to Taino.

They had a long wait for a break in the heavy outbound traffic from Miami International, so it was forty-five minutes later that Wendy noted with a distinct surge of pride that her hands were steady and dry as the plane began its initial descent to the lush, low-key Caribbean paradise called Taino.

The sea below them was mottled, the sapphire blues and tropical greens demarking reefs and sand spits and sheer drops into the abysses of the ocean. It was a sight that would be familiar to everyone in the world within an hour or two.

In three minutes they would exit American airspace

and transit Bahamian territory for a few minutes before turning into Taino's airspace, where the flight would terminate, albeit differently and earlier than anyone save Wendy and Garner Blaylock anticipated.

Harboring the same fear-tinged thrill that had marked every dangerous mission she'd ever flown, Wendy was unable to keep a smile completely off her face as she looked over at her copilot. "He's been awfully quiet."

Jason looked up from his greasy breakfast burrito and hastily swallowed his mouthful. "Who?"

"Dennis." The loathing in her voice was barely perceptible to Wendy's ears, and she knew Jason would never pick up on it. "He's usually poked his head in here at least once by this time."

"Gee, Wendy, that might be because he's not on board," he said with a roll of his eyes. Then, losing what little interest he'd had in the conversation, Jason returned his attention to the disgusting tangle of eggs and cheese and tortillas in his hands.

Doing so, he missed what would be his only chance to see a crack in the legendary composure of Lieutenant Colonel Wendy Watson. Nausea punched her hard and fast, filling every recess in her gut with panic and something even more foreign to her: the certainty of failure.

"What do you mean?" she demanded, her voice held low and steady only through the forceful application of the lessons learned over a lifetime. "He boarded the aircraft with the other passengers. I heard him talking with the crew."

Jason glanced up again, wiping a slash of grease from his chin with a wadded paper napkin. "No you didn't. Cavendish headed back a few hours ago on the

Lear. Four in the morning or something. I thought you knew." He shrugged. "Anyway, what's the big deal?"

Wendy shook her head and unbuckled her seat belt. "Take the controls. I'll be back in a minute."

Ignoring his annoyed curses and the startled expressions on the faces of the crew members she passed, Wendy barged into the crew's head, locked the door, and slumped against the wall. She believed too completely in fate to consider this a coincidence.

This failure will be my legacy.

She swallowed against the bile rising in her throat. No one inside or outside of GAIA would suspect her of complicity. She was certain of that. Her loyalty had never been questioned by anyone, nor would it ever be. But this failure would leave the organization—now her only family—with the mistaken notion that they had a traitor in their midst. Searching for a traitor who did not exist would fracture the bonds of trust that Garner had tempered and strengthened carefully over many years, beginning long before she had joined him. Wendy knew, from her years in the military, that misplaced suspicions led to carelessness, to indiscretions, to real leaks, which inevitably led to discovery.

Two decades of Garner's effort would be jeopardized. Millions of dollars in investments would be compromised. The plans of dozens of men and women who had committed themselves to leading a chastened world back to the doorstep of their Earth Mother would be curtailed. Their beliefs would be mocked and marginalized, their actions demonized, their voices silenced.

It could take another decade, maybe more, to regain what GAIA was about to lose.

The cruelest realization was that even though she

had not been thorough, had not confirmed Dennis's presence on the plane, Wendy had no option but to follow through as planned. But now she would not die as a triumphant martyr to the cause, one whose sacrifice would be celebrated. She would die a failure.

The synchronized bombs she had placed so carefully throughout the fuselage yesterday could not be defused or deactivated, nor could she send a warning to Garner. All onboard communications would be scrutinized when—if—the black box was found. News of an encrypted message sent from the pilot of a private jet to an anonymous Internet dead-drop minutes before a midair explosion would trigger too many questions, inspire too many investigations. She couldn't do that to Garner. She wouldn't.

Wendy took a slow breath, keeping her eyes open and focused as she had always done in the face of danger.

Subterfuge was an option—making her stupid pig of a copilot the scapegoat. She could kill him with one quick blow to the throat, and claim later it was self-defense with no one the wiser; there was barely time enough to begin a rapid descent, to issue a Mayday call and evacuate the passengers and crew, to ditch the plane in the ocean before—

Coldness gripped her, seeped through her with the sureness of death, the implacable knowledge of fate achieved.

There would be no life for her if she aborted the plan. Yes, she would be crowned with the halo of heroics by the media and the world, but Garner would despise her. He had changed her life, had changed *her* by making her see what she had been too blind to see before. Living on the same Earth, breathing the same air while knowing he loathed her, would be intolerable.

She took a steadying breath. Better to complete the task as honorably as she could, even knowing that GAIA, the people who shared the ideals for which she was sacrificing her life, would remember her as committed but ultimately a failure. If her name was mentioned at all in the future, it would be with scorn, or in the context of a cautionary tale. She retched into the bidet, knowing the toilet floor was a better place to die than she deserved.

This flight had been chosen by Garner specifically because of its passenger list and destination. *Everything* had depended upon Dennis's being among the victims.

Wendy stood, cleaned herself up, and returned to the cockpit. She could do no less than die as she had agreed to. At the controls of the aircraft.

She was barely buckled into her seat when the first explosion rocked the plane. Her training took over and Wendy barely blinked against the harsh, sooty fumes before pulling on her breathing mask and goggles. Icy cold air pulled at her as she began to transmit the Mayday call. Next to her, Jason had slammed his equipment onto his face and had already opened the box housing the inflatable vision unit. Within seconds, he had the IVU attached, inflated, and activated, providing them with an unobstructed view of their instruments and chart. Wendy knew the device wouldn't help them for long, and she braced herself for the second set of explosions.

The roar was deafening, and instantly the plane's nose lurched downward at a sickeningly steep angle. Like a rookie, Wendy threw up in her mask as the plane began to plummet toward the water. The momentum of the plane's freefall made it difficult to pull the vomit-filled mask from her face, and as she did her elbow hit something warm and solid. Turning, she saw her copilot's body slumped over the side of his seat. Wendy realized then she would be alive when she hit the water.

Seconds later the detached cockpit began to cartwheel insanely across the waves. A terrible dizziness and searing pain were rapidly replaced by a cold, wet darkness, and then by nothing at all.

CHAPTER

10:35 A.M., Saturday, October 25, off the coast of Taino

Dennis Cavendish was endlessly fascinated by what lay beneath the sea. Not just the life he found there, but the possibilities. From the time he'd strapped on his first snorkel in an unheralded attempt to face another fear, he'd been hooked. He'd quickly graduated from snorkeling to scuba diving, to going on successively deeper, more challenging dives until he'd been able to persuade a small firm to let him dive using a one-atmosphere dive suit.

Sealed inside the bulky, jointed "robot suit," he'd been strapped onto a small platform affixed to the outside of a deep-diving submersible as if he were a piece of machinery rather than a live man dependent on rebreathers and meticulously sealed joints for his survival. The submersible had been lowered from the research boat into the warm, sparkling waters off the Florida coast and released. Unencumbered by any tethers to surface ships, the small, rotund craft had descended steadily through the graduated light and then indescribable darkness to the seafloor eleven hundred feet below the surface.

Once the craft had settled gently onto the silty seafloor, Dennis had been released from his bonds and had taken one step, then another into a world in which he was the alien and the locals were unafraid.

Given the relative distances involved, it was inconceivable to him that more people had "walked" in outer space than on the bottom of the sea at such depths. Dennis's experience had changed his life by awakening him to the realization that the sea wasn't the barren, underwater desert so many assumed it was. It was brimming with life and an energy he couldn't describe.

He'd spent two hours walking in the shifting circle of brilliant light cast by the submersible's headlamp. When he'd arrived back at the surface, Dennis hadn't known how to parlay what he'd just been through into something useful. What he did know was that his time on the seafloor had changed his life's purpose irrevocably.

It was no longer about accumulating money.

It was no longer about facing a challenge.

It was about mastery. Conquering what others declared unconquerable and changing the way the world worked.

Dennis started reading everything he could find on deepwater research. He attended conferences where he was the only one without a string of letters and honorifics after his name. He funded off-the-wall research that earned him public ridicule instead of private riches. He didn't care. He had enough of the latter.

And then a request from a small business looking for an angel investor landed on his desk. The firm was investigating the feasibility of excavating methane hydrate—something he'd never heard of until then—from the seafloor for use as a new, clean fuel.

Dennis hadn't granted them the money. He'd bought the firm outright, knowing instinctively that this was the opportunity he'd been waiting for.

For decades, the big oil companies had raped and plundered the earth and held much of her population in thrall, all the while enjoying profits that became more obscene with each passing year. They weren't alone. Much of heavy industry nurtured Big Oil like a doting aunt, and the financial markets were eager toadies. And now Dennis had the opportunity to destroy oil's stranglehold. The very thought of it induced a feeling in him that was more heady than the finest wine, the best weed, or sex with a porn star.

It was power. Pure, uncomplicated, and it intoxicated him.

He slowed the submersible's speed as it neared the surface and glanced at Victoria. "You can open your eyes now. We're approaching splashup."

Her eyes snapped open, then blinked rapidly when brilliant sunlight streamed into the cabin as the sub crested the surface. "Thank God."

Dennis maneuvered the craft to the submerged platform and landed it. He signaled to the wet suit–clad technicians that they could tie it down.

As soon as the vehicle was secured, the docking platform rose to the level of the walkway, and Dennis began the sequence that would release the air pressure and allow the hatch to open.

"All right, come to papa," he said with a grin as he helped a pale and wobbly-kneed Victoria step onto the dock.

She said nothing, just held on to him for a moment.

"Got your mojo back?" Dennis asked softly. When Victoria nodded, with the faint beginnings of a smile, he released her and they began to walk to the nearby building that housed his office.

At the sound of someone shouting, Dennis's head snapped up. Victoria's assistant was coming toward them at a dead run. When she reached them, she had only to gasp four words—"The plane's gone down"—for both Dennis and Vic to break into a hard sprint headed straight for the offices.

10:38 A.M., Saturday, October 25, Taino

Micki Crenshaw, undersecretary for national security and Victoria's second in command, sat stone-faced in front of a bank of television monitors in Dennis's office. A small telephone headset hung, forgotten, from her left ear. In accordance with the disaster response policies she and Victoria had established, Micki had already shut down all communications systems linking Taino to the outside world, with the exception of the one to their embassy in Washington, D.C.

Right now what mattered was responding to the situation at hand, without the world getting in the way.

Four of the monitors Micki faced were dark; the other two were live. One showed slowed-down satellite footage of a jet flying unremarkably through a blue, cloudless sky until, in the space of a frame, the plane exploded into a blur of smoke that billowed thickly in all directions. Within a few frames, the fuselage separated into two flaming pieces and began to freefall, one segment trailing pale smoke and one trailing black. Seconds later, each piece shattered again. Innumerable smaller objects—seats, luggage, bodies, the distance was so great they were impossible to identify—fell more slowly through the sky, some on fire or smoking, but most without any telltale trails.

In what seemed no time at all, the fiery rain of debris began to pockmark the calm blue-green ocean, sending up graceful, arcing eruptions of white froth. Too soon, it seemed, Nature returned to equilibrium. Some evidence that the aircraft had existed floated gently on the surface of the sea; most sank without a trace. Other than the places where the spilled jet fuel was burning, the easy morning swells swallowed the crash, leaving the scene of the impact almost unremarkable in its ordinariness.

The other monitor showed the head-on view, also slowed down, from the small control tower near the landing strip on Taino. Visual contact had been established only minutes before the accident. Captions along the bottom of the screen indicated the tower and the copilot had been acknowledging the plane's final descent when the copilot's words were cut off in midsentence, replaced seconds later by the pilot's Mayday call. Then the plane exploded, breaking up in full view of the tower and anyone who might be on the beach or a nearby boat.

The full-frontal footage was spectacular, awe-inspiring, and it made Micki's pulse throb with a dreadful excitement. At the same time, watching the loss of life made her stomach clutch and begin to rise into her throat. She'd anticipated that effect, however, and it faded quickly as a feeling simultaneously more primitive and more sophisticated took its place.

Triumph.

We did it. Our time has arrived.

The time for vengeance had arrived, and the Earth *would be* avenged for all the heinous crimes committed upon Her in the name of progress, in the name of convenience. Garner would see to it. He always had. He always would, until he was returned to Her loving embrace to become one with Her again.

Micki closed her eyes and swallowed hard against the urge to laugh out loud at the joy of it. She knew the slightest hint of a smile now would be enough to tip off Victoria to the truth later, after Victoria had taken the time to re-create the event and retrace every movement the flight and ground crews had made. No, Micki knew that right now she had to be as shocked and horrified as the rest of the—

Her gaze shifted to the doorway and she felt the wind knocked out of her as both Victoria and Dennis burst through the door.

Dennis.

Small black pinpricks sparkled at the edges of her vision. Micki knew that in seconds she would faint.

The heady triumph drained out of her as she realized they had failed. Wendy had failed.

Dennis was alive.

I have to get a grip on myself.

Focusing on an unmoving point on the far wall, she took several slow, deep breaths and let her vision clear before she met their eyes.

The expression Dennis wore was a mixture of cold fear and hot fury, and he was panting from either exertion or shock, maybe both. Victoria, as usual, looked unruffled, but her face was pale and her disturbingly blue eyes seemed too big for her small face.

Hiding her anger fed into a renewed strength of purpose. Micki rose slowly and dropped the remote control for the monitors onto the pristine surface of Dennis's desk.

The games are about to begin.

Victoria was two steps behind Dennis when he burst into the office. She was trying to formulate strategies though she had nothing but a single fact to go on: The plane was gone.

"Micki, what happened?" Dennis bellowed.

Micki seemed almost stunned for a moment as they entered the room, but quickly composed herself. Looking as calm as could be hoped for under the circumstances, she reached up to fiddle with and remove her earpiece. She gave Dennis and Victoria a level, detached stare as she came around the desk to meet them.

"Ten minutes ago we lost the *Gaia,* her crew, and all passengers on board, Dennis. It went down four miles inside our territorial boundary. That's all I know," Micki replied, her normally soft and musical Alabama drawl constrained with tension. "I initiated the Code Black response and immediately shut down all communication links between the island and the outside world, with the exception of the secure satellite link to the embassy. I've ordered a team to be sequestered to review the last twenty-four hours of all comms traffic, incoming and outgoing. I've scrambled a search-and-recovery team and ordered the *Sylvia Earle* and the *Wangari Maathai* to sail for the crash site," she said, referring to two of the research vessels attached to the Climate Research Institute. "The *Marjory Stoneman Douglas* was already in the area and should reach the crash site at about the same time as the search team. They might be there already."

Victoria was leaning against the wall, waiting for the adrenaline rush to subside, during Micki's calm recitation of her actions. Micki had done exactly what she should have done, by the book. Victoria shouldn't be surprised, really, considering that they'd run countless tabletop drills for all possible emergencies. That Micki had handled everything so coolly and efficiently showed an extraordinary presence of mind under what were shocking circumstances. Her response was stellar.

Then why do I have chills running down my back?

Victoria kept her eyes trained on Micki, as if she couldn't tear them away. But there was nothing out of the ordinary about Micki. Drawn but calm, she was standing stock-still in front of Dennis's desk, watching him as he paced like a caged animal.

"Do we know what happened?" Dennis barked.

"All we know so far is what we can see," Micki replied quietly, tilting her pretty blond head toward the flat screens mounted on the wall opposite Dennis's desk.

He spun to face them as Micki aimed the remote control at the screens and let the short loops of footage begin.

The images were horrific and mesmerizing.

"What's going on out there now? Can you pull up a live feed?" Victoria asked quietly.

With a nod, Micki pointed the remote at the next screen and clicked it, then pulled Dennis's keyboard toward her and rapidly typed in a sequence.

One of the research boats was on the scene, surrounded by five or so wetsuited security teams on Jet Skis and a few more in inflatables. Bobbing easily on the calm sea, surrounded by debris and dark slicks of spilled fuel, some still burning, they appeared to be waiting for something. Or perhaps just absorbing the chaos.

"Jesus Christ Almighty." Dennis took a short, hard breath. "Get the chopper. I'm going out there."

He began moving toward the door. As he passed her, Victoria reached out and grabbed his upper arms in a grip that threatened to cut off his circulation. "Wait a minute."

"Knock it off. I'm—"

"Dennis, wait," she repeated, her mind racing in too many directions too fast. She looked up at him and knew he was fighting the same smothering confusion. "Nothing is making sense to anyone right now. Just wait for a few minutes. 'Til the fog in our brains clears away a little."

"What the fuck does that mean, Vic?" he snapped. "I need to be out there."

"You might think you need to be out there, but no one else will appreciate it, Dennis. It's your need you're thinking of, not theirs," she pointed out, meeting his glare as calmly as she could. "No one out there needs *you*. Not right now, anyway. You'll only get in their way. It's too chaotic. Even they are still figuring out what to do. There's fire, a fuel spill, a huge debris field—let them assess the situation. It's what they're trained to do. They'll let us know what they need. And I guarantee the last thing they need is a helicopter out there churning up the crash site."

He was breathing as if he'd just finished a sprint. "I'm going out there, Vic."

She clenched her teeth and put as much fire into her eyes as she had in her. "No, you're *not*. You're staying here, Dennis. I swear to God, if I have to pin you down and tie you up, *you are staying here with me*."

"The fuck I am."

Dennis's face, contorted with tension and suffused with anger, let her know his heart rate was approaching the red zone.

"You can't. I won't let you, Dennis. You're the pres—"

He tried again to shrug her off but pulling away didn't dislodge her hands. Hers was a death grip.

"God damn it. Back off, Vic. It was my plane, my people. I'm—"

"Stand down, Dennis," she snapped and gave him a hard shake. "For God's sake, *you were supposed to be on that plane*. Think about that. Whoever planned this didn't know you weren't on board. No one knew except you and me and the pilot who brought you here before dawn." She paused to take a shaky breath and continued in a slightly calmer voice. "Dennis, we don't know what brought the *Gaia* down and we have no idea what's waiting for us out there. There could be other—"

He froze at her words and stared at her, the blood suddenly draining from his face. "You think someone did this?"

"Yes." The word came out of her mouth forcefully, without hesitation or forethought, and the strength of it made her blink. But she didn't doubt herself. She never did when her gut spoke to her. Not for a second.

"But you don't—"

"Until I'm convinced otherwise, you stay on land." Victoria knew her eyes were boring into his.

Dennis stared her down as his breathing became less labored and his color improved. "That's paranoid."

"We went over this less than an hour ago."

"The security at our Miami hangar makes TSA—hell, it makes the Secret Service drool with envy, Vic. No one can get near our planes."

"That depends on how you define 'no one.'" Letting out a hard breath, she released his arms, ready to launch herself at him if he so much as moved. "We need to find out what happened first. Review these tapes in detail—" She waved her hand toward the screens. "We have to find the voice and equipment recorders. Find out if the plane was shot down or if it exploded or just fell out of the sky. All of that could take days, probably longer." She took a final steadying breath and straightened her back, which was still rigid with tension. "But one thing I think we have to assume is that it was sabotage or terrorism. Deliberate in any case. That's gut."

Dennis began to speak and she cut him off. "Don't start arguing with me. An accident is too unlikely. The plane was a month old and had been taken care of like a baby." She turned to Micki. "Other than Dennis, were all expected passengers on board?"

Micki, more wide-eyed now than she had been when they entered the room, nodded. "Yes. I talked to the tower. The copilot checked in with them shortly after they took off. He confirmed that everyone was aboard. I . . . I don't know if he knew Dennis was . . . I didn't ask . . ." she replied, her words ending abruptly in a choked murmur. Micki closed her eyes then and took a deep breath.

Victoria shook off another chill and then returned her attention to her boss, whose color wasn't fully back to normal. "Dennis, think about it. Even without you aboard, the passengers represented companies that produce twenty-one percent of the entire world's gross domestic product. They are the world's largest employers, biggest consumers of natural resources, the biggest polluters. With the exception of Takayashi, they're all Western owned and Western run. A few of the individuals on board had a personal net worth larger than some Third World nations. That all has to mean something." She stopped for a breath, never taking her eyes off him. "*You* were supposed to be on that flight, Dennis. You, who are poised to exploit the world's last, best hope for clean fuel. To think this is a coincidence would be ridiculous."

"No one knows about that except our people, Vic." Dennis folded his arms across his chest, but before his hands disappeared from view, Victoria noted that they were shaking. The sight hit her harder than the images of the plane exploding.

From the edge of her vision, Victoria became aware again of Micki's rapt attention, and forced another degree of cool composure into her voice. "Don't kid yourself, Dennis. Despite all of our efforts, I'm sure there are plenty of people who either know or suspect what we're doing. In light of all that, it would be naive to think this event is anything other than deliberate. And we can't rule out inside cooperation."

"Inside cooperation?" he repeated, looking as though she'd just sucker punched him. "That's asinine. It's—"

"It's anything but," she interrupted quietly. "This is one of those situations that we've been both dreading and anticipating. This is what we've planned for and trained for. It's what you hired me to handle. And now that it's happened, either you listen to me, Dennis, or I'll step aside and let you take care of it yourself. You can't have it both ways."

He was staring at her as if she'd just sprouted another

head. "Vic, what the hell is this? Mutiny? There are people out in that water—my friends are out there and—"

"No, it's not mutiny, Dennis, it's reality. I'm in charge of security, and that includes your personal security as well as that of everyone else here. I want you safe and out of sight for the next twenty-four hours."

He stepped back as if she'd shoved him. "That's crazy. If this was a terrorist attack and if I was the target, I should be visible. To let them know they failed."

"No, you shouldn't. We don't know who *they* are or what they want. We have no information at all right now, and to speculate any further than we already have done is foolish. If you need to hear me concede that there is a possibility that it could have been a catastrophic accident, then sure, I'll concede that." She shrugged. "But it's just as probable—more so—that any one or all of the passengers aboard that plane could have been the target of a hit."

"No one knew—"

"Not likely. Plenty of people knew they were coming here. Plenty of trusted people," she added pointedly. "It may be that no one comes forward to claim responsibility, but in case someone does, we need to let *them* define success. It's the only way we'll be able to determine their agenda."

Victoria paused and, still maintaining eye contact, gently placed a hand on his chest, over his heart. Its beat was strong and just a little too fast.

"You have always trusted me, Dennis," she said, her tone cool but implacable, "and I've never given you cause to do otherwise. Trust me now. We need to go slowly, at least in the immediate short term." She paused and searched his face, then continued more softly, "Consider this: If you'd been on that flight, we wouldn't be able to declare you dead until we either found evidence to support that finding or the recovery effort ended. For once, we have the luxury of time. Not much, but I want to use every second of it to start looking for answers."

Letting her hand drop away from Dennis's chest, Victoria looked at Micki, who was still as immobile as a statue except for her eyes, which flicked from Victoria to Dennis and back. There was an intensity about her that was so high-pitched, Victoria could practically hear it hum.

"Micki, call Miami and get that hangar locked down immediately. I want a list of everyone who went in or out of there from the time that plane arrived there on Thursday. Then get on the phone to our embassy in Washington. I want them to scramble an emergency response team to the hangar today. Right away. We need a press release prepared, so find out who is handling the media up there. But the release doesn't go out until *I* say so, and there are to be no leaks. None. And we need to contact the neighbors," she ordered, using her shorthand for the neighboring countries of Cuba, the U.S., and the Bahamas. "I won't be surprised if they already know, given how much they love surveilling us, but we should inform them officially that there's been an accident. That's it. No speculation, no hints."

Victoria reached up to brush a stray hair from her forehead and was surprised when her hand came away wet. Fisting her hand, she loosely crossed both arms across her chest and glanced at her assistant, who stood in the doorway, crying silently.

"Gemma," Victoria continued, rapid-fire, addressing the assistant, "I need you to get the passengers' names to the embassy staff in Washington and have them start tracking down next of kin. We'll need to airlift any

survivors to Miami, so tell the guys here to get the
Gulfstream ready to serve as an ambulance. Ask the U.S.
State Department if we can coordinate with the NTSB to
send the recovered aircraft parts to them for a joint investigation. We don't have the right facilities for it here.
But *under no circumstances* do we want any of their
ships or personnel entering our waters unless we directly request their presence." She looked at Dennis.
"We're going to have to release the passenger manifest
within the next few hours. There will be hell to pay
when that happens."

He nodded, and Victoria thought that suddenly Dennis didn't look so good.

I was supposed to be on that plane.

*But for a snap decision born of boredom I'd be dead
now. Incinerated.*

As he stood listening to Victoria bark out orders,
Dennis felt a curious detachment wrap itself around
him. He felt as if he were hearing and seeing things in
slow motion, as if time had sped up while his brain and
body had slowed down.

He'd been in enough death-defying situations in his
lifetime to recognize shock when he felt it, and Dennis
knew that the enormity of what had just happened
would take a while to sink in for any man. But he was
more than just a man—he was the head of state of his
little paradise. He couldn't afford to waste time recov-
ering. Taking action, taking control, was imperative.
Yet his brain was frozen in place.

"Come on."

Dennis heard Victoria's voice and knew she was
speaking to him but couldn't find the words to respond.
Then she stepped closer and was peering up at him.

"Dennis," she said, her voice gentle as she gave his arm a tug. "I want you out of here. We'll take care of it."

He nodded. Then, shaking off her hand, he turned and walked stiffly to the door.

She caught up with him as he stepped into the bright subtropical sunshine. The colors, the sounds of the insects and birds, the swish of the palms, the intense heat—the entire setting was as serene as it always was and seemed a cruel betrayal of the horror that had just happened.

The sky ahead of him was a scintillating Caribbean blue unmarred by clouds. He didn't turn around to see the eastern sky behind him. He didn't need to see the trails of dark smoke billowing from the sea only to dissipate to the palest gray and then to invisibility. As if nothing had happened. As if no one had died.

"Dennis? Dennis, we need to put you somewhere." Victoria's voice was low and urgent and her hand encircled his bicep in a firm, gentle grip. "I don't want anyone to see you like this. Will you go to the bunker?"

Dennis looked down at her. She seemed so far away. So small. Her long dark hair and pale, drawn face only seemed to draw attention to her haunting and surreal, slanted blue eyes.

It took some effort to shake his head and form the words. "No. I'll go to my cottage."

"No, Dennis. Let's go to mine." And she urged him toward the palmetto-lined path that led to the small compound of cottages.

CHAPTER

Garner Blaylock looked up from the *Financial Times* and glanced at his watch.

If the bitch followed through, the world should be hearing about it now. Micki would see to that.

There was one way to find out.

He pressed the call button. Almost instantly, the stunning flight attendant who had greeted him when he'd boarded slid open the door that closed off the crew area from the cabin and approached him. He hid a smile as he noticed that her flawless makeup was smudged; her dark eyes were red-rimmed and watery. But her tiara, that blatant symbol of the extent of Dennis Cavendish's arrogance, remained perfectly positioned and sparkling in her carefully tousled nest of dark hair.

"Yes, Monsieur Blaylock?" she said in an accented whisper.

"Dear me, is something wrong?" he asked, feigning concern as he met her eyes.

She immediately lowered her eyes, and her full, movie-star lips quivered for a second before she pressed them together. He watched her take a quick, deep breath and blink back fresh tears before she returned her gaze to his face.

"Just some bad news about some friends, sir. It is of no matter," she replied, stumbling over her words.

He frowned. "Pity. How distressing for you."

"It is of no matter," she repeated, a little too rapidly. "I apologize, sir. Please, what can I do for you?"

"I'd like some more ice water, if I may."

"Certainly. Right away," she replied, and reached forward to pick up the heavy, cut-crystal tumbler from where it sat near his elbow. He allowed his eyes to linger on her voluptuous breasts, showcased magnificently by her uniform jacket's snug fit and low neckline. Everything about her was meant to tantalize, and succeeded brilliantly.

"No." Garner held up his hand to stop her as she began to straighten up, and she looked at him quizzically.

"Sir? Is there something else you'd like? A light snack, or perhaps some lunch?"

"A light snack would be lovely, thank you. No animal products, if you please. And, actually, I've changed my mind about the ice water. I'd prefer Champagne."

She nodded. "Of course. I can offer you the Krug Clos du Mesnil 1995. I also have the Bollinger Blanc de Noirs Vieilles Vignes Françaises 1998, if you prefer."

"I believe I'll start with the Krug." *After all, what better send-off for Dennis Cavendish's sorry ass than to toast it with the most expensive Champagne he has on board?*

"An excellent choice, Monsieur Blaylock. I shall bring it immediately." Forcing a smile, she executed an elegant turn and he watched her walk back to the galley, her fine ass, snug in her skirt, swaying perfectly above long legs that balanced on hooker-height stilettos.

Garner knew he could have her if he wanted her. Perhaps later. Right now, what he wanted was to revel in yet another triumph.

Feeling deep contentment steal over him, Garner leaned back in the plush seat and smiled more widely than he had in a very long time. Turning his head toward the window, he looked past the scattered clouds, tinged with the candy colors of Europe's early sunset, to the Atlantic Ocean, dark blue and sparkling below him. The fish off Taino were feasting right now on an unexpected bounty, and the Earth was getting that much closer to freedom from human tyranny. Sixteen bodies closer.

1:45 P.M., Saturday, October 25, Bolling Air Force Base, Washington, D.C.

The first time that former intelligence operative Tom Taylor saw the footage of Dennis Cavendish's plane exploding, the sight triggered a very typical human reaction: a sharply held breath, an instant emotional numbing, a few seconds of disbelief. Then his training and experience regained supremacy and his brain simply placed the incident at the top of a very long list of twisted, fucked-up things that twisted, fucked-up people did to other, possibly less twisted and even occasionally undeserving people.

But now, after he'd seen the footage twenty or so times, it had lost much of its impact and was just a series of images of yet another plane shattering in an otherwise peaceful sky. Aesthetically, the silent, violent images had a sort of surreality to them. They formed a harsh, arrested-motion instance of beauty, like a pyrotechnic display without the ooh-ahh dazzle. If it weren't for the fact that he knew fifteen probably unsuspecting people had been blown apart in the seconds following the detonations, he would have enjoyed the footage more.

Tom turned to the woman standing nearby. While he had been studying the monitor, she had been looking out the window, which was flanked by the American flag on one side and her diploma from Harvard Law School on the other. Her name—for now, anyway—was Lucy Denton. She was unreasonably sexy in that scary sort of way that Tom had always appreciated. Tall, slim, blond, and icy, with a taut, agile body made bulky by all the custom-fitted body armor she wore, Lucy possessed a formidable intelligence and guts of pure steel, both of which were routinely hidden from public view.

He and Lucy had had some exposure to each other in the past, back when she was on the ground in the intelligence community. That was a long time ago, though, and time had changed almost everything about her except the look in her eye.

Back in the day, Tom used to infuriate Lucy by calling her Rosa Klebb, of *From Russia with Love* fame, or, occasionally, Scary Spyce. Neither nickname had been affectionate or appreciated, but both had been accurate.

Lucy had always been terrifying as hell when she needed to be. Despite her obvious femininity, she had none of the self-doubt or hesitation that tripped up most women, even women involved in deeply covert intelligence operations. Lucy could focus like few other people could. Tom had never known her to avoid doing what needed to be done, to let irrelevant details get in the way. He'd watched her stare down a dead-eyed, bomb-wrapped nine-year-old who had a sweaty trigger finger and a disinclination to disarm. She'd made the kid blink, and in the space of that blink, she'd blown off his hand and popped a neat, round hole between his eyebrows. Afterward, her report coolly described the outcome as a win-win: Paradise had one more martyr in residence; the U.S. had one less asshole to worry about.

Lucy Denton was a woman to be admired. And feared.

Tom wasn't sorry to be working with her again, though they made a bizarre team. These days, she lived on the front page, above the fold, where everything about her—her social life, her fashion sense, her word choice during Senate hearings, and occasionally her meetings with the president—was critiqued by media gasbags and political has-beens. Tom, on the other hand, had become the kind of guy people would rather not know, or even know about. He'd long preferred shadow to light, anonymity to full disclosure. Nobody knew what his real story was and he'd made sure to forget some critical truths about himself. It made his job and his life—and lying about both—easier.

As the image on the screen faded to black, Tom turned to see Lucy's dark eyes fixed on him with an intensity that was seductive and legendary. "Well?"

"No one survived."

"No kidding," she said dryly. "And Cavendish?"

"He wasn't on the plane."

"How do we know that?"

"The usual channels, and we have a source on his maintenance crew who confirmed that Cavendish took off before dawn in one of his other planes. We aren't sure why, but we know he got out of Miami at about four-thirty and touched down on Taino not long afterward." He paused minutely. "We have pictures of him on his dock a few minutes after the explosion."

Her expression didn't change. "You're sure neither of those was the body double he uses?"

"Yes. Dennis is a great guy, a nice boss, and a warped paranoiac, but he doesn't let his flunkies cruise around on his planes without a good reason or go on submarine rides period," Tom replied and received a cool, unamused look in response. "He had his security chief, Victoria Clark, with him on the dock, so it must have been something big that made him want to go south. He doesn't take her along that often."

"Maybe she doesn't want to go that often," Lucy replied. "It's pretty stupid of her to go with him at all. Who's watching the farm when they're both down there?"

"Victoria's second, Micki Crenshaw. We don't have a lot on her, but she didn't make it into the CIA and she flunked out of the FBI after two months. She went to MIT after that, played around in England on a Rhodes Scholarship, and then sort of fell off the radar screen. She's American, Southern, smart."

"Why did she flunk out of the Bureau?"

"Slept with an instructor. Or two."

Tom watched as Lucy let the shadow of a smirk cross her lips for just a second. "Very smart. What about Victoria Clark? Is she a good-guy wannabe, too?" she asked.

"No. She grew up in an orphanage in the Midwest, made it to college on scholarships. Developed a real gift for high-tech network security in the early days. Got through grad school on scholarships. MIT."

"Is that how the two of them know each other? MIT?"

Tom crossed the room and poured himself a glass of water from the carafe on her desk.

"No. They were there at different times. Clark took her talent to Wall Street and rose very quickly to become head of security for two major banks. Then Cavendish made her an offer she didn't refuse and she headed to the island. She hired Crenshaw a few years later. Brought her over from London."

Lucy lifted an eyebrow. "Is that significant?"

"Well, Ms. Crenshaw is also a vegan, and ten years ago was issued a citation for participating in a protest outside of a research lab."

"Is that code for 'we think she's a bad guy now'? Or are we just glad she likes animals?" Lucy asked bluntly.

"She could be. The trail goes cold after that. Until she surfaced on Taino." Tom shrugged. "I wouldn't discount anything."

"Well, that's reassuring," Lucy replied dryly, then paused. "So if Cavendish wasn't on that plane, why haven't we heard from him directly? The secretary of state said she spoke with Taino's ambassador here in D.C., who deflected all questions about whether Cavendish survived. So far no one has officially heard from the man himself. Why?"

"He was probably the key target so Ms. Clark has whisked him out of sight. I'd lay money that she's behind the silence, waiting to see who pops out of the rat hole and takes credit for the fireworks. Victoria Clark is nobody's fool."

"Okay. So, in advance of the rat's emergence, who blew up that jet? And why?" Lucy asked evenly as she unfolded her arms and walked the few steps to her chair. She seated herself gracefully.

Her lack of dithering made Tom want to smile. Even in those first few seconds of seeing the footage, when he'd reacted like a normal human being instead of the spook he was, he'd never considered that it might have been an accident. That Lucy thought the same thing was just going to make being around each other that much easier.

"GAIA," he said flatly.

"Oh, for Christ's sake. Don't blow smoke up my skirt," she snapped.

"Truly an act I've never considered." He was rewarded with a disgusted frown.

"GAIA couldn't pull off something like this. The last thing they tried to blow up was that dam in southern Turkey last summer. If you'll recall, some local farmers got to the would-be geniuses before the police did, and what remained arrived at the forensics lab in a few quart-sized Ziploc bags." Lucy leaned back in her chair, her elbows resting on the arms. "GAIA is full of brutal bastards, but they're not known for their brains. They're the three stooges of the terrorism industry."

"They were," he conceded.

"From what I hear, pigs still rely on four legs to get around and Hell is still a hot place, Taylor."

"Micki Crenshaw attended Oxford the same time Garner Blaylock did. And we have footage of Garner Blaylock with the pilot of the plane a few hours before she took off."

Lucy's eyes widened, but only a little. She remained sitting easily in her chair, her body relaxed, her eyes locked in LASER ON mode. "Garner Blaylock is in prison."

It was an effort for Tom not to smile. "He *was,* in England. But apparently he's been rehabilitated to the Crown's satisfaction. He was released four months ago."

Tom counted four heartbeats before Lucy responded. "Where was he held?"

"Her Majesty's Prison at Full Sutton, with all the other naughty terrorists and assorted really bad guys. I'd say he learned a lot in his five years inside."

Her look turned more acidic, if that was possible. "Spare me the commentary. Go on."

"The pilot was Wendy Watson. First in her class at the Air Force Academy, three tours in Afghanistan, lots of ribbons. Resigned as a lieutenant colonel. Damned good flyer but apparently as stupid as hell when it came to men. She and Blaylock had been seeing each other for about three months. She spent last night at one of the 'secret' apartments GAIA keeps in a pretty nasty part of Miami called Overtown."

Lucy blinked, looking at him as if she didn't hear him correctly. "Are you serious? She stayed with him in *Overtown*? God Almighty."

"You know it?"

"Unfortunately." She shuddered and brushed the topic away with a flick of her hand. "Why was Blaylock staying there? Where did Watson live?"

"GAIA insists on a high return on investment. They spend their pennies on items like pilots, instead of decent safe houses. But it's also a pretty clever security move. Anybody we'd send in to lay down equipment would be pegged instantly as being on what's considered the wrong side of the law in that neighborhood."

She bobbed her head once in agreement.

"Besides, Blaylock is wealthy enough, good-looking enough, and charismatic enough to get his terror babettes to do his bidding without having to flash any bling."

Lucy narrowed her eyes at him. "Did you just say 'babettes'? And *'bling'*?" she asked slowly.

Fucking hell. It had been decades since he'd been even tempted to blush. "Yes. Get over it. Watson lived in a small condo in South Beach."

"And she left that to stay with him in Overtown?" She shook her head. "Love must be blind *and* have no standards. Was his place wired?"

"No. We wired hers a few days after they met, but she didn't spend much time there and he never set foot in the place. He tried very hard to stay well under the radar."

"How long was he here?"

"Fourteen weeks. We tracked him coming in."

Lucy glanced down to check the intact polish coating her fingernails. "Why didn't we bug his place? That step is pretty much covered in Intelligence 101, isn't it?"

"It's refreshing to note that you haven't lost your sense of humor, Madam Director." Tom folded his arms and leaned against the windowsill. "We tried a few times to wire it but couldn't pull it off. Too conspicuous. Besides, GAIA might have trouble with underwater detonation and with finding good help, but they know their electronics. If we'd been successful in bugging it, they'd have known about it pretty quickly, and then they would have moved." He shrugged one shoulder. "We had surveillance cameras and parabolic mikes in place but we didn't get much. She went into the apartment with him at eleven o'clock last night and left at seven-thirty this morning. He was in the doorway when she left. They didn't converse either time when they were outdoors."

"Did you pick up any pillow talk?"

"No. We had mikes trained at all the windows but there was enough white noise in the background to distort any conversation." He paused. "For what it's worth, we didn't expect to get much. He's no fool."

She pursed her lips and looked down at her hands again, then back at him. "Where is he now?"

"He left the apartment shortly after she did. In a characteristic display of his concern for his fellow man, he did a hit-and-run, knocking a little girl off her bike as he swerved to avoid running over a rat. Then he took off in another one of Cavendish's jets. We figure Wendy set that up for him. He was out of U.S. airspace five minutes before the plane blew up. According to the flight plan, Blaylock's trip will terminate in Algiers."

"How's the kid he hit?"

"Out of surgery and in the ICU. Still unconscious."

Lucy was silent for a few seconds. "Why did we let him leave?"

"To see where he's going and what he's going to do next."

"He has plans?"

Tom smiled. "So it appears."

"Alert the UK and the French—and for what it's worth, the Algerians—that we'd like to speak with Mr. Blaylock when he resurfaces." She paused, frowning slightly, and then leaned forward to rest both elbows on her desk, and cradle her chin on the backs of her interlaced fingers. "There's something that doesn't add up here. GAIA is concerned with the environment, and the things they do usually make a point *and* hurt people. Like trying to blow up a dam—it will reverse something humans have imposed on nature and kill a lot of innocent people in the process. So why would Blaylock go for Cavendish's plane? I mean, I know the people on it represented a lot of major players in the business world, so news of their deaths will create tsunami-sized ripples in the financial markets, but that will be a blip. Taking out Cavendish's underwater project would have been a more GAIA-like action."

"The plane was an easier target. An airplane hangar is a place with a lot of moving parts, a lot of variables. There were probably at least sixty people in and out of the place in the last few days, between airport staff and private security staff, maintenance teams, and the flight and ground crews for the various planes. No doubt that among those sixty or so people, at least a few would have been willing to make some money by taking a break or just looking the other way at the right time." Tom shrugged easily. "Of course, it could be that Blaylock doesn't know about the underwater stuff."

"He has to know something. Otherwise why target Cavendish at all? On the world stage, Cavendish is a small potato with a big mouth and a fat wallet. And he hasn't turned that island into a fortress because he's building an underwater theme park down there," Lucy stated flatly.

"If Blaylock is intending to hit the underwater operation, then sending the world economic markets into a panic by killing senior executives of nine major conglomerates is a nice diversion. It's a statement that won't be ignored."

"But it can't further GAIA's agenda."

Tom paused, and smiled at her. "It can if GAIA's agenda has changed."

The thin line of Lucy's lips became thinner. "Has it?"

"It appears to have. Since Blaylock's reemergence,

they've stopped ramming fishing factory ships and setting fire to pesticide-manufacturing plants. They haven't chained themselves to anything, blockaded any-place, spiked a tree, or let caged vermin loose in over a year, and they've stopped pissing and moaning to the press about the inferiority of humans to lower-order spe-cies. For the most part, other than that Turkish fiasco, they've been quiet for about twelve months. Too quiet. We're pretty sure they're regrouping in advance of go-ing global. We'll know more soon. We've got a few peo-ple getting close to the inner circle."

As her gaze latched on to his, it went as cold and dark as a polar night. "*Getting* close?" she repeated. "Why aren't we in there already?"

"Our last team was discovered. One was killed in a hit-and-run two years ago during a WTO protest. The incident got a lot of press. They tried to make it look like we did it, got all the conspiracy nuts raving about it, but it wasn't us doing it to one of their guys. They did it to one of ours." He crossed the room and perched on the corner of her desk, ignoring her obvious annoyance. "Our other officer has been on and off life support for the last eleven months."

In the brief pause that followed his words, Lucy's expression didn't change but Tom watched her bite the inside of her cheek. It was a subtle, unconscious move-ment, and, therefore, revealing.

"What happened?" she asked coolly.

"She went diving with some of the Gaians to recon-noiter the footings of the Golden Gate Bridge. They were thinking of blowing it up. Very original."

Lucy didn't respond.

Tom shrugged and continued, "From the best we can determine, they messed with her gas mixtures before the dive and took their time bringing her back up, giving her a severe case of the bends. She spent seventy-two hours in a decompression chamber while her blood went from foam back to liquid. The whole time she was screaming for the docs to kill her. At the end of it, her brain was ninety percent fried and her body one hundred percent useless." He paused. "We learned that Garner Blaylock ordered it from the safety and comfort of his accommodations at Full Sutton. He thought it would send a bigger message than just cutting her hose and leaving her at the bottom."

Lucy looked down at her hands again and he could see her throat move in a hard swallow. "How many people do we have in there now?"

"Three. Two have been able to get near Blaylock."

"How long have they been in there?"

"One for a few years as a sleeper. He's worked his way up. The other two for less than a year, but they've moved quickly."

"Is there anything else?"

He nodded. "About ten minutes before Cavendish's plane exploded, a large video file was uploaded to one of Taino's satellites and immediately downloaded to the plane."

"Did we get it?"

"Of course."

"What is it?"

"We're still working on decrypting it. Whatever it is, Cavendish wanted to keep it private. The encryption uses an algorithm we haven't seen before. I've sent it to the NSA."

"Let me know what they find. Do we have any update on what's going on underwater?"

Tom shook his head. "They're doing something but

we're not completely sure what. Our seismographs and sonar arrays were picking up some activity that was most likely drilling, but that stopped a few hours ago. Without getting closer, we can't be sure what he's actually up to."

"For Christ's sake, what are your people doing?" Lucy snapped with frigid incredulity. "Every answer you've given me starts with 'I don't know.' What the hell *do* you know?"

"Less than we'd like to," he replied easily. "Within minutes of the crash, Taino powered down all the transponders on its satellites except the most secure link."

"How secure is it?"

"We can't see into it yet."

"Cavendish is one paranoid bastard," she muttered.

Tom smiled. "Enviably so."

Lucy let out a long breath, then reached for a folder on her desk. "Keep in touch," she said dismissively, without looking up. "And let me know if you happen to come across any answers."

"Yes, ma'am," Tom replied and left the room.

7
CHAPTER

2:30 P.M., Saturday, October 25, the White House, Washington, D.C.

"Are they all dead?" President Winslow Benson asked absently, not looking up from the documents he was signing.

"Undoubtedly." Hands in his pockets, Ken Proust rocked back on his heels.

"Have they released the names yet?"

"No."

"But we know who was on the plane."

"Yes."

"So what's going to happen to the markets?" The president moved on to the next paper in the short stack in front of him.

"Chaos at Monday's opening bell. Any slides will correct themselves by the end of the week."

"How are we going to spin it?"

The president's campaign manager hid a smile. "We'll send representatives to the funerals. The tiger team, maybe the first lady. Ramp up the talk on terrorism, demand more money to fight it. Get some talking heads to rhapsodize about your foreign policy expertise and how your opponent has none."

The president nodded. "Timing isn't bad."

"Less than two weeks to the election. I'd say the timing is just about perfect."

The president raised his head. "Whoever wired that

plane had to have done it here. The FBI said it was on the ground for three days in Miami before it took off this morning."

Ken shrugged. "That's the likeliest possibility."

"Makes us look bad. What does TSA have to say about it?"

Shaking his head, Ken answered with another smile. "Not their problem. It was a private hangar. Cavendish's people have complete control of security. But we're launching an investigation anyway. And sending an investigative team to Canada."

"What does Canada have to do with it?" the president demanded, sliding another paper off the shrinking pile.

"The plane was built there."

"For Christ's sake. That's ridiculous. Do we think they had something to do with it?"

"Of course not, but it's good press. Shows how serious we are about domestic terrorists, and how willing we are to help our neighbors."

President Benson leveled a look at his campaign manager and didn't bother to hide his disgust.

"It's Cavendish's problem. Let him send people there," he said, returning his attention to the task at hand. "I think we should investigate *him*. Find out what he's doing and make him look like an asshole in the process." The president stopped again, and Ken felt the heat of those commanding eyes bore into his own for the second time in fifteen seconds. "Was Cavendish on that plane?"

"No, sir. The Taino embassy hasn't released any information about the passenger list but we know he wasn't on the plane. He was supposed to be, according to our information, but he left several hours earlier, on a previously unscheduled flight."

The president smiled coldly. "Make sure that gets out. Send it to FOX. They'll know what to do with it. If Cavendish's people break that first, he'll have left early for some urgent reason. I'd rather have people start to wonder if he knew something and left those people to die, like the chicken shit he is." The president paused. "How many of them were Americans?"

"Six out of the nine passengers, two of the six crew. The pilot and copilot. The pilot was a vet. A woman, and she had a lot of ribbons."

"Kids?"

"No."

President Benson put down the pen in his hand and glanced out the window, then looked back at Ken. "Eight Americans dead, including six leaders of industry and one highly decorated veteran. Make sure that gets worked into the discussion. I want to own part of this story."

Ken chuckled and slid his BlackBerry out of the breast pocket of his suit jacket.

3:15 P.M., Saturday, October 25, Taino

"I really think you should be the one doing this." Micki's usually pleasant voice held a note of petulance.

"I think so, too, however, I've decided that you're going to do it," Victoria replied evenly.

"Come out from behind the curtain, Victoria. By the time this is over, your name and face will be all over the media. It's impossible to hide these days. I'm not even sure it's possible to run."

"You're entirely right, but I'm still going to try. By the way, you've got a little smear of lipstick on your front tooth. No, the other one."

Victoria watched as Micki adjusted her earpiece and

checked that the microphone was clipped securely to the lapel of her suit. The lavender linen was still crisp, and with luck it would remain so until the end of the hastily convened press conference that would be broadcast live via satellite. The black armband—Victoria's best Hermès scarf folded and tied to hide the rest of its colors—had been a stroke of genius.

"You're on in three, two, one—" The cameraman pointed and Micki stared grimly into the camera.

"Good afternoon," she began quietly, her Alabama-inflected accent even more pronounced than usual as she struggled to maintain an even tone and pace. "I am Michelle Crenshaw, undersecretary of national security for The Paradise of Taino and deputy chief operations officer for the Climate Research Institute. I will issue a statement first, and then take your questions." She paused briefly.

"As you know, a Bombardier Global Express jet operating in the service of the government of The Paradise of Taino suffered a midair explosion approximately five hours ago. The flight took off from Miami International Airport at 10:17 this morning and was due to arrive in Taino at 10:42 A.M.

"The explosion occurred as the aircraft was on its final approach at an altitude of one thousand feet. There were fifteen people on board: six crew members and nine passengers. All names are being withheld until the families can be notified. The explosion occurred within the boundaries of the territorial waters of The Paradise of Taino. At this time, search-and-rescue operations are being conducted by Taino security forces, who are fully trained in such procedures." She paused again. "That is all the information we have available for release at this time, but I will answer your questions as best I'm able."

Perhaps because Micki had to keep calm in front of the camera, Victoria felt as though she were tied into knots for both of them. She watched on a small monitor as the jostling, frenzied pack of reporters lined up in front of the microphone hastily set up for them. For at least the tenth time in half as many minutes, she was glad that the journalists were a thousand miles away in Washington, D.C., in the press room of the Taino embassy.

The first to speak was one of the reigning kings of the airwaves who was known for his love of the spotlight. "Secretary Crenshaw, is it true that the passenger list included the CEOs of some of the world's largest companies?"

"We are not releasing any information about the passengers or the crew until their families have been informed of the accident," Micki replied smoothly.

The reporter didn't relinquish his place despite the urging of one of the press secretaries on hand to manage the egos and the information. "Was Dennis Cavendish among those on board?"

"We are not releasing any information about the passengers or the crew. Let's move on."

Victoria felt her eyebrows lift as she watched the reporter actually elbow the embassy staffer aside and grab the microphone stem to prevent anyone from moving him away from it. "There's a rumor that President Cavendish was supposed to be on the plane but left Miami earlier on an unscheduled flight. Is that true?"

"Next question," Micki snapped.

The first reporter's chief rival snatched the microphone as the other man let go of it.

"Secretary Crenshaw, about ten minutes ago, the White House issued a statement saying that it offered to send navy and coast guard search-and-rescue teams to Taino and that you rejected the offer. Can you confirm that?"

"Yes, I'll confirm that the United States did indeed offer assistance, as have the governments of the Bahamas, Cuba, and the United Kingdom. While grateful for the offers of help from all of our larger neighbors and allies, such assistance is not needed at this time. We did thank Presidents Benson and Castro, Prime Ministers Brown and Ingraham, and Governor General Hanna for their offers, and will not hesitate to ask for assistance should we believe it to be necessary. But our own security personnel are well able to handle a situation such as this, and are doing so admirably."

"A follow-up, Secretary Crenshaw, if you'll allow it. Why would you refuse any help? This is hardly the time for secretive—"

"That is your last question, sir. I'm sure your colleagues have equally pressing concerns," Micki replied evenly. "We have the situation under control. The accident happened well within our territorial waters and the debris does not appear to be scattered over a particularly large surface area. Our teams were on the scene within minutes of the accident. The sea is calm, it is still broad daylight, and our personnel are intimately familiar with the area because of their continuous training and patrols. They know the currents and the depth and terrain of the seafloor, and I have no doubt that they will recover far more in far less time than would larger teams of divers unfamiliar with the area.

"Furthermore, as to any secretive behavior, I'll only say it's utter nonsense. Twelve years ago, the territorial waters of Taino were designated as a marine sanctuary.

The area is being considered as a World Heritage site. The presence of many large ships in these waters, even for a short time, would harm the ecosystem we are committed to preserving and protecting. Furthermore, we have requested the United States National Transportation Safety Board to join our personnel in conducting a joint investigation into this incident and in reconstructing the aircraft. President Benson has graciously granted that request."

The microphone was wrenched out of the hands of the smug reporter and set up in front of a beautiful but dangerous celebrity-journalist more renowned for her ability to spin words into weapons than for her mental acuity. "Isn't this taking Dennis Cavendish's over-the-top need for secrecy a little far? If there are any survivors, they've been in shark-infested waters all this time and because of your designation of the area as a marine sanctuary"—she drawled the words sarcastically—"you won't let anyone else in to help save them."

Micki kept her eyes aimed at the camera and allowed her eyebrows to rise at the grating accusation. She let a short, cold pause build before answering. "Dredging up well-loved but utterly ridiculous conspiracy theories at a time such as this does a grave disservice to the present situation and disrespects the bravery and commitment of those undertaking to create the best possible outcome. I would ask that you and your colleagues refrain from including such nonsense in your news reports. Next question."

"Why won't you even tell us if President Cavendish was on that plane? Is he still alive?"

"Next question," Micki repeated, staring resolutely into the camera.

An earnest young reporter, vaguely familiar to Victoria but obviously still in need of a big break to make his career, made an eager grab for the newly freed microphone. "One of the previous questions did bring up an important point, Ms. Crenshaw. The secession of Taino from the Bahamas thirty years ago at the hands of Guthrie Anders, Mr. Cavendish's predecessor, remains contentious in the area. But since buying the island from the Anders family fifteen years ago and setting himself up as the president of a sovereign nation, Dennis Cavendish has almost entirely cut off the rest of the world from knowing what he's doing there—"

"As is his right," Micki replied smoothly. "President Cavendish undertook to firmly establish The Paradise of Taino in order to secure the rights, privileges, and remedies that would not be available to him had he remained simply the owner of an island ultimately governed by someone else. In doing so, President Cavendish has achieved his lifelong dream of establishing a wildlife and marine sanctuary on what may be the only remaining pristine island in the entire Caribbean basin. That is why he put the word 'paradise' in the country's official name, sir. To remind people that it is perhaps the only true paradise left on this planet. His desire to preserve and protect the natural treasures that exist on our island and in our waters is, admittedly, viewed by some ill-informed persons as a craven desire for secrecy. I assure you, it is not that.

"The fact is, simply," she continued, "that the island's wildlife, marine life, and its very nature would be irreparably harmed if President Cavendish were to allow commercial and residential development on Taino, or to allow ecotourist groups or cruise ships to enter our waters or use our port. Our island is not like the Hope Diamond. It cannot be placed in a museum case for all to see. It is a small and fragile living environment and as such must be kept untouched even by those for whom President Cavendish is preserving it. It is a paradox," she admitted with a shrug. "But that, and only that, is the reason we have refused to allow the proffered marine vessels into our waters. Irrespective of their crews' mission, the fact remains that those enormous ships would have a negative impact on our rare and delicate ecosystem."

"But—"

"We know what we are doing, and respectfully request that the world allow us to carry on," she finished firmly. "Next question."

A woman Victoria didn't recognize took the microphone. "Is it true that you have antisubmarine devices to prevent infiltration—"

Knowing she had to bring this circus to an end before Micki lost her cool, Victoria scribbled a hasty message on a whiteboard and held it up.

Micki glanced at the board, took a deep breath, and interrupted the young woman reporter. "There is a lot of speculation about our methods of preserving our rights as a nation. Most of it is the stuff of otherwise idle imaginations," she said calmly. "I must unfortunately conclude this press conference now. I ask that you focus your stories on the serious and tragic event that occurred this morning and direct your energies and imagination toward praying for the best possible outcome as we continue search-and-rescue operations. Thank you for coming. We will return in a few hours with an update."

Micki nodded curtly at the cameraman and remained

looking into the camera with hard-won composure until the red light on the top of it blinked off. Then she leaned back in her chair and slumped as she closed her eyes.

"Well, I feel like I've been rode hard and put away wet, bless their little old, muckraking hearts," she drawled and then opened one eye. "Victoria, you aren't going to make me do that again, are you?"

"No promises. At least they didn't start casting aspersions on the institute."

"If we had given them time for another question, they would have." As Victoria approached, Micki pulled herself to her feet and began removing her lapel microphone.

A tap on Victoria's shoulder drew her attention to her assistant, who was trailing behind her and holding out a sheaf of papers. Victoria took the offering and gave the top sheet a cursory glance as she waved the woman away.

"They haven't found any survivors yet," she murmured in a voice so low only Micki could hear.

"Well, it hasn't been very long since the accident, but were you expecting that we would? You saw the footage, honey. That plane didn't just explode, Vic, it disintegrated. I can't imagine they're going to find much of anything out there." She paused. "It kind of reminded me of the time one of the neighbor boys took his daddy's shotgun and shot a dove that was sitting under a tree in my grandmother's backyard. He used buckshot, not even what you'd use for bird hunting." She ran her hands down her arms, as if warding off a sudden chill. "There wasn't even much blood. It just went *pouf* in a big burst of feathers and noise and smoke, and that was the end of that dove," Micki said in a voice hushed with emotion. "I'll never forget it. It was just *awful*. I cried for days."

Victoria stared, wondering if her second in command's suddenly teary eyes and hoarse whisper were just for effect, a prelude to an inappropriate burst of laughter. It would be just like her—Victoria had always considered Micki to have some odd, but harmless, quirks. This bizarre turn of conversation, which edged the line of good taste, had to be brought on by stress. Maybe.

"A dove?" Victoria repeated, not doing a good job of hiding her incredulity. "Micki, we're talking about a plane full of people. The situations have nothing in common."

Micki met her eyes. "Well, both were a terrible loss of life. I made sure he got hurt later, though."

"Who?"

"My grandmother's neighbor boy."

Victoria watched her warily. "What do you mean?"

"I set some rat traps where he used to hide his dirty magazines under the house. He lost three fingers on his right hand. He didn't do any more hunting after that."

Horrified, and not quite sure she should believe what she was hearing, Victoria took a step back.

Micki noticed and gave her a quick smile, instantly regaining her composure. "That was a long time ago. Kid stuff. Anyway, where's Dennis?"

"Against his will, he's in the bunker," Victoria replied slowly, the lie coming out of her mouth as easily as if it had been the truth.

"Still? How long are you going to keep him there? He's the president. He'll have to come out eventually and make a statement. He can't stay hidden like a possum in a tree."

"I'm not 'keeping him there,'" she snapped. "I've just recommended that he remain out of sight for a while. You don't agree with that?"

"Well, I think it's a bit over the top. It's not like anyone can get at him here. And communications are cut off so no one can find out that he's alive, either. Unless one of us decides to make an announcement," Micki ended dismissively.

"As you're aware, his removal to the bunker is in line with the emergency response procedures," Victoria pointed out coolly. "You agreed with the decision a few hours ago."

Micki was a brilliant technician and troubleshooter, and she'd been intimately involved in crafting and refining their procedures over the years. Though Victoria knew Micki didn't share her own bone-deep paranoia about security issues, she had never encountered this attitude from her deputy before.

What Victoria was not about to tell Micki was that Dennis, in fact, was not in the bunker that he'd built into the side of the island's only peak, a long-dormant volcano. When Victoria had left him a short while ago, he was sitting in her cottage by himself, still shaken to his core.

Known by his friends as well as his enemies as the man who never blinked first, Dennis had made a fortune, built a communications empire, and founded a nation all before he was forty. Victoria had watched as he'd faced down shareholders, stakeholders, stalkers, and government subcommittees without conceding an inch more than he wanted to, and without ever revealing so much as a molecule of fear.

When she'd met him for the first time, Victoria had tried hard not to be dazzled, but it was impossible.

How could anyone not be dazzled when she met one of her personal heroes? All these years later, he still inspired and amazed her. His presence, his complete trust in her, his way of dealing with her—half flirtatious, half fatherly—had only deepened her respect and affection for him. He'd taught her to embrace his way of doing things, to always push any limit she felt like pushing, to take every chance she wanted to take. It was the antithesis of every rule she'd lived by up until then, but she'd absorbed it willingly, eagerly. After all, Dennis had become nearly legendary for taking risks that made others brand him a madman or, more grudgingly, a genius.

And what had she done for this man, who had given so much to her? She had failed him. None of her defenses, none of her precautions had saved him. Dennis had escaped certain death only because he'd been too wound up about the methane-harvesting test to sleep. He'd wanted to go down to the mining operations center and see for himself what was going on. That eagerness, and that alone, had spurred his decision to leave Miami in advance of his invited guests. It had been a whim, a spur-of-the-moment decision made in the early morning hours and executed without forethought. That impetuousness was the only reason he was still alive.

Victoria felt the reverberations of his decision in every dark nook and deep crevice of her psyche. She had failed him. She would never forgive herself. And she would do everything in her power to make sure it never happened again, that she never again felt this degree of self-loathing.

"So, do you?"

With a start, Victoria snapped out of her reverie and met Micki's questioning eyes. "Sorry. Do I what?"

"Have any idea who did this? I saw Gemma just hand you a bunch of papers. They couldn't all be an update from the search teams. I mean, they're not finding any people, so there can't be that much to relate. What is the other news?"

"Nothing critical," she said dismissively. "Details."

"About what?" Micki demanded.

Concerned that her own composure might be approaching a fracture, Victoria gave her deputy a cold stare and said nothing, then turned on her heel and headed for the door.

"Tell me what's going on, Vic," Micki said in an urgent whisper as she followed Victoria.

"A search-and-rescue operation is what's going on, Micki," she snapped. "And this is not the place to discuss anything about it. Now, if you don't mind, there are some pressing matters I have to—"

"Well, fine. I just want to know if the obvious thought has crossed your mind, too."

Victoria stopped short and faced her. "Just what 'obvious thought' would that be?"

Micki glanced at the few people milling around the small room, then grabbed Victoria by the arm and led her, none too gently, outside. She didn't stop until they were several feet away from the building. She leaned a shoulder into the curve of a palm tree and folded her arms across her chest.

"Well, it's controversial. Disturbing, even. But you and I both make our livelihood by being more paranoid than your average crazy person, right? So it shouldn't come as a surprise." Micki stopped, waiting for acquiescence.

Victoria, however, only blinked. Her stomach, churning nonstop for the last few hours, had suddenly solidified into something very cold and very hard.

Whatever Micki was about to say, it wasn't going to be good.

Taking in a deep, exasperated breath, Micki rolled her eyes once, then leveled her gaze straight at Victoria. "Okay. I'll just lay it out like a picnic for you, Vic. Hasn't it crossed your mind yet that maybe Dennis has something to do with this?"

Somehow, Victoria resisted the impulse to double over, but the effect on her thinking was the same as if Micki had sucker punched her. She could feel her jaw drop. She heard herself gasp.

"How can you say that? How can you even think that, Micki? That's insane," Victoria hissed. "Dennis didn't kill those people. They were his *friends*. You saw how he reacted. He's stunned. How can you—"

Micki's mouth formed into a petulant curl. "We're cold, you and I. Isn't that what we've always said, Vic? That you and I have to be willing to seek out the dark places in people's minds by trying to put ourselves in their position? All those tabletop drills we've done, all those extreme scenarios we've drafted—it's never been a game, has it? I thought we always said that the more outlandish the possibility, the more we need to at least consider it. Well, I think this fits the bill."

Victoria stared at her, incredulous.

She's serious. "You can't really think that Dennis would arrange—"

"Well, maybe not *arrange* it, but what if he knew about it, and that's why he left early? I mean, Dennis can be flighty at times, but he's rarely downright rude. And leaving before his guests when they were all expecting to fly with him, well, that's not exactly the done thing, is it?"

Victoria brought her hands up in front of her face,

fingers spread wide, palms facing out. "No. *No!* You're wrong. I mean, yes, I'm always suspicious of random events that break routines or change existing plans," she said, her words coming too fast. "But this is different. Dennis was *not* part of that explosion, Micki. I've known him too long, and his decision to change his plans this morning wasn't random. It was exactly in line with how he operates. You *know* that. You've heard him say, hundreds of times, that being able to make snap decisions is part of the fun of the job. It's the reason he keeps the pilots on call twenty-four hours a day, seven days a week."

"Yeah, I know all that, Vic. Dennis always talks a good game, as much as he plays a good game."

"This is not a game," Victoria snapped, feeling anger course through her and half wishing that, for once, she might not automatically hit the brakes. But she knew she would. She always did. Dennis always teased her about that: *"You don't do "impulsive," do you, Vic,"* he'd laugh.

No. I don't. And I won't start now.

"You know what I mean." Micki's eyes had taken on a challenging gleam.

"No, I don't know what you mean. Your insinuations are disgusting."

Treasonous. Victoria bit her lips to prevent the word from escaping her mouth.

"No, Vic, not disgusting. Disturbing. Frightening, maybe." Micki's breathing was getting a little fast, and the healthy golden tan on her face was deepening in sync with it. "You have him so high on that pedestal, you can't even accept that he might be human. Well, he is. But don't you think that the way he's handling this is just a little out of character? Where's your hero now, Victoria? *In hiding.* The man who has spent the last ten or so years of his life trying to 'change the world's balance of power' is *in hiding*—"

"He wanted to go on the air," Victoria said, her voice low and tight with anger. "I sent him to the bunker. You were there. You saw how he argued with me."

"I'm still surprised that he went. And yes, I saw his reaction, but think about it—maybe he's not overwhelmed with grief. Maybe he's overwhelmed with *guilt*. And I'm not talking about survivor's guilt, I'm talking about a perpetrator's guilt."

Resisting the overpowering urge to spin on her heel and walk away—or to smack Micki's gloating face—Victoria forced herself to slow her breathing and to clear her head. Fighting with Micki wasn't doing anything to help the situation. And she'd always prided herself on her willingness to listen to ideas. This was an unpalatable one, one that sickened her to consider, but shutting Micki down would make the idea fester. Bringing it completely into the open would expose its flaws.

Victoria took one last deep breath and met Micki's burning eyes. "All right. Tell me why you think . . . this." Try as she might, she couldn't bring herself to say the words "Dennis is a killer."

Micki's face took on an expression of surprised satisfaction, and her rigid stance relaxed slightly.

"Thank you. Well, as I said, it's just a possibility. But what made me think of it is the combination of the passenger list and the location. Nine of the world's most powerful business leaders are dead. All personal friends of Dennis's. No one would suspect him. And since it happened inside his territory, he gets to run the show." Micki paused. "He controls the people who determine the outcome."

"I'm not following you, Micki. You still haven't given me a motive."

"Publicity," she whispered.

Victoria felt her jaw sag again and instantly snapped it shut. "That's crazy. That's worse than crazy. Dennis doesn't need to do something this . . . this awful to get publicity."

"Okay, maybe that was the wrong word." Micki shrugged. "Maybe he did it to start momentum building for the methane extraction. He could use this event as a catalyst for restructuring the way the world does business. Out with the old, in with the new," she finished, her voice as callous as it was casual.

Could he—

No. Victoria shook her head as if to wake herself from a bad dream, and then steadied herself. "Micki, I appreciate your willingness to share your ideas with me," she said coolly. "However, I don't find the argument compelling. If anything, what you've just said makes it more apparent that someone outside of Taino, outside of the Climate Research Institute, has learned about the mining project and is taking drastic steps to sabotage it. Our competitors and the nations and consortia that sponsor them are more feasible suspects. Radical ecowarrior-type environmentalists, too, especially the heavily funded ones. Have someone compile a list. Meanwhile, I want you to focus on finding out who might have leaked information—any information—about *Atlantis* and what we're doing down there." She paused minutely. "And please keep your . . . suspicions to yourself."

Her back straight and her jaw clenched, Victoria turned and walked briskly down the path toward her cottage, and Dennis.

She felt as if she were about to be sick. What happened this morning was no accident, of that she was sure. Whoever planned it had known about the habitat, had known what Dennis was doing. The question worrying her was who was behind it. And how he or she had found out about the mining operation.

"Where are you going now?" Micki called.

Victoria stopped and glanced over her shoulder. "My cottage. I'll be back soon."

Micki gave her the ghost of a smile. "I don't suppose you want company?"

"No, I don't suppose that I do. I'd rather you get in touch with the boats and see if anything has changed. I'll be back shortly," Victoria repeated and continued walking.

CHAPTER

3:15 P.M., Saturday, October 25, Gainesville, Florida

Sam sprawled lazily across the enormous brown leather couch that took up most of his living room. He had a beer in one hand, the remote control in the other, a half-eaten bag of barbecue pork rinds resting atop his flat belly, and the remains of a plate of bean burritos and jalapeño cheese grits congealing on the floor next to the couch. There was no one there to yell at him, so he had his head resting on a few of the dozen or so damned throw pillows Cyn had inflicted on him a few months ago, and his feet resting on a short stack of a few more.

Feeling happily dazed at the prospect of having an entire Saturday to himself, he'd abandoned plans to go to the Gators game and parked himself there a few hours ago to begin surfing the pregame shows on the brand-new fifty-inch plasma TV he'd hung in front of the fireplace. Cyn had had a complete hissy fit that he'd hung it in front of the fireplace instead of above it, but he'd stuck to his guns. She didn't live with him—yet— and he wanted the height of the screen to be just right. Besides, he never used the damned fireplace. The only time he'd ever even had the damper open was when a nest of baby squirrels had fallen down from the top and he'd had to get them out.

Right now, he was flicking through the channels during halftime of a game between his alma mater, the Georgia Tech Yellowjackets, and the University of Maryland Terrapins. He paused briefly at the Weather Channel because one of his buddies was displaying uncharacteristic gravitas as he discussed some tornadoes that had just slammed through another trailer park.

What is it with trailer parks and tornadoes?

He continued to flick the remote until his eye was caught by a ticker tape of headlines running along the bottom of a news channel's screen.

PRIVATE JET CRASHES OFF TAINO. NO SURVIVORS RE-PORTED.

Sam took another pull from his beer and decided to wait for the commercials to end so he could see what the story was. He'd been to Taino once, when he was finishing up his Ph.D. He'd applied for a grant from the Climate Research Institute to finance a research trip he'd been trying to put together to study methane releases from ancient lake beds in Siberia. Dennis Cavendish had called Sam personally to discuss his proposal and then had flown him down there for an interview.

Sam smiled at the memory. He'd been in the final throes of getting ready to defend his dissertation and, boy howdy, had he been full of himself. Cavendish's surprise offer of a high-paying job with lots of perks—including eight weeks of annual vacation and a huge bonus if he'd move to the island permanently—had made Sam damned near unbearable, at least according to the girlfriend he had at the time.

There he was, not even in possession of a real Ph.D. yet, and he was having *serious* money dangled in front of him. He'd been tempted, but in the end he'd turned down the job because the island was beautiful and all, but it had an odd feel to it, and the people he'd met with and would be working with were odd, too. They were friendly in a stiff way, and were completely focused on their work, sort of like some of the dweebier colleagues he had in the doctoral program. The kind that got excited over the discovery of a new species of hermaphroditic mud worms.

Besides, it hadn't seemed like there would be much to do on the island except work and surf, which wasn't that bad, except that he'd been twenty-seven and just coming up for air after ten years of nonstop higher education. Sure, he'd wanted to make a name for himself, but he'd also wanted to play and party and fry some of those pumped-up brain cells, not bury himself doing work he could never talk about.

The commercial ended and the news babe came on looking all serious, and began talking in that low, urgent, news-anchor voice.

"We go now to the waters off the eastern Caribbean island known as The Paradise of Taino, where a luxury jet belonging to billionaire Tainoan President Dennis Cavendish crashed at 10:38 this morning, Eastern Standard Time. I-Team reporter Soledad Steinly is there at the crash site. Soledad, what's going on?"

The screen split to show an attractive woman clutching her microphone with one hand and the railing of a ship with the other. She must have been in a heavy chop or on a really small boat because the camera kept losing her. Just watching her made Sam rethink any more pork rinds.

"Thank you, Tiffany. I'm actually about four nautical miles from the crash site and just outside Taino's national boundary. The Taino government is not allowing any outsiders in the area and they aren't providing us with much information. In the three hours we've been here, the number of reporters in the area has probably quadrupled and we've all been sharing what little we know. The story that seems to have the most credibility is that the passengers on the plane were all high-powered business executives headed to Taino at Dennis Cavendish's invitation to see some secret underwater installation he's created. There is, apparently, a large methane deposit under the seafloor around Taino, and it has been rumored for years that President Cavendish has been attempting to mine it."

The female anchor in New York City frowned. "Did you say 'mine' it?"

"Yes, I did."

"Isn't methane a gas? Do you mean he's going to be drilling for it like they do for natural gas?"

"Not exactly." The woman on the boat let go of the railing briefly to look at some index cards in her hand but a wave must have hit the boat because the cards flew out of her hand and fluttered over the side. Her next words were bleeped.

"Oh, I'm sorry! Let me see. The methane that's beneath the seafloor is in a form called methane hydrate, which is a white, very lightweight crystalline form. I've been told its appearance and weight are much like those Styrofoam pellets used as packing material. It has been considered for years to be the answer to the world's energy problems because it burns clean and its only by-products are carbon dioxide and water."

"If it only gives off carbon dioxide and water, it does sound like the answer to a lot of our problems!" Tiffany chirped with a smile, the plane-crash victims forgotten.

Sam stared at the TV screen in mild disbelief. "Carbon dioxide in the atmosphere *is* one of our problems, you moron," he said out loud.

"So, Soledad," Tiffany continued brightly, "if people know the methane is there, why hasn't anyone drilled for it before now?"

Sam rolled his eyes. "Well, damn, honey, maybe because it's beneath four thousand feet of water and a few more hundred feet of rock? And maybe because it's not a liquid you can pump to the surface like oil?" He tipped his beer bottle to his lips. "Bet your next question is about underwater bulldozers."

"Well, Tiffany, apparently, the challenge is getting the methane out of the seafloor and up to the surface.

You can't exactly use bulldozers down there," Soledad said with a smile.

As the women shared a brief laugh, Sam went to the kitchen to get another beer and some Tums.

When he returned, Tiffany was posing questions to an official from the National Transportation Safety Board and getting the same answers: The Taino government wasn't letting any people in or any information out.

I'll get me some information. Sam grabbed his phone and punched in a number.

"The 'Jackets are kickin' your big old Terrapin asses, son," he drawled when Marty—Dr. Martin Collins, professor of environmental science at the University of Maryland, expert on the geochemistry of Caribbean trenches, and Sam's research partner and fraternity brother—picked up the phone. "I think I'm goin' to have me some turtle soup for dinner. *Terp* soup."

"It's halftime, which means there's half a game left to go. And being ahead by a field goal doesn't qualify as kicking our asses," Marty pointed out, his voice as dry as the dust on Sam's TV. "What are you doing watching the game anyway? Doesn't she have you wallpapering a powder room or stenciling rosebuds in your bedroom closet or something?"

Sam winced. There had never been any love lost between Marty and Cyn. Not since the day they met, when Marty had come into town for the weekend and Cyn had insisted on hanging around. And pouring their beers into glasses. And telling them to take their feet off the coffee table. And laughing at Marty's truly putrid Hawaiian hula-girl shirts.

Nobody was allowed to laugh at his shirts.

"She's on a whale-watchin' cruise off the Bahamas

on one of those clipper sailboats. The kind where you pay for the privilege of bein' a crew member," Sam replied. "Went with a bunch of girlfriends this morning."

"Anywhere near Taino?"

"Hell, yeah. They got permission to go divin' with the humpbacks off Taino. Although I'm guessin' that's not going to happen now." Sam wandered out onto his deck, which backed up to a small nature preserve. "You see that stuff about the crash?"

"Yeah. Can't believe the fucking timing," Marty muttered.

"What do you mean?"

"Well, I wasn't supposed to say anything, but I just got a call saying it was all off anyway, so I figure the secrecy is, too. A few of us were going down there for a meeting late next week."

Sam stopped short. "What for?" he demanded. "And why didn't you say anything?"

"I just told you. I couldn't. And I'm not really sure what for. All I know is about a month ago I got this invitation from Dennis Cavendish to attend some sort of conference he was calling a Geo-Marine Summit. I had to sign a confidentiality agreement. They wouldn't tell me who else was going, just that I'd be flown down to Taino on one of his jets this Friday and flown home on Sunday."

"They wouldn't tell you what it was about?" Sam repeated, frowning as he stared absently into the swampy woods.

"Well, come on, Sam, what else could it be about but that methane hydrate gold mine Cavendish is sitting on? He was hot for you eight or nine years ago when you were polishing that reputation of yours. Mine's the one with the high gloss now," Marty said. Sam could practically hear him grinning. "I've been quoted in *The New Yorker* and *Newsweek*. Everybody wants me. I'm Martin Collins, Methane Man."

"You're also even more full of shit than you used to be," Sam pointed out.

"Yeah, but nobody else has figured that out yet, so keep your piehole shut," Marty replied with a laugh.

Squinting into the middle distance and taking a long, thoughtful slug from his beer, Sam paused before asking his next question. "You really think he's going for the methane?"

"Oh, hell, yes." He paused. "This goes nowhere, right?" Marty waited for Sam's grunt of acknowledgment. "I think he's already done it."

Sam frowned. "Done what? Mined it?"

"Yup."

"What makes you think that?"

"Seismic activity, mostly. But, I don't know, maybe it's just a gut feeling. You know, the oddball questions coming up on some loops, some of the research he's been offering to sponsor. Then this weird invitation to the mystery conference. I guess once I figured out who some of the other people invited were, it all made me wonder. That's when I went back to the seismo readings. Some of the activity was just odd enough to make me start to plot it, and I think I see a trend."

"A trend?" Sam repeated.

"I think I might have seen evidence of some tests, Sam," Marty replied bluntly. "Exploratory activity of the drilling kind."

"Are you sure? There haven't been any fluctuations in atmospheric levels there. I've got a grad student doing a dissertation on eastern Caribbean microclimates right now, and she'd have noticed something."

"Well, I'm not looking at that end of the data with a fine-tooth comb, but I'd have noticed a blip. And she's right: There aren't any."

"How can he be mining methane hydrate without any atmospheric release?" Sam demanded. "There would have to be something there. I mean, *something*, Marty."

There was a long silence that Sam knew better than to break.

"Okay," Marty said at last. "You know I'm not crazy, right?"

"Hell, yes, you're crazy. You just called yourself 'Methane Man,'" Sam replied.

"Yeah, well, okay. I'm crazy. Here's what Methane Man thinks Dennis Cavendish is up to."

"What's that?"

"I think he's doing whatever he's doing on the sea-floor." Marty's voice had dropped to a little above a whisper.

Sam blinked, then blinked again. "Say what? Well, of course it—"

"No, you dumb shit, *from* the seafloor," Marty said, interrupting.

Sam paused as he let this sink in. "You think he's got some sort of . . . facility *on the seafloor*?"

"I can't think of any other way he could be doing it, Sam. Over the years, I've looked at a lot of satellite shots of that island and there's no production facility there. There's a volcano, palm trees, sand, a few clusters of small buildings, and a very simple, streamlined, deep-water port, and I know the last thing sounds like an oxymoron. But that is all there is, Sam. There's no mining operation on that island. Nothing visible offshore, either."

"But that island is surrounded by some of the deepest water in the region, Marty. How the hell could he—"

"I don't know. I mean, really, not a fucking clue, Sam," Marty replied, and Sam could practically hear him shrug. "But why else would he have invited me and a bunch of other pointy-headed methane hydrate groupies down there next week? I don't know the whole guest list, but I confirmed three other guys, and just the four of us constitute one serious geek squad, Sammy."

"But how—who the hell would—" Sam stopped, not even sure what questions he wanted to ask. "That's just too wild, Marty. Nobody can build anything that deep. Even the U.S. Navy hasn't attempted anything beyond a few hundred feet, at least anything that I know about."

"Yeah, well." Marty sighed. "Sam? Game's back on."

"Okay," Sam replied absently.

"Think about it for a while," Marty said. "If anything comes to mind, let me know. I can't really come up with any other conclusion."

"Well, yeah, okay, I will."

"Hell, there goes the kickoff."

The click as Marty hung up on him snapped Sam's mind back to the present, and he wandered back into his house and parked himself in front of the TV. In the real scheme of things, what Dennis Cavendish was or wasn't doing on his island wasn't quite as important at the moment as what the Yellowjackets were doing to the Terps. He rearranged the stack of silk pillows beneath his head and brought up the volume.

3:35 P.M., Saturday, October 25, Taino

Not entirely recovered from her upsetting conversation with Micki, Victoria let herself into her cottage. All of the large, screenless windows in the room were open, admitting a breeze that retained heavy hints of the acrid odor of burning jet fuel and little else. Even the frangipani that curled up and around the windows and doors couldn't obliterate it.

Dennis was standing in the doorway to her private lanai.

He still looked like hell.

"How are you holding up?" she asked quietly as she moved to his side.

He looked down at her with a hollow expression in his eyes. "I won't lie to you, Vic. I'm numb."

"Why don't we sit down for a minute?" She urged him toward the small table nestled in a corner of the patio and then stopped short. "Oh."

A thin layer of greasy black dust lay on the bamboo furniture, and the broad shafts of sunlight that pierced the canopy of palms and catalpas held particles that spun and swirled but didn't sparkle as they fell. They were matte and dark, reflecting nothing but the horror that spawned them.

"I've never faced a situation that left me not knowing what to do, Vic. Never. It's like my brain is paralyzed."

She said nothing, just looked at him with an expression she kept as neutral as she could. It was as if she hardly knew the man standing in front of her. Frustration and grief had replaced the adrenaline-fueled anger that had rushed through him at first. She knew it was a natural progression, but it was a dangerous one.

Neither one of them could afford to let grief take precedence. Not when there were countries interested in more than altruism, with ships and crews at the ready to invade her space. She needed Dennis sharp, decisive, and in command, not frozen.

Leaving her standing in the dappled sunlight, Dennis turned and walked to the other side of the room where he stood silently in front of open French doors that led to a wide, waving communal lawn of sea oats and sawgrass, and eventually the beach.

"They almost got me, Vic. Came damned close."

She had to bite her lips against the raw emotion in his voice. "Yes, but they failed. That's the important thing. And they don't know it yet. That's important, too."

"What will they do when they find out?"

"That depends on who they are. But whoever they are, they'll try again if it means that much to them. You know that. This isn't the first attempt, Dennis."

"It was the best so far."

Snap out of it, damn you. "What do you want to do?" Victoria made sure her voice was as quiet as it always was, but she could hear evidence of the strain she'd been under for the last few hours. It felt like days since she'd watched the footage of the plane coming down.

"I want to do the same thing to the bastards who tried to do this to me."

Okay, maybe you are coming back online. "I meant now."

"I know what you meant." He let out a long breath. "What did the neighbors say?"

"They're providing the assistance we've asked for. Keeping them away from the crash site will likely be our biggest challenge."

He turned and looked at her. "I wouldn't be surprised if one of them had a hand in it just to get in here for a look around."

Victoria gave him a hard stare. "State-sponsored terrorism? Too convenient, Dennis, and too ridiculous."

"Is it?" He lifted an eyebrow at her. "I've been thinking, and for all of our security precautions and background screening, for all of our encryption and double-blind controls on information transfer, for all of your constant surveillance, do you really think we haven't been infiltrated somehow? I don't mean electronically, I mean by someone. That we have an enemy in our midst."

"Of course I've considered it. At the hangar in Miami, yes, perhaps we have been penetrated, but here on the island? No. We're secure. I know no security system is perfect, but we've taken system redundancy to the extreme, as you well know. And only you and I know the extent of that redundancy," she replied easily, lifting one slim, dark eyebrow of her own. "Other than a few, a very few people in Washington, no one living outside of this island knows about the mining operation, Dennis. They may have their suspicions, but no one can *know* anything. Half the people living in *Atlantis* don't know what the other half are doing."

"I'd like to believe that, Vic. I'm glad you're so confident." He turned back to look at the beach.

Victoria crossed her arms and walked to the doors and stood next to him, careful not to lean against the wall. The more she looked around, the more it appeared that everything was covered with the greasy soot.

"Don't kid yourself. You're not glad. You're horrified. And you don't pay me to be confident, you pay me to be paranoid, and I'm exceptionally good at it. I won't deny that this—"

"Act of terrorism," he interjected. "That's what we're calling it, isn't it?"

"This incident," she continued, "is highly suspicious as well as tragic. The consequences are already rippling across the world literally at the speed of light. Or the speed of television, anyway. Charlie has been fencing with the press for hours," she said, referring to Charlie Deen, Dennis's oldest friend and his Georgetown-based ambassador to the United States. "But I'm not entirely convinced that a real insider is involved."

"Humor me. Who inside this organization could have been involved?"

She shrugged tightly and wondered what he would say if she told him he topped Micki's list of suspects. "That's the question of the day, isn't it? I've already requested all the work records associated with the plane from the day its components started being fabricated until the day we took delivery. We need far more basic information about the aircraft and what happened to it before we can start making conjectures. The first batch of—" She'd been about to say "debris" when the realization that the remains of fifteen people were mingled with the wreckage of the plane flashed into her mind. She stopped and swallowed hard, waving a hand in dismissal as she collected herself.

"The first batch of recovered material has already been brought ashore and is being labeled and packed for delivery to the NTSB in Miami. It should be on its way in a matter of hours. Charlie has arranged for a private hangar to be used as the staging area for reconstruction and . . . and as a morgue," she finished, stumbling over the last words and hating herself for it.

Be cold.

"We've arranged for the families of the victims to stay at Kamelame Cay on Andros if they would like to come down for . . . whatever. To see the site. We've arranged with the captain of the *Ma Belle* to have it available to them—"

"What's that?"

"A yacht. With a helipad, so they can be closer to the site if they'd prefer."

A soft tap on the door preceded its opening, and Dennis watched as Victoria's assistant poked her head into the cottage.

"Excuse me, Victoria." Gemma shifted her red-rimmed eyes to Dennis. "I have the office of the American secretary of state on the phone, sir. She's patched through the embassy in Washington. She'd like to speak with you."

"I'll bet she would," Dennis said with a hard laugh. "Unfortunately, we haven't decided yet whether I'm still alive."

"I understand that, sir. But I was told to convey to you that it's urgent," she added softly, her eyes flicking between her boss and her boss's boss.

"Gemma, please tell the secretary that *I* will return her call when my current meeting ends," Victoria interjected smoothly, pleased that Hurricane Dennis was regaining some force, if only in fits and starts.

Gemma nodded and shut the door, leaving them alone once again.

Dennis watched the door as it closed. "I'm sure the old tart is frothing at the mouth because we won't let them in."

"No doubt. And she's not the only one. The British have a carrier group doing exercises in the Central Atlantic and have offered assistance."

"Well, they can just bugger off, as they're so fond of saying." He let out a hard breath and closed his eyes. "I need to go on television, Vic, and let them know they missed."

"I know. And you will. Just not now."

"I want to tell them that they killed close friends of mine, Vic. And that I won't forget that."

"Unfortunately, you're not allowed to have friends at a time like this. You have to think beyond that," she said coldly.

"The world financial markets will be in chaos by the opening bell Monday and dozens, if not hundreds, of companies are already. And you want me to hide in my tree house and flip off the world." He glared at her. "I need to get my presidential ass out there for the world to see."

She gave him the hardest look he'd ever gotten from her. "I'm glad you're back from the edge, Dennis, but if your presidential ass is known to be intact, we may lose our best chance at finding out who did this. I want you to stay here and stay out of sight." She paused. "I've decided to send Micki up to Washington. I think it will be better for everyone if she's up there. That way Charlie will have someone—"

"Fuck that." He glared back at her. "Micki is a pain in the ass. She can't think and talk at the same time. I'm not going to have her talking to anyone who matters. You go up there. She can handle things here for a day or two. That way she can't screw anything up. You've got everything locked down, anyway. You go."

Victoria's eyes widened. "I can't go. *I* need to be here."

"No you don't," Dennis stated. "I'm here. You just tell Micki what to do and she can run things. We're not going to have any answers for at least twenty-four hours anyway. The crews on the water have their orders and the security is tighter than it's ever been. It will be okay."

"But—"

"Why are you arguing? That was an order."

Speechless at the imperiousness of his tone, Victoria could only stare at him, his set jaw, his furious eyes. Her mind was frozen with the thought that her belief in Dennis all these years might have been misplaced, that Micki might actually be right.

She nodded, feeling almost sick to her stomach. "I'll have Gemma get it organized right away. If it's all right with you, I'll return that call to the secretary of state."

CHAPTER

4:45 P.M., Saturday, October 25, Gainesville, Florida

The phone rang and Sam immediately lowered the television's volume as CYNTHIA DAVISON appeared on the pop-up banner shadowing the Georgia Tech sidelines. "Hey, darlin'."

"Hi." Her voice betrayed her excitement.

"What's up? You on the boat yet?"

"We've been on the boat for a few hours already. We're about thirty miles south-southeast of the tip of Miami." Her voice dropped in a conspiratorial rush. "Sam, guess what? I've already been in touch with the station and they want me to try to cover the crash. The captain is—"

"Now just hang on a minute, Cyn. What do you

mean you're goin' to cover the crash? You can't be anywhere near that plane crash yet."

"Oh, sorry, Sam. I'm just really excited. No, we're not near it. Not yet. But we will be. Soon."

He took a deep breath and rolled his eyes. "I hate to rain on your picnic, sweetheart, but they said on the news they're not lettin' anyone near it. I know you were supposed to be allowed into Taino's waters for a dive, but a friend of mine was invited down there for next week and his trip just got canceled, so I don't think you're goin' to get anywhere near it. They've sealed the area."

There was a pause in their conversation that let Sam know a storm was imminent. He stood up and walked toward the kitchen. Turning his back on the TV was a painful decision, because the 'Jackets were on the fifteen-yard line, but he couldn't pay attention to Cyn *and* the game, and Cyn would kill him if she realized she was the second horse in that race. Under the circumstances.

"Well, you *are* raining on my *parade*, Sam. And we *are* heading over to Taino," she snapped. "I mean, it's the ocean, Sam. No one can 'seal the area.'"

The tone in her voice was the one he hated most: her bossy, determined, just-watch-me tone. The attitude that went with it had propelled her to the level of senior producer in a growing market in just a few years, and Sam was sure it would end up causing her big trouble one day. Maybe today.

"The crash site is inside Taino's territorial waters, Cyn, and they're not lettin' anyone in. They're not even lettin' coast guard or navy rescue teams in. It's all over the news. You're not goin' to get in there, darlin'," he insisted. "Just back off. Head over to one of the Bahama islands. Just enjoy your vacation."

"*Back off?* Are you crazy? We've already been granted permission to get into the area," she hissed.

"That was before the accident. Taino's security force is out in spades, darlin', and I don't care if y'all are hanging off the masts in your bikinis and passin' out piña coladas, y'all are not goin' to get past those guys. Those Taino people aren't even lettin' helicopters cross their airspace, for cryin' out loud. CNN and FOX are talking about tryin' to get live satellite footage from the military or NOAA. Cyn, darlin', you won't get in," he repeated.

Her pause was ominous, and when she spoke, her voice was cold. "I'm sorry I called."

Hell's bells. Sam took a deep breath.

"Cyn, don't be like that," he said, his easy voice belying the effort it took to make it that way. "I just don't want you to get in trouble or get hurt. Taino's security guys aren't a bunch of retiree rent-a-cops. CNN is saying they're all former SEALs, with a few candy-asses from the Mossad in the mix for good measure."

"Oh, get real. You know what their day-to-day job is? They zip around on Wave Runners keeping sailboats away from a bunch of fish and a few coral reefs," she snapped. "Taino doesn't have a navy. That 'private security force' is a collection of burned-out surfers armed with bullhorns and spotlights. They won't bother us. We're on a clipper cruise. We're tourists."

"Well, the rest of your girlfriends might be, but you just told me that you're the press now, and if I know you as well as I think I do, you took your cameras with you, with all those fancy lenses. They'll know what you're up to, Cyn."

"As far as they're concerned, we're harmless. And we're *expected*."

Sam rolled his eyes again at her bullheadedness, and knew it was ridiculous to argue further, especially at international cell phone rates. "Whatever you say, Cyn. How was your flight?"

"Fine," she replied. "Having a great time. Wish you were here."

He winced at the acid in her tone. "Sounds like it. Well, darlin', call me again when you've had your adventures on the high seas. Tell me where to wire the bail money."

"Not funny." A short pause was followed by a heavy sigh. "I don't want to hang up mad at you, Sam."

"I know. That's 'cause you love me and you can't wait to marry me. So just say you're sorry and promise me you won't do anything stupid. Call me a wuss, darlin', but I don't want you telling our grandchildren any stories about the time silly ol' granny got harpooned by a cop on a Jet Ski."

Another short pause ensued. "I have to go now. Bye, Sam."

"I love you, Cyn."

He waited until he heard the click that disconnected the call, then, shaking his head with annoyance, he placed the handset in its dock and walked out to his pool to do a few dozen laps. It was a nationally televised game. He'd be back on the couch before the fourth quarter started.

4:45 P.M., Saturday, October 25, Taino

Fresh from seeing Victoria take off in one of the Gulfstreams, Micki parked her golf cart outside the small, low-slung building that housed the security group and went straight to her office. Shutting the door, she walked to her desk, brought up her secure e-mail, and created a

new message to an internal address. With all communications to the outside world shut down except for their
one ultrasecure link, she knew every incoming and outgoing message was being scrutinized by several levels of
her staff. There was no point in trying to send a message
to any address that didn't end in Taino's identifier; it
would never make it past the perimeter she and Victoria
had so carefully set up.

On the address line, Micki hurriedly typed the in-
house e-mail alias she'd set up for Garner months ago,
and then put *Thanks!* in the message line. Moving to
the text area, she began typing rapidly.

Hi

Thanks for your message. Everyone on the island is
okay. Devastated but pulling ourselves together.

Dennis was supposed to be on the plane, but
thankfully wasn't. Swamped right now—VC is on
her way to DC and will be back tomorrow.

I hope you are okay.

I'll be in touch.

Micki

The message would be read by someone on her staff,
but she knew nobody would pay too much attention to
it. After all, the message was innocuous, it was being
sent to an internal address, and it was coming from the
person who, now that Victoria was in midair, was in
charge of security for the island.

Not that anyone would recognize the recipient's
name. Dennis's reach was extensive, with small pockets of people working around the globe on various pet

projects. No one but Dennis, Victoria, and Micki knew exactly who was working where or on what, so creating a ghost employee hadn't been difficult.

The e-mail would leave Micki's computer and almost instantly enter the mailbox for the alias account on the Washington-based network of the Climate Research Institute. That network was distinct from the one on the island, and would be functioning at a different level of security. The arrival of the message in the dummy mailbox would execute code that would hide the message from the security filters before sending it out to a series of e-mail dead-drops. The message would bounce around the world twice, arriving in Garner's e-mail application with an untraceable return address within minutes.

Micki knew that Garner wouldn't be pleased with what she had to say; he'd wanted Dennis dead. But the situation as it now stood had defaulted to the best possible option. Instead of having to neutralize Victoria, Micki would have to neutralize Dennis, and once she did, she'd be in control and the second phase of the operation could commence.

Micki clicked SEND and then sat back in her chair with a smile. It felt so good to be doing a job she could be proud of.

CHAPTER

7:30 P.M., Saturday, October 25, Washington, D.C.
Proudly bearing the colors and seal of The Paradise of
Taino, the sleek Gulfstream G350 touched down at
Reagan National Airport in Washington, D.C., and tax-
ied to a private hangar. As she expected, Victoria was
met at the foot of the jet's steps by a member of the
Taino embassy staff, U.S. Customs officials, and a small
contingent of tense people who said they were from the
U.S. Department of State. She knew that was unlikely.
Under the circumstances, that agency's claims would
have been trumped by Homeland Security.

Victoria and the two embassy attachés who met her
were ushered politely into a small conference room and
invited to sit down, which she just as politely declined
to do. She instructed one of the embassy staffers to ac-
company her small carry-on to the Customs and Im-
migration area and then turned her attention to the tall
young woman from State, who was clearly not present
by choice.

"Welcome back to the United States, Secretary
Clark," she said awkwardly.

"Thank you."

The woman hesitated for just a moment before she
got to the point. "Secretary Clark, I'm sure you understand that the department of state and some of our other
domestic agencies share your concerns regarding the
crash of Flight—"

"Of course I do, Ms.—" Victoria interrupted smoothly with a slightly raised eyebrow. "I'm so sorry. I know it's only been a few minutes, but I've forgotten your name."

"It's Elizabeth Keene, ma'am."

Victoria slid her sunglasses off her face to make eye contact with the woman, and was gratified by the split second of startled surprise that showed itself on Elizabeth Keene's ivory-smooth Ivy League face.

Ol' Blue Eyes, indeed.

With well-practiced patience, Victoria smiled faintly and gave a gentle, casual tweak to the sleeve of her black suit. It was Moschino Couture and didn't need tweaking, but Victoria knew the movement would underscore the impression she gave of ease and composure, something the other woman was clearly lacking.

It never hurt to have interrogators off base from the start, even inept ones.

"Thank you, Ms. Keene. We're very appreciative of President Benson's generous offers of assistance and will certainly pass on appropriate information as we assemble it. However, at the moment, we have little to share. It's very early in the investigation. We're still trying to recover from the shock of seeing the plane come down and of losing so many colleagues. The Climate Research Institute is a small organization and very tightly knit."

"Yes, ma'am—"

"So I'm sure you understand my desire to get to the embassy as quickly as possible. My presence was requested by our ambassador and he and his staff are waiting for me," Victoria continued with pointed politeness.

"Yes, ma'am—"

"Feel free to have your representatives call the embassy later this evening, or tomorrow. I'm sure I'll have some information to share. Right now, I must be going. Please convey to the secretary my most profound thanks for such a gracious reception." In one smooth motion, she began to turn toward the door.

"Ms. Clark."

The voice was not particularly deep, nor did its tone possess any particular urgency. But there was a dark chill in it, and Victoria knew without needing to be told that it came from the lean, well-built man in the corner, the one who very casually had not been introduced. The one who looked like he'd had a lot of experience fading into the woodwork until it was time to make himself known.

The one who had "spook" written all over him.

Victoria stopped immediately, but made sure she did so gracefully. Turning to face him, she met his dark eyes with practiced calm. She was not at all surprised to find that he had stepped forward or that the others had taken a step back, giving him center stage and the power it afforded.

"I don't believe we've been introduced," she replied.

The faintest shadow of a smile crossed his cold but youthful face. "I'm Tom Taylor."

His gaze was shuttered, but she had no doubt that it could burn like a laser as needed.

"How do you do, Mr. Taylor?"

"I've been better, Ms. Clark."

"I'm sorry to hear it."

The pause that followed her words lasted long enough to have the others in the room shifting their weight and clearing their throats.

"I understand your hurry, but I'd like to talk with you

about this morning's accident sooner rather than later. Would you mind if I accompanied you to the embassy? That way I won't have to delay your arrival," he said as though several minutes hadn't ticked by.

She lifted an eyebrow. "That's rather unorthodox, Mr. Taylor. Surely we can set up—"

"These are unusual circumstances. I have a car waiting."

She counted four slow, steady heartbeats. "Very well." She flicked her gaze to Elizabeth Keene, who looked both confused and relieved. "I trust this meets with your approval?"

"Yes. Thank you. I'll be in touch with you later, Secretary Clark."

Victoria gave a slight nod, then turned toward the door. "Mr. Taylor," she said, tilting her head toward the door, "please don't trouble your driver. My car is this way."

Tom didn't know much about Victoria Clark other than that she'd come from tough circumstances to rise to the top of her profession as quickly as anyone with no connections could. According to the thin dossier he'd reviewed, her intelligence and professional abilities were unquestioned. What interested him more than her accomplishments, however, was that people who had worked for her universally ascribed something more to her than simply smarts. Some called it intuition, others more imaginative terms, but the end result was that she was held in high esteem by her colleagues and was rarely challenged. And was just as rarely wrong in her decisions.

The descriptions and few pictures included in the file, mostly from old passports and driver's licenses, hadn't done her justice. She was stunning: dark, petite, and obviously in great shape; every movement she made was graceful and controlled. But it was her eyes—almond-shaped, with irises of dark, brilliant blue—that sent her looks beyond beautiful and over the edge of exotic. Her cool confidence sharpened that edge.

Tom was looking forward to finding her flaws.

He was partly amused and partly impressed, though not surprised, that she betrayed not even the slightest hint of nerves as she directed the remaining attaché from Taino's embassy to sit in the front seat of the town car and left word that the other should take a cab back to Georgetown with her luggage.

She fell silent as they headed through the maze of airport roads toward the George Washington Parkway. As they turned onto the GWP, she raised the panel that separated them from the driver, then swiveled to face Tom. Those deep and startling blue eyes met his.

A slight smile appeared on her face as she spoke. "What's on your mind, Mr. Taylor?"

Tom returned the smile. "Terrorism, Ms. Clark. It's what's on my mind most of the time these days."

"May I infer that you think this morning's accident is—"

"It was no accident."

"You sound very sure of yourself."

"And you sound remarkably unsurprised."

"I'll admit that seeing the plane come down was a shock and a tragedy for everyone on Taino, but I don't surprise easily, Mr. Taylor. Call it part of my charm." She lifted one shoulder in an elegant shrug. "Tell me what makes *you* so sure today's tragedy wasn't an accident."

"I hope I'm not being too forward if I say that your performance is enchanting."

She said nothing and her expression remained fixed and calm, but she couldn't stop the annoyance that flashed in those eyes.

So she is human.

He reached into the breast pocket of his suit coat and pulled out his BlackBerry. It took him less than a minute to pull up the photos of Blaylock and Wendy Watson. He passed it to her. "Does anyone in these pictures look familiar to you, Ms. Clark?"

"Of course I know Lieutenant Colonel Watson. She was a consummate professional, President Cavendish's chief pilot, and a well-respected member of the staff. She'll be greatly missed." She frowned slightly. "I don't recognize the man with her, although he seems familiar. I think I may have seen his face—"

"On the news? Or maybe on a post office wall?" Tom offered with feigned helpfulness. "Move forward to the next picture. He's a bit younger in that one."

Victoria hesitated before doing so, and as she looked at Garner Blaylock's mug shot her eyes widened slightly. The face in the picture was bearded and the hair was shorter, nearly shaved.

As she handed Tom his BlackBerry, her eyes met his and he saw something resembling fear in them.

That's right, honey. You've just met your first mistake. And it's a beauty.

Tom took the gadget out of her unresisting hands, returned it to sleep mode, then slid it back into his breast pocket. "Looks like your memory just got better. His name is Garner Blaylock, the brain power behind a British organization called GAIA."

"The environmental group?"

He smiled at her and it was almost genuine. "He'd be delighted at your description. He likes people to call GAIA that."

"What should I call it?"

"Call it anything you like. In the circles I move in, we call them terrorists."

Tom watched her run the tip of her tongue over her lips. Nothing else moved.

"They're ecoterrorists, then?"

"If you need to be that precise, yes."

"I thought radical environmentalism died out years ago. After your people infiltrated the Earth Liberation Front and prosecuted some of them, it seemed like other groups took the hint and abandoned the red-paint-throwing and tree-spiking variety of activism in favor of politicking and rubbing shoulders with sympathetic celebrities."

So you've done your homework. "Some of the groups, like ELF, died out. Others splintered. True believers like Blaylock went dormant until a new generation decided avenging the ills brought on by the industrialized world would be a fun way to spend idle afternoons," he replied. "This time around, the activities didn't remain the brain-child of tree huggers and suburbanites who put on their plaid shirts for a few days of playing weekend warrior. The message this time penetrated the brains of kids who shrinks like to call 'disaffected urban youth.' Punks and low-lifes, in other words. Inner-city tenement dwellers with no money and a lot of attitude who hooked up with suburban delinquents in possession of a bad combination of money, brains, and what they consider to be righteous anger, who think their high-tops and iPods should have come to them without an environmental price tag and who want to punish those who ran up the bill."

He shrugged. "Most of these pseudo environmental-terrorist organizations still adhere to the old Earth First! model of a loose organizational structure and no formal hierarchy. They rely on local, small-time lunatics to fill the void and cause the trouble. GAIA is different. Blaylock is too smart and too much of a narcissist for that. He founded GAIA while he was in his mid-twenties. Its organizational structure is fairly flat, and Blaylock controls everything. His public persona is a starry-eyed romantic seeking utopian harmony, but beneath that façade, he's a control freak and a sociopath, bent on destroying whatever industry creates. And he has a private source of money, which is one thing most of them don't have." Tom paused. "You're not curious about that?"

"Should I be?"

"I would think you'd be curious about anything that might have to do with the plane crash."

He watched a muscle work in her cheek.

"Okay. Where did he get the money?"

Tom sat back and folded his arms across his chest. "His adoptive parents died under unusual circumstances very shortly after he graduated with an honors degree from Oxford. He was their only heir, since their two biological children had died tragically while in their teens."

"Was he investigated for their murders?"

"No, but we're pressuring the British to review the circumstances of their deaths."

"You said they were his adoptive parents?" Victoria asked.

"Yes. The Blaylocks adopted him when he was about five. From Romania. He was an orphan."

From the corner of his eye, Tom saw one of Victoria's hands clench almost imperceptibly.

Is that sympathy for the devil, orphan girl? There's only one way to find out.

"Pretty interesting, huh?" he continued, keeping his voice casual but his eyes watchful as he pricked her a little harder. "Those amazing Romanian orphanages. No affection, practically no attention given to those kids. It's amazing so many of them survived." He paused. "I guess you could say a lot of them actually thrived. After all, those *orphanages*"—he repeated the word deliberately—"were the breeding ground for many of today's best hackers and thugs. They nurtured a whole generation of cold-blooded, free-range sociopaths unencumbered by morality or ethics. They live by the law of survival of the fittest. I doubt Stalin could have done better."

A harsh, dull flush had crept up Victoria's neck and she was holding her body so stiff he could feel the hot tension radiating from her.

"How does this relate to what has happened off Taino this morning, Mr. Taylor?" she asked, her voice remarkably cool as she glanced at the slim gold watch encircling her wrist. "What is Garner Blaylock's connection to Lieutenant Colonel Watson?"

"We believe Blaylock recruited Wendy Watson and that she had a role in bringing down your plane this morning," he said bluntly. "The plane she'd named *Gaia*."

Victoria's head snapped up and cold blue fire sparked in her eyes as they met his. "I find your statements inflammatory and highly offensive, Mr. Taylor. Wendy Watson was a highly decorated officer in the United States Air Force before she came to work for President Cavendish. She wasn't radical in any respect. She was also, as are all of our staff, thoroughly investigated prior to being offered her job, and routinely and closely monitored afterward," she said. "I fail to see why, based on the strength of one photograph, you can conjecture that Lieutenant Colonel Watson was working for Garner Blaylock's organization or had developed some sort of relationship with him."

He lasered a look at her that conveyed every bit of his exasperation. "Ms. Clark, do I seem that stupid? Just own it. You fucked up. Big-time."

"If I make a mistake, Mr. Taylor, I do own it," she snapped. "In the four years that I knew her, Wendy Watson never expressed any opinion about the environment. In fact, she spent most of her adult life being a loyal member of an organization that performed activities that could easily be described as destructive to the environment—at least to Afghanistan's environment. She was no pushover, Mr. Taylor, but a highly decorated career military officer with many dangerous and successful combat search-and-rescue missions to her credit. She was hardly the type to fall for some romantic, New Age, environmental rhetoric spouted—"

"To the contrary, she was just his type."

Victoria frowned at him. "Wendy Watson was an exceptionally intelligent woman, and a woman of tremendous personal integrity. I know that for a fact. As I said, I conduct exhaustive background investigations on the people who come to work for us, and—" She paused and took a measured breath in a late attempt to regain the composure she'd lost. "She was perhaps atypical for a combat-hardened pilot in that she wasn't in it for the excitement. She was no adrenaline junkie and didn't fit the 'warrior' stereotype. She was quite the opposite, very practical and stoic and steady. She hadn't had many romantic relationships and all of them were brief and extremely circumspect."

"Are you saying she never got laid? Easy score for Blaylock then. Gratitude can be a big turn-on for some guys."

Victoria's eyes turned hot and furious for a split second. "What I am saying," she snapped, "is that she was certainly not a woman to be taken in by a mane of golden hair, a hard body, and an English accent, nor by any ridiculous, radical propaganda."

Tom smiled at her, keeping it cold. "Think that about her if you like, but I'd advise you not to underestimate Garner Blaylock. He's a modern-day Svengali and could charm the chastity belt off Granny Clampett."

Victoria didn't even blink. "If you were aiming for droll, you missed, Mr. Taylor. I'm neither offended nor amused."

"I'll have to try harder, I guess." He shrugged. "Blaylock's got the psychology down pat; he knows the right words to say and when and how to say them. He doesn't blink without knowing exactly what effect it will have on his audience. Most of his minions are women, usually smart and good-looking. As improbable as it sounds, when he starts talking to people about 'nurturing natural magic,' about the need to 'reenchant the earth' and 'disrupt the anthropogenic constraints on the universal life force,' they go slack-jawed and believe him."

She took in a deep breath. "Fascinating, Mr. Taylor, really. But Wendy would not—"

"Forget what you think she *would* and *would not* do, Ms. Clark. I'm telling you what she *did*," Tom replied forcefully, resting one hand on the seat between them and leaning toward her. He could see Victoria stiffen again, but she didn't back away.

Yeah, honey, you're tough. But I'm tougher.

"By the way, would you like to know how Blaylock left the country this morning?" Tom asked.

"I'd like to know why you let him leave if he's a suspect," she shot back.

"We weren't sure what exactly he was up to. And he was out of U.S. airspace before your plane blew up." He paused. "He was on his way to northern Africa. In one of *your* Gulfstreams, Ms. Clark. They touched down in Spain for refueling, and he's probably on the ground in Algiers by now—enjoying a victory fuck with one of the legendary Taino stewardesses," he added, just for effect.

She jerked back in her seat as if he'd pushed her and then everything about her froze, except her eyes, which widened considerably. "One of *our* planes? You're mistaken."

"To the contrary, it's confirmed. And if you check into it, I imagine you'll discover the trip was arranged courtesy of Wendy Watson." He paused. "But let's get back to Blaylock's operation, shall we? He recruited most of his babe-alicious army in the U.K. and Western Europe, but now they're scattered around the globe. They're one-woman sleeper cells, collecting information and passing it on. It's a pretty brilliant scheme. These foot soldiers are essentially invisible, even to security forces. No one expects beautiful, intelligent women to be terrorists." Tom shrugged.

When Victoria didn't respond, he continued, "His women are all highly educated, not the type you would expect to fall for that kind of green, flowery, universal life force crap, and every one I've seen pictures of is pretty damned hot. He seems to prefer blondes, but he doesn't discriminate. And he does a hell of a job recruiting them. They're tightly meshed with him through emotional and, more often than not, sexual bonds and they're absolutely loyal. They believe everything he tells them and will do anything he asks. Despite, or perhaps even because of, her 'integrity,' your stoic, sexless Wendy would have been a meager challenge for him."

He watched Victoria simmer.

"Mr. Taylor, let's leave Wendy and her alleged involvement out of this for the moment. Why would Garner Blaylock target Taino this way? President Cavendish has a long and illustrious record of fostering the environment—"

She stopped talking as he shook his head and let out a heavy breath. "Ms. Clark, let me be the first to tell you that you lie like shit and you can't do 'disingenuous.'"

Her eyebrows flicked upward but she said nothing and didn't drop her gaze.

"We both know Dennis Cavendish is as much of a narcissist and possibly as much of a sociopath as Garner Blaylock, and he's doing just as good a job creating his own bizarre little reality. Cavendish might own lots of mountains and forests and pretty meadows around the world, and a beautiful Caribbean island, but he has never saved or fostered anything unless he could make lots of money doing it. And Blaylock has targeted your projects before."

Victoria had relaxed somewhat, but kept her eyes on him, her hands loose in her lap. "In small ways."

"Think of who was on that plane and what industries they represented," Tom continued harshly. "Between their primary businesses and their subsidiaries, they included agribusiness, aviation, manufacturing, banking, paper, biopharmaceuticals. And where were they headed? To the private island of the man the greens

love to hate because he's stolen their platform and prof-
ited hugely from it. Why were these titans of industry
headed to Dennis Cavendish's island paradise, where
no industry is allowed to exist?" He paused and gave
her a smile designed to chill rather than warm. "That
wasn't rhetorical, Vicky. Don't be shy about filling in
that blank."

"Please, Mr. Taylor, feel free to call me Secretary
Clark," she said easily. "And the answer to your question is Taino state business."

"Eight of the people on that plane were American
citizens, as are you, Ms. Clark."

"My status is immaterial. And their citizenship doesn't
play into this situation, either."

"Don't delude yourself."

"I never do."

"Where's Dennis Cavendish?"

The change in subject caused her pupils to dilate
suddenly, an involuntary action immediately disguised
with a slow, controlled blink.

As they crossed the Potomac, Victoria turned her
face to the window and squinted at the sunlight splin-
tering the river's dark surface. "Mr. Taylor, this conversation is over."

"Ms. Clark, this conversation has barely begun. Was
he on that plane?"

"That's classified information."

"Unclassify it."

"We'll release the passenger list when the search-
and-rescue operation is complete."

Tom leaned back against the leather seat, not taking
his eyes off her. "You don't strike me as the type to believe in fairy tales, Ms. Clark. We both know no one
survived that crash."

She looked at him and said nothing.

"We could have another pissing match over whose footage is better, but I'd win, Ms. Clark. We were watching your little banana republic this morning, as we have been, twenty-four/seven, for a long time. Other than the cockpit, which, well, you saw what happened to that—other than that, the largest thing we saw hit the water was a strut from the landing gear. That's what I thought it was, anyway. Someone else thought it was the lower half of a woman's leg." He shrugged. "Your 'search-and-rescue' operation is approaching twelve hours. Small plane, small scatter, small number of bodies to find. If there were anyone to be found, you would have found them by now. Why are you delaying any announcements? Why so secretive?"

He paused to let her reply, which she didn't, so he sighed and folded his arms across his chest. "You're the security expert, Ms. Clark. The computer wizard, the princess of paranoia. Here I was thinking we were going to have a real insightful conversation, a meeting of the minds. But I have to say that your silence on some of these topics is mighty interesting."

"I'm delighted to hear it."

"So why were those people on that plane?"

She gave him a tight smile. "You're getting tiresome."

"And you're getting closer to being denied diplomatic or any other kind of immunity if the attorney general decides to open a criminal investigation. There's no question that we have jurisdiction. That plane took off from Miami."

She actually smiled at him then. "Your threats aren't very subtle, nor do they frighten me, Mr. Taylor. But I'll tell you this; the passengers on that plane were personal acquaintances of President Cavendish. He had invited them to his home for a few days."

"Why?"

"Why not?"

"There's no golf course on Taino, no spa, no fishing boats, no luxury hotel. No swimming pool. No tennis courts. Just a few ungroomed trails to the volcano's rather lush crater. In fact, there's nothing for wealthy, hard-driving visitors to your island to do other than visit your very well-equipped dock, which is home to a small fleet of state-of-the-art submersibles, including the one you climbed out of one minute and twenty seconds after the plane exploded. So I'm thinking that perhaps President Cavendish wanted to show his 'acquaintances' the rather large structure he's built on the seafloor. You know the one I'm talking about. The one that's situated near the largest methane-hydrate deposit in this hemisphere, if not in the entire world." He paused and let the weight of his knowledge settle into her brain.

Although her face had gone a bit pale, her expression became steely and her eyes chilled to something measurable in degrees Kelvin.

He continued his revelations in a casual tone. "Even the scope of conversation among the locals is rather limited, I'd imagine. What could thirty or so of the foremost experts on hydrogeology, underwater mining, deep-sea habitats, and a few other narrow field specialties have to discuss with nine people who control a very large percentage of the world's wealth? Perhaps the group would also include the thirty or so other experts who arrived on the island a few months ago and then promptly disappeared—the ones who were last seen by us as they climbed aboard your largest submersible.

That wasn't a Disney ride you were taking them on, was it? One that would give new meaning to the title *Pirates of the Caribbean*?"

Throughout his recitation, her expression had not changed. Those blue eyes remained icy and calm.

"Is your silence my cue for applause?" she said after a long pause.

"Not at all, Ms. Clark. It's your cue to start providing some answers."

She said nothing, just turned her head to the window.

Victoria knew that Tom Taylor's conversation was meant to shock her, to confuse her into revealing what he wanted to know, which was everything. He was good at it, and the effort to keep their multilayered dialogue functioning on her terms was nothing less than exhausting. She was glad that they were nearing the embassy's compound.

As the limousine turned the corner of M Street in Georgetown, Victoria took one look out the window and felt her already battered spirits plunge. Fighting her way through the crush of television vans, camera crews, and reporters swarming in the street outside the embassy was the last thing she wanted to do. But if she didn't exit the car outside the gates, she'd have to either throw him out of the car or bring the uncharming Mr. Taylor inside the gates. The latter was an action that could arguably be considered an invitation and she knew better than to invite a federal agent onto sovereign territory. He'd be like kudzu in a garden; she'd never be rid of him.

Using the intercom, she asked the driver to circle the block, then turned to her companion.

"Can my driver drop you off someplace, Mr. Taylor?"

"I was hoping to hang around with you for a little longer."

This is getting old. She smiled coolly. "Thank you for the compliment. Unfortunately, I have pressing matters to attend to, as you can imagine. The driver will drop you off at your office, your home; wherever you wish."

"My office will be fine, thanks," he said after a short pause, then reached into his pocket and pulled out a business card, which he handed to her. "Feel free to get in touch with me any time you want to have another chat, Ms. Clark."

The card provided only his name and a phone number. No title, no agency.

She met his eyes again. "Of course. And you know how to get in touch with me, should you want anything."

He nodded once and then they both looked away, falling silent as the driver fought his way once again through the scrum of reporters. The embassy gates opened slowly. Steel-jawed, impassive, and openly armed, the embassy's security staff stood along the fence line, keeping their eyes moving over the crowd and occasionally murmuring into the slim microphones hugging their cheeks.

When the car came to a stop, Victoria looked at him.

"Just tell the driver where to take you, Mr. Taylor."

"Thank you, Ms. Clark. Keep in touch."

She didn't wait for anyone to open the car's heavy, armored door for her, but a phalanx of security personnel surrounded her the moment her feet touched the brick driveway. They hustled her beyond the boundary of the gate and through the elegant porte cochere that fronted the building.

Leaving the noise of the street and the protective

swarm of agents behind her, Victoria passed through the doors of the mansion and across the threshold of the ten-thousand-square-foot, immaculately renovated Georgian mansion. The ornate front door closed behind her with a muted thud.

The building exuded the calm hush of a bank vault though she knew the tension levels were well beyond high. The young woman who had opened the door had to hurry to keep up with her, and ushered Victoria into the elevator and up to the elegant third-floor bedroom suite that was always held in readiness for her.

At the doorway to her suite, Victoria turned to the aide. "Please tell Ambassador Deen that I'm here. I'll be available to meet with him in about half an hour. Have my luggage brought up as soon as it arrives."

Safely inside her room, Victoria stood with her eyes gently shut, acknowledging the first moment of solitude she'd had since early morning. It was then, in the artificial calm, that the accumulated weight of the day's tragedy and tension reached a critical mass with no warning, and she had no chance to buffer herself against it.

Fifteen people dead, torn apart and incinerated. Making Dennis inert. Spawning Micki's hysterical accusations and Tom Taylor's grim assertions.

She squeezed her eyes shut, wishing she could turn off the voices shouting in her head.

The Benson administration's hateful leaks. The media's desperate, craven need for information, for scandal, for images of bloodied bodies.

"Meanwhile, I still have hundreds of people to protect, including thirty-six on the ocean floor. I don't know their vulnerability, and I can't ensure their safety," she said out loud in a harsh whisper. "And I don't know who I can count on anymore, or who I can trust."

Slumping against the closed door, she felt tears well in her eyes and spill over as a hard, cold mass of hated emotion bloomed in her chest, constricting her breath and forcing her to double over.

Fifteen people. I failed them. I let them die.

Tearing at her sleek suit, she pulled it off with clumsy hands as she stumbled to the bathroom. Turning on the shower, she stepped in as soon as she was naked, not bothering to wait until the water was warm. She needed to clear her mind. She needed to hide her tears.

She needed to wash the blood from her hands.

CHAPTER

7:30 P.M., Saturday, October 25, Taino

Micki moved into the open doorway that led into Dennis's office. She had to clear her throat twice before he looked up. He looked like hell. A five-o'clock shadow had begun to stubble his chin and cheeks, and his face, usually handsome and full of energy, was dull and slack.

"When did you get back from the bunker?" she asked, moving into his office.

"I never went. I was in Victoria's bungalow for a

while, then I came here." He paused. "I've been calling the families."

The realization that Victoria had deliberately lied to her struck Micki like a blow, and her body responded with a surge of anger. The lie was a first. It would be the last.

"Trust is critical, but proof takes precedence."

How many times had Victoria said that? Thousands, over the years. Well, those words were about to bite her. Micki would make sure of it.

Looking at Dennis, Micki raised her eyebrows and kept her voice even. "Does Victoria know that you've been calling the families?"

"No. And I don't give a rat's ass, either. How are things going?"

"I've been getting hourly reports from the boats. They've picked up a lot of debris, but they haven't found any survivors," she said quietly, settling into a chair. "Dennis, has Victoria discussed any of her thoughts about who might have done this? Or planned it?"

"How could she? It's too early. We don't know anything yet."

Micki nodded silently and glanced down at her hands.

"Has she discussed anything with you?" he asked after a moment.

Micki looked up and met his eyes. "No. Not really." She shrugged. "Some nutty idea about ecoterrorists. It didn't make a lick of sense to me. But when I brought up the possibility that whoever did it might have had inside help, she shut me down cold. It was so unlike her." She pulled her brows together into a small frown.

"With all of her layers of defense—"

"Oh, I wasn't implying any laxness on her part,"

Micki rushed to assure him. "But I just found it so odd that she wouldn't even entertain a conversation about an infiltration."

Dennis leaned back in his chair, glaring at her. "Cut the bullshit, Micki. What are you getting at?"

"Well, I mean, she's the one who taught me never to overlook something just because it might seem outlandish." She paused and bit her lip for effect. She didn't have to fake the heat that rose in her face. Adrenaline was pouring into her veins at the thought of what she was about to do.

"This is so hard to say," she stammered. "But I just don't think I could rest if I don't say it. What if—what if Victoria was part of it?"

Dennis didn't hesitate. "That's preposterous."

Heart pounding, Micki looked at him with every shred of emotion she could summon. "I know it sounds preposterous, Dennis, but don't you think we have to entertain every possibility, no matter *how* crazy? Isn't that the foundation of our entire security platform?"

"We might as well suspect you or me of complicity, Micki. Victoria did not bring down that plane."

"Not intentionally, maybe, but what if she did something that helped someone get through—"

"No," he said coldly.

"Well, why did she want to get off the island so quickly?" Micki almost shouted, pushing herself to her feet. "She's needed here—"

"She didn't want to go to D.C. She was going to send you. I told her to go instead."

The news jolted her. "She was going to send me? She never said anything about that."

"It was a spur-of-the-moment decision."

I'll bet it was. Filled with a sudden, cool clarity, Micki lowered herself back into her chair. "There's some-thing you should know, Dennis. It didn't make sense to me until just now," she said, making her voice eerily subdued. "After she took off, I checked my e-mail. There was a message sent from my computer this evening that I didn't send."

Dennis frowned. "What?"

"There was a message sent from my machine that I didn't send," she repeated. "It was signed by me but I didn't write it and I don't recognize the name it was sent to."

"You think someone broke your password?"

She met his eyes. "Not someone. Victoria. It had to be. No one else has her level of access to the system. Even I don't."

"What did the e-mail say?"

"It just thanked someone for his or her concern and said that you were still alive." She made herself swal-low hard. "It was sent to an internal address, but I didn't recognize the name of the recipient, so I checked the personnel records. There is no such person, Dennis, and the mailbox for that name has executables that for-ward all mail it receives to other mailboxes."

His gaze bored into her. "What are you saying?"

"I'm saying we need to watch Victoria just like we're watching everyone else, Dennis," she answered after a long moment. "I don't think she should be allowed to leave Washington until we know for sure she isn't the mole."

**7:45 P.M., Saturday, October 25, aboard the
Wangari Maathai, off the coast of Taino**

Leaning against the doorjamb in the cockpit of the *Wan-gari Maathai*, his research-boat-turned-rescue-vessel,

Captain Simon Broadhurst picked up the radio handset and called to the captain of his ship's twin, the *Marjory Stoneman Douglas,* whom he could see standing on the deck of her ship.

An unseen member of her crew called to her and, stopping to give Simon a tired wave, she turned to go into the bridge.

"This is Maggy on the *Marjory, Wangari.* Go ahead."

"Simon here. Any news?"

"Lots of metal and upholstery. Luggage. Some—"

Captain Maggy Patterson paused and Simon knew without her having to say it that pulling dismembered human body parts from the water had taken its toll on her.

"Got a few ourselves," he said, clipping his words. "Would you like to do the inventory, or shall I?"

"Oh, God." Maggy choked out the words.

"Right. I'll do it, then. E-mail me a list, Patterson. Not much left to be retrieved out here. This is the *Wangari* out."

"I'll send the list," Maggy replied. "Thanks, Simon. *Marjory* out."

Simon checked in with the other search boat and, in minutes, was looking at a gruesome, updated inventory of the body parts the searchers had found and were storing in the ships' onboard refrigeration units.

Most of the victims were accounted for, at least in part. Simon shuddered at the unintentionally macabre pun. None of the bodies had been intact.

A mixture of anger and grief knifed through him, not for the first time today, and sent his head into his hands. He'd seen the plane coming in, its elegant, streamlined white body vivid against the tropical blue sky. Seconds later, it became a memory suffused in smoke and fire, and he'd spent the day picking body parts and seat cushions out of the water where it had fallen.

This is insanity.

A sudden wave of exhaustion washed over him, leaving him feeling uncomfortably vulnerable. To stave off any emotion—a useless expenditure of energy under the circumstances—Simon looked at his watch and swore under his breath. He'd been on the water for nearly twelve hours. He brought his gaze up to the sea, still slicked with rainbowed patches of jet fuel, and made a decision. Picking up the radio handset again, he called ashore for permission to change the operation from search and rescue to search and recovery.

7:45 P.M., Saturday, October 25, Gainesville, Florida

Not sure whether he was more bored or annoyed, Sam flicked the television remote and sent the screen to darkness, then slumped against the back of the couch. He glanced idly through his ground-floor living room windows and watched the palm trees in his front yard swaying gently in the breeze. The street lights behind them cast languid shadows across the room's walls, the dark screen of his television, and his body.

Ordinarily the shifting light bothered him and he just kept his blinds shut. Tonight, though, he wasn't thinking about it. He'd been trying for two hours to get through to Cyn on her BlackBerry. His calls kept getting sent to voice mail and she never called back. Undoubtedly she'd shut the damned thing off, and he was seriously pissed about it.

She might be furious at him, but she'd never not returned a call before. At least not for this long. And she couldn't be that busy. She wasn't official crew and the weather was perfectly calm where she was. The nearest thing to a storm was a small tropical depression a couple of hundred miles to the east, probably the last gasp of an otherwise uneventful hurricane season.

She must really be furious at him. Or in jail.

If she'd convinced her girlfriends and the captain of the boat to go along with her cockeyed plans to trespass into a restricted zone, she could be somewhere on Taino, or on a ship, locked up or being questioned.

He blinked once and stared hard out the window at the dark sky.

Locked up. Getting engaged and arrested in the same day. Wouldn't that just beat all?

Who the hell knew what they did to trespassers on Taino? Dennis Cavendish was well known for being a privacy freak. And on that Caribbean speck of volcanic rock, he was the law. From what little Sam knew about it, Taino was the current poster child for banana republics, ruled by an autocrat and guarded by highly trained but no doubt extremely bored ex-military guys. Who probably hated journalists.

Damn it. He reached for the phone again and dialed the number of the television station where Cyn worked as a news producer. At the first sound of the automated greeting, he punched in the extension of her boss and his occasional pool-shooting partner.

"Matt Frits." The bored, abrupt voice made Sam's mouth tilt upward at the corners. It was the first time he'd smiled since Cyn had wakened him with a kiss this morning.

"Dude."

"Don't give me that 'dude' shit, Briscoe," the station manager snorted. "You're almost as old as I am."

"Not at heart, my man. Besides, I'm trying to remain

cool and hip to maintain my appeal to my students," Sam protested with a forced laugh, pacing the room and eventually coming to a stop at the window. He leaned against it.

"Fine. Get a 'Kurt Cobain Lives' tattoo on your forehead and pierce a few visible body parts. But when you talk to me, talk like a freaking grown-up."

"Ouch."

"Now that we've gotten the pleasantries out of the way, what can I do for you, Sam?"

"I'm wonderin' if you've heard from Cyn lately."

"Not since this morning, when she was begging for permission to break a few international laws and put my ass in a boiling water bath."

"What did you tell her?"

"That she wasn't Gainesville, Florida's answer to Christiane Amanpour. What the hell do you think I told her?"

Sam rolled his eyes. "Yeah. But I mean, what did you actually say to her?"

"I reminded her that she was my producer and on vacation, not an investigative reporter on assignment. I told her anything she did down there was as a free agent, that I don't do hostage negotiation, and that bail for employees isn't in my budget," he said bluntly. "She went in anyway, didn't she?"

Sam clenched his gut against a distinct slamming sensation. Cyn lied to him when she said she'd gotten the station's okay.

A few hours after you agree to marry me, you're lyin' to me. Damn it, woman, what the hell are you up to?

It was what Cyn mockingly called "an Oprah moment"; a moment in time that exes refer to in tabloid, tell-all interviews, or in tawdry barroom confessions: It was the moment Sam knew their relationship was over.

It's so like Cyn to make it happen from a distance.

He cleared his throat. "She told me that you okayed it."

"My fat, lily-white ass I did," Matt snapped. "That kind of publicity I don't need. Not that I thought for a second she'd do anything other than what she wanted to do but, for the record, Sam, I told her unambiguously to stay the hell away from the crash site and anything else having to do with Taino, and let the networks handle it. They're the ones with the bail funds and satellite coverage." He paused. "You argued?"

"Let's call it a difference of opinion. You know Her Highness when she's determined."

"And now she's not answering her phone."

It was a statement, not a question, and Sam looked up to the shifting light on the ceiling. "Yeah."

Damn her. For much of their relationship—most of it, maybe—he'd been lazy and she'd been horny. Lately, though, he'd begun to think that three years of fun times and easy boundaries wasn't enough, that all the convenience of their relationship had left a few gaps that he now wanted filled.

With a rueful smile, Sam admitted to himself that he knew getting serious about her would be dangerous. It was plain stupid because Cyn had made it clear that she didn't ever want to be in a relationship that would require more than merely pulling up stakes at the end.

Matt had known her much longer than he had, and had had the foresight to tell Sam to steer clear of her three years ago. It was advice Sam had ignored with a smile. He should have known better. She'd even let him know this morning he'd made a mistake in proposing to her.

Sam Hill Briscoe, you're some kind of fool. A woman who doesn't want to wear her engagement ring thirty seconds after getting it doesn't want to get married.

He'd met Cyn in New York; he'd been at a weather conference at Columbia University and had taken a behind-the-scenes tour at one of the television networks' flagship stations. She'd been finishing her master's degree in broadcast journalism and serving as an intern at the station. They'd met in the canteen, and had spent every minute of their free time together for the next two days. A year later, she'd given him a call, saying she'd just landed a job in Gainesville and if he wasn't married, was he still interested?

He'd been bowled over by her long legs and boundless confidence, and the easy, laughing way she completely lived up to her nickname: Cyn.

"Synonymous with sin," she'd said the first time they met.

It hadn't been just a flirtatious comment. As a woman, and as a lover, she was hot, moody, unpredictable, tempting, and inventive. It was a delicious and exhausting combination most of the time. Except for times like the present, when the extrication from another of her self-inflicted messes made his life complicated.

"You okay?" Matt asked cautiously.

Sam knew the last thing Matt wanted to do was get involved in anything remotely personal so he tried to inject a smile into his voice. "Yeah. I've been tryin' to get through to her most of the day. My calls just go straight into voice mail." He let out a heavy breath. "Hell, Matt, her hands can't be full of piña coladas all the time. She might be just putting me on *Ignore,* but I'm beginnin' to think something's not right."

Matt sighed heavily into the phone and muttered, "Like I need this. All right, buddy, let me make some phone calls. I'll have her call you if I get through. But I warn you, by the time you talk to her, I will have chewed off at least half her ass, so don't be expecting any thanks for being the concerned boyfriend."

Fiancé. "I'll plead the Fifth. Thanks, Matt."

CHAPTER

8:00 P.M., Saturday, October 25, *Atlantis,* **off the western coast of Taino**

Marie LaSalle sat in the snug, streamlined quarters that comprised her private office and personal living space. It was in the habitat pod next to the control center and, since she was the most senior person on the staff, her part of the modular unit was slightly larger than the rest of the staff quarters. It was comfortably decorated to her specifications and, while not spacious, it didn't feel cramped. Despite that, and despite loving what she was doing, she still sometimes missed having the ability to step out of the door and feel sun on her face and a black sand beach beneath her feet. Now was one of those times.

She sipped the flute of sparkling water she'd poured for herself. Had the day progressed as originally intended, it would have been delicate bubbles of vintage Champagne bursting gently on her tongue. Instead, the mood of the day had been somber, the conversations quiet and occasionally grim.

Even so, the cold truth was that the news of the plane crash had had little actual impact on the personnel in *Atlantis*. A small bolt of shocked dismay had struck Marie when she received the news; her response was echoed by her crew. She had led a moment of silence for the victims, and then everyone had returned to their tasks with markedly less animation than they had displayed moments before.

Had any outsider, even Dennis, been present, he or she would no doubt have considered the crew's reaction cold and unfeeling. That would have been an accurate but unfair characterization. These highly focused scientists were long used to working at the boundary where reality met the imagination, where technology met untried possibilities. Emotions held but a small place in their lives. The ability to disengage was one of the more crucial traits required of everyone who had been selected to spend months at a time living in close quarters at a depth of four thousand feet. And no one in *Atlantis* had been personally acquainted with the flight crew or the passengers. The amount of emotional energy any of them would expend grieving for people they didn't know was minuscule.

That's not to say the news of the accident didn't have an effect on every person in *Atlantis*. Unquestionably it did, but more upsetting to them than the loss of fifteen lives was the specter of technological failure; in *Atlantis* everyone lived within the ever-present, never-mentioned shadow of death, instantaneous and horrible and only inches—and seconds—away.

Four thousand feet beneath the sea, they were an alien society, a civilization unto themselves.

The only material comfort that they relied on surface-dwellers to provide was food, and there was a month's supply of that on hand at all times. Everything else was taken care of on site. Special seafloor power arrays converted the limitless energy of strong ocean currents into the electricity that kept the entire structure functioning. Special rebreathing units scrubbed and recirculated the air; an oxygen generator took care of the rest. A desalination plant ensured potable water. Every contingency had been planned for, every need satisfied, every small luxury accommodated. Dennis had seen to it personally.

Underwater habitats had fascinated him for decades. He'd never doubted that people could live and work under the sea. It had been done successfully on a small scale since the early 1960s. But Jacques Cousteau's Conshelf projects, the U.S. Navy's Sealabs, and even the interagency Tektite projects had pushed the limits only so far. Dennis believed that thirty-odd years had been enough time to play in the shallows; it was time to take the habitats from sixty feet and six hundred feet to more challenging depths, and to put them to uses beyond mere research and within reach of more than just a few marine biologists.

In one of their earliest conversations, Dennis had told Marie—had vowed—that his structures would not only be viable long-term habitats, but that they would change the way the world worked. He had already begun to assemble a team of cowboy scientists and renegade engineers who could rise to his irresistible challenge. She'd been one of the earliest employees at the institute, and one of *Atlantis*'s earliest proponents.

Part of the miracle of *Atlantis* was that it had taken only a decade to design and build.

Every step of the design and planning of *Atlantis* had been undertaken with Dennis at the helm. His childlike enthusiasm had swept everyone along in its tide. Every person working on the project had been handpicked by Dennis, who'd used grant money, scholarships, and design competitions as lures to bring the best innovative thinkers and creative minds to him.

The result was a daring experiment that no government or corporation could ever have achieved. Sweeping aside the strangleholds routinely placed on creativity—regulations and worries over liabilities—Dennis had forged ahead, demanding loyalty, ingenuity, and hard work from his people. His only inviolable command was to make it safe and functional, because each member of the team was going to have to live in it for a few weeks at a time. The result was magnificent, a tribute to pushing the limits of the collective imagination.

And she, Marie LeSalle, was running it, entrusted by Dennis Cavendish to bring *Atlantis* to its rightful place in human history. She closed her eyes and let the realization flow over her. This day was as much about her perseverance as it was about his.

With the success they'd been striving for so imminent, trying to maintain a suitably somber attitude was next to impossible, despite the morning's tragedy. Marie had finally had to excuse herself for a brief, private celebration. She knew she deserved it and harbored a hidden but simmering resentment that anything, even the death of fifteen people, had intruded on her triumph.

For the last several hours, she had maintained only the barest hint of a smile as she stood before the array of computer monitors in *Atlantis*'s control center watching her staff move in a muted ballet as they finalized the project's operational details.

The methodology they'd devised for actually mining the crystals had been so simple, similar at first to techniques used for undersea recovery of petroleum and natural gas. They sank a well bore several hundred feet beneath the crust, below the methane hydrate, and triggered a small, controlled explosion that put holes in the end of the pipeline to provide access to the material. At this point in the process, the operation moved to the fringes of known technology.

Topsiders had for years theorized that the best method for harvesting the methane would be to pump superheated water into the cavity. The methane hydrate ice crystals, warmed from below, would be altered and the released gas would be able to be harvested and moved to the surface, where it would be transferred to tanks for purification, storage, and distribution. The critical problem had always been getting enough water into the cavity—and keeping that water at the right temperature as it was pumped for thousands of feet through a frigid environment. The engineering costs would be prohibitive; the loss of heat through the pipes would be massive; the logistics of bringing such an operation online would be daunting.

Locating the entire operation right there on the seafloor neatly eliminated the problem.

Which is why, during the past day, Marie's team had been forcing a specially created stabilizing chemical into the clathrate deposit, which would enable the first-ever large-scale, safe harvesting of methane hydrate crystals. The chemical, officially named "dennisium" in honor of the man himself, facilitated the retrieval at several stages. Injected at high pressure into the caches of intact methane hydrate crystals, it made the crystals brittle, and therefore prone to separating at significantly lower temperatures, which meant the temperature of the water they induced could be significantly lower than previously projected—in fact, it didn't have to be much warmer than seawater. Once the stabilized, lightweight crystals were successfully harvested, they would be transferred to the surface.

And Dennis would bring the energy industry to its knees.

In the privacy of her quarters, Marie knew her triumph was justified, if perhaps insensitive at that particular moment. She and her team had overcome some of the greatest obstacles humans and technology had ever faced to design this operation and bring it to full functionality. Extraordinary distances, extreme pressure, frigid temperatures, and fast and often unpredictable currents had been but a few of the challenges they'd faced and surmounted. Her team had prevailed, although the sea had not given way easily.

Feeling the heady rhythm of superiority pulse through her, Marie tapped a few keys on the small laptop on the table in front of her. Instantly, the screen became her window to the outside world as she brought up real-time video footage of the mining operation as captured by cameras mounted outside the habitat's pods.

The sight never failed to leave her both awed and humbled.

Throughout the years it had taken to build the habitat and then the mining operation, the sea had continually asserted its presence. A never-ending swirl of sea "snow," minute bits of skeletal remains, decayed matter, and other jetsam, drifted, now and always, through swaths of brightness cast by powerful spotlights mounted on the habitat's superstructure. Myriad bizarrely configured fish, octopi, the occasional curious shark or whale, and other fantastic, less recognizable sea creatures emerged from the impenetrable shadows that hugged the edges of the light to swim or drift among the struts, tanks, and machinery that comprised the submarine seascape.

Bizarre deep-water coral and sponges had already encased some of the pillars, which now appeared to be the spires of an undersea cathedral. Sea worms wound sinuously, ethereally among them. Tiny insectlike crustaceans moved through the water in dizzying, seemingly mechanized bursts of minute motion, in sharp contrast to the balletic glide of squid and the delicate wanderings of starfish along the seafloor. It was a view that could hypnotize her, and sometimes Marie thought it was as though the sea had given its approval to the intrusive, alien structure, and had bestowed an unearthly elegance on such a high-tech, industrial vista.

She closed her eyes for the briefest of moments and let quiet triumph wash over her. Never in her career had a project been such a challenge, never had one given her such a sense of personal pride. This was the crowning achievement of her career, of her life. Nothing could possibly surpass it.

Their success—*her* success—tomorrow would have effects that would ripple across the world and across time.

The team she and Dennis had put together, the team they had nurtured, would introduce to the world a new fossil fuel: methane hydrate. Retrieving the precious crystals would not irreparably destroy massive amounts of the earth's surface. When the methane hydrate was burned to generate power, its only byproducts would be carbon dioxide and water. The crystals needed no belching, polluting refineries to become usable. Handled properly, the crystals could be transported easily and safely, with no risk of befouling coastlines in the event of an accident.

Whenever Dennis decided to announce it, news of the discovery of hundreds of millions of cubic meters of methane hydrate crystals beneath the Caribbean seafloor would enliven the world's financial markets; the news that the cache was already being mined would stun them. But only for a few seconds. Someone, somewhere—Wall Street, London, Hong Kong, Dubai—would realize that the balance of world power was about to shift. Then the trading frenzy would begin.

Announcing the mining operation was an enormous risk. Going public would put the Taino installation into the crosshairs of the petroleum industry, the natural gas, coal, and hydroelectric power industries, and the nuclear power industry, all of which would be waiting for, hoping for, and possibly plotting its failure. *Atlantis* would become the newest target for terrorism.

Even without the potential for human-generated danger, *Atlantis* was still at risk because Nature itself could rebel.

Atlantis lay in the deepest part of the Caribbean Sea, near a fault line between two tectonic plates. The area was well known for its seismic activity—earthquakes and volcanic eruptions were familiar events in the region. Taino itself was a volcanic island.

Marie took the knowledge in stride. The potential effects of an earthquake of a magnitude 7 on the Richter scale had been used as a measure against the amount of torsion and shaking the rig and habitat could withstand.

The compartmentalized design enabled damaged sections to be sealed off and jettisoned so as to minimize any damage to the remaining structure. The huge struts of the drilling platform were tethered to the seafloor, yet allowed for significant flexibility in the event of unusually strong currents, even the sucking pressures of a tsunami. The harvesting and transfer installation was braced against collapse. Every conceivable scenario had been considered, every vulnerability addressed. The result was a masterpiece of materials, design, and construction.

A pop-up message from one of her team brought Marie's attention back to the images on the screens in front of her. As she read the message, she erupted into unrestrained laughter.

The final in situ tests of the liberation and extraction procedures had been completed and the results were being analyzed.

Barring any last-minute problems, her team would begin changing the course of the world's history in just a few hours.

CHAPTER

9:00 P.M., Saturday, October 25, off the eastern coast of Taino

Cyn and her friends and the entire crew of the *Floating Dutchman* lounged on the deck as the boat rocked easily in the soft swells of the calm, dark sea. No one was admiring the far-flung stardust that lit up the night sky or commenting on the occasional splashes that punctuated the heavy, humid silence. They were all too busy watching a patch of ocean just a few miles off their starboard side, which had been lit to an obscene brightness by Taino's search-and-rescue teams. The mood on the party boat was an odd mixture of patience and frustration; there were more people than there were binoculars and they had to take turns watching the flurry of activity going on within that distant blur of light.

Though the captain had dropped the sails a good distance from the fray, the clipper had plenty of company. There were several military ships loitering nearby, and a ragtag fleet of small pleasure craft, commercial fishing boats. Even a few yachts—probably chartered by the networks—bobbed and weaved through the water.

"Can't we get any closer?" Cyn demanded with a petulance that her camera crew in Gainesville would have recognized as dangerous. The captain of the clipper, the delectably Dutch and sun-streaked Günter, however, shook his head slowly, then shrugged.

First Matt, then Sam, now this joker. What the hell is it with rule-bound men?

"Why not? Other boats are," she insisted.

"Because I'm the captain and I said so," he said easily in heavily accented English.

"Where's your sense of adventure?"

The look he gave her was cool and unfazed. "We tried, and we'll try again tomorrow, like I said. But for now, we're staying here. I don't want to get any closer in the dark. Why don't all of you ladies just relax and drink?"

He straightened from where he was leaning against the railing and walked toward the bow, shaking his head at his first mate and muttering something unintelligible. Then Cyn saw the captain roll his eyes and anger burned through her.

"Take us closer," she snapped. "We deserve to see what's going on."

He turned to face her again. "You think that if you like. But getting closer is not going to happen. Instead, I suggest you do what you came here to do. Get drunk. Go skinny-dipping. Enjoy the weather. That is what you're paying for, not to see body parts in the water and get jet fuel all over the hull of my boat," he said over his shoulder as he disappeared below deck.

"He's got a point, Cyn," Stephanie said quietly as she passed the binoculars to her neighbor.

Cyn looked at her oldest friend with something close to shock. "Oh? And what's that? And, by the way, when did you become such a wimp?"

"I'm not a wimp," Stephanie shot back. "For heaven's sake, Cyn, people *died* over there. I mean, okay, I'm human and I'm curious like everyone else, but I really don't need to see anything close up. Do you?"

"Yeah, I do. I don't want to see headless torsos floating by," Cyn replied, mostly to see Stephanie cringe, "but I'd like to see what they're doing."

"They're pulling pieces of bodies and an airplane out of the water. If you need to watch that, you have a pretty weird sense of fun," Stephanie snapped. "Now, would you just drop it? We're not going over there, okay? We're on vacation. *I'm* on vacation. I want to have fun, not play the faithful assistant in your *CSI: Caribbean* fantasy. Can't you just turn it off for once?"

Cyn gave her oldest friend a smug look. "Okay, fine. Let's do what the captain says. Let's have fun. In fact, let's go for a moonlit skinny-dip."

Without another word, she stood up, stripped off the few articles of clothing she was wearing, swung her legs over the railing, and launched herself from the side of the boat in a graceful arc.

The water was relatively warm; nevertheless the shock of it bit through her. By the time she'd surfaced and caught her breath, the shouting from on deck had begun. Ignoring the voices, some angry, some clearly concerned, Cyn struck out in an easy crawl toward the lights.

She knew she wouldn't make it very far before the captain launched the small inflatable that they'd been towing and chased after her.

Indeed, only a few minutes elapsed before it passed a few feet from her, manned by Günter himself and another crew member who looked as if he'd rather not be there. The craft swung around to block her passage. Cyn stopped swimming and met the captain's furious gaze.

"Get the hell in this boat," he ordered after he cut the engine.

"I feel like having a swim, just like you suggested." She turned onto her back, figuring the sight of her pale body against the dark water might distract him or at least diffuse his anger. "Why don't you join me?"

"Get in this boat," he repeated coldly, his accent growing stronger.

"Hey, I'm the customer, remember? And I feel like taking a moonlight swim," she said, willing her teeth not to chatter.

"Lady, you get in this boat or I'll leave you here."

She smiled at him. "You can't do that."

"Very well. I'll come in there and I'll get you aboard any way I have to. You understand that?"

The temperature of the water and the sheer fury on his face finally cooled her own temper, and the sheer ridiculousness of her actions began to seep into her brain. Without any further arguing, but without showing any sign of repentance, Cyn swam the few feet to the small boat. She was instantly and roughly hauled over the side.

The inflatable's sharp-edged seams scraped her everywhere. Once in the boat, she pulled herself to a sitting position on the cold, wet rubber floor and wrapped her arms around herself for warmth during the brief, breezy trip back to the boat.

No one on the clipper said anything as she climbed aboard. Only a few made eye contact and that only briefly. She went straight below deck to the cabin she shared with Stephanie. Other than nipping to the small head for a quick shower, she stayed in her room, dressed and ready to go back. She just didn't have the nerve. But it wasn't until Stephanie entered the room bearing the clothes Cyn had left scattered on the deck that Cyn began feeling guilty. Stephanie's overpowering silence was throbbing with anger.

"Thanks," Cyn said quietly, taking the neatly folded clothes from her friend's hands.

"That was some stunt."

"Yeah. Sorry," Cyn mumbled.

She received a quiet snort in response.

"It was stupid, okay? I said I'm sorry," Cyn said again, unable to keep the defensiveness out of her voice.

"Günter just said that he's taking us back to port when the sun comes up," Stephanie snapped, finally looking at her.

"He can't do that," Cyn protested. "We paid for—"

"Yeah. *We* paid for the trip, Cyn. All of us, not just you. But you and your damned stupid ideas ruined the trip for everyone. And *he* can do whatever he wants to. He's the captain of this boat, and we all signed statements that we would respect his command and defer to his judgment regarding safety issues blah, blah, blah. So now we're all going back to port because of you. You and your damned *story*." Stephanie stopped and sucked in a deep breath. "We've been planning this trip for months, Cyn. None of us have any more vacation time left this year. But did you think of any of that before you went off and ruined it for the rest of us? Of course not. You just wanted the big show. Great performance. I hope you're happy."

Stephanie never got mad at her, no matter what she did. It was one of the things that Cyn liked best about her.

It took her a minute to find her voice. "Steph—"

Her oldest friend turned away and reached for the backpack on her bunk. "I don't want to hear it, okay? All I want to do is go to sleep, if you don't mind. And I'd like to spend my *one night* on the Caribbean in peace, so could you just leave? Go up on deck and talk to someone else. Maybe throw yourself overboard again just for fun, and see if anyone comes after you this time. Or, gee, you could apologize to everyone else and try to convince Günter that you'll behave yourself from now on. There's a thought, if your stupid ego can handle some adult behavior, *Cynthia*."

Feeling uncomfortable and in the wrong for perhaps the first time in her life, Cyn left the cabin without another word. Two of the other passengers—she wasn't entirely sure if she could still call them her friends—passed her in the narrow corridor. They didn't speak or make eye contact.

She walked up the short flight of steps to the deck, which was mostly empty. The only person she could see was the captain, leaning against the railing in the bow. She took her time making her way over to him.

"I want to apologize," she said awkwardly, coming to a stop a few feet behind him.

He spared her a cold glance before looking back to the dark horizon. "Start whenever you're ready."

Jerk. She shifted on her feet. "I shouldn't have done that and I'm sorry."

"That's the best you can come up with?"

She clenched her teeth against the annoyance that she knew no one else would consider justified under the circumstances. "I shouldn't have bugged you to get closer to the crash site, I shouldn't have challenged you, and I shouldn't have gone into the water."

"That's right."

A pause built that seemed to last forever.

"Anything else?"

She took a breath. "Stephanie said that you're talking about heading back to port tomorrow."

"I wasn't talking about it. I said that's what we're doing."

"Don't."

He turned to look at her, finally. His eyes were hard and his face tight. "What?"

Heat flooded her face. "Don't do that. I mean, please don't," she said, almost choking on the unfamiliar taste of humiliation. "I'm the one who fucked up. You shouldn't punish everyone because of it. It's their vacation, too."

"Nice of you to remember that." He turned away again. "Unfortunately for them, my order stands."

If I were going to marry Sam—which I'm not—I'd be entitled to a last hurrah. So that would make this just a vacation fling. With a purpose.

Flipping her still-damp hair over her shoulder, Cyn took a step closer to the captain and leaned a tentative hip against the rail. "Look, I know you're furious. That's obvious. But isn't there anything I can do to make up for what I did earlier? I've apologized, but that apparently isn't worth much to you. I don't want to ruin this trip for everyone. It means a lot to them to be here, so tell me what I need to do. There has to be something I can do to make you realize that I'm sincerely sorry."

"Or maybe something *I* could do to let you earn my forgiveness?" he asked, unimpressed.

"Maybe," she said after a moment, not liking the prickle that raced up her spine or the look in his eyes. There was a sudden ruthlessness there and it wasn't the sexy kind. "Depends on what you have in mind."

He glanced around the deck, then tilted his head toward the stern. "There's a nice breeze tonight. Maybe I could tie you to a long rope and throw you overboard, then unfurl the sails and take you for a ride through the wake. Hmm? Maybe naked, too, since you like that so much."

She didn't let herself recoil and instead sent him a

look as chilling as his words. "Sounds like a blast, but how about we keep the activities within the Geneva Convention?" she said, unable to keep the sarcasm out of her voice.

He turned to face her again; his expression had changed slightly. It hadn't exactly softened but it wasn't as harsh as it had been.

"What are you really offering me, Cynthia? Not an apology. What then? Money? Or sex?" he asked bluntly.

"Which one would help the situation?" she asked, holding his gaze for a few heartbeats.

His laugh was short and unamused. "I don't need any more money, and I get offered sex all the time. By women with better bodies and less attitude than you."

Now that we've got that out of the way. She smiled and, pushing any thought of Sam and his proposal from her conscience, reached up casually to brush her hair from her face, making the movement as sensual and inviting as she could.

"I'm glad to hear that you don't need the money. As for the sex, well, judging by the looks you've been giving me all day, I'd say you don't think my body is too bad," she said, feeling every bit as brazen as her words.

Günter deliberately let his gaze slide down the front of her with disdain that was palpable. "No, not too bad."

You son of a bitch. "As for attitude—" Cyn shrugged and didn't break eye contact. "I've got a very good attitude toward sex, Günter. The only real trouble is that I get bored very easily, and I hate being bored."

The intensity of his hot, still-angry eyes bored through her. "Why should I care about that? I am not some boy toy interested in providing you with relief from boredom or anything else. The burden is on *you* to please *me*. And I'm not easy to please."

"I can tell. And that's a good thing, because I've already demonstrated how much I love a challenge." She paused. "I'll be in your cabin whenever you're ready, Captain," she finished in a whisper, then turned to walk away, knowing his eyes were following her.

9:15 P.M., Saturday, October 25, Embassy of Taino, Washington, D.C.

Neither the cry-out nor the shower had helped much. The day felt a week old when Victoria was ushered into the second-floor office of Ambassador Charlie Deen, Dennis's friend, confidant, and go-to man for many years, and one of the calmest, most easygoing men she'd ever known. She came to a stop near one of the wing chairs and remained standing, too tense to sit, until he ended his phone call.

Their eyes met. He looked as weary as she felt.

"That was Dennis."

"How is he doing?"

"Mad as hell that you still want him under wraps."

"But he's staying under wraps?" she asked.

Charlie nodded. "Barely. He's been on the phone with the families of the passengers."

Victoria felt a surge of anger rush through her, pushing away the exhaustion threatening to dull her brain. "Why did he do that? He might as well have—"

"They were his friends, Vic. He knows them. He knows their kids, their husbands and wives." He shrugged. "You've got him hog-tied, and he's not a man to put up with that for long."

"He couldn't wait a few more hours? There's nothing to tell them, anyway," she snapped, and let herself drop into a chair. "Other than that they were on the plane when it went down."

"Have the feds contacted you again?"

"You mean since I stepped out of the car?" She gave him a grim smile. "No, but they will. They're pretty sure they know who's behind it, although the motives are a bit dodgy. You've heard of Garner Blaylock?"

Charlie nodded. "The tree hugger."

"Ecoterrorist," Victoria said crisply. "With an army of brainwashed Bond girls who carry out his whims, apparently."

Charlie laughed. "Seriously?"

Victoria shrugged. "That's what my new best friend in Washington thinks."

"Who's that?"

"Some spook named Tom Taylor."

"Never heard of him."

"I'm sure no one has. I doubt it's his real name. He's one of those professionally anonymous people. But he's adamant that Blaylock was behind the plane crash." She pulled in a deep breath. "He has pictures of Blaylock with Wendy. And he said Blaylock was flown out of the country on one of our jets this morning."

Charlie frowned and tapped the manila folder in front of him. "This report states flight plans were filed and executed for a trip from Miami to Algiers via Spain this morning. Authorized by Wendy."

Great. Victoria closed her eyes.

"What does he think Blaylock's motives are?" Charlie asked.

"The mining operation," she replied bluntly.

"They know about it? The feds, I mean?"

Victoria met his eyes. "It's not much of a leap, Charlie. I'm not sure how much they know, but it's an open secret that the methane is down there, and they know we're doing something requiring a lot of heavy equipment and creative minds. He admitted the U.S. has had us under satellite surveillance for months. I'm sure they don't know how we're doing it or when. Short of having someone on the payroll, they can't know those things."

"Do you suppose they have someone on the payroll?" he asked after a moment.

"I've been mulling that over, Charlie, and I just don't see it. I'm sure we don't have any American moles. Or free-range terrorists. Other than Wendy, I mean. That she was involved is a strong possibility based on what Taylor told me." She stopped and shrugged. "What keeps stopping me from buying into it is the suicidal aspect. There were no indications of that sort of instability in her."

"Pharmaceuticals?"

Victoria shook her head. "According to Mr. Taylor, Blaylock's weapons of choice are sex and emotional blackmail. Two more things that don't fit Wendy Watson's profile."

"People change." Charlie leaned back in his chair. "If they're right about Blaylock and his group being behind it, and about them being aware of the mining, the motives are pretty clear. Kill the industrialists who kill the environment. And use Wendy to do it. Would you call that symmetry or dramatic irony?"

She ignored the question. "Then why wouldn't Blaylock come forward and take credit for the crash? We haven't released the passenger list yet, so he could trump us by revealing who was on the plane. Only a few people know the rescue operation has become a recovery op." She leaned her head against the back of the chair. "By morning, things will have changed. The

CEOs of nine major conglomerates, each of which have greater annual revenue than the GDP of several small nations, will be declared missing and presumed dead. The Asian markets will open with a roar. Other than the 'glory' of having perpetrated an act of terrorism with global implications, I don't see what's in it for Blaylock."

"Possibly stopping or delaying the mining operation."

"If he knows about it."

"At this point, if he's involved in any way, he knows about it. Realistically, Vic, how long before the world knows about it? It's supposed to begin tomorrow."

"Speculation is already rife, Charlie, but it's just that: speculation. We're the only people who know for sure what's going on down there. Even the Americans aren't completely certain."

Charlie said nothing for a few minutes, then glanced down at some papers on his desk.

"How sure are you that no one else knows about it?" he asked quietly.

The hair on the back of her neck went rigid as seconds ticked by and he didn't meet her eyes.

"Wendy was the only weak link, Charlie," she said fiercely. "Not only is she dead, but she knew nothing about the mining operation or the habitat. She couldn't have told him anything. She never remained on the island for any length of time, and she didn't associate with anyone from the island except for the people who took care of the planes and the other aviation personnel. She and the flight crew were based in Miami." She paused. "Do you know something?"

"No. But I have a real bad feeling about this. If the Americans are saying that she wasn't a random pickup in some bar, that she was targeted—well, it makes sense, Vic. Wendy never struck me as suicidal, either. And she didn't seem to be the type to fall for a load of flowery, airy-fairy shit about an earth mother, but it could be that's exactly what she did." Charlie shrugged. "Otherwise you're saying Blaylock, a blatant psychopath and convicted terrorist, met her, bonked her, and then decided 'oh, what the hell, let's see if I can get her to blow up a plane.'"

Victoria felt her stomach plummet. "He's a convicted terrorist?"

"Oh, your copper didn't tell you that? Yes, the Brits threw him in prison for a few years. I can't remember exactly what for."

She wanted to put her head in her hands and wake up from this nightmare. Instead, she just kept her gaze trained on Charlie. "If Blaylock did target Wendy, he's had our organization under close surveillance for some time—" she said slowly.

"Unless he had someone inside doing the watching for him."

His words were like a slap and she barely stopped herself from recoiling.

"So what made him decide to watch us?" he asked, his eyes boring into hers.

Victoria blinked. "Charlie, it's not like we've never heard of Garner Blaylock. We've been one of his targets for a while. Ten years ago his group tried to stop the wind turbine farm Dennis wanted to build off the south coast of England."

"He was small-time then. Now he brings down a plane full of people, and you think he's targeting *Atlantis*. That's a big change in tactics, Vic. It's a big change in the scale of his attempts. What's behind it? Why us, and why now?" His voice was as hard and sharp as flint, and Victoria stared at him for a moment, the sinking feeling in her stomach reinforcing a new sense of dread. This wasn't the Charlie she knew.

She spread her hands, palms up, as if presenting him with her words. "Blaylock knows that Dennis is a very vocal proponent of alternative energy. Dennis constantly talks about wind, solar, tidal, and other energy technologies and has begun to mention methane hydrate in the last few months. Blaylock also knows that Dennis funds energy research. It wouldn't be much of a leap to assume that Dennis is involved in applied research on methane-hydrate harvesting. And a simple Google search would mention a suspected deposit in the trench near Taino."

Charlie shook his head. "Not good enough, Vic. It still doesn't explain how he would have gotten his timing down."

"Don't make the mistake of assuming Garner Blaylock is acting from a rational point of view, Charlie. His timing could be a fluke."

"How long did this American intel guy tell you Wendy had been involved with Blaylock?"

"A few months."

"He had to be awfully persuasive if it only took him a few months to convince Wendy, of all people, to go postal and kill a planeload of people and herself. And what about the time he needed to plan it and execute it? It doesn't make sense to me, Vic."

"It wasn't just any plane full of people, Charlie. It was—"

"I know who was on the plane," he said tiredly, lowering his gaze to the top of the desk, "and what they represented. But companies rebound and so do markets, and this will be old news to most people by next week. There will be an earthquake somewhere, or a wildfire, or some movie star will go into rehab or have a baby, and the world will dismiss this plane crash as yesterday's news. But if the Americans are right and Blaylock knows what we're doing, then he will continue trying to stop it. Shut us down. And he would also have realized a while ago that the only way to get close enough to the operation to harm it is with inside help." He looked up at her again. "If he knew that much about our organization and structure, he also knew Wendy Watson wasn't the person to get him inside information."

Victoria stared at him and found it hard to breathe as a hard churn began inside her. "You think someone set her up."

"Yes, and not just 'someone,' Vic. Someone high up."

They looked at each other as a cold silence settled in the room. Neither had to say what was on their mind: that that "someone" was still in the organization.

"On Taino, or here in the embassy?" Victoria asked quietly.

"On Taino," he replied.

"Who?" she asked, feeling a chill settle over her as the uneasiness that had been haunting her all day set up a sentry in her brain.

"Someone who knew Wendy, who knew what would work on her, who knew her vulnerabilities." Now Charlie's gaze met hers unflinchingly. "There are only two people in the organization who have access to that information. They are also the only ones who know nearly everything there is to know about the operation—and, therefore, have the means to cripple it. You are one of them. Micki is the other."

Without a gasp or a startled exhalation, Victoria's breath simply stopped and her field of view shrank to just Charlie's face, just his cool, dark, neutral eyes.

"You left. She stayed behind. Either one of you could be the mole, or you could both be complicit."

"Charlie, you can't be serious. You don't suspect me," she said in a choked whisper.

"Were Dennis to have been killed, you would have become the titular head of state."

"But he's not dead. And I was with him when we heard of the explosion—" she breathed.

"Dennis was supposed to be on that plane, Victoria. He surprised everyone by *not* being on that plane, even you, I'd guess. Very few people know he didn't make the flight, but you haven't released that information to the public. Instead, you've released virtually no information and you have persuaded him to remain out of sight of the world for twenty-four hours. Micki's there to ensure that that happens." He paused, and in the space of that moment, Victoria saw his eyes harden. "If he were assassinated now, few people would be the wiser."

She swallowed, if only to get some moisture into her suddenly dry mouth. "You think I want to kill Dennis? For what?"

"I don't know the answer to that, Vic. You'll have to tell me, or prove to me that you're not the one who did this. Until then, you're under house arrest. On Dennis's orders."

Shocked almost beyond the ability to speak, her heart pounding in her chest, she stared at him and rose slowly to her feet. "Charlie, you can't—"

"I'm sorry, Victoria. I wish I could see other possibilities, but there aren't any others to see." He stood, came around the desk, and escorted her to the door. "I suggest we meet again first thing in the morning. If I need you before then, I'll send for you."

Feeling caught in a rushing, nightmarish void of her own making, Victoria found herself flanked by her own carefully blank-faced security staff. They silently escorted her back to her suite, then left.

She sank into one of the slipper chairs near the silently burning fireplace and stared at the swaying, jumping flames. She had no idea how much time passed before she was able to begin the struggle to make sense of what had just happened.

Finally, with a shaking hand, she reached for the telephone sitting on the small table next to her.

"Good evening, Secretary Clark. How may I help you?" The female voice on the other end was crisp and professional.

I'm not even allowed to place my own calls.

She wondered if someone was posted outside the door, but felt too dispirited to check. Closing her eyes, Victoria willed away the nausea puckering her stomach. "I'd like to place a call to Taino. To President Cavendish's private line, please. Scrambled to Level One," she added, indicating that the highest level of security should be employed.

"One moment."

Knowing the call was being recorded, if not actively monitored, Victoria concentrated on her breathing, her mind racing too fast for any coherent thoughts to form.

"Please hold, Secretary Clark. President Cavendish will be on the line shortly."

"Thank you." Ten minutes passed before Dennis picked up the call.

"Yes?" His voice was abrupt, his fury obvious.

"Dennis, what are you doing?" Victoria blurted, her voice a hoarse rasp. "Charlie has me under house arrest. You told him I'm behind the crash. That I want to kill you." Bending over double in the chair, her head sinking to below her knees, Victoria drew in a tortured breath. But she couldn't stop her voice from breaking. "How could you think that? What's happened to you?"

"I am not interested in questions from you. I'm interested in answers. Do you have any?" he snapped.

Victoria straightened, then rose shakily to her feet and moved to the window. She'd selected the window coatings herself. Any electronic signals attempting to penetrate it from inside or out would be randomly scattered and absorbed. The room was completely secure. And, now, that security was being used against her.

Resting her head against the cool glass, Victoria pulled in another deep breath. "On the trip from the airport to the embassy, I had a long conversation with someone from one of the American intelligence agencies. He's pretty certain an ecoterrorist group was behind the bombing of the plane. There's evidence that Wendy was involved," she said bluntly. "That she was somehow convinced to, I don't know, give someone access to the plane, or—" She faltered to a stop.

Her words were met with a short silence. Then, "Wendy wouldn't have killed herself."

Sidestepping that argument for the moment, Victoria continued carefully, "The group is known as GAIA. It's based out of England and its leader is Garner Blaylock. We've encountered them before. The group takes the principles of that Earth First! group and pushes them farther into the land of crazy. They believe the earth is a living thing and that humans are to blame for destroying it and must be made to pay. They've been launching attacks on agribusiness and pharma conglomerates for years—"

"Wendy Watson would not have killed herself, Vic," Dennis repeated, interrupting her. "She didn't make it through the Air Force Academy and all those years in Afghanistan to blow herself up like some fucking suicide bomber. Not for some long-haired pissant eco-fucking-terrorist."

"She might not have known what he intended to do. She might not even have known who Blaylock was. The agent made it sound like she was targeted. Maybe she was, was just swept off her feet and he got the information out of her that he needed. Your travel schedule. When you were flying and on which plane. That's all he would have needed." Victoria stopped and pressed one hand against her stomach as if to quell the nausea, then continued shakily, "I don't know. None of us know exactly what happened, Dennis, except that that plane is down and you were supposed to be on it. The agent I spoke with believes that you were the primary target of that plane crash. If GAIA learns that you aren't dead, they could try again, Dennis," she finished slowly.

"Thanks to you, they already know that I'm alive, don't they?"

She frowned and stared at her reflection in the darkened glass. "What are you talking about?"

"The message you sent right before you left the island. To someone named Gigi Blaine."

"I don't know anyone by that name. I don't recall there being anyone by that name connected with Taino or the institute," Victoria replied slowly.

"That's because Gigi Blaine doesn't exist. But the name is similar to—what did you say the GAIA leader's name was?"

She felt her eyes widen as the nausea returned with a punch.

"Garner Blaylock," she replied slowly. "Dennis, I didn't send any messages before I left. I didn't tell anyone to send anything for me. And I haven't told anyone that you're still alive."

"The message showed up on Micki's e-mail." His voice, if not his words, was an accusation.

Trying to keep her frayed patience intact, Victoria mentally counted to three before answering. "Then she must have sent it, Dennis. Or someone else sent it from her computer. Did you ask her about it?"

"She's the one who found it. And she didn't send it."

Victoria shivered suddenly, as if an icy hand had gripped her by the neck. "Dennis, did Micki tell you that she suspects me . . . that I knew about . . . that I had something to do with the crash?" she asked, fumbling the words. She fell back against the window frame as her knees began to buckle.

"Yes."

"And you believe her?" she whispered.

The silence lasted way too long. "Yes."

Oh, God. Victoria closed her eyes, feeling a void open inside her.

"Dennis." She choked on the word and had to stop for a breath before going on. "Dennis, in eight, nearly nine years, when have I ever given you cause to doubt me? To distrust me? What could I have possibly done to make you believe Micki—"

"Too many bad calls today, Vic."

"For God's sake, Dennis," she hissed, screwing her eyes shut to keep the tears in. "For God's sake, what was I supposed to do? That plane crash was an assassination attempt. We both know that now, don't we?

Don't we? You were a target. Garner Blaylock *had* to know you would be on that plane." She took a deep breath. Despite it, her voice still shook as she continued. "The crash was a shock to us all, Dennis. Maybe in retrospect I didn't make the best decisions this morning, but I *had to* make decisions. You weren't fit to lead."

Her words met only a cold, stony silence.

"How can you think I would betray you?" she asked, her voice harsh as she pushed the words past the hard, aching lump in her throat.

"Somebody did, Vic."

"It wasn't me. I swear to you on everything I hold dear that it wasn't me, Dennis."

"There's only one other person who could and that's Micki. You are the only people who would have access to the— Let me guess. You think she's behind it," Dennis said, his voice heavy with sarcasm and scorn.

Victoria swallowed hard and attempted to keep her tone even. "She could be. I don't know what her motives would be, but she'd have the means and the opportunity. Micki knows the system almost as well as I do. If she put enough effort into it, she might have been able to circumvent some of the security parameters. Get information out. Meet up with people—"

"Not as easily as you could, though. Why did you want to send her away?"

"Because I thought she was losing it," Victoria snapped, her voice rising. "When Micki started to accuse you of killing those people for the sake of publicity—"

"What the hell are you talking about?" he demanded.

"I'm telling you what she said to me right before I met with you in my cottage. She said she suspected you brought down that plane to draw attention to your plans. That it was a bizarre publicity stunt because the extraction operations are so close to becoming a reality. It was crazy and I told her so, but she wouldn't let it go."

"You're the—"

"Dennis, be careful," Victoria interrupted as a frigid tendril of fear began curling through her. "You just said that it had to be one of us, either Micki or me, and I think you're right. I'll admit that. If we were being targeted and someone on the outside was looking for a weak spot in the organization, Wendy wouldn't have been an obvious or a logical choice. Even we, who knew her, are having a hard time believing it could be true; someone from outside would never consider her. But someone inside might have seen things in her— vulnerabilities, maybe, or beliefs that we never questioned." She let out a hard, frustrated breath. "Micki would have had access to Wendy's personal information, her psychological profile. They could have become friendly. I don't—"

"So you think Micki— What is this, Vic, some sort of sick game the two of you have cooked up? You're both in on it—"

"Dennis, listen to me. Nobody outside knows for sure what we're doing. Not even the Americans. And if no one knows, no one has any reason to attack us. But if Blaylock does know about the drilling, if he's been told that we're starting an operation that he doesn't agree with, that he would think is a violation of some, I don't know, natural order, then that alone might be enough reason for him to want to kill you—" As the words came out of her mouth, Micki's choking confession echoed in her brain and Victoria felt as if the wind had been knocked out of her.

"And that was the end of that dove. I'll never forget it. It was just awful. I cried for days."

And then she'd crippled the boy without a glimmer of remorse.

It's her.

"Dennis," Victoria hissed sharply, the horror of realization stealing over her. "It *is* Micki. She's the mole. It can't be anyone else. She's behind the plane crash."

The silence on the other end of the phone seemed interminably long, and with every second that ticked by, the constriction in Victoria's chest began to ease.

Dennis would believe her. He always had.

She straightened against the window, feeling clarity return.

She would get word to the security teams on Taino and Micki would be taken into custody before she realized what had happened. Whatever plans she might have in store—

"Vic, consider yourself relieved of your duties. Charlie will accept your resignation and debrief you. You'll remain in custody."

His words, uttered coldly and clearly, pierced her like a shiv to the lung and she couldn't breathe.

"Dennis, no—" Her words were strangled as emotion too overwhelming to suppress engulfed her. "You're . . . you're wrong. Those people . . . the institute . . . No, Dennis, I would never—" A huge, wracking sob, alien and painful, tore through her. "I'm . . . you're my family, Dennis."

"No, Victoria. I'm not. I'm your boss," he said in a tone that froze her. "You're an employee who killed fifteen people and tried to fuck me over. You're sick and twisted and you thought you'd get away with it.

I don't know who's paying you, but you won't bring me down. Not now. Not ever."

The line went dead and Victoria let the phone drop from her hand.

Still gasping for breath, she staggered across the room to the bed. Collapsing onto it, she curled into a ball and, with her mouth pressed against the hand-made quilt, began to scream. She wasn't sure how much time passed before the rage, the pain, and the disbelief numbed her and she dragged herself into the shower.

CHAPTER

10:30 P.M., Saturday, October 25, Gainesville, Florida

Phone pressed to his ear, Sam paced the new wood floors in his kitchen. They were Cyn's idea, of course. He hadn't really given a damn that the original floor was no-wax flooring in a pattern that was "so eighties." The little geese wearing light blue bow ties or yellow bonnets as they marched around the squares hadn't really bothered him. In fact, until Cyn pointed them out, he wasn't sure he'd ever noticed them. It was a floor, for pity's sake. You walked on it, spilled on it, occasionally washed it. And it had been in pretty much perfect shape. But to Cyn, it was a "statement." So he'd had it ripped up and replaced with a sinfully expensive, appropriately "green" bamboo floor. Sure it looked nice, but it was still a floor. He still walked on it, spilled on it, and occasionally washed it. And now she was starting to bug him about replacing the cabinets.

Woman, if you ever want to get your way again, you had better not come home crowing about getting past Taino's borders.

"Yeah, okay, we lost. Happy?" Marty muttered by way of a greeting.

There probably had never been a time when Sam had talked to Marty without a cold beer in his hand. Good times and Marty had always been a natural pair, like socks and shoes, beaches and sand, wind and rain. This conversation was going to be a first. But he had to get the pleasantries out of the way, so Sam made sure a grin was evident in his voice.

"Hell, yes, I'm happy. Not that I ever thought I'd be otherwise. Maybe y'all oughtta change your name from the Terps to the Twerps. Y'all looked like a bunch of high-schoolers out there in the fourth quarter. And I don't mean Texas high-schoolers, either. I mean *Yankee* high-schoolers."

"Are you done? Can I hang up now?"

Sam's grin faded. "No. Actually, I'm callin' about something we were talkin' about earlier. About Taino. You have a minute? I mean, if you're not consolin' some cheerleader—"

"Jealous?" Marty drawled.

"Not really."

Marty laughed. "Liar. Yeah, I got a minute. What did you want to know?"

Sam stopped pacing and leaned his shoulder against the edge of the sliding doors that led to his deck. "Well, that whole wild-ass story you told me about Dennis Cavendish minin' methane at four thousand feet has sorta been chewin' on my brain."

"Yeah?" Marty said cautiously.

"How is that even possible?"

"Lots of money, lots of equipment."

"No, smart-ass, I meant how could he get it out? The stuff is down there pretty damned deep. I mean, it's down a couple hundred feet even once you hit solid ground. It's not like oil. It's a solid, so pressure isn't goin' to help drive it to the surface, and you can't get in there with diggers. And it's methane. It's volatile. So how does he get it out?"

"Well, there have been a few theories floated for getting it out. Basically, all you need to do is get into the reserve and pump superheated water into it. The heat would liberate the gas from the crystals and then you harvest the gas."

"Well, I'll be damned, Marty. Is that all? Just push a big ol' honkin' pipe through four thousand feet of freezing cold water and pump a few million gallons of boiling water through it to melt the ice?" Sam said, his voice heavy with sarcasm.

"Look, I said it was a theory, okay? I don't think anyone's tried to do it. It would cost an obscene amount of money to even attempt it. Cavendish has that and isn't shy about spending it, but it's a completely impractical idea. The volatility of the gas is the biggest danger. I mean, there's the whole explosion issue, but any kind of big release—without an explosion—is a huge environmental fuckup. And even if he worked around all of those things somehow, I know for sure Cavendish isn't bringing it up because there isn't a production plant in evidence on his island. He'd need a power plant to generate the hot water, and facilities for purification, storage, and distribution, none of which he has."

"Where is it then? On the seafloor?" Sam asked bluntly.

A silence built that Sam was not about to break. Eventually, Marty cleared his throat. "It sounds crazy, really crazy, but . . . yeah. Maybe that's where it is."

Sam felt laughter coming on but it died as he realized there wasn't a shred of amusement in Marty's voice. "Run by remote control?"

"It would have to be. That wouldn't be such a big deal, though. You know, the whole thing could be fabricated and assembled on land and then sunk and placed, just like an oil rig. And there are plenty of small offshore oil rigs that are run remotely. People fly out as needed."

"Yeah, but the first offshore rig ever built didn't operate remotely. It had people on it twenty-four/seven," Sam interjected.

"True, but the first few generations of spacecraft did. And now there are spacecraft flying millions of miles away from earth, functioning just fine, and they're controlled remotely. I can't see why it would have to be any different with an operation on the seafloor. Theoretically, anyway."

"Except that oil rigs and spacecraft rely on radio signals to communicate, Marty. Once you go underwater like that, you're relyin' on cables," Sam pointed out.

"Well, yeah, cables. Not always, though. Anyway, so what? If something needs to be fixed, just send someone down in a submersible, or in one of those one-atmosphere diving suits. Hell, it can't be that much different than sending an astronaut out on a space walk to do repairs. I think undersea and outer space projects have a lot of similarities. Similar challenges anyway."

Sam stopped pacing. "You've thought about this, Marty. Either that or you know something you're not tellin' me."

"I don't know anything," he protested. "I get paid to come up with theories."

"Not about underwater mining operations, you don't. Tell me what else you think that dude is up to."

"I don't know anything. Look, everything I've just said is pure speculation, okay? If this crash had happened two weeks from now, I might have been able to answer more questions because I'd already be back from the island," Marty said, stifling a yawn. "And I don't even know for sure that the man is actually doing anything with all that methane. But it just seems kinda odd that he'd be sitting on top of it and not messing around with it, not trying to get it out of there. We've both met him. He's half genius and half lunatic. And he owns the island."

"Well, I can't argue with the genius-lunatic idea," Sam drawled. "He's an original."

"Have you heard from Her Highness?" Marty asked after a moment.

"Yeah. Almost wish I hadn't," Sam muttered. "She's hell-bent on turnin' into an investigative reporter and pokin' around that crash."

"Bad move."

"No damned kiddin', Methane Man." Sam sighed and rubbed a hand over his face. "Listen, buddy, thanks for the information. For a crazy man, you're okay."

"I aim to please," Marty replied with a grin in his voice. "Later, Sam."

After he ended the call, Sam remained at the door

for a few minutes, then wandered back to his office. Sitting down in front of his computer, he logged on to his favorite search engine and typed in the words "methane hydrate."

5:10 A.M., Sunday, October 26, Annaba, Algeria

Garner Blaylock wasn't sure what awakened him, but knew that jet lag being what it was, he was unlikely to fall back to sleep any time soon. He rolled over and let his eyes adjust to the shades of darkness in the unfamiliar room. The darkest shapes were furniture. The filigreed striations on the walls had to be moonlight coming through the carved shutters. There was no artificial light brightening the sky this far outside of Annaba's French-influenced city center. No man-made sound polluted the dawn, either. He heard only the soft susurrus of the trees and shrubs moving in the early-morning breeze, and the grunts and cries of animals following their instincts.

He'd leased the remote villa set in the slowly rising uplands beyond Annaba a few months ago, after being assured it came with all the amenities a wealthy European businessman—as Garner had described himself—could possibly want: privacy, luxury, armed security guards, and the woman in his bed.

He gave the warm, slick, female body next to him an almost gentle shove. The summer's heat hadn't completely disappeared and the autumn rains weren't in full force yet, which left the weather overly warm and humid for this late in the year. That environment was compounded inside the room, making it too easy to remain in the sex-and-jet-lag-induced torpor in which he found himself.

Get up.

Despite his determination to become fully awake, he felt his eyes drift shut.

Seconds later, they opened again. Tired as he was, it was too damned hot to be this close to anything that sweated or smelled so heavily of sandalwood. The woman—he hadn't bothered to ask her name—was too cloying by half.

"There you go, love. Over a bit more." With a feminine but unladylike noise, she rolled away, leaving him more room to spread out on the low bed.

It didn't matter. Less than a minute later he was on his feet, prowling the cool tile floor of the unfamiliar room as sure-footed as a cat, forcing himself into full wakefulness. There was too much to do.

A few members of Garner's inner circle had arrived at the villa weeks ago to finish their work undisturbed by the annoyances of Western Europe. Police, politics, prudery—none of those had any relevance here. Here in the northeastern corner of Algeria, where the Mediterranean Sea hugged North Africa's coast, locals were extremely amenable to looking the other way, if ensuring that became necessary. And, lately, it had become quite necessary.

Phase one had gone off almost exactly as planned. Micki's e-mail had confirmed the turmoil, although Garner wasn't entirely sure if he should be surprised that weak-minded Wendy had not come through for him as thoroughly as she ought. The deed was done, however, so it scarcely mattered. The exact coordinates had been hit at the right time and altitude and the small but effective bombs had detonated precisely in sequence, sending several of humanity's foremost perpetrators of crimes against Nature to a terrifying, fiery death, which had been caught on tape and in vivid color.

Garner stopped pacing for a moment and let a quiet laugh slither through the silence. The visuals had been lovely. Utterly, fucking lovely, with elegant streams of smoke and flames brilliant against a pristine sky, and the light rain of the remains of the sinners falling like macabre confetti to feed the fish.

This manifestation of his drive and his genius had stunned the world, perhaps even more than had the World Trade Center's demise. Such a small number of people had died yesterday, yet those few deaths were having an enormous effect.

He felt his smile fade as the taste behind it became bitter. It was triumph, but it wasn't enough. Not nearly enough, even though the aftermath was unfolding exactly as he'd planned. Cavendish's people had been prompt in issuing their first information-free press release— he'd been delighted at the quixotic touch of irony as he watched Micki so calmly deliver her lies.

Without additional encouragement, the babble issuing from the world's news organizations worked in ceaseless synchronicity to create rumors and foment panic even as their talking heads sat in their studios urging calm against the backdrop of somber riffs, which had temporarily replaced the programs' usual, inane theme music. As entertaining as all of that was, Garner knew the real humor was to be found in the Oval Office, 10 Downing Street, the Élysée Palace, and the Kremlin, and in the halls of their respective legislative bodies.

Garner pushed open the louvered doors at one end of the long room and walked onto the balcony. Leaning his naked body against the cool iron of the curved railing, he breathed deeply, taking into his lungs the hot, acrid breath of North Africa.

All around the globe, heads of state and their high-ranking underlings were rushing to avail themselves of a new opportunity to flaunt their gravitas and dust off their tired, bombastic remarks about terrorism being a fact of life, security being at the top of the international agenda, and the need for constant vigilance on the part of Everyman.

The problem with the politicians' favorite argument was that Everyman wasn't the target, and they knew it. And that's why Everyman was fucking clueless about what terrorism was and how it worked and why it worked. And why governments were impotent against it.

At some point, Everyman would have to cop to the fact that the self-proclaimed warriors leading their nations with chest-thumping abandon were like eunuchs pointing out the size of their biceps to anyone who would listen. At some point, Everyman would tire of the rhetoric and demand to see the size of their balls, and then the game would be over. And the truly righteous, the potent, the change-makers would have won.

Refreshed by the thought, Garner stalked back to the low bed and flipped the woman over, ignoring her startled shriek.

To the victors go the spoils of war.

CHAPTER

Dennis sat at his desk after a mostly sleepless night and watched the morning breeze flirt with a short stack of papers that were held in place by a large chunk of volcanic glass. The sun was well up and it was going to be another sultry day in paradise.

My shattered paradise.

In the time since he'd spoken to Victoria, Dennis had been regaining his senses. And his sense of anger was building faster than anything else.

The connection the Americans had made to that prick Blaylock made sense, and it pissed Dennis off to no end that it hadn't occurred to him first. Blaylock had been a thorn in Dennis's side on many occasions over the years by trying to block development and acquisition deals, and by engaging in negative publicity over how "green" the institute's research really was—or wasn't.

Blaylock was smart, but he was also a cocky son of a bitch with vicious streak that he neatly covered up with that House of Lords accent and a heart that bled freely and on cue every time there was a camera nearby.

Animal testing. Foxhunting. Factory farming. Overfishing. Pesticide development.

Blaylock had pushed his sticky fingers into every hot-button environmental issue that could generate both publicity and cash flow. Dennis had always found it somewhat surprising that Blaylock also targeted alternative energy, since it didn't directly affect his precious fauna. That Blaylock might know about the mining operation was more than surprising; it was God-damned frightening—primarily because he would have had to find out about it from an insider.

And the timing of Blaylock's actions, if he indeed had been the one to order the destruction of Dennis's plane, could only point to either Micki or Victoria.

Micki's recklessness was counterbalanced by Victoria's extreme caution; where Micki dared, Victoria planned. From that perspective, either could have been Blaylock's mole. But Dennis knew Micki wasn't smart enough to pull off something like that, and Victoria had always struck him as less capable of being bought.

Not knowing which woman had betrayed him was maddening. It made him feel impotent.

Dennis stood and walked to the window, seeing and not seeing the palms moving languorously in the early heat. There were two things he knew for sure: Whoever had done this was clearly insane, and that person would not stop until some additional goal—Dennis's death, the destruction of the mining operation, maybe both—had been accomplished. All he could do now was to keep pushing both women until one of them revealed herself to be both an accomplished liar and a cold-blooded killer.

A quiet tap at his door preceded the entrance of his assistant, Leanne, bearing a full, steaming cup of coffee.

"I thought you might be ready for a fresh one," she said with a hesitant smile.

"You read my mind, as usual," he replied, forcing a smile. "Thank you."

She came to stop at the edge of his desk and picked up the nearly empty mug that sat there, replacing it with the new one.

"May I just say how very sorry I am, sir? Everything was so crazy yesterday that I never took a moment to say it." Her voice was a near-whisper and her eyes were watery when he met her gaze.

She'd worked for him for nearly two decades and knew him almost as well as he knew himself. Dennis picked up her free hand and kissed the back of it; it was an unlikely gesture, but one that felt right. "Thank you, Leanne. It's a hard time for all of us. And this may only be the beginning."

Her eyes widened and her fingers curled around his in a snug grip. "The beginning of what?"

He returned a slight squeeze of her hand before releasing it. "I don't know. But enough people, including me, think that I was the real target of that plane crash, and that whoever did it may not stop there."

"Oh—"

He stopped her alarmed exclamation with a hand raised slowly. "There's no point in speculating. We just have to be more vigilant. Thanks for the coffee, Leanne. Right now I have to get back to work."

With a perfunctory smile, she left his office as quietly as she'd come in and Dennis was once again alone with his thoughts, and his demons.

In direct rebellion against Victoria's strong, and in his opinion, ridiculous—possibly treasonous—desire to have him sequestered like some warty has-been who needed protection, Dennis had returned to his office almost immediately after she'd left the island the previous evening. He'd remained there for much of the night, resuming the command that was rightfully his. He'd been surprised that Micki had hung around after delivering her bomb of an accusation, but little more had been said about it. No doubt she'd been waiting for him to make the next move. He had, by calling Charlie, but he hadn't informed Micki of that.

He'd also decided not to tell Micki what had transpired during the call with Victoria, but he'd summoned her immediately after he hung up, curious to see if she'd been monitoring his conversation. If she had, she'd given no indication of it and had simply done everything he'd asked her to do. He'd finally managed to catch a few hours of sleep, only to be up and at his desk again long before dawn.

Micki had appeared not long after he'd set foot in his office. He'd given a cold reception to her annoyingly casual and unproductive report on the overnight progress of the search-and-recovery operations. She'd taken the hint and absented herself to the low cluster of buildings nearer the beach to check up on some communications issues that had erupted on the secure network in the last few hours.

Looking up, Dennis glanced at the large television screens mounted on the wall opposite his desk. They were dark at the moment, taken offline deliberately so the comms team could do some troubleshooting. It was an uncomfortable and eerie feeling to be so completely cut off from the rest of the world. He didn't like it.

Being on a tiny island with a very small population comprised mostly of scientists, engineers, and other assorted high-tech gurus, Dennis had sunk enormous quantities of money into his communications systems. There were backup systems for the backup systems, and security for the primary and redundant networks was tighter than the clichéd drum. That Micki hadn't been overly concerned at the unexplained troubles on their highly secure, heavily protected link with the outside world chafed at him; even knowing that it normally took a lot to rattle her didn't assuage him. No matter how temporary the downtime would be, it was beyond frustrating. It was disconcerting. And dangerous.

Dennis shook off the thought and brought his mind back to the text on his laptop screen. Still trying to make sense of the crash, during the long, mostly sleepless night, he'd begun composing notes for the remarks that he was going to make—Victoria's inevitable outrage be damned.

He'd known every person killed in the crash. The pilots and cabin crew had been handpicked by him, had worked for him, traveled with him. Some had been with him before he'd owned Taino, before he'd set up the Climate Research Institute. They weren't quite family, but they'd been good people, intelligent, professional, loyal. Warm, energetic. Damned good people. He rubbed a hand over his exhausted eyes. The passengers had been his friends; he'd known some for a time that was measurable in decades.

And they were dead because they'd accepted his invitation.

That's why he'd called the families last night. Screw the security argument for keeping him out of sight. Whether or not terrorist actions had brought down his plane, those families deserved to hear about their loved ones' fate from *him*. Not from some embassy staffer in Washington, not even from Victoria, who wouldn't know what to do with an emotion if she ever allowed herself to feel one.

Whatever Victoria thought the world needed to know or not know, Dennis knew the world needed to see him alive and in real time, needed to hear from his own lips the somber news that there were no survivors. He'd never shied away from any challenge in his life, and breaking this news to the world was not going to be his first failure. And if the people who blew up his plane were watching—well, if nothing else, it would be one hell of a way to show those fuckers who they were messing with.

He typed a few more words, then hit save—and watched his screen go blank.

"Leanne," he called, and saw his senior assistant appear in the doorway that separated their offices. "Did you do something to the local network connection?"

"No, sir. Mine just died, too," she replied calmly. "I'll run down to the beach and find out what's going on."

Dennis nodded absently and brought up the automatic backup copy of the file, which had stored itself somewhere on the laptop's hard drive. Absorbed in writing his speech, he was only marginally aware that time was passing. When his assistant returned, he looked up to realize that half an hour had gone by.

"What's the latest? I've been working locally. Have they fixed it yet?" he asked.

"No, sir. It's next in the queue."

Both of his eyebrows rose. *"Next in the queue?"* he repeated. "What the hell is going on down there? What can be so important that they have to triage the network?"

"Well, sir, it seems everything is down. I mean, not deliberately this time. They tried to bring the external communication links up and then everything started failing." Leanne hesitated, faltering as the next words left her mouth. "And now the comms to the habitat are down."

Dennis stared at her, wondering if he'd heard correctly.

"When the fuck did that happen?" he demanded. "We're taking the operation to live testing in a few hours. Tell Micki—forget it. I'll call her myself. What's the number down there in the comms hut? That's where she is, isn't she?" He grabbed one of the cell phones on his desk.

"Yes, she is, sir, but the—"

She stopped talking as Dennis yanked the silent telephone away from his ear and stared at it, then looked back at her.

No phone service.

No computer networks.

No way to let anyone know what's happening on the island.

An ominous coldness settled in his gut. "You're sure she's down there?"

"Yes, sir, I just saw her."

He stood up and, without another word, headed for the beach and some answers.

The normal muted hum of voices and equipment in the only air-conditioned building on the island had been replaced by a fierce tension that Dennis could feel the minute he walked in. He saw Micki leaning over the shoulder of the best communications engineer they had, peering at a monitor. The director of communications was by her side.

"Micki."

She turned and slowly straightened up, then walked toward him. "Hey. I was just about to come get you."

"What the hell is going on?"

"To put it bluntly, we're having catastrophic failure of every network. They're crashin' like dominoes, fallin' over in slow motion," she drawled with an understated shrug that made Dennis's already-surging blood flow faster.

"What are you doing about it?" he demanded.

Meeting his gaze with a stony look, she took his arm and ushered him outside.

"Obviously, Dennis, some of the team are trying to prevent the remaining networks from crashing and the rest are trying to find out what's going wrong. When we brought down the external networks yesterday morning, we did it quickly but strictly according to protocol. We left the one supersecure channel open. Then, right before Victoria left, we began reopening some of the other critical channels. That was also done very carefully." She shrugged again. "With nothing much to go on, we're attempting to determine if these new failures are related to any of those actions, but so far we can't find any logical or even discernible reason why this is happening. We don't know why the electronics started acting up overnight and we don't know why we can't bring them back online."

"Things just don't stop working for no reason, Micki."

"I *know* that, Dennis," she said with obvious annoyance. "I'm going to get some people looking into whether it could be something physical. Maybe some of that heavy soot dirtied up some equipment topside, or some debris or jet fuel got into some underwater equipment. We just have to keep looking."

He glanced toward the water, so blue and calm, and frowned. The Brits, the Cubans, and the Americans were practically slavering at the thought of getting their mitts on his information, his equipment, his people. It was damned near a miracle that he'd kept them away from his playground this long. "Are we being jammed somehow, maybe from that God-damned traffic out there? Because if the neighbors are fucking around with us—"

"There's no evidence that we're being jammed. That was the first thing we looked at."

Making a concerted effort to control his temper, Dennis asked, "What about the backup systems?"

"All but one have gone down."

"You *pulled* them down, you mean," he snapped.

She nodded after the space of a heartbeat. "Yes. I pulled them down because they were having the same troubles as the primary network. The one remaining is still experiencing those issues."

"Leanne said we've lost contact with *Atlantis*."

Micki hesitated again, then nodded. "Yes, a few minutes ago. But Marie was apprised of the problems we'd been having, just in case."

"What do you mean, 'just in case'? Did you know this could happen?"

"Well, yes, Dennis, something like this could happen at any time," she replied with some impatience, her drawl getting thicker with every word. "A computer network is a complex system comprisin' lots of variables, which means it can fail at any time for any number of reasons. Satellite uplinks and downlinks, the fiberoptic cable to the habitat, wireless connections topside—there are a lot of vulnerabilities and a lot of potential points of failure. But the probability of this sort of catastrophic failure was so low, Dennis." She took in a deep breath. "When things began to fail in such odd ways, the first thing we did was put everyone on high alert. The boats, the habitat, the port—"

"What did Victoria say?" he asked, watching her carefully.

For the first time, Micki's gaze left his face. "The external network went dark before we were able to reach everyone. Washington."

An icy burn in his stomach worked its way into his esophagus and stalled there, searing his chest.

"You didn't contact Washington? They don't know what's happening?" he asked in disbelief.

"They have to know by now that we've gone dark, but I wasn't able to warn them that we might ahead of time, or inform them of the communications troubles we were havin'." She looked at him again as her chin rose. "I couldn't have known when this started how widespread the problem would be, Dennis. If I had, I would have let Washington know first."

Micki's voice had gone from calm to defensive and her eyes were displaying poorly hidden nervousness. But it was her body language that disturbed him, the way her hands had become restless, the way her feet shifted as she rebalanced her weight. He didn't know what it signified, but all that movement was unlike her.

Dennis studied her and attempted again to control the anger that was churning in him.

"We need everything back online," he said at last. "It's almost time for Marie to initiate the first live test. We need to be in contact with everyone topside and in *Atlantis*." He paused. "How long has *Atlantis* been offline?"

"Less than ten minutes."

They both knew that the first rule of the habitat was to shut down everything and abandon the structure if they were unable to communicate with the surface for more than thirty minutes.

Bringing everything back online after an emergency shutdown will take weeks.

Impotent fury was boiling over inside him. He wanted to shake her, and settled for clenching his fists instead. "Micki, what the fuck is going on? You're acting like we're helpless."

"At the moment, we are," she snapped. "We're doing everything we can to get back online."

"Fuck that. You're not here to—"

At that moment, the door to the communications building opened and the director stuck his head out. "We've lost communications with the boats."

"Oh, for Christ's sake," Dennis exploded. "The boats are on *radio* channels. We can't lose that. They have nothing to do with the network."

"Well, the radio channels are still open," the engineer admitted. "We haven't been using them because of the likelihood of being monitored by all the uninvited company. But our secure lines are encrypted; they bounce off a backup transponder we leased on a maritime bird."

"On a leased satellite?" Dennis looked back to Micki. "How the hell does a problem happen with that?"

"It happens *on the ground*," she snapped, her voice rising. "It's not the transponders that are the problem. The problem is on the island and the boats. The problem is in the system."

"Okay, thanks," Dennis said, glancing at the engineer, who was watching them impassively.

The other man withdrew into the building and the door closed.

"How much of this is connected to what happened yesterday, Micki?" he asked bluntly. "And I'm not talking about any God-damned jet fuel contamination or dirty air filters."

Micki met his eyes. "I'm not a believer in coincidences, Dennis. Are you?"

"So the plane was a diversion and the real target is *Atlantis*?"

"Seems logical." She hesitated and glanced away. "I heard one of the guys muttering that it's almost as if a command were executed that changed the codes. Or code. He might have said 'code,' as in it might have been that software was rewritten rather than just a code in the software was changed."

Her words ricocheted through his brain. *"A command was executed that changed the codes."*

"What are you doing about it?" he demanded.

"Well, nothing right now," she snapped. "The only thing anyone could do is review the monitor logs, but I wouldn't know where to tell someone to start looking. It would be a waste of time."

"Why?"

"Well, it could be that someone went in yesterday and messed around, but it could also be a rogue executable that's causing all this trouble. A logic bomb could have been embedded days ago, or even months ago, with a trigger set to activate at a certain date and time."

"Who's authorized to do that? Get into the code and change it, I mean?"

She paused and gave him a look that chilled him. "There are about four programmers who are authorized to do it, Dennis, but all of them need either Victoria or me to log them on and log them off. And I haven't logged anyone on in months."

His cold anger turned to hot fear, but he refused to show it. "Damn it, Micki. Stop giving me the runaround. Give me some fucking answers."

She tilted her head and gave him an oddly calm look.

"I'm trying to, Dennis, but, unfortunately, I think that the person with the good answers made a fast getaway. She's probably having breakfast in some upscale café overlooking the Potomac right about now."

He said nothing, just stared at her.

"Look, I know she's your little pet, Dennis, and I know what I said last night really pissed you off. So I really hate to say this, but she's the only one who could be behind something like this." Micki grabbed his arm and glared at him with hot, furious eyes. "She wrote the rules. She knew the codes, the software, the—"

"Get in touch with *Atlantis*. It will take too long to send someone down in a sub, so ping them with sonar. Use Morse code or the underwater telephone. I don't care what the hell you have to do, but I want the habitat locked down and all those people evacuated topside immediately. I don't know what the hell is going on, but I'm not going to let anyone hurt the operation," he said grimly.

Without another word, Dennis yanked his arm from her grasp, then turned and began walking toward the cottage that housed his office. His field of vision had narrowed to the path and not much more, and all of it was tinged with red.

Damn it to hell, why can't I tell who's lying? Why don't I know who wants me dead?

Seconds later, Micki was beside him again, frowning and a little out of breath. "Where are you going?"

"I'm going to my office, and then I'm going to the airstrip. And then I'm going to Washington," he said in a voice so low it was almost a growl.

"Don't, Dennis," she said, something so close to panic in her voice that he stopped and looked at her. Her eyes were wide with alarm.

"Why not?"

"We need you here," she burst out, clutching both of his forearms. "I need you here. The mining operation— What am I supposed to— Dennis, you can't—"

"Don't fucking tell me what I can't do, Micki. And get the hell out of my way." He pushed past her and into the building, leaving her standing on the pergola-covered walkway. As he passed the window near his assistant's desk, he watched Micki turn and sprint toward the low cottage on the other side of the path, which housed her office.

After one quick look at his face as he crossed the small anteroom, Leanne rose and followed Dennis into his office.

"I don't know what the hell Micki is up to but I'm not going to wait on her. Get down to the comms shack and tell them to ping the habitat and issue an emergency evac order. Then send someone over to the dock to let them know to expect everyone to be coming up on the subs," Dennis said over his shoulder as he rounded the corner of his desk. Before he was even sitting down, he began tapping at his keyboard. "Get whichever pilot is on call and tell him we're flying. I want to leave for D.C. as soon as I can, on whatever jet is going to get me there the fastest."

When there was no response from his assistant, he looked up in annoyance. Leanne was standing in the doorway to his office, wide-eyed, her mouth forming a silent "O" as she stared past him at what he knew was a blank wall behind his desk.

"What?" he demanded, leaping to his feet. He froze and caught his breath as a bizarre sensation of dizziness passed through him.

A crash made him spin around to see the tall, heavy crystal vase that Leanne kept filled with flowers on his credenza now lying in a few large pieces in a puddle on the floor.

"How the hell did that—"

"Earthquake," the woman breathed as she turned and ran to the doorway, bracing herself in it.

God Almighty. The drilling. Something's gone wrong.

"This isn't fucking California, Leanne. Nothing's going to fall on you. Get the hell outside," he said, shoving her out the door and sprinting for the beach.

CHAPTER

8:45 A.M., Sunday, October 26, Taino

The first bomb detonated with a muted pop that registered as a small blip on every seismograph within two thousand miles. A few seconds later, those spikes on the seismographs lengthened as the undersea cliff's facewall shattered like a mirror tapped with the back of a spoon, with hundreds of fissures simultaneously snaking across the rock in all directions.

Gentle puffs of dust emerged from the cracks into the absolute blackness of the depths, turning within seconds to terrifying billows reminiscent of thick smoke as pulverized rock was forced from its place in the wall into the now-frenzied churn of the water column. A roar louder than that of a descending jet erupted in the frigid, dense water. Concussive sound waves sped simultaneously in all directions, instantly bursting the delicate sound arrays in the bodies of sharks, dolphins, and humpback whales that lived in pristine security at the foot of the island sanctuary, deafening the people in the habitat, and startling the submariners eavesdropping miles away beyond the mesh barriers.

Tsunami watchers throughout the Caribbean and Central Atlantic scrambled for their computer keyboards as automated alert systems began to spew high-priority warnings.

Barely two minutes later, the same scenario—the detonation, the shattered facewall, the thunderous roar— was repeated a short distance away, unleashing chaos of apocalyptic dimensions.

Pockets of air, hidden for millennia deep within the caves that had pockmarked the cliff's face, exploded as the rock surrounding them fell away. Bubbles churned the water column that was already choked with dense, billowing masses of sand, rock dust, and gravel. Huge slices of rock were sheared from the wall by the explosions. Some slid straight down along the disintegrating face of the cliff, others somersaulted away from the wall in movements that would have been described as balletic in their grace had any human been there to witness them.

It only took minutes for the first enormous, free-falling slabs of ancient stone and fossils to reach *Atlantis*. The first impact decided the fate of the habitat and its residents.

CHAPTER

8:45 A.M., Sunday, October 26, Taino

The instant the hypersensitive seismograph in the habitat's operations center recorded the first shudder of rock, alarms sounded and Marie knew that her brush with glory, and likely her life, was over.

The noise of the sirens and the roar of the earthquake filled the air so completely that thought was impossible. Knowing that this wasn't a drill and that they might have only seconds to save themselves, the crew had to rely on their training.

Without bothering to shut down or secure their terminals, everyone abandoned their workstations and fled in panic to their assigned submersibles, which were docked at strategic places around the habitat and kept continually pressurized and charged for immediate departures under emergency circumstances.

By the time Marie's group had reached the airlock at the entrance of their submersible, each of the habitat's modular pods had been sealed off. An eerily calm automated voice was relating the damage and destruction that was taking place. Far from reassuring, the disembodied voice added an absurd surreality to the moment.

The brazen roar of effervescing water and collapsing steel resounded through the structure. The structure shuddered with each massive blow; between the strikes, the crew could clearly hear the staccato rain of gravel and rock pummeling the exterior skin. It was as sharp and terrifying to hear as machine-gun fire at close range.

Marie pressed her thumb to a small screen to open the submersible's hatch and glanced behind her. The crew who had followed her, all highly trained scientists and engineers, cowered in the tiny space of the airlock. One of the women had fallen to her knees, hands over her ears, and was rocking while sobbing unintelligible words that held the cadence of the Twenty-third Psalm. Another, almost catatonic with fear, had her arms folded tightly to her chest. Her fists opened and closed spasmodically, her fingernails raking bloody bands into the bare flesh of her upper arms. The men were just as bad, one sobbing and two rigid with terror.

Fools. "Move," Marie snapped at the woman on the floor. "You have no time to pray. Follow me."

To a person, they remained frozen, staring at her, fear transforming their features into grotesque masks.

With a violence she'd never imagined she possessed, Marie lunged forward and grabbed two people, dragging them to the opening door of the submersible.

"Get in," she ordered in a harsh whisper, knowing she had perhaps seconds to spare. "You will die if you don't. Get in."

The two she'd assaulted seemed to regain their senses. They practically fell over the threshold into the small sub and scrambled into seats.

The other three did nothing. Marie's brain, suffused with adrenaline, was focused on flight, not fight, and her heart was pumping too fast to allow for any more compassion. "Get in the sub," she shouted as the pod shuddered ominously. Almost instantly, the structure shook again and the piercing scream of shearing metal stabbed into Marie's brain.

"I am leaving. Stay here and you will die," she spat. She flung herself into the sub and gave the group one last look. Wide-eyed with terror, no one moved.

After pulling the heavy hatch closed, Mariè threw herself into the pilot's seat and wasted no time starting the sub's motor and initiating the sequence that would disengage the sub from the loading bay. She ignored the suffocating smell of human fear that permeated the small space, tuned out the sobbing of the man and woman strapped into the small seats behind her, and refused to look through the hatch's porthole to see if any of those she'd left behind had roused themselves.

It was too late for them. They'd made their choice.

She and the others had chosen to live and whatever she had to do, she would fight for that. Gritting her teeth, unconsciously murmuring prayers she hadn't thought of since childhood, Marie moved by rote through the sequences she'd practiced endlessly during her training.

She began to carefully inch the freed submersible away from the habitat's failing, buckling structure. Having to navigate using only the instruments was another torment in the Hell she faced, but she had no choice. The visibility on the other side of the porthole was nil and, at this depth, the slightest impact with the habitat—or even a minor collision with any of the falling rock—would mean instant, horrifying death.

She was so focused on her task that the sound of a voice coming through her headphones startled her for a second. The feeling was followed immediately by a wave of relief: they weren't alone. Their "underwater telephone"—a hull-mounted transducer that enabled them to send heavily encrypted messages over short distances using high frequencies—hadn't been destroyed.

"Atlantis Alpha, over. Atlantis Alpha, over. Please reply."

The voice was slightly garbled against a background dense with white noise.

Never so glad to hear anything in her entire life, Marie grabbed the transmitter with a grip that could have crushed it and replied. "Contact, Atlantis Alpha. This is Atlantis Delta. Three aboard. Transiting away Sub Bay One-Zero."

"Copy, Atlantis Delta. We're clear of the structure. Heading due west and climbing. Five aboard. Atlantis Alpha over."

"Copy, Atlantis Alpha. Atlantis Beta reporting. Two aboard. Clear of the structure. Moving west-southwest."

Marie bit her lips until she felt the sharp sting of her flesh breaking. The blood welled warm from the puncture and the taste of it seemed overpowering.

Ten people.

Only ten of the thirty-six currently onsite had gotten away. There should have been more; had the others on duty not succumbed to fear, they'd have had a chance at survival. Their other colleagues, who had been off shift and probably asleep in the living quarters on the opposite side of the habitat, hadn't had a chance. Though the diameter of the modular, ring-shaped structure was only eighty feet, the side of the habitat that contained the living quarters had been critically closer to the torrent of boulders. Marie had heard the automated damage control system report the destruction of those pods during the first few seconds of chaos.

When the head-up display on the cockpit's dashboard indicated she was completely clear of the structure, instinct drove her to instantly put the submersible into a tight banking turn and maneuver the craft through the roiling turbulence toward the open sea. She had to get far away from the chaos of the island's waters, which were becoming ever more dense with debris from what had to be a landslide. Whatever had triggered it, the rain of boulders and gravel meant that portions of the four thousand vertical feet of walls above the habitat were turning to rubble. Moving away far and fast was her only hope.

Although every second she survived boosted Marie's confidence that they might survive, there was no sense of sanctuary inside the tight quarters of the submersible. Even with the brilliant megawatt searchlights on, utter darkness masked everything outside except the violent swirls of abrasive rock dust that smashed into the sub, rocking it, scouring it. Visibility beyond the now heavily abraded convex portholes was zero. In some ways, their blindness to the chaos outside was a blessing.

That thought had barely formed in her head when, in front of the sub and much too close, Marie suddenly saw a hulking silhouette loom into view. The image was blurred, as if it were a dark and ghostly hologram against a wall of darkest black, but she knew without any doubt that she was looking at the pipeline and its superstructure swaying drunkenly in the churning water.

She had sent the sub toward the mining operation instead of the open sea.

A panicked glance at the inertial navigation system display confirmed her worst fear: The sub had somehow lost its bearings. The delicate electronics linking the gyroscopes to the onboard computer had crashed.

Steering clear of this ripening Hell would be nothing short of miraculous.

Anger fueled her frustration and fear and, switching to manual override, she performed an emergency reboot, hardly daring to take her eyes off the dim nightmare playing out before her eyes.

The soft, reassuring beeps that indicated the computer was once again functioning had barely penetrated the tense atmosphere in the sub when Marie began to punch in new coordinates. Glancing up from the keypad, Marie saw a huge, black, amorphous object strike one of the support towers, wrenching it away from the enormous pipeline. She watched in mute horror as the pipeline and its entire support structure lurched precariously and then, impossibly, snapped.

The graceful descent of the mining platform's limbs and the ensuing rush of water being sucked into the massive pipe was an amazing sight. One that, should she live, would haunt her forever.

Choking back searing tears of terror and loss, every muscle and tendon in her body rigid, Marie steadied the small sub on its new course away from the habitat, away from everything she'd spent so many years designing, building, bringing to life.

CHAPTER

8:57 A.M., Sunday, October 26, Taino

No material ever devised, no structure ever conceived could have withstood the furious, deadly force of the massive boulders that fell from thousands of feet above the mining edifice. The pipeline that would have been hailed in a matter of days as a modern marvel of design and engineering was wrenched loose from its mooring. Once loosened, it became lethally vulnerable to the seduction of gravity and the torment of deep-ocean currents.

Ripped free of its fortified nest on the seafloor, the structure fell, leaving a gaping, sucking gash in its place. Frenzied from the force of the explosions and implosions going on around it, and bearing within it thousands of tons of crushed rock and twisted metal spears, seawater rushed into the fragile seafloor gap, widening the fissure.

Violently released from the unimaginably enormous pressure of supporting trillions of tons of the earth's crust, and suddenly flooded by an unnatural surge of seawater, the large, frozen, pale, clathrate-structured crystals of methane hydrate burst through the deep, narrow trajectory that had been so carefully crafted by the now defunct pipeline. The newly freed, lightweight crystals rushed into the water column, creating an upward avalanche of destructive, churning solids lighter and more deadly than earthly ice.

Tainted by the crew of *Atlantis* with chemicals intended to stabilize them, the crystals shattered, their components separating and recombining. The altered substance rose through the water at vicious speed, becoming ever lighter until the crystals dissolved into nothing more than ancient water and bubbles of methane gas that had been created when the earth was little more than a spinning ball of cooling rock. Freed of the confines of tangibility, the methane gas rose higher and faster, destroying the density of the water column.

From the moment the first rush of crystals burst from their icy, hidden Paleozoic cavern into the alien warmth and fluidity of the water column, every unsuspecting creature that moved into the path of the rushing bubbles, whether boneless or skeletal, warm-blooded or cold, single-celled or sentient, was doomed to a horrific death.

The unimaginable pressures their bodies relied upon for survival vanished without preparation or warning. Amoebas and shrimps, squids, sharks and jellyfish exploded and the torn remnants of their bodies sank without grace to the seafloor. Even the leviathans of the deep, the great whales, with their ability to dive thousands of feet and return to the surface rapidly and safely, crossed the boundaries of the methane chimney and burst into smeared and bloody clouds of matter that had no form, no shape, no longer any purpose but to decay.

CHAPTER

8:59 A.M., Sunday, October 26, off the coast of Taino

Only moments had passed, but Marie was far enough away from the structure for her nerves to have steadied and her mind to have cleared, if only minutely. Her inability to make contact with the surface was of concern, but of greater concern was getting herself out of danger, which meant out of the sea and onto dry land. Irrespective of what had triggered the landslide—a terrestrial volcanic eruption, a submarine earthquake, or something more sinister—Marie knew that remaining any longer than necessary in a small underwater vehicle with finite power and air supplies and limited communication channels was foolhardy.

Her body drenched in sweat and her system awash with adrenaline, Marie maintained contact with the other, no doubt equally terrified pilots, reporting her position and plans, and requesting that they do the same. After only a few brief, tense exchanges, both other subs went silent in rapid succession, one with the pilot in mid-message.

The sudden silence would not allow her the kindness of pretending either craft was still functional. The knowledge that Marie and her two companions were all that remained of *Atlantis* hit Marie like a hard blow to her gut. All she could do was clench her trembling muscles against the horror she felt and the loud roar of the sea's fury pounding in her ears, and focus on her own survival.

"We appear to be out of range of the rockfall," she said in a voice that was reasonably calm. "Are you still with me?"

Choked assurances were followed instantly by loud, unrestrained sobbing. Anger spiked within her. She wished she hadn't spoken.

Marie steered the submersible into a slow, ascending turn as she increased its speed to maximum. Her intent was to return to the topside port as quickly as possible. The turbidity of the water began to lessen slightly as the vessel rose slowly through the four thousand feet she had to traverse, but she kept the lights on as a precaution should any other vehicles be approaching the area for reconnaissance or recovery.

It was only because of those lights that she saw the sparkling veil that lay directly in her path.

For a split second, she thought it must be a hallucination caused by extreme anxiety or a head injury she was unaware of. Instinctively, she slowed the sub and watched as the water before her seemed to shimmer and sparkle and move sinuously in the murky light, as if it were alive. Marie forced herself to blink, to take an instantaneous inventory of her surroundings, her body, her reality. Everything was normal, yet the vision grew more distinct as the sub drew closer to it.

It wasn't until she was too near the specter to change the sub's course that she realized the shimmer wasn't a trick of the mind, but a massive, never-ending stream of bubbles soaring through the water.

She stared through the thick, heavily scratched window, her blood thumping almost painfully through her veins.

Bubbles don't belong in the water column.

For an instant, it was as if time stopped. She could hear in her mind her own words, spoken decades ago in a younger voice, inside of a classroom.

"A bubble is a spherical defect or void formed by a gas within an enveloping medium, frequently a liquid."

A terrified glance at the vehicle's inertial navigation system revealed that they were almost directly over the pipeline.

The pipeline she'd watched collapse.

A scream of abject horror ripped from her throat as Marie realized she was witnessing the nightmare scenario she'd spent years working to prevent: the uncontrolled discharge of methane gas into the environment.

The ghostly mist of bubbles before her was the natural result of the altered crystals melting into the water column; nothing could stop the bubbles' progress through the water and into the air. There, the methane would linger for years, eventually destroying the atmosphere and, subsequently, all life on the planet that atmosphere sheathed.

There was no time for another thought or even another prayer as she frantically worked the controls of the sub in an attempt to change its course, and her own fate. But her efforts were to no avail as the perturbations of the water and her own panicked actions played havoc with the vehicle's sensitive electronics. The sub pitched and rolled uncontrollably in the turbulence immediately outside the degraded water column. In seconds the sub had crossed the illusory, unnatural boundary into the upwelling pillar of bubbles where the overwhelming volume of methane gas had diluted the density of the water until it was dramatically different from that of the water surrounding it.

Death, when it happened, was horrific but quick.

The submersible fell like a heavy stone thrown into a still pond, plummeting toward the seafloor. Within seconds, it was wrenched by a bone-shaking impact; it echoed with an eardrum-shattering boom and a screaming hiss. Marie was barely cognizant of the sub's rupture in the nanosecond before her own body became one with the dark, roiling, rushing sea.

The vehicle became a rain of inanimate particles, the remains of its occupants indistinguishable from anything else that had ever lived or breathed. In an instant, they were transformed into a gruesome amalgam of warm mammalian flesh and cold machinery, a grim, bloody cloud of technology and humanity and dreams.

9:00 A.M., Sunday, October 26, off the coast of Taino

After listening to Sam's latest message—he'd gone from sweet to concerned to downright pissed off over the last twenty-four hours—Cyn powered off her crackberry and tossed it into the duffel at the end of her bunk.

She had to force herself to feel justified in ignoring his calls. Fighting off the guilt that was chewing at her brain went with the territory.

You'll see, Sammy. Especially when I come home with the biggest story of my career. You'll see how wrong you were to try to stop me.

The last image of him—sleepy, tousled, gorgeous—crashed into her fantasy. As did the ring he'd offered her.

Nothing has changed. We are so over. We were over before this trip started.

"Deal with it," she snapped under her breath. She pulled her hair into a ponytail and headed to the deck, stopping at the top step to take a deep breath and let the world wash over her.

The setting was beyond idyllic. The water lapping at the boat was sapphire for as far as she could see. The sun was behind her, rising toward the center of a sky that held only a few harmless, gold-edged clouds. Its heat and light burnished the six hard, almost-naked bodies of the lithe young men who crewed the boat as they went about their duties.

Of course, all of those young men had glanced at her and then pointedly looked away, and she knew better than to expect anything remotely like conversation from her girlfriends. But Cyn refused to dwell on any of that, just as she refused to dwell on Sam and his demands. She was even able to block out the fairly sordid memories of how she'd spent the night and chose instead to focus exclusively on the results she'd procured.

While Günter had never said he accepted her apology, a rigorous, frequently debasing expenditure of

Cyn's energy and imagination had gotten him to rescind his decision to leave the area. And, not long before dawn, she had been able to persuade him to follow through on his original promise to take the boat inside the territorial boundary of Taino.

Cyn moved across the deck to the starboard railing. Despite feeling the frigid disdain of everyone around her, she found herself on the verge of completely inappropriate laughter at the sheer absurdity of her situation.

Here she was lolling in the middle of Any Girl's idyll—sun, water, hard-bodied near-naked men—and her blood was pumping for a reason unrelated to any of it.

The clipper had spent the last few hours drifting through the mostly empty waters to the west of Taino. The crash had happened off the island's eastern coast, and that's where all the action was. In fact, by the time Günter had gotten the boat under way and they'd left the area, the number of vessels, mostly pleasure craft, had more than doubled from the day before and the U.S. Coast Guard was getting a bit aggressive in its unilateral decision to play international water cop.

It could have been, as Günter said, that the coast guard was getting antsy because the sea was getting slightly choppier as a storm centered on the other side of the Bahamas supposedly gained strength, but Cyn didn't believe it. All the military posturing going on indicated to her that something big was going down, something bigger than just the crash of a private jet, and she was determined to get closer than anyone else to see exactly what that something was. She'd convinced Günter that, with all eyes on the other side of the island—including the point-and-shoot news helicopters and photographers with extremely long-range telephoto lenses—their best chance to get a scoop was to sail in from behind, hugging the coast.

She knew that waiting patiently at the border and following the rules was not how you got the news; you got the news by being bold and, yeah, by breaking the rules.

When Günter announced his decision not to head back to port, everyone on the boat had been relieved and there had been smiles all around. When he went a bit further and told them he'd decided to break Tainoan law and head to the site, the response had been more subdued, but no one had complained. The only thing missing from the scene was anything that hinted of any thanks to Cyn for her efforts or the results they'd garnered.

Not that what the others might or might not have been thinking of her mattered a damn to Cyn. Overall, a few hours of weird sex with a gorgeous, angry man was a small price to pay for getting the story she—and only she—was going to get.

Cyn couldn't hide her smile as she realized that everything hinged on the next few minutes. They were coming about in their first attempt to breach the off-limits waters of Taino.

She stood at the rail beside Stephanie, still sullen and angry, and Grace, who was marginally more friendly. They had been friends all through college and had indulged in their share of cold-shouldering over the years. And, despite their silence, Cyn knew they were as buzzed as she was as they clustered together and scanned the horizon, keeping one ear open for any barked order from Günter.

Enjoying the surge of cool wind on her face as the

boat cut through the water under full sail, Cyn glanced back at the captain as she heard him call for Pieter, the first mate, in a stream of unintelligible Dutch. The only word she could make out was "sonar." After watching him for a minute to see if she could discern what was happening, she turned back to the horizon. They were now inside Taino's waters and rapidly approaching the first jutting edge of the island's southern headland.

"Oh, God. We're in trouble now," Stephanie muttered, causing Cyn to turn around.

Approaching the boat were two wetsuited people on Jet Skis. The wakes revealed they had just emerged from a small, nearly hidden cove along the shore.

There was a low shout, and almost immediately the boat began to slow as the sails dropped.

"You." Günter spoke from close behind her.

Cyn started, then composed herself and said, calmly, "What?"

"You get in the inflatable and go over there and talk to them. I am not about to get arrested. You got us into this, you can get us out. Why don't you use your press card?" he finished grimly.

An unhealthy churn started in the lower section of her stomach as Cyn walked to the stern of the boat. One of the silent Dutchmen helped her down the ladder; another waited in the small rubber dinghy.

She made it into the rocking inflatable, landing unceremoniously on her butt as the sailor gunned the engine and arced away from the clipper before she'd secured a seat.

In a few minutes the crew member cut the engine as the slowing Jet Skis pulled alongside the inflatable.

The Taino security agent nearest the inflatable shoved his goggles up to just above his eyebrows. "You're in restricted waters. We have to ask you to leave. This area is secure."

The security guy's Gomer Pyle accent might have been amusing if he hadn't been built like the side of a barn and covered in a clinging, black wetsuit with a gun-shaped lump strapped to one thigh and a sheathed but brutish-looking knife strapped to the other, and sporting what looked like body armor beneath the straps of his high-tech life vest.

Okay. I'm intimidated. Cyn tried to smile. "We're on a clipper cruise. We were given permission—"

"No, ma'am. All visitor permissions have been suspended. You would have been notified about that. You must leave the area immediately." He didn't have to raise his voice or even get aggressive. There was no way Cyn or any other rational human being would have argued with him, or his silent, female colleague, who was similarly dressed and just as heavily armed.

"Hey, I think we'll leave. No offense," Cyn replied with a weak smile.

"Thank you, ma'am. You just head toward the open water. We'll go tell your captain what we told you. The crew can pick you up out there."

The sailor next to Cyn was moving to restart the motor when a loud shout from the deck of Günter's ship reached them and all of them—security team, sailor, and Cyn—turned toward the clipper. Everyone on the boat seemed to be moving like scurrying insects, and Cyn's eyes followed their pointing arms to a sight so incomprehensible that at first she thought she was hallucinating.

Cyn watched incredulously as a section of the surface of the sea erupted into crashing, burping turbulence a few hundred yards away from the boat's stern.

The patch swelled and churned, filling the air with a low, unearthly growl that gradually became more of a roar.

The choppy sea surrounding the frothing patch was calm by comparison.

The raw sound of Velcro being torn apart yanked Cyn back to the present and she turned to see both security agents lifting binoculars to their eyes.

"What is it? I mean, that can't be from a whale, can it? No whale is that big." The words burst out of her mouth before she could stop herself.

"No, ma'am. Looks more like a submarine emptying its tanks in a hurry," the woman agent replied. "But there are no subs over there."

"It could be an underwater volcano," the sailor offered in broken English, peering at the patch through the small binoculars he'd taken from the inflatable's safety kit.

"That's no volcanic eruption. It's too small, and there's no ash or solids coming up," the woman snapped, her voice rapid-fire with nerves. "Whatever that's coming from is—"

As suddenly as it had begun, whatever it was stopped and the water returned to normal.

No one said anything for a full minute, as they looked to one another for silent confirmation that they'd actually seen what they saw.

A hoarse, panicked shout from the sailor made Cyn swing her head toward the clipper's bow in time to see a large circle of water turning to what looked like foam very close—too close—to the boat. The circle was expanding rapidly in all directions, turning paradise into a watery shop of horrors.

At a shout from Günter, the people clustered in the

bow jumped into action. They raced around the deck, trying to raise the sails and get the boat under way even as it drifted closer to the turbulent patch.

"Those are my friends on that boat," Cyn growled as she grabbed the binoculars from the Dutch sailor's hands. As she brought them into focus, she saw Grace fling a hand to her chest and begin clawing at her throat as her eyes went wide and she took on the expression made famous by Edvard Munch's *The Scream*.

Cyn watched her girlfriend's face go purply blue. Grace fell to the deck, body convulsing, eyes still wide with panic. Bloody foam appeared at the sides of her gaping mouth. Neither of the two women Grace had been working alongside stopped to help as her body flipped through the rails and into the water. Those women had also fallen, clutching their throats, their bodies seizing and arching spastically into shapes Cyn had never seen a human body attain.

Cyn was frozen physically and emotionally, hearing but not absorbing the sailor's almost frantic attempts to start the inflatable's motor and the security guards' orders to stop. Cyn kept staring—not at her clearly dead friends but beyond them at the surface of the water.

From where she sat one hundred yards away looking through binoculars, the ocean's surface looked like fine white foam. It wasn't churning as furiously as the other patch had been. It was effervescing smoothly, like much dish soap in a rapidly filling sink.

Cyn watched in mute horror as the patch continued to widen. It edged closer to the clipper, which kept moving toward it despite Günter's visible heroics as he wrestled with the wheel and bellowed orders at the terrified surviving passengers and feverishly working crew.

The creeping foam met the clipper's bow. The ornately carved prow of the ship tilted into the foam and the stern rose out of the water in defiance of logic. The screams of the people on deck reached her ears as she saw them pitch forward, soaring parallel to the upended deck until they, and the boat, disappeared from view.

Letting loose a primeval shriek, the Dutch sailor gunned the engine and the inflatable lurched forward, bow completely out of the water. Cyn fell backward, grabbing at the sides for security. She realized in a stark, panic-filled moment that the little vessel was heading straight for the deadly foam.

Without making any conscious decision to move, Cyn flung herself over the side, landing on water as hard as concrete and bouncing violently before sinking into the wet coolness. Between the inflatable's wake and the slight wind, churning water swamped her. Choking, gasping, she sought to brush the seawater out of her eyes, retch it out of her throat.

A large hand gripped her upper arm and pulled. Pain ripped a scream from her; pinpoints of blackness swam into the edges of her vision. Instantly the hand released her and then she felt it slide around her other arm. This time there was no pain.

Another hand slid into her armpit and she felt herself being hauled out of the water and onto the saddle of a Jet Ski. One arm hung uselessly at her side at an unnatural angle. Blood streamed from her leg on the same side of her body.

"Are you all right, ma'am?"

The security guard's face floated before her, frightening and fantastical with the pushed-up goggles looking like bulging, insect eyes emerging from his forehead.

She nodded, still choking, and then felt herself drift forward, blackness claiming her mind.

The two additional security guards who'd been dispatched from the crash site to deal with the trespassers rounded a small point on the south end of the island. Seconds later they brought their Jet Skis to a stop with a pair of hard banking half-turns a few hundred yards short of where their colleagues bobbed. Both shoved their goggles onto their foreheads and pulled off the hoods of their wetsuits before slowly turning to stare at each other. Despite their experience and training, both were wide-eyed and breathing heavily.

"What the fuck is that?" the first officer asked, turning back to the bizarre scene unfolding before him. A former Navy SEAL, he figured he'd seen just about everything there was to see, but this had beat all. Like something out of a brain-bending horror flick, whatever was out there causing the sea to foam up had just swallowed an eighty-foot clipper ship and a small inflatable without hesitation.

"No fuckin' idea, but I'm not goin' anywhere near it," his colleague drawled, her voice revealing every bit of twisted, unbelieving wonder that he was also feeling.

He looked at her again. They'd known each other for a decade, and she'd been his commanding officer on a few SEAL missions before they both opted to work in the private sector.

"Chicken?"

"You want me to start cluckin', sailor? God-damned right I'm chicken," she snorted, her Texas attitude resurfacing. "I don't know what's goin' on over there, but I never seen seawater looks like shavin' cream."

"What should we do?"

"You do what you like, son. I know where your next of kin live. But I say we get Barker and Timmons and that civilian and head back to port on the double. Then I'll write a report and send it up the line, and the egg-heads can figure it out. If this isn't what you call a Situation FUBAR, I don't know what is," she drawled, then pulled her hood over her head again and secured her goggles.

Revving her engine, she made the Jet Ski leap forward toward the area where their colleagues sat in, no doubt, stunned disbelief. Her partner shook his head one more time at the white patch of water in an otherwise blue sea, then followed her lead.

CHAPTER

9:00 A.M., Sunday, October 26, Taino

Dennis stood absolutely still, adrenaline roaring through his body for the second time that day as he stared at the bank of monitors that framed his desk. Most of them were blank, as they had been for the last few hours. They should have been providing him with a shark's-eye view of the habitat and the mining operation or, with the tap of a keystroke, showing him exactly what was going on in the habitat's control room, at the surface docks, on his beach, or in the pilot house of any one of his research ships. The monitors should have been displaying real-time readings of the systems and operations of the habitat—its air quality, its power consumption, its personnel roster. Instead, they were dark.

He looked at Micki, who had arrived in his office seconds after the tremor. She'd convinced him to stay put while she made a quick trip to the comms hut to see what she could find out. Now that she'd returned, he could see that her face had gone ashy beneath her golden-girl tan. Her eyes were huge and she was trembling visibly.

"What the fuck is going on?" Dennis had intended to shout, but instead his words were muted and his voice hoarse. It was as if every muscle in his body had gone rigid. Even breathing seemed difficult.

"Initial reports indicate that an underwater landslide occurred at roughly two thousand feet." Micki's voice was raspy with emotion and her hands were flexing and clutching at air as they hung at her sides.

"An earthquake? Hardly anything up here moved—"

"No quake. No epicenter. Just a landslide," she whispered.

"With no warning?"

I'm in a daze. Dennis blinked and tried to shake off the numbness. *I'm conscious but inert, with no synapses firing and no will left to summon. I can't do a fucking thing except fight to breathe. It's madness.*

He couldn't pull his gaze from Micki's face. Something was wrong. Not just with him. With her. Her face. Her expression. There was shock there and something else he couldn't quite identify, but it scared the hell out of him.

There were thirty-six people down there. They may be dead. And she's . . . studying me.

"Where did it happen?" he asked.

"On the western slope, about two thousand feet directly above *Atlantis*," she whispered. "Some people were able to evacuate. The emergency signals from three submersibles came through. Just three. We lost the signals from two of them within twelve minutes. We lost the signal from the third—Marie's—about two minutes later. None of the other subs managed to—" Micki stopped and closed her eyes as a shudder ran through her body.

Swallowing hard was a deliberate, labored motion. Then she pulled in a slow, deep breath. "We have a few minutes of video footage from the external cameras. We lost the signal around the same time the turbidity got bad. The footage shows boulders hitting the habitat. You can see one pod of the habitat implode just before the signal goes dead."

Horror crashed into Dennis's gut with the power of a brass-knuckled roundhouse and he bent over, clutching the corner of his desk and wondering if he was going to puke.

"God Almighty." He sank, practically fell into his chair. The crew—his people, his pioneers—gone. Gone. Horribly dead, their bodies unrecoverable, their lives and dreams irreplaceable.

"God Almighty, Micki," he said again, his voice a harsh rasp in his throat. "Are you sure we don't have any Maydays? Something weak? Are you sure that none of the—"

"There's no audio to speak of." She waved a hand abruptly, distractedly. "A few seconds, a few interchanges relating position and head count, that's about it. They were too deep, too far away to pick up much and what's there is hardly intelligible over the background noise. Then the signals crashed. All we can confirm is that only three subs detached, Dennis. Their sonar was pinging as expected, and those signals were picked up by the guys at the dock. Then they went dark."

Dennis blinked to clear his vision, then lifted his hand to his face when that didn't work. To his surprise, it came away wet. "That wall was stable. We had it assayed. We checked it with everything—ground-penetrating radar." He shook his head in disbelief. "It was stable, Micki."

"Was it?"

He raised his head to look at her. Her tone—

"This is a volcanic island sitting at the edge of a trench at the end of one of the most seismically volatile regions in the Caribbean," she pointed out in a voice gone a little high and breathless. "The stability of that wall and everything else down there is relative. In some ways, this accident should come as no surprise. You were drilling into sediment you knew was riddled with fault lines. You were disrupting—" She stopped, and he watched in growing horror as her color deepened, her breathing became tighter.

Before he could speak, before she could continue, the door to his office was flung open with a crash and Andi, the daytime supervisor of the topside monitoring station, burst into the room, her eyes wild and streaming.

"The mining operation." Her voice broke in a breathy shriek. "The pipeline's been hit. It's discharging," she panted, nearing hyperventilation. "The hydrate is vaporizing in the water column. It's broken the surface. Atmospheric sensors are going wild."

Her first words had brought Dennis to his feet. Her last words enabled him to find his voice.

"*It's what?*" he demanded.

"Vaporizing," she repeated. "Loss of pressure is forcing the clathrate out of the cavity, shooting it to the surface. It's breaking down as it rises—" She stopped and sagged against the doorjamb, fighting for each breath. "The wind. Is blowing. Onshore."

Galvanized by the news, Micki dragged Andi, now swaying on her feet, to the nearest chair and pushed her into it, then made her cover her mouth and nose with her hands and breathe deeply. Over the now-sobbing woman's head, Micki's eyes met Dennis's.

"Look what man hath wrought," she said softly. "From the depths of the Earth, you shall reap both your material reward and your eternal fate."

She's lost it.

Dennis stared into her eyes, watching the shock he'd seen in them earlier dissipate, and be replaced by a furious heat.

"What the hell are you talking about? Snap out of it, Micki. I need you to keep it together. We've got a crisis—"

Her attractive face split by a cold, terrifying smile, Micki took her hands off Andi's shoulders and walked toward him with the feral grace of a jaguar closing in for the kill. Without realizing he did so, Dennis backed up a step.

"That's right, Dennis. You be afraid of me. You should be. Because the party is over."

"What are you talking about?"

Her expression grew more intense, and anger seemed to seethe around her. "You know perfectly well what I'm talking about, Dennis. But if you insist on playing dumb, I'll enlighten you. You got greedy, Dennis. You had to tamper with Nature just like those other people did, the ones you were bringing here. Your executive *audience*. Y'all got greedy, and they died because of it. You will, too, and so will a lot of people. People who don't even know they deserve it."

"What people? What are you talking about, Micki?"

She gave a tight, jagged shrug. "Swimmers, people on boats and who live near the shore. Oh, and not just people, Dennis. You're going to kill innocent creatures, too. Whales. Dolphins." Micki's demented gaze bored into his eyes, her expression sending a river of ice down his spine. "Ships are going to drop like stones into the sea. Aircraft will fall out of the sky like your big jet did yesterday, but with much less fuss and drama. No flames, just here one minute, gone the next." She snapped her fingers and the sharp crack of it seemed to shatter the very air in the room.

Dennis stared at her, his bloodstream running hot and full of adrenaline. "You're sick."

"And you would know all about that kind of sickness, wouldn't you, Dennis? Oh, don't move, precious. Stay right where you are. I have so much more to tell you," she said as he started to cross the room toward her. "The winds are calm right now, Dennis, and coming from the west. They're blowing inshore from the site of your little mishap. That means your precious, invisible cloud of poison will reach land very soon. But that will change in a little while. The wind will change and then your deadly cloud will move into the west, to the U.S." Her mouth twisted into a frown, as if she'd suddenly tasted something bad.

"All the pretty parasites on the beaches of the Florida Keys, all the people on sidewalks, in cars, in the buildings will die. They'll be fast but ugly deaths. I wish they would be the only creatures to die but, unfortunately, everything will die, Dennis. The birds, the animals, and the insects. Anything that needs oxygen to breathe will die. And then the plants will die, because there won't be anything left to produce the carbon dioxide they need," she continued in a slow voice that was hypnotic with insanity.

She was describing the worst-case scenario. How did she even know about it? He hadn't told her everything.

"No, Micki," he said, trying to keep his own voice calm. "No one on land will die. No animals. Methane is lighter than air. It will rise—"

"Shut up," she shouted. "Just shut up. Do you think I'm a fool, Dennis? I know all about your additive, Dennis, your precious dennisium—"

His gut puckered, then lurched, at her use of the term.

The chemical composition, even the name of his creation, was a heavily guarded secret. Only he and Victoria and a handful of people—most of them now dead—knew about it.

Micki wasn't one of them.

At Victoria's insistence, he'd kept Micki out of the inner loop.

Victoria. He stared at Micki as if at a ghost, a monster.

Mother of God, what have I done?

A harsh, ugly laugh burst out of her. "Surprised, aren't you? You might as well understand now that you have no secrets from me, Dennis. Neither does the lovely Victoria." She shook her head. "I know all about the precious secret that was going to make you king of the world. You know, for all your intelligence, you're so predictable. You couldn't resist naming it after yourself, could you? How trite."

"There is no—"

"Oh, shut up, Dennis," she snapped. "I just told you I *know* about it. I know what it is and what it does. How you've pumped tons of it into the Earth. How it's supposed to stabilize the methane hydrate and allow it to remain solid at higher than normal temperatures. And I know that the one little drawback to using it is that when those crystals eventually vaporize, the adulterated methane is heavier than air."

He said nothing, just watched her preen.

"Your whole revolutionary idea, the one that was going to change the world, depended on keeping the temperature and pressure stable until you had all your lovely methane crystals safely topside, didn't it? Poor Dennis. All that equipment, destroyed. All that time and effort, all that brain power, gone. Your grand experiment is dead beyond all reason. It's completely out of control." She grinned, and gave another short laugh before she continued.

"Your precious methane, your 'clean' fuel, is being injected into the atmosphere under pressure. Hundreds of millions of cubic feet of it, remember? In its natural state, it's dangerous, but it's also lighter than air, so it would have just drifted up into the atmosphere," she said in a singsong voice and let her words fade away. Then Micki paused and stared at him, her gaze hard, in contrast to her tone. "And it would have collected at the poles, trapping more and more heat, exacerbating the environmental damage the rest of your criminally arrogant predecessors started.

"Of course, Mr. President," she said, her voice seeming to scorch the air with its acid, "even if you had left all that lovely methane hydrate pure and tried to bring it up in its natural state, the accident still would have happened. The world still would want to crucify you for bringing the Earth to an early death. The people still would want to hang you high for all to see, to watch you die for the crime of filling the atmosphere with cataclysmic quantities of a deadly greenhouse gas."

Micki paused again. "But leaving those crystals alone wasn't grand enough for you, was it? You had to 'improve' them. So all of it is coming up on its own now, Dennis. Pumped full of your precious dennisium and vaporizing on its way to the surface. And once it reaches the surface, the methane won't rise as quickly through the oxygen and accumulate, will it? It will hug the water and diffuse the oxygen, pushing it up and out of the way. It's coming up so fast, Dennis, that the lovely easterly Caribbean breezes will just keep spreading it toward the west." She shrugged nonchalantly before continuing. "And we both know that anything that moves into that methane-enriched, oxygen-deficient area will die instantly, won't it, President Cavendish?"

Dennis stared at her in horrified fascination.

"Well, you always said you wanted to change the world." Micki sighed. "Of course, eventually the additive will dissipate and *then* the pure methane will rise, and collect at the poles, and start superheating the world." She paused and her normal, beautiful smile lit up her face, extending to her mad, sparkling eyes. "The world will become a wasteland. Earth's devastation will be on your hands, Dennis. Just think of it. Your legacy will be the death of the world as we know it."

Keeping his gaze trained on Micki, he noticed a small, blurred movement behind her. Forgotten on the chair in the back of the room, Andi had dropped her hands to her lap; her mouth hung open as she listened to Micki's crazed monologue. Now she had eased out of the chair and to her feet, and was moving slowly to the door. Dennis dared not shift his eyes away from Micki, knowing that to do so would alert her to Andi's escape.

"Micki, you're losing your—"

"No." Her voice was as harsh as a slap as she took a step toward him. "I'm losing nothing. Long ago *you* lost your chance to do the right thing. You gave it up; you abdicated your responsibility to the Earth. You said you were going to balance the dynamics of life, to re-align the economics of living. That sort of arrogance always deserves vengeance, but you were given the benefit of the doubt. We gave you time to prove your-self, Dennis, and you failed us. All you ever intended to do was make money and rape the Earth again in the process."

Andi had made her way to the door and now lunged through it like the hounds of Hell were on her heels. Micki didn't flinch, didn't turn around to see what the commotion was.

"Let her go. She's dead anyway," she said carelessly.

"What do you mean?"

"You'll kill her in a few minutes."

Disbelief warred with fear as her words sank into Dennis's brain, as the look in her eyes grew more heated.

"You did this," he said. "It will be your legacy, Micki, not mine. You're insane."

She began walking toward him. "You're mistaken. It's your doing, Dennis. I'm only a cog in the universe, an actor carrying out a critical role. But I didn't do this alone. There are more people in this world who hate you and what you stand for than just me. And you're hardly fit to call me insane, what with all your big, bad-ass plans to change the world." She shook her head with a look almost like wonder on her face. "I guess you never got the memo, Dennis, but the world isn't yours to change. The world simply *is,* and She's teachin' you the hard way to leave Her alone." She reached the edge of his desk and perched on the corner of it. "I believe you called this a crisis a little while ago. I have to disagree, Dennis. This is a *disaster.* This is a global Bhopal. People will die more slowly but just as horribly. And it's all your fault."

"Who are you? Who are you working with? Who told you to do this?"

"Why, bless your heart, Dennis, I'm who I always have been, and it hardly matters who else worked with me to accomplish this." She lifted a languid hand and pointed toward the window and the volcanic peak that rose in the distance. "I suggest we head toward your bunker while there's still enough oxygen to breathe. There are hazmat suits there, and a filtered air supply. And your precious independent backup communications system."

"I can't leave my—"

"Of course you can. They don't matter any more. No one else matters, Dennis. It's just you and me, darlin'. And your life is in my hands. Now get movin'." And to back up her quietly fierce command, she pulled a Taser from the back waistband of her shorts and pointed it at him.

CHAPTER

"Mr. President."

The soft voice wasn't his wife's, and it wasn't his valet's. Winslow Benson blinked in the darkness and made out the shape of his campaign manager. "For Christ's sake, Ken, what are you doing?"

"Sir, I'm sorry to disturb you, but I think we need to go back to Washington."

The president pushed himself into a sitting position and rubbed a hand over his face. "What happened? What time is it?"

"It's a little after nine, sir."

They'd been in the air for just over an hour. He couldn't have been napping for more than twenty minutes. Seemed like the only place he could ever get any sleep any more was aboard the flying White House. He fought a yawn.

"This better be worth my while, Ken. What happened?" he repeated.

"The cruiser stationed off the coast of Taino has reported seismic activity in the area. It's been confirmed by NOAA and the USGS."

"So?"

"It's not your basic submarine earthquake, sir. The early satellite footage coming in is pretty strange."

"Strange how?" Win snapped. "Who's seen it?"

"Navy Intel and the NRO. It's being analyzed, but no one who's seen it has been able to say what's going on."

"Any of our people hurt?"

"No, sir. We were nowhere near it."

"Good. So what's the problem?" He yawned again and stretched. It had been a late night spent with a circle of power donors to his campaign. *Thank God this dog-and-pony show is almost over.*

"Whatever happened occurred near the area where we think Cavendish is doing his exploratory drilling for the methane hydrate. If there was an accident related to that it could have—" Ken paused with the barest hint of triumph. "It could have a serious negative environmental impact with long-reaching consequences."

The president stared at his campaign manager with open disgust. "Who the hell have you been listening to? Al Gore?" He snorted. "Look, Ken, I'm not in the mood for this ecobullshit. Send it to Lucy and let her deal with it. I don't care what Katy Wirth or the Joint Chiefs say. Lucy is the only one who doesn't have her thumb up her ass where Cavendish is concerned. Get me some coffee. And tell the colonel to turn this plane around."

9:35 A.M., Sunday, October 26, off the western coast of Taino

The small pod of humpback whales, mostly heavily pregnant females or mothers with still-nursing calves, were among the first of their group to arrive in the Caribbean Sea, where they would spend the winter. Their long journey from the cold, high latitudes was over and their early appearance had delighted thousands of shipboard onlookers as the whales traveled toward the warm waters of the lower latitudes.

Some nearly sixty feet long and weighing thirty tons,

the huge creatures moved in elegant arcs through the warm sea, rolling playfully and displaying their pleated throats and long, graceful flippers that were one-third the length of their body. Having reached their destination after weeks of traveling down the eastern coast of North America, the whales were at leisure to enjoy themselves in the relative sanctuary of Taino's protected waters.

Some crested the surface and instantly blurred the air with fountains of exhaled breath, each blow emptying a gigantic body of nearly all of its breath in less than a second, and refilling those lungs nearly as fast. Others, more playful perhaps or just following instinct, surged out of the water, their towering shapes streaming water as they curved and twisted before crashing majestically back into the waves with a showy display of enormous, distinctive flukes before disappearing from sight.

Their instincts led them to avoid the strange column of hissing water as they swam between it and the shoreline of Taino, but nothing could have warned them of what lay in wait for them at the surface.

Several of the creatures broke the water at the same time, mothers and their young, and in the fragment of a second that it took for them to empty and replenish their air supply, they began to thrash maniacally. Flippers, flukes, and huge, writhing bodies pounded the sea in helpless torment before death rapidly stilled their efforts.

Aware of a threat they could not see and could not defend against, other pod members rose to the surface. They, too, were killed instantly as the methane that had displaced the air at the sea's surface entered their bodies, searing their lung tissue and causing the massive mammals to convulse, thrashing the calm blue surface of the sea. The terrifying chaos ended quickly, leaving the carcasses of the lifeless leviathans floating in once-again calm waters.

Panicked by the frenzy of their companions, the last few whales surfaced as well, just beyond the invisible boundary of the poisoned air. All the movement in the water pushed some of the corpses toward the living.

Instinct drove most of the herd to move on, away from whatever unseen predator had decimated their group. But instincts just as strong drove the few mothers who had avoided the methane to remain with their dead calves, gently bumping them in hope of a response and protecting them from the sleek, circling forms of familiar enemies who knew opportunity lay amid the commotion.

9:40 A.M., Sunday, October 26, Embassy of Taino, Washington, D.C.

The overwhelming sense of powerlessness that had reared its ugly, long-remembered face last night had frozen into implacability. There was no way Victoria was going to accept with any sort of grace the role of puppet after being the puppetmaster, and so it was an angry but subdued Victoria who arrived immediately upon request in Charlie Deen's office. The aide who'd escorted her closed the door behind her and Victoria came to a stop in front of one of the wing chairs. She didn't sit down, she just stared at the back of Charlie's balding head until he finally turned around to acknowledge her presence.

Swiveling from his place at the windows, one hand holding a phone to his ear, he gestured with the other that he'd be done shortly.

Several minutes later, having uttered only a low "Keep me informed" the entire time she was in his office, he ended the call and turned fully to face her. Despite her fury, Victoria's heart lurched when she saw his pallor, the redness around his eyes.

"My God, Charlie, what is it?" she asked, rooted in place.

He stared at her for a few long seconds, his throat working, his cheeks flexing as he struggled to maintain his composure.

"There's been an underwater landslide on the western side of the island."

Atlantis.

Victoria's body went rigid and she reached out to grasp the arm of the chair for support.

"An earthquake? What happened?"

"Not an earthquake. They're sure of that, but that's about all they are sure of. Seismographs picked up two separate concussive events near the face wall at about two thousand feet below the surface. They triggered a landslide."

Her stomach flipped. "What do you mean by 'concussive events'?"

He shrugged. "I don't know. That's all I've been told. So far our guys are looking into the stability of the wall. There are faults there, and some parts of those slopes were honeycombed with caves. If the rock wasn't stable, one could have collapsed and set another into collapse, and then the whole thing broke up."

Her insides in turmoil, she stared at him and tried to remain calm. "These 'events' happened in sequence?"

"They happened less than two minutes apart and about three hundred feet apart," he said, distractedly.

"When?"

"About forty-five minutes ago"

Victoria's breath caught in her throat. "*Forty-five minutes?* And you're just finding out about it? Why didn't—"

He looked at her with almost vacant eyes. "The communications systems on the island failed before the blasts," he replied.

At his words, she found herself holding her breath, and staring at him with eyes that she knew had gone wide. "They can't fail. There are layers of backups. They can't fail," she repeated, her words a burning whisper.

"They *did* fail," he said flatly, and rubbed a hand over his exhausted face. "They're still down."

She felt a wobble in her knees, then the cushioned surface of the chair behind her met the back of her thighs and she came to rest on its surface with a soft thump. "Who were you talking to just now?"

"Simon Broadhurst, from the *Wangari Maathai*. He was calling from aboard a U.S. Navy ship that's hanging around the crash site. He was in touch with the topside communications team pretty soon after it happened, but they were using open radio channels, so they didn't say much. It took him a while to get the U.S. Navy's help."

Good God. Bureaucracy at a time like this. "Has anyone heard from the habitat?" she asked.

Victoria watched as Charlie squeezed his eyes shut and pulled in a deep breath, shaking his head.

"It's gone," he said as if the words were choking him. "Crushed. There's some footage. It went in minutes." He took a breath. "The landslide happened on the slope directly above it. Three subs were able to evacuate, but topside lost contact with them soon afterward. There's no indication that anyone survived. We're just hoping they'll surface somewhere."

Charlie's words drove all coherent thought from her head as she stared at him, her stomach clenching, her breath hard to find.

Gone. The people. The building—

She'd been in the habitat a little over twenty-four hours ago, and now it and everyone in it was gone.

She looked up at the frozen-faced ambassador. "Where's Dennis?"

"No one has heard from him. As I said, communications went down."

"But there should be one channel up," Victoria protested. "Charlie, it's automated."

"It's down. It's all down," he repeated sharply.

"No, Charlie. Micki would—" She took a deep breath and made herself focus, and realized that Micki could be injured. Or dead.

Or in charge.

She shook away the thought. "We can open a channel from here. Akil knows how to do it."

Charlie shook his head. "He's been trying since before the landslide, ever since the network went dark. Nothing is bringing it back online. We initiated emergency procedures and they didn't work, either."

"That's ridiculous. They have to work," Victoria snapped. "We run tabletop scenarios all the time. We did exercises this week in advance of the mining—" She stopped and looked at him, feeling the blood drain from her face. "What about the mining operation? The rig. Is it okay?"

Charlie shook his head very slightly and rubbed another hand over his shiny, bewildered face. "No word yet." He paused, choked to a stop. "For Christ's sake, Vic, tell me if you had anything to do with this."

"I didn't," she replied forcefully, pulling herself to her feet and crossing the room to stand in front of his desk. "I didn't. You've got to believe me, Charlie."

"How can I, Vic? You're here, and you shouldn't be. And everything on the island—"

"Charlie, I told you last night that the Americans know who brought down our plane," she said, leaning onto his desk. "*Wendy* was the weak link, and Micki. Not me."

"Do you think the plane and, and this . . . are related?" he asked as the loathing she'd seen in his eyes last night slowly returned.

Victoria refused to look away. "At this point, Charlie, I'd say that's a given. I don't believe in coincidences, and a failure of this magnitude is no accident. *But it's not my doing,*" she said, her voice low and almost shaking with tension. "Give me access to the systems. I'll get the island back online. There are back doors—"

"We've tried them."

"No, there are others. Ones that only I know about."

He raised an eyebrow and the disgusted satisfaction in his eyes made her feel dirty.

"I'm the queen of paranoia, right?" she hissed. "Isn't that what Dennis has always called me? Well, I am paranoid, but I'm not a criminal, Charlie. And I'm not a traitor. Right now I'm the only one who can help you. Trust me, Charlie, and let me do what I need to do."

"I need to think about it."

She let out a harsh breath and slammed her palm onto the table, shocking them both.

"Fine," she snapped. "You go ahead and *think about it* while everyone who's still alive down there might be dying. What more do you know? Or what are you willing to tell me?" When he didn't respond, she straightened her back and forced energy she didn't possess into her voice. "Despite its location, there hasn't been seismic activity on or beneath that slope since records have been kept. I suggest you tell whoever is analyzing those events to consider causes other than seismic."

"Tell me what you know, Victoria."

"Oh, for God's sake, Charlie, I don't know anything. All we can do is try to piece things together," she snapped and spun away from his desk in anger. "I'm going to help you, if only to clear my name."

"Vic—"

She turned back to face him. "Look, we're all stretched to the edges right now, but even if no one else can see things clearly, you and I have to. If I *were* the one who planned all this, I wouldn't be here now, would I? But I am. So I'm telling you again that I was not and am not involved with any of this. So get over it." She stopped for two deep breaths, then continued. "Here's what I know: One of our planes exploded yesterday morning, only a few miles offshore. The Americans are pretty sure GAIA is involved. And now, almost exactly twenty-four hours later, as the mining operation is about to commence its live test, this happens. There's only one possible option, Charlie: terrorism. Maybe it wasn't Dennis who was the target. Maybe it was *Atlantis* and the mining operation all the time."

"No one knows about them."

"So we thought." She folded her arms across her chest and leveled her gaze at him. "Consider this. I don't care if it is a seismic region. How many landslides have two 'concussive' triggers that happen two minutes apart, and almost exactly three hundred feet apart? On a pockmarked undersea cliff wall that was declared stable independently by several world-renowned marine geologists? Here's an idea: Let's call them detonations and see if that changes anything for you."

"Who could have planted anything there other than you?"

She flinched and tried to ignore the venom in his remark. "Only another insider could. No one else could have gotten near that wall. We all know there's no such thing as a totally secure system. Even the most secure system—and I'd say that the island qualifies for that description—every secure system has some degree of porosity. I tried damned hard to plug every open pore, but if I couldn't see it, I couldn't plug it. Which means that anyone who *could* see it—or who had created it— could exploit it."

"There would have been too much planning involved. It would take months to put this together. Maybe more time than that. Who could go that long without being detected? And who would know where to look?"

The "other than you" was silent this time.

Determined not to show any more anger, Victoria raised an eyebrow slowly and meaningfully. "Yes, it would have taken a lot of planning, and a lot of stealth to continually circumvent all of the security measures we have in place. However, if someone *were* able to sidestep all of our security and never did anything to arouse suspicion, he or she would have had plenty of time to do whatever was necessary," she replied, her voice cold. Turning her back to him, she began to pace the breadth of the room.

"So who could do that?"

Victoria stopped and faced him. "Micki. Or Dennis."

A long silence built between them until Charlie broke it. "*Micki* could have planted the bombs?"

"Anyone with access to a dive suit and well-honed

homicidal tendencies could have planted them. So could a trained dolphin. Or a well-built robot." She shrugged. "But I vote for Micki."

"Despite all of your background checks, could a competitor have gotten to her?"

She shook her head. "Industrial espionage doesn't make sense as a motive. Any competitor would want the people—the knowledge and experience. A competitor might sabotage the habitat to make the personnel come topside. You know—introduce Legionnaire's disease into the air supply or do something else that would get the crew out of there fast and make them feel that Dennis wasn't taking good enough care of them. The competition wouldn't kill them or destroy the structure. Either would be counterproductive."

"This isn't a better mousetrap, Vic," Charlie snapped. "There's a hell of a lot of money at stake. Tens of billions already spent, hundreds of billions more to be made when the methane is brought to the surface."

"What are you getting at?"

His gaze was cold and hard as it met her own. "If someone can penetrate our security and plant bombs underwater, they may already have gotten all the information they need."

She stared at him, her chest tightening and burning with her held breath, and wished his words, his meaning hadn't sunk in.

22

CHAPTER

Up early with Cyn on his mind and no distractions, Sam had gone for a long run around Lake Alice, and then, still twitchy, had headed into his office. Sunday mornings during football season were always quiet, but with a home-game victory the day before, it was even more so. Victory parties always knocked the campus comatose.

Before he'd left his house, he'd pulled together all of the information he'd found about Caribbean methane-hydrate deposits and e-mailed it to his office account. Upon arrival, he'd started trolling through specialized databases that he could only access on campus, and was still at it. Long ago Sam had taped to the edge of his computer monitor a quote cribbed from Justice Potter Stewart, which Sam had always said defined his own research methodology: "I know it when I see it."

At the moment, the line fit his quest more than he would have liked. Sam had no idea what he was looking for, and was waiting for something to jump out at him. But the only thing jumping in his office that morning was him nearly jumping out of his skin when he heard a quiet tap at the door.

"You gotta get a grip, son," he muttered as his heart rate began to return to normal and he swiveled in his chair. He didn't have to get up to twist the doorknob and pull open the heavy door, but when he saw who was standing there, he wished he'd been on his feet.

Just what I need. My relationship with the woman I love is heading for the rocks and here comes a mermaid to get my mind off things.

Sabina Haskin, one of Sam's atmospheric science doctoral students, was framed by the doorway, looking hesitant, alluring, and confused at the same time. Sam had to admit that it wasn't a look too many women could pull off, but it was a good look on her. Then again, any look was a good look on Sabina. She was Salma Hayek, J-Lo, and Penelope Cruz rolled into one incredibly compact, gorgeous, lush woman with dark eyes that could swallow a man whole, and an accent that was an orgasm for the ears. And she had brains. Serious brains. And lots of 'em.

The combination had the capacity to make Sam forget his own name. But he was her dissertation advisor, much to the disgust of his married colleagues, and therefore he tried very hard to counteract the Sabina Effect. Playing the geek and remembering the four months he spent doing postdoc work on one of Greenland's ice sheets occasionally helped. But, with Cyn away and infuriating him from a distance, a sprinkle of saltpeter in his Wheaties would have been in order this morning if he'd known a meeting with Sabina was in the cards.

"Hi, Sabina. What can I do for you?" Sam asked in his most noncommittal voice.

"Good morning, Professor Briscoe."

Breesco. She said it so softly, so hesitantly in that sultry voice of hers. Every time he heard her say his name, he wondered if he'd have the will to put up a fight if she ever actually came on to him.

"I was just fetching some new data from the satellites for my research and I found some things that seem funny."

"It's Sunday morning, Sabina," he said in a mildly scolding tone. "You're supposed to be sleeping off a hangover, not working in the weather lab."

She smiled and looked away. "I decided to do a little work. You don't mind?"

He shrugged with a faint smile. "It's your time. What did you get?"

She took a step through the door and handed him the slim manila folder she held in her hands. "Some of the gas chromatography readings from Region Nine went haywar a little while ago and have remained that way. See? Right there. The methane." She pointed to a line toward the bottom of the folded dot-matrix sheet.

"Hay*wire,*" he said absently, scanning.

"Yes, thank you. Hay*wire.*"

Sam squinted at the page, looked back at the page's margin to make sure he was following the data correctly. Then he blinked. Twice.

Sure enough, just about an hour ago the atmospheric methane level had suddenly shot up to one hundred times its normal concentration in the northern Caribbean, from 1,700 parts per billion to 170,000 parts per billion.

Which was scary as hell and made absolutely no sense.

"What are the coordinates?" he asked absently, still staring at the numbers. When she told him, he plugged the location into his computer, then stared at the screen in disbelief. "That's Taino."

"I know. It makes no sense. Is it maybe a mistake? Or something to do with that airplane that crashed yesterday?"

"No, it wouldn't have anything to do with the plane going down. Let me contact the guys up at GISS," he murmured, using the shorthand name for the Goddard Institute for Space Science, NASA's atmospheric research group, which was headquartered at Columbia University. "There has to be some explanation for an anomaly this big. It's probably a software glitch. I think there was some maintenance done on some of their satellites recently. Thanks for bringing this to me, Sabina. I'll let you know what I find out."

"You're welcome."

Several seconds ticked by before he looked up, though he'd been aware all along that she was still standing in the doorway. "Is there something else, Sabina?"

The look on her face was unmistakably "yes," and she started to say something, then stopped. Instead, she gave him a tight smile, shook her head, and left. He stared at the space she'd just vacated and wondered if this nonsense with Cyn would lead him to determine the strength of his moral fiber before the weekend was over.

He was looking up contact information for his colleague at GISS when his cell phone rang. A glance at the caller ID set his stomach into a slow burn.

Sam grabbed the handset. "Hey, Marty."

"Hey, Sam. You got a minute?"

The cold, leftover chicken tacos he'd wolfed down for breakfast lurched in his stomach as his brain registered the gravity in Marty's voice. "Sure, I got a minute. What's up?"

"You checked the GISS data this morning?"

Sam leaned forward, elbows on his desk, frowning. "I just saw it. In fact, I was looking up Jimbo's number when you called. Something's got to be wrong with the—"

"Save your nickel. I just talked to him. They're already running the hardware and software diagnostics for the second time."

Sam felt his stomach flip. "Why for a second time?"

"The first set showed everything to be working just fine."

Sam shook his head and walked to the windowsill to lean against it. "I don't buy it. Something's got to be wrong. Those numbers don't make sense, Marty."

"They're consistent, though."

"It's an anomaly. A spike."

"Can't be. The volume shot up, that's for damned sure, but it's been consistent at the new level since it was recorded," Marty replied patiently. "That's not how we define an anomaly."

"What are you thinking? Some deep-sea monster let one rip?"

Silence from Marty in the face of adolescent bathroom humor wasn't a good sign. Sam cleared his throat. "What are you thinking?"

"One of the oceanography guys was all fired up about some underwater event that happened close to the time that the spike occurred, at the southern tip of the Tongue of the Ocean," he said, naming the bizarrely shaped, mile-deep trench that hugged the Bahamian island of Andros—and Taino.

Which is right where Cyn is if she's following her God-damned plan.

Sam rubbed a hand along the jaw he hadn't bothered to shave for two days. "What sort of event are we talkin' about?"

"Two small jolts. We're not sure what they were, but

whatever they were, they precipitated an underwater landslide."

Sam squeezed his eyes shut for just a minute. *This is just too damned weird.*

"So these jolts—nobody's callin' them earthquakes?" he asked slowly.

"Too shallow. They happened at about two thousand feet. Practically at the surface," Marty replied.

"So what do they have to do with the spike in atmospheric methane?" Sam asked bluntly. "Are you tryin' to tell me that the landslide cracked open the seafloor above the deposit?"

"Yeah."

Sam recoiled at the speed of the reply. "Come on, Marty. You just said what happened wasn't an earthquake and, believe me, no landslide is goin' to open a fissure a few hundred feet deep," Sam stated flatly. "The odds of that happening are bad, Marty. Real bad. You'd have a better chance of winning the Powerball twice in a month using the same numbers."

"What if," Marty said after a short pause.

"No, Marty, there is no 'what if.'" Sam pushed a hand through his hair and knocked off the Gators cap he'd forgotten he was wearing. "Look, if a rupture in that methane bed is what's causing this spike, we're not talkin' about some crack in the seafloor. We're talkin' about one hell of a big canyon that's opened up down there." He shook his head as if his friend were standing in front of him. "We got methane spewin' out of the ocean like a wildcat oil well and you're tellin' me it wasn't an earthquake that did it. Well, I'm here tellin' you that there aren't rocks heavy enough to do that sort of damage in a landslide. And you don't need me tellin' you this. You know it yourself."

"Could a bomb? Could that do it?" Marty asked quietly.

Sam felt as if his feet had suddenly become rooted to the floor. "Say what?"

"A bomb. Something detonated underwater. All the background noise from the landslide could mask a bomb's concussion."

Sam stared straight ahead, not liking the weird churn in his gut. "Maybe, but it would have to be one big fucker of a bomb, and set off deep. But that would mean the landslide was triggered deliberately, too."

"Okay, what if."

This is getting surreal. "Oh, for cryin' out loud, Marty. Who the hell would want to blow up the seafloor?" Sam demanded.

"Somebody who wanted to blow up a methane-hydrate mining operation," Marty replied quietly, and Sam stopped breathing. He couldn't even form a coherent thought.

"You still there?" Marty asked after a moment of silence had passed.

"I think so," Sam said weakly, leaning against the windowsill that wasn't quite deep enough to serve as a seat. "You think the methane deposit was breached by Cavendish?"

"And the landslide broke up the equipment. What if." Marty's voice was quiet and deadly serious.

Sam shook his head. "Shit, Marty. I mean—*shit.*"

"Yeah." Marty let out an audible breath. "Think, Sam. There are some weird stories circulating about what's going on down there. I'm trying to get my hands on some video of what's happening, but with that plane crash yesterday morning, everybody wants the same thing and at GISS they've queued everybody who got in before the server crashed. I'm on a few other lists, too, but haven't been able to cop any priority. When I get the data, I'll copy you on it, okay? You can look at it yourself."

This is turning into one hell of a day. Sam rubbed his suddenly burning eyes. "Well, hell, yes, I'll look at it. But what are you thinking we're going to see, Marty?"

"Bubbles breaking at the surface, if nothing else. If the numbers are right and there really is methane coming up that fast and at that volume," Marty said slowly, "it's got to be messing with the water column."

"Yeah."

"It's damn close to that crash site, Sam, and there are a hell of a lot of ships nearby. If I'm wrong and it is a fissure, like you said, the release won't stay localized. The differential in the density of the water column— well, it could get real ugly real fast, Sam."

Sam didn't need to hear more. He knew what his friend was thinking. All that gas fizzing through the water column could cause what some researchers had termed the Bermuda Triangle effect; too much gas released under pressure would turn the water to foam, and foam can't support a ship. Anything in the water column would sink like a stone. And anything requiring a specific pressure, like a body, would burst as it sank.

And Cyn was there, right there, on a boat. Right down there where all this crazy shit was going on. The thought made his stomach heave, and bile backed up into his throat, burning it.

"—and that gas is just going to keep rising," Marty was saying as Sam refocused on the conversation. "It could mess with the air column if the wind doesn't disperse it fast enough. And the winds are pretty calm right now. But if that tropical depression kicks up, we could be in for—"

"I gotta call you back, Marty," Sam said abruptly.

"Something wrong?"

"Maybe," he said distractedly, wanting only to hang up on his friend and get his God-damned girlfriend on the phone. "Last time I talked to her, Cyn was tryin' to convince the captain to take them to the crash site."

"She'll never get there."

"Well, I haven't been able to get her on the phone since yesterday, and nobody's called me or the station asking for bail money or where to ship her body," he said with an attempt at humor that fell flat.

"Hey, she's okay, Sam. Cyn is a nut, but she's not stupid," Marty said after a long pause.

"No, she's not," he agreed quietly. "I'll get back to you, man. Thanks for callin'."

CHAPTER

10:15 A.M., Sunday, October 26, Embassy of Taino, Washington, D.C.

Victoria had known as she watched the sun rise that this day was never going to end. She'd barely slept last night, and her conversation with Charlie hadn't done her any favors. She was exhausted beyond words and it wasn't anywhere near noon. She would have to get a second wind soon or she wouldn't make it through the afternoon.

Charlie had grudgingly allowed her back into the brain of the embassy, and she wasn't about to mess it up. Given what his opinion of her had become, Victoria knew there wouldn't be any more chances if something went wrong.

She rolled her shoulders and looked at Andy Trump, the embassy's chief of information technology, hoping that her tiredness wasn't apparent to him—or to Charlie, who had wandered in a few minutes ago and was leaning against the back wall of the office with his arms folded.

Such a comforting presence. Victoria wanted to roll her eyes.

Andy was a good guy and a genius when it came to setting up and securing computer networks. She'd hired him herself four years ago, and they'd never encountered a situation that he couldn't fix.

Right now, his business casual clothes were rumpled, stress was etched into his face, and she knew he was just as frazzled as she was. He'd been called in to the office as soon as the communications links with the island had gone down five hours ago, and had been working nonstop to reestablish them. Nothing had worked. Even the emergency links refused to come online.

"Andy, have your teams run the diagnostics again. Hardware and software," she said, keeping a sigh out of her voice. "Networks, especially networks *you* design, don't just stop working for no reason."

"Victoria, we've run the diagnostics. The transponders are fine. The commands we're transmitting to the island have all the proper codes within the agreed-upon parameters. We are infection free," he said, as if he hadn't already said the same thing several times this morning. "I am one hundred percent certain that the problem is on the ground down there. Either the ground stations have been damaged, or they've been shut down, or some codes have been changed."

"There's no reason for the ground stations to be taken offline, Andy. Micki would never order that, not without notifying us first and definitely not without a good reason," Victoria replied, wishing she could believe her own words. "And she'd never take down the backups at the same time as the default systems. Especially not under these circumstances. She knows we need them."

Without getting up from his chair, Andy leaned forward and gently shut his office door, then leaned back and met her eyes. "Vic, let me be blunt. Whatever's going on down there is not happening by accident. Things have been powered down and turned off. The island has gone dark on purpose. We can't even get through using cellular traffic, which, as you know, relies on a different transponder on a different bird and uses different receiving equipment on the ground." Andrew folded his arms across his chest and let them rest on his not-inconsiderable paunch. "Orem's checked the weather and there's nothing going on. Barely even a breeze, no lightning strikes, no volcanic eruptions, no crazy geomagnetic, flux density, planetary-alignment, alien-entity, New Age psychobabble crap. *Nothing* is going on. And Tropical Storm Whoever is nowhere near Taino."

Feeling what little energy she had left draining out of her, Victoria drew in a breath and kept her voice even. "Go on."

"I think we have to start thinking about bad things," he said simply.

"Like what?" Charlie asked from his place leaning against the wall.

Andy didn't take his eyes off Victoria, and she could feel the intensity behind their deep, tired brownness. "That someone has changed the command codes or the security codes or both."

"Who could do that?" Charlie asked, and Victoria knew he was deliberately not looking at her.

"Me, Victoria, Micki, in a heartbeat," Andy said. "With more time, anyone with a lot of know-how. And lots of people down there have both the time and the talent."

"Is that true?" Charlie demanded. "You both said it was secure. Now you're both saying it isn't."

Meeting Charlie's eyes, Victoria replied coolly. "Andy's right, Charlie. It's possible that someone down there could have hacked the system but the probability is extremely small." She paused and Andy nodded, turning to look at Charlie.

"We wrote our own software, custom-built the network, and reinforced its perimeters with so many blind alleys and dead ends that you literally need a roadmap to find your way around to the important modules. The command codes—" Andy began.

"What are those?"

"Commands are the lines of code that identify tasks and define their execution," Victoria replied. "With regard to the communication satellites, commands are what we send up to them and telemetry is the data that the satellites send back to our ground units to detail how the equipment has processed and responded to the commands. If everything is going smoothly, it's described in full. If tasks fail or have to be aborted, the data tell us when, why, and how."

"But commands can be overwritten?" Charlie asked.

"Yes. Anyone who knows the software and has a fairly high degree of coding skills could write new commands, but getting them into the system would be extremely difficult because of our security structures," she continued. "The commands are not protected by run-of-the-mill passwords; these passwords are upward of twenty characters long and they change every thirty seconds. So to access the command encoder unit, you have to have the correct random password generator." She slipped her hand into the pocket of the suit jacket she'd slung over the back of the chair in front of her and pulled out a small device that resembled a stick drive. "I have one, Dennis has one, and Micki has one. And there are two more, located in safe places off-island. These are the only devices that can provide access to the system at such a high level."

Charlie's mouth flattened into a thin line and anger flared in his eyes as he realized it had been in her possession the entire time. He hadn't known about it, so he hadn't been able to seize it.

"So if someone has gotten their hands on this, they could get into the system," she said, slipping the device back into her pocket. "But then they would have to get past the encryption. Without the proper encryption key, you'd need a supercomputer and a few weeks at least to crack the algorithm. *But* even if someone could get past all of those barriers, we still have someone pulling hammer duty twenty-four/seven," she finished.

"What's hammer duty?" Charlie asked warily.

Andy smothered a laugh.

"It's our security method of last resort," Victoria

replied. "Someone sits in the secure area that houses the command encoder unit and the command decoder unit. Those are the black boxes that translate everything into and out of the encrypted code that passes through the satellite transponders and network routers. The person on duty is attached to the unit with a bracelet—more or less a handcuff with a long lead—and there's a balpeen hammer nearby. If there's a physical threat to either unit, he or she smashes the units, making the codes unrecoverable."

Charlie's eyes widened. "Oh, for Christ's sake, Vic. You're kidding, right?"

"No, I'm not."

"That's kind of primitive. Why not just eliminate the threat? Give the person a gun."

Victoria looked at him, her eyebrows aloft. "The people who work near the units aren't security personnel, Charlie. They're computer geeks. They eat, breathe, and sleep computers, and the only guns they're likely ever to have handled are virtual ones in Warcraft or something similar. Giving them a real gun and leaving them alone for four or five hours at a stretch is likely to make them attempt a game of quick-draw and they could end up shooting themselves, each other, or the units. We can make another unit if we have to, but getting a good programmer isn't as easy as you might think. Besides, an attacker might have a weapon of his own, but no black box is going to survive an attack with a hammer."

"That's nuts."

"Well, I'll agree that it sounds nuts, but it's more than just physical security, it's computer security. Not all threats to the machines are physical. If something goes wrong with one of the units, a gunslinger couldn't assess and fix it," she finished pointedly. "Bottom line: Our communications system security is tight."

"So what about Micki?" Andy asked.

Victoria turned to him. "What about Micki?"

"Tag, she's it. Obviously."

You don't have to convince me of that.

Victoria said nothing as she stood up and met Charlie's eyes once more. "Unless you have other plans for me, I intend to fly back to Taino this afternoon. And then I'll get everything back online." She glanced to Andy. "Meanwhile, I'd like you to keep trying to make it work."

As Andy shrugged and swiveled to face the array of monitors on his desk, Victoria and Charlie left the room.

"Bold plan of action for someone under house arrest," Charlie said as they walked toward the staircase that would take them back to his second-floor office. "Give me that little thing you showed off in there."

She slid it out of her pocket and handed it to him. "Be careful with it. If Micki and Dennis are—" She couldn't bring herself to say "dead." "If they're not inclined to share theirs with me when I get back, I won't be able to do much," she said casually. "Are you going to try to stop me from going?"

"I'm not sure."

Neither spoke again until they were in his office with the door closed.

"Going back is the only way to find out if Micki is behind any of this, Charlie. Depending on what's going on down there, she and Dennis might be hostages, or they could be dead," she said bluntly.

"Or Micki could be waiting for her accomplice to return."

Stay cool.

Victoria drew in a slow, deep breath. "The snide comments are getting old, Charlie. If I had anything to do with the plane crash or the landslide, do you think I'd be *here*?" She swept a hand to encompass the room, then sat in one of the wing chairs and looked straight at him. "I'd be in Northern Africa with Garner Blaylock. Why can't you just accept the fact that you and Dennis are wrong, and that I'm your only hope to fix things? At least let me go back and try."

"I am letting you try—from here." Charlie moved away from the window and toward Victoria. "We need to be brought back online, Vic. The media are going nuts because we can't give them any new information. They're calling this an 'information blackout' and implying that we're doing it deliberately. They can't hear about an equipment failure without creating fifteen different conspiracies. The fact that our personnel have started visiting the U.S. ships in the area so they can use the Americans' equipment to contact us doesn't seem to matter. And President Benson is enjoying every minute of it. He cut a trip short this morning and said it was because of a heightened terror risk. Ken Proust was on FOX a little while ago and I swear the guy was nearly having an orgasm. And his flunkies are swarming over this like rats on garbage day."

"What's life without a conspiracy?" Victoria replied wryly.

"I have to go back downstairs to the press room. I get to play sitting duck for a few more doorknobs who want to boost their ratings," he muttered, buttoning the top button of his shirt and straightening his loosened tie.

"Who is it this time?"

"I'm not sure. Someone from our staff has been on

nearly every news-related show there is this morning. Could be Martha Stewart at this point."

"She tapes ahead of time. Besides, there's no way to gift wrap this." Victoria met Charlie's eyes. "May I make a suggestion?"

He nodded.

"Shave," she said lightly.

The shadow of a smile crossed his mouth. "I did already."

"Do it again."

"Doesn't a five o'clock shadow make me look tireless?"

"Well, considering it's nowhere near five o'clock yet, it just makes you look tired. Like you've been drinking too much coffee and would have preferred whiskey."

"That's pretty damned close to the truth."

A sharp rap at the door was followed immediately by the entrance of Tim Cotton, Charlie's senior advisor, who strode into the office and let the door slam behind him. Both Victoria and Charlie looked at him in surprise.

"Sorry for barging in, Vic. I know you're due downstairs, Charlie, but you need to hear this," Tim said without preamble as he walked straight to the large desk and reached for the phone.

"What?" Charlie asked.

"I'll let her tell it." Tim activated the speaker phone, then punched in a code to pick up a waiting call. "You know Captain Maggy Patterson. She commands the *Marjory Stoneman Douglas,* one of—"

"One of our research ships. Of course I know her," Victoria interjected.

Tim nodded curtly. "She's running the search-and-recovery operation at the crash site," he said to Charlie. "Captain Patterson, are you there?"

"Yes, sir."

"I have Ms. Clark and Ambassador Deen in the room. Please go ahead."

"About an hour and a half ago, I dispatched two teams of officers to investigate a report of a pleasure boat inside our waters, tacking around the southern end of the island. Our teams were on Jet Skis, and had established visual contact with the trespassing sailboat when they noticed a disturbance on the sea surface," the captain began, her voice scratchy and fading in and out over the tenuous connection. "They reported that the surface appeared to be bubbling."

"Bubbling?" Victoria and Charlie said in unison and looked at each other for confirmation that they'd heard it correctly.

"Yes, ma'am, sir. 'Bubbling' was their term. That stopped within minutes, they said, but then another area of the surface nearby erupted into something that resembled foam."

"Captain, did I hear you correctly? Did you say 'foam'?" Charlie asked.

"Yes, sir. Foam. One of the teams was about two hundred yards away from the boat they were approaching when they observed the phenomena. The other team was closer. Both events occurred between their vessels and the sailboat. Both teams report watching the foamy patch getting bigger and bigger, spreading outward over the sea surface. One team described it as appearing like dish soap foaming in a sink, the other said it resembled the head of a beer. Both stated it was coming up from beneath the surface and it didn't generate waves or high seas." The captain paused. "One of our officers had established radio contact with the boat. She was an eighty-foot clipper cruise boat, the *Floating Dutchman*. British flag, out of Andros in the Bahamas. The captain had dispatched a crew member and a civilian passenger in an inflatable to meet our officers. Shortly afterward, the captain of the clipper issued a Mayday call."

She paused again for the time it might take to suck in a deep breath. "Sir, ma'am, the officers who were closer to the clipper said that the captain was trying to steer away from the foam but the area was expanding and—" Her voice broke and she stopped speaking.

"Maggy, what happened?" Victoria demanded when the woman didn't continue.

Her voice was shaky as she resumed. "They—all of them—said that the foam reached the boat and—"

"And what?"

"The clipper fell into it, as if it were tipping over the edge of something," the captain said, her voice revealing tears and the same stunned disbelief that Victoria felt slam through her, that she saw wash over Charlie Deen's face.

Silence roared in Victoria's ears, drowning out all but the faintest hint that the captain was still speaking.

"I'm sorry, Maggy, I missed what you just said. Could you repeat what you said after you said the boat capsized?" she said, willing her pulse to slow, her voice not to shake.

"It didn't *capsize*, Ms. Clark," the captain replied forcefully. "It *disappeared*. As if it fell off the edge of a cliff, is how my security teams described it. It went down. The crew member who was piloting the inflatable took off straight for the disturbed area. The civilian threw herself overboard and we have her in custody. She has corroborated everything our team said."

"And these officers are credible, Captain? They weren't under the influence of anything? The stress of the operation—" Charlie asked, his brow furrowed.

"With all due respect, sir, these officers are entirely credible or I wouldn't be talking to you now. I've known them for several years. They're all former SEALs, and all of them have Navy Crosses among their honors. If they say it happened, it happened, and it happened the way they say it did."

Victoria looked from Charlie's ashen face to the equally pale visage of his advisor. "Thank you, Maggy. Is there anything else?"

"One thing, ma'am. Before the boat disappeared, two of the officers had time to get out their binoculars to do some recon. They stated that it appeared as if the persons on deck suffered some sort of sudden, very violent seizures just before the boat . . . sank. It happened very quickly."

"Thank you. Where are you now?" Victoria's voice trailed off on the last word.

"Aboard a U.S. Navy ship, the *Eutaw Springs*. We haven't had external comms for several hours, so the commander let us come aboard to handle that."

And eavesdrop his altruistic heart out. Victoria gritted her teeth. "Thanks, Maggy."

Ending the call, Victoria leaned back in her chair and looked at the two silent men standing before her. "What's going on?" she asked them softly.

Neither offered a reply.

10:25 A.M., Sunday, October 26, Bolling Air Force Base, Washington, D.C.

Tom Taylor opened the e-mail that had just come in marked HIGH PRIORITY. He read it, blinked, checked his heartbeat against the second hand of the small crystal clock on his desk, then read it again. Then he picked up his phone and punched a series of numbers on the keypad.

"What do you mean by 'the sea surface has turned to foam'?" he asked, forgoing any greeting when his call was answered.

"Too much gas injected into liquid at high pressure will—"

"I didn't ask you what foam is or what causes it," Tom snapped, cutting off the nameless, faceless CIA drone on the other end of the line. "I know that. What I want to know is how can a one-hundred-square-foot section of very deep ocean turn into fucking *foam*?"

"We can't answer that, sir. It's a phenomenon that's never been observed on this scale—"

"Are you telling me that it's been observed on a smaller scale?" he demanded.

"Not by us, sir. It's been hypothesized."

"Why? What the hell would make someone think that the ocean would ever turn to foam?" Tom pushed a hand through his hair.

"That area of the ocean sits above a methane-hydrate bed. It's been posited over the years that submarine methane releases might have played a role in the disappearance of vessels at sea. It's highly speculative at this point, sir, and we're still investigating the situation. But we're pretty sure that the gas causing this foaming effect is methane based. Something similar has been observed in the Arctic. By Russians."

Tom had frozen in place at the first mention of the chemical. "You think methane is causing this?" he repeated softly.

"Something methane based. The gas we've detected

over the site is not pure. We're trying to analyze it, but we can't identify the other components."

"Why not?"

There was a brief pause on the other end of the line. It wasn't long enough to be overtly insulting, but it was long enough for Tom to realize that the analyst on the other end of the phone was getting bored with the conversation. "Well, sir, we can't identify it because our equipment doesn't recognize its properties."

"Thank you. Keep me informed of any developments," Tom snapped. "And you call me first. You got that?"

Tom waited for a reply, then disconnected, and punched in the cell phone number that Victoria Clark had given him.

10:30 A.M., Sunday, October 26, Embassy of Taino, Washington, D.C.

Charlie and Tim left for the press room, and Victoria went back to her suite. She had barely started to wrap her mind around the increasingly bizarre situation she was facing when her cell phone rang. Gritting her teeth and wishing for a single undisturbed minute so she could just breathe, she picked it up and looked at the small blue screen. UNKNOWN CALLER was spelled out in deepest black. She was sorely tempted to let the call go to voice mail; she was that sick of unknowns.

Not bothering to take a deep breath because she knew nothing would help to settle her nerves, she pressed a button and lifted the phone to her ear. "Victoria Clark."

"Ms. Clark."

The voice was all too recognizable and made her already flat mood deflate further.

"Mr. Taylor. What can I do for you?"

"You can tell me what your fearless leader is up to on the seafloor," he snapped.

"Mr. Taylor, this isn't a secure line."

"Then call me from a secure phone at the number I gave you yesterday. Immediately."

Staring at the silent phone in her hand, Victoria felt a fresh wave of hot anger run through her. *I've had enough of being pushed around.*

She walked to the telephone sitting on the desk and grabbed the handset.

"May I help you, Secretary Clark?"

"Yes. I need a secure line," she said crisply, knowing that Charlie had removed any such privacy from the list of luxuries to which she was entitled.

"Please tell me the number you wish to call."

Forcing herself to remain calm, she read the number off the card and waited for the connection. She was gripping the handset so hard her hand started to ache before the call was answered—which was before the first ring had ended.

"Mr. Taylor, it's Victoria Clark. May I ask just what you are—"

"I'm talking about the methane that's churning to the surface and turning the sea to foam approximately one mile off Taino's southwestern shore," he snapped.

She caught her breath. Her mouth was too dry to formulate a reply, not that she'd be able to speak anyway given the fear squeezing her chest.

A methane release could only mean one thing: Something was catastrophically wrong with the mining operation. There was no other explanation. The structures were designed to ensure that every movement of the material was through sealed and reinforced conduits. The entire operation was engineered to shut down if any failure was detected anywhere in the system.

"I take it that you know what I'm talking about," Tom continued after a minute pause. "I want to know what the hell Cavendish is up to, and I want to know *now*. Because whatever it is, it's gone seriously wrong, Ms. Clark. An unidentified methane-based compound is rising from the seafloor to the surface at high pressure, and it's turning the sea surface to foam in the process. I've got NASA spinning some satellites that usually analyze atmospheres in other *galaxies* to focus on your pissant little island because no one can figure out what the fuck is coming out of your territorial waters. Now, tell me what he's up to," he finished in a terse and deadly voice.

"This is the first I've heard of it," she rasped, her heart beating as though it were about to explode out of her chest.

"That's bullshit."

"No, it's the truth. I just got off the phone with our—I just heard about the foam and the sailboat. Honestly. This is the first I've heard of the methane," she said.

"But you're not surprised to hear it."

"Mr. Taylor, I don't know what you're thinking—"

"I'm thinking that you had better get your butt over here and tell my people what the hell is in that gas and what it's going to do."

"I'll have to get back to you. I need to get the answers—"

"Wait a minute," he demanded, interrupting her. "What did you just say about a sailboat?"

She froze, practically felt molecules colliding as everything in her came to an abrupt stop. "What?"

"Don't fuck with me, Victoria," he snarled. "You're

seconds away from being declared an enemy combatant. And I'll personally come over there, throw you into handcuffs and leg irons, and haul you out of that building."

"Back off," she snapped. "We're both being broadsided here, so don't threaten me."

"Tell me what you know."

She pulled in a short breath. "Two of our security officers were dealing with a sailboat that entered a restricted area. It went too near the area of the eruption—"

"What eruption?" he barked.

"The methane. The foam. It—they watched it fall," she finished lamely as the horror penetrated her imagination and threatened to crack her hard-won control.

"What fell?"

"The boat. It sank. They said it fell into the foam and disappeared," she replied, sinking into the chair next to her. "They said it was like watching the boat fall over a cliff."

Seconds ticked by as neither of them spoke. Her hands were shaking so badly that she had to use both to hold on to the phone.

"Anything else?" Tom said at last. His voice had resumed his typical emotionless nonchalance, and Victoria shuddered.

Swallowing hard, she said, "One of the officers said it appeared as though the people on board were experiencing some sort of seizure as the boat approached the—"

"Seizure?"

"That was the word the officer used," she said quietly.

"I want you to come over to our offices. I'll send a car."

She sat bolt upright in her chair. "Absolutely not. I'm

needed here. And I'm heading back to the island later today."

"Like hell you are."

"I'm a representative of a sovereign nation, in case you've forgotten," she snapped.

"You're also an American citizen who may be involved with terrorist activity," he shot back. "You'd be better off coming in on your own, Victoria. I really don't want to stage a Delta Force extraction in Georgetown."

As ludicrous as his threat sounded, she didn't doubt his sincerity in making it. Or his ability to carry it out.

"Okay, look," she said slowly. "Arguing with each other isn't going to help the situation. I'm needed here." She paused. "Mr. Taylor, the embassy has lost all contact with the island. So have our search crews. We've been trying to reestablish communication for the last few hours. Nothing we've tried has worked. I have to be here."

"Keep me apprised," he growled. "I'll be expecting to hear from you within the hour."

"You will."

She ended the call and sat at the desk, frozen, staring at the golden leaves on the tree outside her window.

"Dennis," she whispered. "What have you done?"

CHAPTER

The volcano that was the heart of Taino was long dormant. Some scientists had even assured Dennis that it was extinct. The last eruption on Taino had happened hundreds of years ago, and in the centuries since, the deep central crater had become lush with plants and wildlife, an ecosystem unto itself. Time and weather had worn away some of the lip of the crater, and the volcano's gently sloping lava walls rose only several hundred feet. They were covered by luxuriant growth that was, for the most part, undisturbed until the land flattened out to meet the sea.

All human activity on the island took place along the coast. The volcano rose steeply from the sea at the northern end of island and sloped more gently toward the south. At the southeastern tip of the island, centuries of storms and currents had carved a deepwater port, where the institute's research vessels and the occasional supply ship could dock. To the west of the port, the calm, warm waters of the Caribbean lapped a black sand beach. Not far from the water's edge sat a small compound of simple residences and low-slung offices. The southern wall of the volcano was the thickest, and given that it was also the most convenient to his compound, that's where Dennis had built a bunker.

The shelter had been built almost as an exercise in imagination. Dennis never really thought he'd need the bunker for anything other than perhaps shelter from the occasional hurricane. Still, he'd wanted a bunker, so he built one.

After months of careful blasting, excavation, and construction, the space was habitable. The entire structure functioned independently of the main residential compound near the beach. It was blastproof, floodproof, and self-sufficient, with running water, a purified air supply, and solar-, wind-, and wave-generated electricity. The bunker was comfortably furnished and didn't lack for luxuries, and its command-and-control center was an identical copy of the island's primary system and continually updated in real time. When Dennis was inside it, he felt invincible, like he owned the world instead of just his island. He'd always known the bunker was only part necessity and mostly folly, but more than that, it was a novelty. The bunker had even helped enhance his mystique abroad. And yes, he'd made occasional use of it for some not quite mission-critical adventures, including a few with Micki a few years ago, although under significantly different circumstances.

Right now, however, the space was being put to its true use: protecting him from a harmful situation developing outside the ancient lava walls. Unfortunately, the enemy was inside with him.

Dennis sat in a chair made for relaxing, his body perfectly still, his breathing controlled, and his mind clearer than it had been at any time since early yesterday morning. He was seething with anger, his muscles bunched like a cat ready to pounce and adrenaline rushing like a river through his bloodstream. He was watching Micki. She sat across the airy, well-lit room from him, smiling as if everything that had transpired was a joke, a prank that had been executed without a flaw.

"Chill out, Dennis," she drawled, her low, lilting voice rich with laughter. "Isn't that what you usually do when you're here? Or was that only with me?"

"Murderous bitch."

Her smile faded. "And you? What about the lives you've ended or destroyed?"

"I've saved—"

"You've saved nothing," she stated, cutting off his reply. "You told the world that's what you were going to do: save a pristine ecosystem, save the marine life. They were empty words, Dennis. You knew when you uttered them that you were lying. You have destroyed what you said you would save, and now you've killed all the people you brought here under false pretenses." She shrugged. "They were fools for believing you; they deserved what they got. You can't defy Nature and expect to survive the experience."

He began to push himself out of his chair and she casually raised the Taser and aimed it at his chest. "Sit yourself down, darlin'. I'll tell you when you can get up."

Slowly, Dennis resumed his seat. "They didn't deserve any of what happened to them. You killed them in cold blood."

She laughed and shifted in her chair, her warm caramel eyes never leaving his face. "I didn't put those people on that plane, and I didn't put those people in a canister under the sea, either. It was your mindless need for domination that did. Your need to boast about how you would harness and constrain Nature to suit your bottom line. That's what killed those people, Dennis. Your ego."

"And what about all the people here on Taino who will die? Your colleagues. Your friends."

"Friends? No, Dennis, not my friends." She shrugged carelessly. "They're just as bad as you. They came here out of greed, not to save the Earth or Her creatures. Their deaths are your doing. And they won't be missed, just like you won't be missed."

Her voice, the way she'd draped herself over the chair, the way she held her drink—everything about her was calm and easy, as if they were having an inconsequential chat on a lazy afternoon. Calm and self-assured, she didn't even have the decency to be cocky.

Dennis had to admit that he found her nonchalance unnerving, but he was determined not to let it affect him. He'd lost enough time as it was. Right now he had to focus, to find her blind spot and exploit it.

"What about you, Micki? Will you survive? If what you described is actually happening out there, we'll both die. We can't stay in here indefinitely. The space isn't designed for that. Our supplies will run out."

She tilted her head and looked at him with an almost gentle gaze. "Oh, of course we'll both die, sugar. Don't you fret about that," she said, her voice softening as her drawl became deeper. "Maybe we'll go out there together and take a last deep breath of the poison you've spewed into the air. That would be a fitting end for you, wouldn't it? You murder the environment and then let it murder you."

Dennis said nothing and she laughed again.

"You don't think I'll do it, do you? Of course I will. I'm not afraid to die, Dennis. I'll be happy to go. I've done my bit for the world. I'm satisfied. I have no regrets." Micki cocked her head and looked at him almost flirtatiously. "But I can tell that you're afraid of what's ahead of you. Probably wonderin' if you said enough prayers as a child. Well, darlin', don't worry your head about it." Her voice dropped to a gentle whisper. "I'm your Earth Angel, here to assure you that your death will be empty, Dennis, and that you will die wanting to live on. Your last thought will be regret."

If it weren't for the Taser dangling loosely from the long, elegant fingers draped over the armrest of her chair, Dennis would have crossed the room then and killed her. He'd have cheerfully grabbed her by the slender, honey-sweet column of her throat and crushed the breath out of her.

With no regrets.

11:15 A.M., Sunday, October 26, Gainesville, Florida

"Look, I know you guys have a lot of other things on your plate right now, but this is literally life and death," Sam pleaded with the Taino embassy worker bee on the other end of the phone. He was on his deck, pacing the short distance from the steps to the sliding glass door of his bedroom. It was a miracle he hadn't worn a groove in the planks that made up the floor. He'd been on the phone with every agency he could think of ever since he'd left the office after talking to Marty.

"Sir, I have no information to give you in answer to your question."

"Can you transfer me to someone who does?" he said, striving for calm.

"I am that someone," the woman said, frustration finally creeping into her voice. "I have no information about any pleasure craft or persons taken into custody today."

"Look, even CNN is talkin' about a boat that's gone missin', for Christ's sake," he exploded. He leaned one hand on the deck's railing and curled his fingers around it to keep it from punching something. "How the hell can you not know about it? It happened in your territorial waters just a few hours ago."

"Because I'm in Washington, D.C., not on the beach in Taino with a pair of binoculars," she snapped. "And there's no reason to curse at me. I'm trying to be helpful but you refuse to pay attention to what I'm saying. I don't have the information you're looking for."

He unclenched his fist and slapped his open palm onto the railing of the deck. "Well, someone has to, ma'am. Who else can I talk to? There has to be someone."

"Try calling the company that chartered the boat your girlfriend was on, or try the Royal Bahamas Defence Force. That's the Bahamian coast guard."

"I did. The charter company hasn't heard from the captain for ten hours. He should have checked in by now. The Bahamians couldn't tell me anything, and the U.S. Coast Guard and the navy don't have any information, either. Look, lady, if the boat was in your waters, then *your* people would have found it," he growled. "What would they have done with the crew if today was a normal day?"

"We wouldn't do anything with the crew. Our security personnel would escort the vessel out of the area and file a report."

"Well, would it kill you to find out if they did that?" he practically shouted, pushing his hand through his hair and sitting on the top rail of his deck.

The woman on the other end of the call let out a large, exasperated breath and her voice, when she spoke, was heavy with forced patience. "As I've told you several times already, sir, we're having some communication difficulties. Why don't you give me your name and telephone number and I will contact you if I hear any information regarding a pleasure boat. Would that work for you?"

"Fine," he said, then stood up abruptly. "Well, actually, no, that won't work for me. We both know you'll never call me with anything. You're probably not even goin' to write down my number."

"I resent that," she said stiffly. "Unfortunately, you just lost your best chance for getting any information. Goodbye."

He heard the click and found himself staring at the silent handset.

"Well, that didn't work too well."

With a start, Sam jerked his head to look in the direction of the soft voice and saw Sabina standing on the middle step leading to the deck from his backyard.

What the hell is she doing here? He stared at her while his mind pulled itself back to the moment. "Uh, hi. I didn't know you were there."

She smiled. "I just got here. May I come up?"

He set the phone on the round table that sported a striped umbrella and four citronella candles, courtesy of Cyn, and two freshly emptied Coors bottles, courtesy of Cyn's failure to call in. "Sure. What can I do for you?"

"Nothing. I was hoping I could do something for you," she said, walking toward him with a smile that had gone hesitant.

Oh, shit. "Um, I, ah—" He ran his hand through his hair again. He wasn't sure how to ask Sabina to leave, but he knew that the last thing he needed was a distraction, much less one that looked, walked, and smelled like Sabina.

"Um, Sabina, this isn't a good time—"

She glanced away from him as she set her purse on the table. "I've been monitoring that change in the atmospheric methane values since I told you about it. I think it could be getting troublesome. I wanted to get your opinion on it. I tried calling you a few times, but I couldn't get through." She looked up at him, and shrugged with a smile. "It might be important. I hope you don't mind that I came over."

Sam stared at her, blinked, and tried to focus on her words rather than her other attributes.

"Uh." He cleared his throat. "What do you mean by 'troublesome'?"

She dropped her hand to the table and opened the thick manila folder that had escaped his notice. "The numbers are odd. But they are consistently odd, so I think they may be accurate."

She moved around the small table to stand next to him, holding the sheaf of green-and-white striped printouts in her hands. "Here are the values since ten o'clock this morning. Here is what I find odd. Methane in its pure state is lighter than air, and so should rise. This isn't rising. It's hugging the water," she said, pointing to the rows of small print. "The winds have been calm and steady down there and are predicted to remain so until this evening. So the concentration isn't diminishing too much and the methane seems to be spreading laterally as it moves across the water. The wind is taking it almost directly toward the shore. There is a storm to the east, though, and the winds near the island are already beginning to change direction. That will blow the methane away from Taino and toward the Florida Keys."

Sam scanned the printouts. She was right. The numbers *were* odd. More than odd. They were crazy.

He glanced at her. "Is something else showing up in the gas?"

"I haven't yet identified anything else but the gas is not pure methane. The hydrate beds in this region— can this be some variant of methane? Have the beds ever been sampled?"

Sam shook his head as he continued to review the printouts, dropping to the next page, and then the next. "The water's too deep and Taino won't let anyone in except people associated with its own Climate Research Institute. And if they've done tests, they aren't sayin'." He frowned as he kept reading. "It could be a more pure form, like what they found in that Siberian lake bed a few years ago. But if it was purer, it would rise faster, not slower." *And we'd be heading for some serious atmospheric trouble.*

"Then could something be mixed into it?"

"If there was something else in it, it would have shown up in the data," he muttered.

"So it's just an anomaly?" Sabina asked, with such doubt in her voice that Sam looked up.

"What are you getting at?" he asked.

"Shouldn't we do something to find out why the gas is behaving that way?"

"Something like what?"

She hesitated. "Well, tell someone."

"Tell who? And tell them what? NASA's aware of what's going on. GISS has been on it since it began. NOAA knows about it, too."

"But is anyone doing anything?"

Sam put the papers on the table and looked at her. "Sabina, what are you talking about?"

Even with her brows pulled together in a frown, the woman was stunning.

She let out an abrupt breath in frustration. "Well, if the gas is not rising, it's hugging the waterline. That would mean it's creating an oxygen-depleted atmosphere at sea level, wouldn't it? I mean, the concentration of methane is high. And if it's not diffusing as it's blowing toward shore, wouldn't it start to have an effect on . . . things?"

He stared at her blankly.

"If there is too much methane in the mixture of air, wouldn't people on the beach and on boats die when they breathed it in?" she said, her voice deepening and cracking a little.

"Well, I suppose so, in theory. But—"

"Oh, bugger this," she snapped. Letting out a harsh breath, she reached out and flipped over several pages in the folder, then jammed her finger onto a page presenting a table. "I *graphed* it, Professor Briscoe. There's a plume forming, and there's nothing to stop it. The wind currents—" She flipped to the next sheet, a map of the area. "This tropical high is stationary, but"—she pointed—"*this* storm is building. The winds generally shift to the north-northwest here." She moved her finger along the map. "And the next significant land masses are the Florida Keys, approximately fifty miles away. People live there. And they will die if this plume does not diffuse."

She looked up at him, tears shimmering in her eyes. "If I am wrong, please tell me. Please."

Shaken, Sam stared at her. "I need to review—"

She shook her head. "No. No. Just tell me if I'm right or if I'm overlooking something, Dr. Briscoe. It's a beautiful weekend and the big fantasy festival is under way in the Keys. There are thousands of people in the Keys now, on the beaches, in boats. If I'm right, then they are all in trouble."

That's the fucking understatement of the year. How the hell could I not have seen this?

Grabbing the folder of papers in one hand and Sabina's wrist with the other, he pulled her through the sliding doors and into the kitchen.

"Who else have you talked to about this?" he demanded.

"No one. There's no one around."

"Okay. Good." He dropped her hand as he went to the dining room and strode over to the table where his laptop sat humming quietly. "Pull yourself together, Sabina. I need to introduce you to a friend of mine," he said, sliding into the chair in front of his computer and beginning to type. "You ever had an urge to go to Washington, D.C.?"

6:30 P.M., Sunday, October 26, Annaba, Algeria

Sprawled on the low-slung sofa in the luxurious living area of his cliffside villa, Garner Blaylock watched the serious faces parade before him on the American cable news channel's split screen. TERROR ON TAINO, a suitably sensationalistic title, was splashed in lurid red on a banner across the bottom of the screen, just above the ticker that continually fed the public's appetite for disaster. Other networks were using similar labels to frighten and, therefore, lure viewers. NIGHTMARE IN PARADISE had been another good one. CARIBBEAN CHAOS was the weakest.

For sheer entertainment value, the total package of hysteria, lack of information, and wild speculation was better than anything he'd watched in a long time. The reporters' desperate desires to get the latest information about the crash and landslide was almost as intense as it had been on September 11, and almost as fruitless.

What made the media scrum all the more amusing was that no one really knew what questions to ask or which expert to grill. The lineup had changed with the incidents. First there had been the aviation experts and so-called terrorism experts, then the diplomats and politicians, and finally the sailors and fishermen who had seen the plane come down and were eager to tell their inane, unnewsworthy stories in return for fifteen minutes of fame. After the landslide, the networks had scrambled to find earthquake experts, oceanographers, hydrogeologists, and tsunami experts willing to have microphones shoved in their faces.

Despite all this entertainment, Garner's patience was fraying. So far the media were all keeping quiet about what he considered an unexpected validation of his actions, the methane release. There had been a report of the bodies of twelve humpback whales found floating in the vicinity—regrettable casualties—but the so-called journalists were blaming the deaths on the landslide, not methane.

The lack of attention was inexcusable. The methane release posed more danger to more people than anything else GAIA had ever done. It deserved the most acute interest. Yet not a single one of the parasites had mentioned it.

It was just further proof that the slimy bastards were colluding; there was no doubt in Garner's mind that every atmospheric scientist on the planet knew what was happening by now, yet no one was saying anything. Even the Internet was silent on the subject. It was more than bizarre. It was revealing. The total silence on the subject could only mean one of two things: Either they were scared shitless or they were waiting for someone to claim responsibility for what was going on.

He stood up and stalked to the window, not seeing the lush landscape that was falling slowly into shadow. The thought of being outmaneuvered by the ignorati made him seethe.

Spinning in his tracks, he stalked back to the room he'd set up as his office.

If they're waiting for a message, I'll bloody well give them one.

25
CHAPTER

11:30 A.M., Sunday, October 26, off the east coast of Islamorada, in the Florida Keys

Fishin' for Trouble, his father's luxurious fifty-foot fishing boat, rode the light swell easily. Griffin Bradshaw, twenty-five, drowsy, sated, and sprawled next to his naked, sleeping girlfriend on the sunlight-flooded deck, enjoyed the motion. The warm breeze and easy rocking should have had him sleeping like a baby, but instead the sensations were keeping him awake. The fact that he couldn't fall into a deep sleep came as a vague surprise. Considering all the sun, beer, and sex that he'd been indulging in for the last twenty-four hours, he was fairly amazed he could even move, or think.

He stretched and sat up, then gingerly pulled himself to his feet. "Indulgence" was the word of the day. He was a couple of months into his last year of law school and he was going to enjoy every free moment he could squeeze out of it. Reality was waiting for him onshore as soon as he graduated; he would be joining the work-force without any break. A sought-after job at a top law firm in Miami awaited him, as did a brand-new South Beach condo. His father had bought the high-rise unit for him a year ago, while it was still on the drawing board, and the construction was nearly done. His mother was going to decorate it, and he'd move into it the week-end he graduated.

Life is good and only getting better.

The nearest other boat was a few hundred yards away, so he saw no reason to consider putting on any clothes. He rolled his shoulders and walked to the bow, then sank to the deck to watch the sky. It was a pure, eye-popping tropical blue and almost cloudless. The air was so hot that even the faint breeze didn't help to cool him down.

A series of heavy splashes pulled his attention to-ward the starboard side. He couldn't see any distur-bance from where he sat, but just because it had sounded as it if were close didn't mean it was. Sound carried over water, that much he knew. It had been so clear though, and fairly loud, as if something heavy had fallen clumsily into the water and then thrashed for a few seconds.

After a minute, he dismissed the sound as just an er-rant wave, closed his eyes and tilted his face to the sun again.

Almost immediately, he heard the noise again. Grif-fin stood up this time, turning his head sharply. Some-thing *was* thrashing in the water. He could see something cresting, then being pulled under the surface.

Sharks enjoying a midday snack.

A little uneasy, he sat back down, coughing slightly as he detected an odd stink in the air.

Must be the gut gas of whatever that shark just ripped open.

Before the thought was complete, the back of his throat began burning, and he felt almost light-headed. Figuring that it was a combination of the sun and probably still being a little buzzed from all the partying he'd done last night, Griffin stood up carefully and began to make his way to the stern and his girlfriend. Being flat on his back would help.

Feeling even more dizzy, he grabbed the low handrail to steady himself but a glance over the side made him stop short. The bodies of three dolphins floated in the dark, sparkling water, bumping gently against the hull, white bellies up.

He inhaled deeply to clear his head, and the breath seared his lungs.

The panicked shout he intended came out instead as a dull, scraping bray, and he fell to his knees, leaning over the rail at a precarious angle. Choking, needing air, he instinctively took another deep breath. The toxic atmosphere flooded his lungs and he clutched his throat, tearing at his skin.

The lack of oxygen in his brain made his equilibrium falter, his vision blur and darken. His last sensation was of pitching head first over the rail, his terror complete.

Before he hit the water, bouncing off the nearest dolphin, Griffin Bradshaw was dead.

11:35 A.M., Sunday, October 26, aboard the *Marjory Stoneman Douglas,* off the coast of Taino
Cyn lay in the claustrophobically small room that boasted three bunks stacked vertically on each of three

walls. The other wall held a collection of nine lockers and the door, which at the moment was locked. She'd been brought to the boat on a Jet Ski. Between the excruciating pain of her broken arm and the shock of seeing what had happened to Günter's boat, much of that trip was a blur.

She'd been hauled aboard the research vessel and someone who wasn't a doctor had set her arm and put it in a stiff sling. Then the captain of the boat, a woman, and an English guy who was the captain of another boat, had grilled her for much too long about who she was and why she was there and what she'd seen. Then the guy who wasn't a doctor had handed her some Vicodin and told someone else to take her to the cabin.

Right now, confinement was okay with her. They'd have to take her to a hospital at some point, but as long as they kept the drugs flowing, the pain in her arm was a dull throb, and rest of her couldn't get too excited about too much. The steady rocking of the boat and the intermittent hum of voices was relaxing. Sleep seemed like a good thing.

11:45 A.M., Sunday, October 26, Bolling Air Force Base, Washington, D.C.

It was getting late, and all he'd had to eat so far was a stale muffin from the cafeteria early that morning. Not that Tom was particularly hungry, but it would have been nice to have something in his stomach to absorb all the coffee he'd drunk in the past six hours.

"In other words, there's been no significant addition to the information we had early this morning." Lucy's voice was cool and quiet, and more damning because of it.

Tom Taylor fought the urge to run a frustrated hand over his face. "Depends on how you define 'significant'—relevant to the problems or the solutions."

"I define it as anything that will move us closer to having some answers."

"In that case, no. We've gotten more information that has led us to a lot more questions, some of which are of particular interest."

"Such as?"

He glanced at the BlackBerry in his hand as he began to answer her, but stopped before he could finish the first syllable. With only the barest glance up at her, he began walking to her desk. "Are you logged on to an external network?"

"Why?" she demanded.

"Looks like Garner got bored a few minutes ago," he muttered, sitting down at her desk and tapping a key to bring the screen to life. He looked up as she came to a stop next to him. "You really should lock down your computer when you're not at your desk."

"I'm four feet away from it," she ground out.

"Yes, but now I'm driving. What if I'd been a bad guy? You'd be tied up in the corner and I'd be reading the last few Presidential Daily Briefings."

"Damn it. Get away from there," she ordered, but he was already logged on to the Web and navigating to the URL that had appeared on his BlackBerry.

"Well, would you look at that. He's taking credit where credit is due."

Lucy forgot her anger and bent closer to the screen, her head close to Tom's.

The digitized image was of the highest quality, as GAIA's messages always were. Garner Blaylock's vanity would settle for nothing less. So much of his message relied on his charisma, his personality, his person, and he knew how to maximize it.

He stood on what appeared to be a stone-walled terrace that rose above a low-slung village. The first fiery streaks of a sunset glowed behind him, throwing into relief his defiant, pirate-king stance. Powerfully built, evenly tanned, and bare-chested, Garner Blaylock stared into the camera, his eyes full of blistering anger, his mouth set, his shoulder-length, dark blond hair blowing in the evening wind.

Tom clicked on the play button and leaned back in Lucy's chair to watch the performance.

"Yesterday, the Western media declared that a tragedy has befallen the world," Blaylock began, the audio synchronized perfectly with the video. "They are right, but they have labeled the wrong event. The real tragedy is not that the pointless lives of six airplane crew members ended and that nine demons of the industrialized world have been eradicated. I take credit for that—full credit. My organization, GAIA, took those lives in order to bring to the world's attention a greater evil, one that has led to a tragedy of epic, eternal proportions."

He paused and swept back his rock-star hair with an elegance that would put a dancer to shame. "Why were so many so-called titans of industry on one plane, headed to a small island that has no industry? That is the question everyone is asking and that only I can answer."

He paused for effect, then continued, "Dennis Cavendish was going to show them his latest project, a project designed to make him even wealthier than he already is by raping the Earth to provide humans with more fuel. *Fuel*. Cavendish has devised a way to mine methane hydrate from the seafloor, which would keep in motion the world's death march toward oblivion.

"And the irony is that his underwater operation, which he was preparing to tout as the only source of 'clean' fuel, a fuel that would allow polluter nations and rapine industries to maintain their status quo, has now become the world's biggest nightmare, one from which the Earth and Her inhabitants will never awaken. The landslide that happened in Taino earlier today was triggered by bombs placed by my people. That landslide destroyed Cavendish's plans. The near pristine waters of Taino are now spewing methane into the atmosphere. This will increase global warming faster than any worst-case scenario has ever predicted."

He smiled into the camera, a smile so beautiful, so beatific, it belonged on a cathedral wall. "We can all thank Dennis Cavendish and the miserable parasites who died on his plane for providing an up-close and personal lesson in what a 'scorched earth' approach to business really means."

The video faded to black. A few seconds later, the GAIA logo appeared, ghostlike, over a full-color, real-time loop of the Taino jet exploding.

"In my professional opinion, we're fucked," Tom said.

"Get him," Lucy said coldly. "I don't care how, and I don't care where. I want him in custody as quickly as we can arrange it. Alive, if necessary."

Before he could respond, the intercom on Lucy's desk buzzed and her assistant quietly announced that President Benson was on the phone and would like to speak with her.

Tom was a few steps outside of Lucy's office when his cell phone rang.

"Tom Taylor."

"Mr. Taylor, it's Victoria Clark. Have you seen the video that Garner—"

"Yes. I think we need to talk, Ms. Clark."

There was the briefest of pauses and something in that silence made him stop midstride.

"I agree," she said quietly.

"Will you come to my office, or will you allow me to come to yours?"

"Let me check with Ambassador Deen and get back to you," she said after a strained moment that had the hair on the back of Tom's neck standing upright.

"I'll be waiting for your call."

1:05 P.M., Sunday, October 26, off the coast of Taino

Cyn leaned against the side of the inflatable and tried to suck in as much fresh air as she could. Not that she wanted to diminish the still-wonderful effects of the painkiller, but she knew there weren't going to be fun times ahead. This wasn't the way she'd wanted to get onto Taino but she'd been assured that there was a real doctor there, who had a real X-ray machine and could set her arm properly. She'd been told that after her arm was seen to she'd have to speak to several people, maybe even Dennis Cavendish himself. And when she'd been questioned by whoever wanted to question her, she'd be released to the custody of the U.S. Navy.

And a good time was had by all. Pouting, Cyn braced herself against the pounding of the boat. Despite the drugs, she could feel every bump and bounce in her injured arm.

The boat slowed and she watched the armed guy driving it start to frown. He grabbed the radio unit strapped to his shoulder and murmured something into it, then waited for a reply. The boat neared the dock now, and he slowed it further. Without taking his eyes off the land, he repeated his radio call. Abruptly he brought the engine to idle, grabbed the binoculars Velcroed to the side of the small craft, brought them to his eyes, and stared just past her shoulder.

As wary and alert as she could be in her altered state, Cyn knew something was wrong. She turned her body to face the shore just as the man at the helm sharply ordered her to turn around and get to the floor. He gunned the engine and threw the boat into a tight 180-degree turn, racing back to the ship they'd just left—and away from the twisted, lifeless bodies littering the dock and the beach.

She closed her eyes and tried focus on the pain shooting up her arm every time the boat slammed into another wave. It was more comforting than trying to figure out when her vacation had turned into a trip to the island of death.

1:10 P.M., Sunday, October 26, Embassy of Taino, Washington, D.C.

Nearly two hours after she'd spoken with Tom Taylor, Victoria stood in a small, bare room near the embassy's security offices in one of the building's lower levels. Across from her stood one of her own staff members, a woman who, until a few moments ago, had been familiar to her only on paper but was now unlikely ever to be forgotten.

Mustering what dignity she could, Victoria slipped on her blouse and buttoned it as she stepped into her shoes.

"I'm very sorry, Secretary Clark," the woman said

for what had to be the twentieth time. "It was Ambassador Deen's order."

"Yes, you've said that," Victoria replied evenly, wanting to destroy Charlie Deen. She had expected her purse and briefcase to be searched before she was allowed to go—accompanied by an aide who was more like a guard—to meet with Tom Taylor at the DNI's office. Even being patted down or wanded would not have come as a surprise. A full strip search, however badly executed, had been overkill, and had solidified her resolve.

She wouldn't be coming back.

Victoria gently swung her drift of long hair off her shoulder and felt it brush against the silk that covered her back once again.

The security officer handed her her small purse and briefcase, and escorted her to one of the side doors of the embassy. Handed off to her "aide," Victoria waited while the Americans' car passed through the gates and onto embassy property. When it came to a slow stop, she walked forward and climbed into the car's back seat. The aide followed, and they both returned the polite greeting from the otherwise silent federal agent who had been sent to fetch them.

Only the most perfunctory conversation took place during the twenty-minute drive to Bolling Air Force Base. Located near the southeastern tip of the District on the Maryland side, the base was standard-issue military: a collection of mismatched, mostly drab buildings of gray or beige that were marked by numbers when they were marked at all.

At the entrance gate, the military police checked the IDs of the driver and both passengers, used mirrors to look under the car, swept the floors with their flashlights, and gave the trunk a cursory search. It was all done quickly and quietly, and then they were waved through the gate with a smart salute.

Victoria wasn't sure how she was going to manage it, but she knew she had to quickly concoct a story plausible enough to allow her to ditch her babysitter.

The agent pulled up into a reserved slot in front of an unremarkable building in the center of the base. He escorted the two women through twin sets of doors that led to the lobby, which was no more than a vestibule containing a security checkpoint, then left after a curt goodbye.

Tom was standing on the other side of the checkpoint's Plexiglas wall. Wearing a neutral expression, he waited for each of them to go through the routine of having their identification confirmed and the contents of their bags and pockets reviewed. Victoria, as the senior ranking official, went through the metal detector and turnstile first, and was just shaking Tom's hand when she realized that her babysitter hadn't cleared yet.

Clearly annoyed, the woman had slipped off her shoes as requested and was in the process of removing her hair clip. Her irritation turned into full-blown alarm when Tom casually instructed the security staff to escort her to the tenth-floor conference room when she cleared, then slipped a hand under Victoria's elbow and led her down the bare, linoleum-floored corridor toward the elevators.

Shouts from the woman that she had to stay with Victoria were ignored by all as the American military police efficiently moved the woman out of the vestibule to a private screening room.

Enjoying the first shred of humor she'd encountered in more than twenty-four hours, Victoria looked at Tom with a hint of a smile once they were in the privacy of the elevator. "Is that standard?"

"I don't think that's been tried since the Russians were still called the Soviets," he said dryly. "She'll be treated with the utmost courtesy and sent home in about an hour, in case you're curious."

"Is there a tenth-floor conference room?"

"There isn't a tenth floor."

Victoria smiled more broadly. "So what does that mean?"

"That her invitation has been revoked. When did Charlie Deen decide you needed a sitter?"

"I've been under house arrest since yesterday evening."

His only visible response was a raised eyebrow. "Then why are you here?"

"I'm very persuasive. And he didn't want any bad press. Or you on the embassy premises."

"I'm wounded. What does he think you've done?"

Her smile faded. "He and Dennis are convinced that I'm Garner Blaylock's mole."

His other eyebrow went up. "Are you?"

Victoria rolled her eyes, inwardly gratified at his mild incredulity. She said nothing more until they'd gotten off the elevator on the eighth, and top, floor.

The décor was significantly not military. The corridor was carpeted and hushed, the walls were, no doubt, blastproof, rebar-reinforced concrete block. But unlike the walls on the ground floor, these were covered with drywall, wainscoting, and attractive colors of paint. And paintings that were probably on loan from the National Gallery.

The conference room Tom led her to was not large, but held an attractive table and comfortable chairs, and had a stunning view up the Potomac. She could see the Capitol dome sparkling in the midday sun.

Tom indicated that she should take a seat, and then seated himself.

"You're an American, so you don't need asylum. Do you want protection?" he asked bluntly.

"Yes."

"Done. We'll put you up at one of the hotels downtown, with an around-the-clock security detail. So, other than curing your cabin fever, what did you want to talk about, Ms. Clark?"

"The weather," she said, leaning back in the stiff chair and meeting his eyes. "You were right about the mining operation. So was Garner Blaylock. As I told you, communications with the island were cut off completely early this morning, so what I'm going to tell you is based on our worst-case scenarios. I believe what we predicted is happening." She paused for a heartbeat to rein in the emotion that was threatening her voice. "The foam is being caused by a methane leak on the seafloor, which happened when the landslide knocked out our underwater habitat and apparently dislodged the drilling apparatus. I am not sure if that was part of Blaylock's plan—the release, I mean—but I have to assume it was. We had all the infrastructure in place, Mr. Taylor, and were to begin a live test. If Blaylock's mole was highly placed, he or she would know that."

He displayed no surprise at anything she said, merely nodded slightly. "I think we can safely assume the mole is a she. There are very few men in Blaylock's organization. Do you know who it is?"

"The only person it could possibly be is my deputy, Micki Crenshaw. She knows just about everything there is to know about Taino, the institute, and the technology. She is still on the island, or was when I left."

"No one's left the island."

"There is a fleet of submersibles—" Victoria began.

"Ms. Clark, no one has left that island," Tom repeated softly. "Tell me about Micki Crenshaw."

For all his ease with her, Victoria knew she was in federal custody and had put herself there voluntarily. There was no point in getting annoyed with him. She folded her hands and leaned forward. "As I said, this morning all communication with Taino went dark, even the backup systems and the emergency systems. Only she could have done that."

He corrected her: "About an hour ago, we picked up something pinging a satellite in low-earth orbit. It lasted for less than a minute and terminated as soon as a signal was returned, so we presume it was a test. We're going to continue to monitor it. Now, tell me what the worst-case scenario is when methane leaks from the seafloor to the surface."

Not dropping eye contact, Victoria reached around to the back of her head and unclipped the two multigigabyte lipstick drives she'd fastened into her hair, close to her scalp, and handed them to him. "These will provide all the details you want."

He raised his eyebrows at her as his hand closed around the small drives. "Do you always carry this kind of insurance?"

"Never. I had a bad feeling about this trip, Mr. Taylor. I wanted to send Micki up here, get her off the island. President Cavendish insisted I go instead. I actually brought these in case there was trouble on the island."

"In your hair?"

"I took a chance. Believe me when I say my scalp is the only place the embassy staff didn't search," she said dryly.

"What's on them?"

"Everything," she said crisply. "They contain years worth of research into methane-hydrate mining, information about the habitat and mining operations, and full briefings on our worst-case disaster scenarios."

"What's the condensed version?" he asked, slipping them into the pocket of his suit jacket.

"The methane rises into the atmosphere and stays there, functioning as a greenhouse gas many times more potent than carbon dioxide. Global warming will accelerate in proportion to the amount of methane that accumulates." She paused. "That is, if it's pure."

"Which this methane isn't?"

She met his eyes. "No, it's not. And I think you already know that."

He nodded once. "What's in it? And what does it do?"

"It's a proprietary compound. I don't know what it's made of, but it's meant to stabilize the methane. It makes the gas dense, and therefore safer to handle. Pure methane is highly volatile, lighter than air. This isn't."

"It won't go into the atmosphere? Isn't that a good thing?"

Feeling a wave of shame wash over her, she had to look away. "No. It's bad, Mr. Taylor. It's going to hug the surface for a while before it rises. It's going to create an oxygen-deficient atmosphere wherever it goes—across the surface of the water or the land," she finished in a voice that had gone low with emotion. "Lots of people are going to die."

CHAPTER

1:30 P.M., Sunday, October 26, aboard the
***Marjory Stoneman Douglas*, off the eastern coast
of Taino**

For the second time in a few hours, Captain Simon
Broadhurst had left his own ship, the *Wangari Maathai,*
to board the *Marjory,* only to hear stories that chilled
him to his very core. The first, about the sea turning to
foam and eating ships, he'd believed reluctantly and
only because he knew four of the five people involved
and had questioned them separately.

This time, the thought of dead bodies on the island
left him incredulous. Lack of sleep and the stress of
running the search-and-rescue, and then search-and-
recovery, operations had left him exhausted, with very
little imagination and absolutely no sense of humor. Radio contact with the base on the island had been intermittent and on an as-needed basis ever since the secure
channels had gone down early this morning. But surely
if someone or, more frightening, some*thing,* had killed
people on the island, anyone who had escaped that fate
would have contacted him.

Unless everyone was dead.

The thought made a shudder run through him. He
shook it off and focused a hard glare on the stoned,
sunburned civilian with one arm in a sling who sat in
front of him, and then shifted it to the security staffer
who sat opposite her at the small table.

"Did you see the seagulls?" the woman asked with no preamble, and both Simon and the officer turned to look at her. Between her American accent and painkiller-slurred words Simon could barely understand her.

"I beg your pardon?" he asked coolly.

"I was asking him," the woman said, and pointed a limp finger at the officer. "He was looking at the beach with binoculars. I'm just wondering if he saw the seagulls in the water."

Not hiding his exasperation, Simon ignored her and turned his attention back to the officer.

"Hey, don't dismiss me," the woman said, speaking as if moving her mouth were difficult. "Your people gave me the drugs. This isn't how I usually operate, Admiral."

"Thank you for the promotion, but it's 'captain,' ma'am. What about the seagulls?" Simon asked sarcastically. "Were they pretty?"

"They were dead."

Her words made him do a double take. Intelligence flashed behind the woman's dilated pupils and glazed look.

"Dead?"

"Yes. Dead. About a dozen of them. Maybe more. Floating in the water. How do you suppose a whole flock of seagulls dies, Captain? Fly into the mast of a sailboat?"

He swallowed the sharp reply that immediately came to mind. "How do you think they died, ma'am?"

"Same way the people on my boat died before it sank out of sight and the same way the people on the beach died. I think they breathed something that killed them," she said slowly. "I couldn't see the faces of the people on the beach, but I saw their bodies. Curled up in balls or crumpled up with their hands near their throats."

Simon looked at the security officer, who was nodding at the woman's words.

"Carlson, is this true?"

The officer nodded. "Yes, sir. Their hands were near their throats and chests, and most of their mouths were open. The ones whose faces I could see."

Holy buggery fuck. What's out there? Simon gritted his teeth and looked at the woman.

"The foamy patch where my boat sank was just on the other side of where we were going to dock, isn't it? The dock is kind of on the tip of the island, right? The clipper was coming around the tip when that foamy patch appeared. I think something is in the air near that foam, Captain, blowing around. And whatever is causing that foam is killing anything that breathes it in."

"Thank you, Miss . . . ?"

"Davison. Cynthia Davison."

"Thank you, Ms. Davison." Simon stood up abruptly. "Patterson. A moment," he said, looking at Maggy Patterson, captain of the *Marjory* and wide-eyed observer of the conversation.

She followed him out of the small room.

"I'm giving you command of the search-and-recovery operation, effective immediately. Jones will assume command of the *Wangari* until I return," he said, crisply and quietly.

Surprisingly, Maggy Patterson didn't nod in agreement.

"Where are you going?" she demanded, clearly not pleased.

You're questioning me? He frowned at her. "I'm going to take one of the security teams and go around the north head of the island. If we can land safely, we'll try to make it to the bunker to see if anyone is there."

"You're crazy," she said thinly. "The whole island could be toxic."

"I believe that's 'you're crazy, sir,'" he snapped. "If I don't return within two hours, you can assume we're dead. That's all, Patterson. You have your orders."

"Not so fast, *sir*," she snapped back at him. "You need to get clearance from Victoria Clark for something like this. We don't know what's happening on the island other than a lot of weird deaths. Don't you dare add your name to that list."

"I didn't know you cared, Patterson," he said dryly.

"Knock it off. Send two of the security guys. That's what they're trained for. You need to stay here," she insisted.

The air was tense between them as they stood in the tiny corridor glaring at each other.

"Or I'll have you confined to quarters," she said, her words low and fierce. "You're standing on *my* boat."

Simon smiled at her coldly. "Thanks for your input, Patterson. I believe we'll adjourn this discussion until a later date. In the meantime, I must return to my ship."

Twenty minutes later, a reconnaissance team, fitted with full masks and scuba tanks, peeled away from the *Wangari Maathai* in an inflatable with Simon Broadhurst at the helm. He waved jauntily to an obviously fuming Maggy Patterson, who was standing in the stern of the *Marjory* as they zoomed past.

2:00 P.M., Sunday, October 26, Taino

Handcuffed at the wrists and ankles to a chair, Dennis didn't have much choice but to watch Micki and be sickened by her.

They were in the bunker's security office, surrounded by computers that were all online and humming, and completely out of reach. He concealed his frustration, impotence, and fury; revealing any of it would only give Micki more to be glad about.

Still as calm and unfazed as if she had nothing more pressing on her mind than a typical day at work, Micki activated the backup security system. As she waited for the cameras to come online, she glanced over her shoulder and grinned at Dennis.

"Well, in just a few seconds we'll get to see if all those worst-case scenarios were right, won't we?" She turned her attention back to the monitor in front of her, and tapped a few keys. "Let's start with the offices."

The camera panned slowly, impassively, revealing a vista that was increasingly horrific, and Micki gave a small squeal of delight. Laughing and triumphant, she clicked the mouse to change the view and then sped her way through the images from each of the many cameras installed on the island.

The bodies of her colleagues littered the offices and the walkways that connected the compound's low-slung buildings. More corpses were strewn on the docks of Taino's port and floated in the placid water those docks surmounted.

"Ah, success is so sweet, isn't it?" she said, after she'd completed one loop of images. She got up from the chair and stretched as if to loosen stiff muscles. The movement pulled her T-shirt above the waistband of her shorts, revealing a tanned, taut stomach that, at one time, Dennis had known intimately.

He turned away.

"What, Dennis? I'm not allowed my moment in the sun? That's hardly fair. I recall—quite vividly—that you used to be rather brazen about celebratin' your victories, no matter how small," Micki said, lowering her face so that it was level with his own. Her eyes were hot and her smile was all about sex and conquest.

Under other circumstances—

"This isn't a victory, Micki," Dennis said between clenched teeth, his arms and legs straining instinctively but impotently against the metal biting into his skin.

"Oh, but it is. It's a victory for the Earth," she purred, running her hands up his forearms, then over his biceps and shoulders, not stopping until her hands were cupped around his face. "I can see now why power is the ultimate aphrodisiac. The sight of them"—she tipped her head toward the monitor without breaking eye contact with him—"and the reality of you sittin' here like this . . . I've never been much for playin' with toys, but I have to admit that I'm beginnin' to understand why some people like it," she finished, her words a hot, damp whisper against his ear.

The toned curves she pressed against him, the earthy heat she radiated, caused an age-old battle in his brain and elsewhere; it was a battle Dennis had often fought, but had never before sought to lose.

"Don't fuck with me, Micki," he snarled, jerking his head away from hers.

She pulled back slightly until they were face to face again. "You keep forgetting that you're not in charge anymore, Dennis. So I'll fuck with you if I want to," she said, her voice calm and even slightly amused. She dipped her head again and Dennis felt the slick, hot tip of her tongue slide along his neck. It generated a response he couldn't prevent. Or ignore.

She straightened then and stood before him. Giving a quick glance to his lap, she let out a filthy, wicked laugh and stretched again, this time only for effect. Ending her performance with a melodramatic sigh, she turned on her heel and walked to the door of the security office.

"I'm goin' to go take a shower, darlin'. You just stay there and make yourself comfortable. I won't be too long." She smiled and flirtatiously waggled a few fingers at him, then disappeared.

Her presence lingered in the air as Dennis stared in speechless rage at the empty doorway. The hatred he felt for her defied words. Pulsing in his head was a murderous need to damage her for what she'd done to him and to his universe.

From the edge of his vision, the dull flash of the images appearing in sequence on the monitor's screen recaptured his attention and, reluctantly, he turned to face them again. The pictures turned Dennis's stomach but something, a sense of responsibility perhaps, or the unfamiliar and overwhelming sense of failure, prevented him from looking away. He watched the surveillance footage advance in a slow, staccato slide show, polling each camera in turn and presenting the scenes in full-color, five-second clips. The impersonal stillness of the images was haunting. Only the changing time stamp indicated that the world had not ended for everyone.

Tears filled Dennis's eyes and dripped unchecked down his clenched, aching cheeks as he looked at the screen. Those people had been his people, his staff, Micki's colleagues, who only hours before had been highly valued, brilliant professionals working toward a shared goal. Now, their stiff, cyanotic corpses were splayed grotesquely on outdoor gravel paths, across bamboo floors, in desk chairs. The positions of their bodies revealed the horror of their sudden deaths. Each face was frozen in a twisted, terrified rictus. Wide-open eyes bulged. Mouths hung open in screams now silenced or in last, vain attempts to inhale nontoxic air. Heads were thrown back as now stilled hands clawed at throats, leaving darkened, bloody tracks.

What aerobic bacteria that could survive in such a low-oxygen atmosphere had already begun to act upon the flesh and hasten its decomposition. Despite the tropical heat, however, no flies had alighted on the bodies, no ants or beetles or rodents had begun their gruesome tasks. For every animal, bird, and insect had also perished, enveloped by the poison cloud. They lay around the human corpses, just as still, just as silent.

The tapes offered no audio. It was just as well. Dennis knew that the only sounds to be heard beyond the walls of his bunker were the roar of the generators that were extending his own life, the whisper of the deadly wind moving through the fronds hanging limp from the branches of dying trees, and the susurrus of the tainted sea.

He had no idea how long he sat there, watching the endless, hypnotic loop of terrible images, evidence of the tranquil aftermath of unabashed madness.

"They're dead, Dennis. Get over it."

Dennis slowly turned to see Micki standing in the doorway. Her thin dress clung to her still-damp body and her hair fell in long, wet curls over her shoulders, dripping strategically onto her breasts and rendering sheer the single layer of fabric that covered them. His body overruled his brain's revulsion and responded to the sight of her.

She was a damned good-looking woman, sexy beyond reason.

When Dennis pulled his gaze away from the lushness of her body to focus on her face, he saw that her eyes were bright with amusement, her mouth curled in a mocking, knowing smile.

"So, sugar, has the survival instinct started to kick in?" Micki asked, her voice lower, more sultry than it had been a moment before. "I had a feelin' it might."

He said nothing, just held her gaze and willed his body to revile her.

"Oh, come on, Dennis," she said, a soft, cajoling note in her voice as she moved toward him in a languid stroll. "There are only the two of us here, with no possibility of escape or salvation. I mean, if you want to get it all over with, we could go outside and take a deep breath right now, or we could just relax and have some fun while we see what happens."

She came to a stop with a shrug, and the loose, open neckline of her short dress slid closer to the outer edge of her shoulder.

He curled his hands into angry fists. "You don't need to get in touch with anyone?" he asked. "Like your *boss*?"

She smiled. "I'm my own boss here, Dennis. But yes, there are people I need to contact. And I already have."

"I thought you said communications were down."

"Well, that e-mail I sent before everything went down got through just fine." She laughed. "I can't believe you believed me when I said Victoria sent that. You must really have been out of your wits. Anyway, it's only the island comms that are down. But I'm linked to a different satellite and sent another message just a few minutes ago, darlin'. Ours—mine, that is, not yours—is in a low-earth orbit, so it has come and gone and won't be within transceivin' range for a while." She walked farther into the room and boldly sashayed right by him, giving him a scorching look as she did so. "The link was perfectly clear, and the transmissions were fast.

Too bad you weren't around. But then, you might know when to log on again if you had been, and we can't have that."

"Where's the dish?"

She draped herself onto the chair next to his. The hem of her dress was high on her thighs, and the fabric flared out as she slowly twirled from side to side in the swivel chair.

"Too many questions, Dennis," she said with a flirtatious smile.

What the hell is she up to? "Why are you afraid to answer them?"

"Afraid? I'm not afraid of anything, Dennis. Not you, not your questions. The answer to the one you just asked is simply none of your business."

"Of course it's my business. But even if it weren't, I don't understand why you won't tell me. As you've said, neither of us will survive this. It's not possible for me to escape and you have no desire to. We might as well indulge in all the deathbed confessions we can." He shrugged and watched as she brought her swiveling to a stop directly opposite him, then slowly, sexily lifted and extended a leg to cross one knee over the other.

Whatever game it is you want to play, you miserable, murdering bitch, I intend to win it.

Changing his tactics, Dennis leaned back in his chair, smiled, and let his eyes wander over her body at a leisurely pace, lingering deliberately over her more interesting curves.

"I've always considered you one of the most beautiful women I've ever seen, Micki."

She laughed, partly with delight and partly with derision. "Is that your idea of a deathbed confession?"

"Not at all. It's a statement of fact. You're gorgeous.

Sexy." He moved his bound hands, making the metal handcuffs rattle. "Erotic."

She lifted an eyebrow. "So you like that, do you?"

"I might." He forced himself to keep smiling. "I've known a lot of women. Slept with a lot of women. You're unique among them."

"I should say I am. And I'm glad you finally have sex on your mind."

He lowered his voice and let his eyes wander again. "I thought it was on *your* mind. You're the one who brought up the survival instinct."

"It is on my mind, but I want to hear your confession," she replied, leaning back in her chair. "I want to find out what the man who had everything and lost it all will miss the most. Hmm? Countin' all your money? Makin' money? What will you miss the most when you're dead, Dennis?"

"Making love to beautiful women," he said without hesitation.

She laughed out loud. "Like me, I suppose. Good answer for a man with a one-track mind."

"I don't have a one-track mind, I'm just a man."

"Who's hoping for a last hurrah?"

Dennis jangled the handcuffs again. "As much as you are."

Micki didn't move, didn't reply. She just watched him in silence for a moment and fingered the pocket of her dress. The outline of the streamlined Taser was evident against her hip.

Come on, Micki. Let's play my *game and see who wins.*

He quirked an eyebrow at her and gave a short laugh. "You've called me greedy and arrogant, and you're not the first woman to do that, but you know me too well to make the mistake of thinking I'm stupid. You don't need the Taser. I'm not going to hurt you, Micki. You know that's not the way I work," he said, his voice gone low. "I admit that I was angry earlier. It was the shock. But I've wised up. You didn't leave me with any other options." He shrugged. "You could have killed me a dozen times over by now. Frankly, I'm not sure why you haven't. I suppose it doesn't matter. We both know I'm dependent on you for every minute that's left of my life. Everything I need to survive is in your head. Hurting you would be counterproductive."

She continued to watch him in silence, her hand still resting on the Taser.

"Why not have a last hurrah? There's not a hell of a lot else to do." He paused. "And since you've taken on the role of hostess, I think you owe it to me to keep me entertained. Don't you? I doubt either of us has forgotten how much fun we used to have together."

Dennis slowly turned up his palms as if in surrender. It was several long minutes before Micki extended one of her own and touched him. Then she leaned across the chair and brought her face to his. He allowed himself to smile as she lowered her face to his for a long, deep, slow kiss.

It would be one of her last.

CHAPTER

2:20 P.M., Sunday, October 26, Taino

After sweeping the area with high-powered binoculars as they made their approach, Simon Broadhurst and the two security agents with him beached the inflatable on the narrow strip of sand along the northern tip of the island. Wearing full masks and breathing through regulators from the tanks strapped to their backs, the men stepped out of the small boat and fanned out, using a crouching run to make themselves smaller targets. All the while, they kept their eyes moving and senses alert.

Their mission was to quickly survey the island and determine if anyone had survived. But they all knew that some survivors—if there were any—might not want to be found. They carried their guns at the ready, out of their waterproof sheaths. After a few tense but uneventful moments on the beach, Simon realized that the sounds of birdsong and droning insects meant that not everything on the island had died. Unlike what had been reported on the south end of the island, here no bird carcasses littered the beach, no dead fish floated in the water.

Cautiously pulling the regulator out of his mouth, Simon took a short, shallow breath.

Nothing.

"The air is clear. Whatever is on the other end of the island hasn't made it here yet," he called to the other two men as he closed the tank's valve and pushed the mask onto his forehead. The security agents did the same as they kept their gazes on the dense undergrowth that closely bordered the beach.

Feeling triumphant and oddly calm, Simon reached for the radio unit strapped to his shoulder and called in a quick report to a still-fuming Maggy Patterson.

The three men regrouped to make a quick study of the steep rise before them, thickly covered with vegetation. There was one narrow, groomed path that led from the beach to the bunker—a path intended as an emergency evacuation route *from* the bunker. Its sheer ledges and long drops hadn't been an issue during training, when they were descending the trail in full camo gear. Climbing it in wetsuits with full air tanks on their backs was going to be a royal bitch.

"Well, lads, let's get this party started," Simon muttered, and led his team across the sand.

4:30 P.M., Sunday, October 26, Taino

A sated, exhausted Dennis rolled onto his back in the custom-made bed in the bunker's bedroom suite. Sex with Micki had always been measurable on the Richter scale, but today it had taken some determination to be able to look past the reality that the woman in his bed was an eerie combination of cold-blooded killer and hot-blooded lover.

"I think that's called going out with a bang," he said, looking at her face. *Not that I'm going anywhere. But you will be.*

"Oh, I could have sworn I heard a few whimpers, too," Micki mumbled, her eyes closed, her long blond hair a wild mess flung across the sheets.

"Only a few?" Dennis ran a hand down Micki's long, lean, very naked body.

"No more. Not now," she said, rolling away.

"Do you have to be somewhere?" he asked with a laugh.

Micki slowly pushed herself upright, leaning on one hand as the other brushed her hair out of her eyes. "As a matter of fact, I do."

"Soon?"

"Too many questions," she said crisply.

"Well, is there time for a bath before you dash off to wherever you're going?"

She hesitated. "A shower."

"Baths are more fun," Dennis said, lifting a section of her hair and wrapping it around his hand. He wondered briefly if it would be strong enough to strangle her. "After all, Micki, it's not like we have to conserve water. There's a thirty-day supply, and we won't be here that long."

"I don't have time for a bath," she said, swinging her legs off the bed.

"How about you go do your thing and I'll run the bath? You won't be long," he said, sliding closer to her and nuzzling her neck. "When you come back we can pick up where we left off."

"You think I'm going to leave you here?" she asked, looking over her shoulder with raised eyebrows. "Alone?"

He feigned surprise. "Well, you already told me you don't want me knowing where your dish is. The one programmed to connect to your LEO satellite. So I didn't think you would take me with you." He paused and narrowed his eyes at her. "Or were you intending to kill me now, so soon after sex? Like a black widow."

She blinked, and then a sly smile crossed her mouth. "Perhaps I am."

He returned her smile. *You crazy bitch.*

"The hell with that," he murmured, then moved his head and began to trail his lips down her spine. "There are a few more good times to be had. When I'm too tired for sex you can kill me. How about that?"

"Sounds good, Dennis, except for one small thing. I have no way to lock you up other than those handcuffs."

He shrugged and began to play with her hair again. "You don't have to lock me up, Micki. Just turn on the cameras and the motion sensors. If I leave the bedroom area, the alarm will go off and you'll be able to see where I am. But for the record, I'm not planning to go anywhere." He shrugged again. "There's nowhere to go. Stepping outside would mean instant death, and you've changed all the codes on the systems, so I can't contact anyone on the outside anyway."

"So you're going to be a good guy and stay here because I ask you to," she said, her voice heavy with sarcasm.

"What other options do I have?" he asked.

She considered it as she lifted her dress from the floor and slipped it over her head.

"All right, I'll give it a try," she said easily as she stood up and walked to the door. "I won't be long. You stay here. The alarms and cameras will be on. If you attempt to leave this room, I'll find you and kill you."

Her unnatural calm sent an involuntary chill through Dennis. He smiled against it.

"It's a deal. I'll run the bath." He paused and lifted an eyebrow as he added some heat to his grin. "Make sure you come back by way of the wine cellar. Bring back a bottle of something cold and bubbly. There's some good stuff in there. We might as well celebrate our last few hours of life in style."

"Not a bad idea," she murmured. Then, without a backward glance, Micki left the bedroom, closing the door behind her. Less than a minute later, the small, glowing light on the alarm control panel changed from green to red. The alarm system was on. Exit doors were armed, motion sensors were activated, and cameras were rolling.

When, after ten minutes, none of the door alarms sounded, Dennis knew Micki had taken the precaution of purposely disarming one door to the outside. The system log and surveillance footage would show which one.

Hiding his smile from the hidden cameras, whose coverage encompassed his entire bedroom, Dennis got off the bed, balanced a moment on still-weak knees, then walked gingerly into the large bathroom. He turned on the taps and began to fill the deep tub.

The tub was full and he was in it by the time he saw the light on the alarm system's control panel revert to green. Seconds later Micki entered the bathroom, bearing a bottle of vintage Cristal and two flutes, which she set onto the polished obsidian countertop.

"You kept your word," she said, peeling off her dress and letting it swish gently to the floor.

"Of course I did. I always do. I'm counting on you doing the same," he said with a grin as she climbed into the water.

"I don't recall makin' you any promises," she replied. "Except to kill you."

"Well, maybe you can just promise me that it will be quick and painless, then," he said softly as he slid his arms around her warm, pliant body and brought her close for a lingering kiss.

Breaking off a long moment later, he glanced across

the room at the Champagne sweating elegantly in the room's steamy air.

"There's only one thing that could make this moment better," he said, releasing Micki and standing up. "And it's almost within reach."

From the wall of mirrors in front of him, he watched her smile widen as he climbed out of the tub and walked, naked and dripping, across the cool, polished lava-rock floor to where the wine stood on the counter. He reached for the bottle and unwrapped the foil collar and then, deliberately making eye contact with her, eased the cork out of the bottle with a soft hiss.

After carefully filling one of the Baccarat flutes she'd brought with her, Dennis put down the bottle, dried his hands, and turned to face her.

She frowned. "Where's mine?"

"You don't get one."

"What?" She began to rise out of the tub, her eyes wide with alarm.

"No, don't get out of the tub." He held up a hand and spoke in a soothing voice. "When I said there was only one thing that could make this moment better, Micki, I wasn't talking about the wine." He bent down and fished the Taser from the pocket of the dress that lay near his feet. Then, with a cold smile, he lifted the flute of wine in a toast.

"I was talking about solitude."

He watched her expression change from panic to terror as he aimed the fifty-thousand-volt device at her and pulled the trigger.

The prongs embedded themselves in the side of her neck. Her scream lasted until the splash, but her body convulsed for several minutes. Whether that was due to the single powerful shock he'd administered or because her muscles were unable to respond to any voluntary commands and she was, therefore, drowning, he wasn't sure. Actually, he didn't care.

Feeling more satisfied with himself than he had in a long time, Dennis calmly took a sip of wine and watched her body flail with increasingly less vigor.

It didn't take long for the splashing to stop. Wanting to ensure that there would be no more unpleasant surprises at her hands, Dennis remained in the room watching her body float face down in the water until he'd finished two leisurely glasses of Champagne.

Then he dressed and made his way to the control room where he reviewed all the footage from the closed-circuit security cameras she'd activated at his suggestion. In no time, he found footage of Micki going out the door, retrieving a case of equipment, and setting up a small antenna apparatus. Dennis slowed down the images and zoomed in as she keyed in her passwords and coordinates, then he sat back, smiling, and took another satisfied sip of wine.

She'd done it all in the open without wearing a hazmat suit.

Which made perfect sense now that he thought about it. He didn't have to stay in the bunker. Under such calm conditions, the adulterated methane would hug the surface as it moved to the west and not come near the high, northern tip of the island unless those conditions changed.

He was about to stop the videotape when he saw her head snap to the left as if something had alerted her. Reaching into the dark case that had held the equipment, she withdrew a large handgun and rose slowly to her feet. Bringing it up in front of her, both hands gripping it, arms fully extended, she called out. There was no audio with the footage, but Dennis could tell from her stance that Micki had not been afraid.

He stared in disbelief as three men wearing the uniform wet suits of his security team emerged from the dense vegetation several yards away from her. They wore air tanks on their backs; their masks were off. They all had their arms in the air and the center one, the leader, spoke to Micki with a smile on his face as he lowered his arms.

Before Dennis had a chance to put names to their faces, Micki popped off three shots, leaving a small round hole in each man's forehead and spattering the trees and shrubs behind them with a dark red spray interspersed with blobs of lighter-colored goo. All three bodies rocked backward and dropped in crumpled heaps at the edge of the clearing.

Micki calmly lowered the gun, walked to the bodies, methodically removed the radio units from their shoulders, and threw the units far into the brush. Then she returned to her position, kneeling in front of the laptop she'd hooked up to the satellite equipment, and continued her transmission.

As he watched her carefully repack the antenna array into its box, Dennis set the wineglass onto the desk with hands that shook from a mixture of shock and fury.

This madness has to stop.

CHAPTER 28

It was a nice, quiet afternoon. The wind had picked up a little but it was still warm and Linda Carson had just sat down for what felt like the first time that day. With a grin, her husband eased open the screw top of a bottle of a New Zealand sauvignon blanc, poured some into a travel mug, and handed it to her. They toasted each other silently.

Both kids had only just fallen asleep for their nap and the minivan's windows were closed for the moment against even the quiet, drowsy sounds of a sultry afternoon in the Keys. Linda would open them in a few minutes and raise the special screens they had bought, but not until she was positive the soft rustle of the trees, the whining drone of the crickets, and the symphony of frogs wouldn't wake the children.

Right now Hunter and Chloë were still in what she and Dan called "the red zone." For the next few minutes, *anything* could wake them. The slightest human noise—the creak of a lawn chair, a parental cough or whisper—would instantly wake the babies, which would mean that Linda would have to endure another half hour of singing "Twinkle, Twinkle, Little Star" in a breathy whisper and Dan would have to listen to it. Better that the two of them just stayed quiet for a few more minutes until the children were deeply asleep.

This place, a small clearing in the midst of a little thicket of scrubby pine and wildly overgrown hibiscus only twenty feet from the road, was completely hidden. It was their favorite spot in the world. It wasn't actually a legal campsite, situated as it was on the edge of the Crocodile Lake National Wildlife Refuge, but a legal campsite wasn't what they had been looking for when they'd come here one moonlit night during spring break ten years ago. They'd only known each other for a few hours at that point, and had been looking for a quiet, private nook or cranny for some urgently required bonking.

It was so private and so romantic that they'd kept coming back, year after year, despite being able to afford to book into any of the resort hotels nearby. This was their little Eden—they'd celebrated new jobs here, gotten engaged here, spent their wedding night here while en route to Key West, conceived both kids here. In ten years of reasonably frequent visits, no one had ever bothered them.

The vehicles they drove had changed over the years, from Dan's Camaro, to Linda's Camry, to his Explorer, to the Range Rover he'd bought her when they got married, and now the luxury minivan they'd bought last year. With an infant and a toddler to accommodate now, it was getting a little cramped, but staying in the van was safer than pitching a tent and less obvious than parking an RV would have been.

Linda jumped as they heard a series of small, unlikely noises coming from the woods behind them. Even though the small crashes didn't sound like human footsteps, she'd never known any animal to be so noisy. There was no urgency to the sounds, just the noise of brush and branches being pushed aside clumsily. With a reassuring look, Dan picked up her hand and kissed the back of it, and she returned his smile.

A frown crossed his face then and he dropped her hand to cover his mouth as he began to cough. A second later Linda felt a strange, burning tickle at the back of her own throat. Dan stood up, knocking over the folding chair he'd been sitting in, not caring that it banged into the side of the vehicle and instantly triggered screams from both children.

Coughing herself, and feeling a deeply uncomfortable tightness in her lungs, Linda stood up to go to the babies, but stopped in horror as she saw Dan bend almost double as he gasped for breath.

Unable to speak for the dryness in her throat, Linda moved to Dan's side in time to break his fall, and flung him onto his back as soon as he was on the ground. His eyes were bulging and his hands clawed frantically at his shirt until they went limp and the fight went out of him. Before her disbelieving eyes, Dan's face began turning bizarrely dark and bluish against the mop of white-blond curls surrounding it. Recognizing death, Linda tried to scream, but creating sound had become impossible.

Reaching for the car's fender to support herself as she tried to drag herself to her feet, Linda could think only of getting away from whatever was attacking her, of getting into the car where her babies were and taking them away from there. Reaching for the door handle, she fell, her hand only partially easing her hard landing on the sandy ground. Her lungs were on fire and her brain was frozen with fear as she stared at the door handle, just out of reach.

Her vision dimmed then, and the sound of the babies' cries grew faint, and then she heard nothing at all.

Strapped in their car seats and cocooned inside the closed vehicle, Hunter and Chloë Carson continued to breathe unpoisoned air, and they continued to wail.

29
CHAPTER

4:25 P.M., Sunday, October 26, Bolling Air Force Base, Washington, D.C.

"I really don't care about regulations at this point, sir," Sam said, trying as best he could to keep his voice from rising in the face of military implacability.

And imbecility, from his point of view. He hadn't busted his ass and his credit limit to get from Gainesville to Washington just to stare at the unadorned walls of a small, bare room in the security building next to the front gate of Bolling Air Force Base. Nor had he counted on spending so damned much time trying to make his point to a crew-cutted and uniformed guy who was probably ten years younger than him and whose expression hadn't changed in fifteen minutes. It said "Don't even try to fuck with me" loud and clear.

Sam was ignoring it.

"I've got to get in to see the director of national intelligence. It's a matter of national security, a matter of life and death," Sam repeated for what had to be the tenth time. "And I mean that literally."

"So you've said. But you can't go on base unless

someone is expecting you and you're cleared. I can't clear you now. It's Sunday afternoon."

"Your *computers* don't work on Sunday?" Sam asked, not hiding his derision. "The annual defense budget is how many trillion dollars, and y'all give *machinery* a day off?"

"Sam." With just the one word, Marty let Sam know that he was acting like a prick, that Marty was losing patience with the whole idea, and that Sam would be better off just shutting up.

Sam turned to glare at his friend. *You could get your ass over here and help me.*

Marty, who was sitting in a hard chair against the wall and looking mostly pissed off and only slightly scared shitless, very subtly moved his head from side to side, then looked away. Annoyed anew, Sam looked back at the military cop in front of him.

Having Sabina here might have helped.

"Okay, I understand what you're sayin'," he lied, trying to put as conciliatory a note as he could muster into his voice. "But, look, you've already searched our stuff and frisked us. You know we're not carryin' anything illegal or dangerous. And I'm sure you've already run our Social Security numbers, so you know we're not felons. I'm tryin' to make it clear that I'm not a whackjob or some kind of crazy person—"

The cop said nothing, only lifted an eyebrow.

Well, thank you, son, that says it all.

Sam took a deep breath and started over. "Look, sir, you've got my ID. It says right there that I'm Sam Briscoe, Professor Sam Hill Briscoe of the University of Florida's School of Natural Resources and Environment. I'm a teacher and a researcher, not a terrorist or anything else." He paused and gave the cop a good ol' boy smile. "Let me tell you somethin' else. Do you know why I'm Sam and not Samuel? Because I was named for Uncle Sam, that's why, and Uncle Sam isn't Uncle Samuel. He's just Uncle Sam. And do you know why I was named that? Because I was born in Americus, Georgia, and my parents thought it was a nice thing to do. And I've got two sisters, named Libby and Jessie— Liberty and Justice." He nodded. "So there's my patriotism right there. I'm true blue straight from the womb. So I'm not about to do anything crazy, I've just got to get in to see the—"

"I know. The director of national intelligence. And I'm telling you that you can't." The cop's lips barely moved but his mile-wide shoulders went back a little and the fingers that were as thick as sausages refolded themselves on the table in front of him.

"Well, can you at least call her? She's got to be here. *You* may not know about this, but there's a seriously big-ass crisis going on fifty miles off the Keys," Sam replied, his frustration level rising again. "Can't you just call her office and see if she'll let me in? Please? Sir."

Clearly unimpressed, the cop stood up, gave both of them a hard, scathing look, and then left the room.

"Well, that went well."

Sam stood up and turned to face Marty, who was looking back at him with a face as dark as a thundercloud. "How else are you supposed to deal with—"

"Watch it, Sam. The room is probably bugged," Marty interrupted.

Sam glared at him. "I was goin' to say 'How else are you supposed to deal with the military but by tryin' to pull rank?' That's all."

"You don't have any rank to pull, Sam. You're a

civilian," Marty replied in the same sarcastic tone of voice and stood up to begin pacing around the small room. "What the hell did you mean by coming up here? And why the hell did you have to drag me into it?"

"I didn't *drag* you into anything. You *offered* to pick me up at the airport."

"Well, I didn't know you were going to go postal," Marty snapped. "When you called, you said you were coming up here because you needed to talk to some people. You conveniently neglected to tell me who it was or that they didn't know you were coming. You might as well be trying to get in to see the president." Marty shook his head in disgust. "What the hell were you thinking?"

"I was thinkin' of tryin' to get someone to get movin' on this catastrophe in the makin'."

Marty rolled his eyes. "You think they don't know about it? Or that they should have contacted you to ask your opinion or let you know what they're doing about it? God Almighty, Sam, sometimes you're a complete and utter idiot. Not to mention a total prick."

"Well, thank you very much, *Methane Man*," Sam shot over his shoulder.

Just then the door opened and the military cop who had been in the room earlier walked in, flanked by two other uniformed military police officers.

Marty shot Sam a murderous look but even without that Sam's stomach would have still plummeted to somewhere around his kneecaps.

"Dr. Briscoe, the director of national intelligence will see you in her office. These officers will escort you."

It took Sam a few seconds to process the fact that he wasn't about to take a one-way ride on the Gitmo Express. "She's goin' to see us?"

"Yes, sir, that's what I said. There's a car waiting outside. Please go with these officers."

"Thanks, man," Sam said, grabbing his backpack off the floor and practically galloping to the door. He stuck his hand out to the cop. "No hard feelings."

The cop looked at Sam's hand, then at his face, and didn't say a thing.

Dropping his hand to his side, Sam looked at Marty, who had joined him at the door. Without another word, they took the neon-orange adhesive-backed temporary security tags they were handed and stuck them onto their shirts, then left the room behind one of the military police officers. The other closed ranks behind them.

No one spoke as they climbed into a large SUV parked outside the rear entrance of the building with its roof-mounted blue lights flashing. The short trip through the streets and mostly empty parking lots of the base was quick. They entered a nondescript building, then were whisked through security and escorted into the elevator and to the top floor in near-complete silence.

No pissed-off girlfriend, no phalanx of university brass, no team of armed and annoyed military police officers could ever be as intimidating as the three people facing Sam when he walked into Director Lucy Denton's office.

"Good afternoon, Dr. Briscoe, Dr. Martin. I'm Lucy Denton. This is Mr. Taylor, and this is Ms. Clark, secretary of national security for Taino," the director said, not rising from her place behind her desk. "Please have a seat."

Looking around, Sam had to admit that the office of the director of national intelligence was almost comfortable. The room's color scheme was just a little too cool, the chair's seat just a little too short, the tight, exhausted faces of the two women and dead-eyed gaze of the one man just a little too grim.

Lucy Denton smiled at Sam. She seemed almost friendly. He didn't know much about her. In interviews and articles, her background was never discussed, just alluded to in vague terms. So Sam, like most members of the public, knew her only as Queen of the Spooks, with the face of an angel and, reputedly, the compassion of one of Hell's coldest minions.

"Dr. Briscoe, Dr. Collins, let me thank you for making the trip to see me. I apologize for the somewhat chilly reception you received initially, and I'm very glad that you persevered. Rest assured, there won't be any charges filed."

Still a little stunned, Sam nodded once to accept her thanks and apology, surprised not only that she had offered either, but that she'd done so with such cool grace. Between the situation in the Caribbean and his own audacity in barging up to Washington to bang on doors until someone listened to him, he was damn near shaking in his boots. Lucy Denton's controlled calmness was downright eerie under the circumstances.

"You're an atmospheric scientist, Dr. Briscoe?'"

"Yes, ma'am."

"And you're a geologist, Dr. Collins?"

"Sort of. I study the geochemistry of Eastern Caribbean trenches. It pulls in a lot of disciplines."

She nodded. "And you're both here because you are aware of the atmospheric anomaly we're experiencing in the wake of the plane crash near Taino?"

What brand of bullshit is this? Sam and Marty glanced at each other.

"With all due respect, Director Denton, that's no anomaly and it's not related to the crash. It's a methane eruption," Marty said, looking steadily at her. "That area of the seafloor sits on top of a huge bed of methane hydrate, and this morning's seismic activity must have opened some sort of fissure that's allowing the methane to escape."

"What seismic activity?" she asked.

Sam thought Marty made an admirable attempt to keep the disgust off his face as he replied. "There were two seismic events in that exact region this morning. It appears that the first underwater event—I'm calling it an explosion—"

"Excuse me, but why would you call it an explosion?" Director Denton's expression didn't change, but from the corner of his eye, Sam caught Victoria Clark glance quickly at the third man in the room, Tom Taylor.

"Because that's what it seems like to me. The signature of the event indicated that it definitely wasn't an earthquake," Marty said bluntly. "Neither was the second event, the one that opened up the fissure. The first event happened in an area where there are a lot of underwater cliffs. It most likely triggered a small landslide. The second event could have been another explosion, or part of the wall collapsing spontaneously. With all the activity that was already under way, it's hard to tell. But the combined effect would have caused a change in subterranean pressures, which could destabilize parts of the ocean floor, opening a fissure or widening a shallow one that already existed."

"Doesn't that happen all the time with submarine earthquakes?" Director Denton asked.

Marty shifted in his chair. "Not like this. Not into a methane bed. See, a sudden opening into a methane hydrate bed would allow seawater to mingle with the crystals and change them to a gaseous state *in situ*. At those depths, gas would be expelled as if it were under high pressure—because it is." He fumbled and caught himself. "Under extremely high pressure, I mean. The water would continue to fill the void left in the cavity." He stopped and shrugged.

"Then what?" Tom Taylor asked.

"I'm not sure," Marty replied after a minute. "The thing is, there are a whole bunch of things going on down there right now that no one has seen before. We can only go on conjecture and hypothesis. I think this activity is putting stress on otherwise relatively stable fault lines, as well as on features we call 'pockmarks,' which are essentially partial tunnels into the clathrate beds."

Nobody said anything for a few seconds, then Sam looked at Marty. "In English this time."

Marty gave him a tight smile and turned back to face Lucy Denton. "Okay, in plain words, I think the second event happened because an existing fault gave way. Considering that the Caribbean is a highly seismic area with several tectonic plates rubbing against each other, especially right there, it's something that could be repeated. And that could be a problem."

"So what you're saying is that more of these events could happen, which could open more of these fissures and release more methane into the ocean and atmosphere?" Lucy Denton asked.

"Yes, that's what I'm saying."

Hardly aware he was holding his breath, Sam looked at the three officials in the room, one from Taino and two from the U.S., waiting for a reaction that, after a minute, he realized wasn't going to happen.

What the hell is wrong with you people?

"Director Denton," Sam said earnestly, "the size and volume of the methane-hydrate beds down there haven't been fully determined. All we know is that a serious amount of methane is entering the atmosphere right now. If a pockmark collapses, we'll have more. This is serious trouble, y'all. *Serious* trouble. Like on a planetary scale."

"Feel free to elaborate on that, Dr. Briscoe," Tom Taylor said dryly.

"Well, thank you, I will." Sam stood up and paced to the nearest wall, then turned abruptly and jammed his hands into the front pockets of his jeans. "Okay. Here's something to feed the number crunchers: The earth's atmosphere contains approximately three gigatons of methane. That's three *billion* metric tons. Nine zeroes. Big number. But it's still only considered a trace element. That three gigatons translates to about seventeen hundred parts per billion. Breathing that in the standard mixture of everything else in the atmosphere isn't a problem. Problems happen when that number rises too high. For instance, sediment cores dating back to about fifty-five million years ago indicate an event in which a few *thousand* G-tons of methane were released into the atmosphere and the ocean in a relatively short time frame. The event is called the Paleocene Eocene Thermal Maximum because it warmed up the oceans by about five degrees Celsius at intermediate depths."

He looked at them to determine if they were following him, then caught himself.

They're not college freshman. They have a stake in this.

Taking a quick breath, he continued. "The best guess

is that the release took roughly one thousand years. I know. That sounds like a long time. But the effect of atmospheric methane fluctuations gets more interesting when you look at something called the Permian Mass Extinction, which happened about 250 million years ago, when only some of the very earliest dinosaur-type critters were draggin' their tails through the swamps." He stopped and shrugged.

"To save you a lot of technospeak, I'll describe the event by sayin' that the oceans burped, so to speak, on a huge scale. There's a pretty damned tootin' high level of confidence that that burp—which was a *rapid* increase in the level of atmospheric methane—is what killed off about ninety-five percent of the marine species that existed at the time and about seventy percent of the land species, and it happened pretty damned tootin' fast. Marty here can provide more information on this, but some scientists have speculated that what caused that 'burp' was a clathrate 'melt': an enormous release of undersea methane hydrate, which is *exactly* what we've got goin' on down near Taino. And when I say enormous, I'm talkin' to the tune of maybe *ten thousand* gigatons. That's thirteen zeroes, in case you're interested. To put that in perspective, the atmospheric level of methane sittin' on top of Taino right now is *170,000 parts* per billion—one hundred times what it should be. Now, yes, that's gonna diffuse, eventually, but that's still a hell of a lot of methane. Pardon the language. If that fissure keeps spewin' the way it is, we're in for a real mess of trouble."

He had been gratified to hear the woman from Taino, Victoria Clark, give a little gasp of shock when he mentioned the numbers. Director Denton, however, just blinked, and Tom Taylor glanced at his watch.

"If you don't mind, could you define 'pretty damned tootin' fast'?" Taylor asked.

Sam glared at him for a minute as politely as he could, then let out a frustrated breath. Marty began talking before Sam could get a word out.

"Mr. Taylor, what Sam and I are talking about here is considered fast in geologic time, but it doesn't really matter. The point is that during both events nearly all terrestrial and marine life on earth was killed very rapidly, in real time. Especially near the coastlines. And the reason they died is because oxygen-dependent creatures *can't breathe methane*." Marty paused. "We can't say for sure exactly how fast the gas was released during the Permian event, but it was fast. Bubbles don't linger, they rise and burst. The release was massive and sudden, and so were the results."

"Okay, I've got a better analogy than an ocean burp," Sam said. "Different gas but the same result. Do y'all remember hearing about a real nasty event in Africa about a decade ago, at Lake Nyos in Cameroon? No? Well, a whole village, about eighteen hundred people and all their animals, got wiped out overnight by a massive carbon dioxide release from the bottom of a volcanic lake. A 350-foot-tall fountain of carbon dioxide and water erupted in the middle of the lake, creating a wave that surged seventy-five feet up the shores. The cloud killed things in a radius of fifteen miles. The eruption in Cameroon lasted for a few hours, but its effect was immediate. Everything in the village was alive at sunset and dead by morning, okay? Could have killed them all in ten minutes, could have taken an hour or two, but they all died."

Sam tossed up his hands and stalked away from the desk and their carefully bland faces. "Think about it.

Two hundred and fifty million years ago the wind currents were different; so were the ocean currents. Everything was different then. The continents weren't where they are now and there was only one anyway. Didn't matter." He stopped pacing and threw his arms open wide, his voice rising. "The methane stuck around in the atmosphere, migrated around the entire planet pretty damned quickly, displacin' the oxygen as it moved, and things began dyin' off. It took a little while but pretty soon plants, critters, anything that needed oxygen was turnin' back to pure carbon."

He crossed the room again and, placing his hands on Lucy Denton's desk, leaned onto them and nearly into her face. To her credit she didn't flinch. She didn't even blink.

"Ma'am, what Marty and I are tellin' you is that *methane doesn't just go away*." He straightened up and took a deep breath.

At last, Victoria Clark spoke up. "It has to diffuse as it mixes with the air, though. Doesn't it? The concentration—"

Sam nodded, cutting her off. "Sure, Ms. Clark, it will diffuse if there isn't much of it. But there's a lot of it comin' out of your waters right now. The long-term effects are going to be nasty, but the short-term effects are downright scary as hell." He paused. "They're linked. The long-term and short-term effects are linked. There's something called the 'Clathrate Gun Hypothesis,' which someone came up with after studying that Permian event I just told you about. The theory is that if a methane-hydrate release achieves a critical mass, it could create an uncontrollable feedback loop; the warming atmosphere will cause the oceans to warm, which will cause more methane to be released. Okay, the loop is a hypothesis, but what methane will do to the temperature of the atmosphere is a *fact*. Methane lingers in the atmosphere *as methane* for about eight years, and it's about twenty times more effective as a greenhouse gas than carbon dioxide is. And after those eight years, it oxidizes to *become* carbon dioxide, and that remains in the atmosphere for about a century."

He paused and stared straight at Victoria Clark. "That means the effect of the releases that are happenin' *right now* off your little island will be with us forever. So not only will what's bubblin' up out of the ocean kill a lot of things that try to breathe while they're caught in that plume blowin' off your island, Ms. Clark, but all that methane is goin' to hang around for years, as obvious as a horse turd in the milk pitcher." He caught himself and grimaced. "Beg pardon, again. But my point is, what's happenin' is goin' to kill a lot of people in the path of that plume right quick, and make life damned miserable for the rest of us for a long time."

"You know what volume of methane is entering the atmosphere from this release. We know how large the deposit was that we drilled into. If we could—" Victoria Clark stopped suddenly and her eyes darted to Tom Taylor's face. Sam looked from Victoria to Tom to Marty, whose eyes had gone wide and whose mouth had sagged open a little.

"Did you say you *drilled into* the methane bed?" Marty asked.

Victoria hesitated, then nodded. "Yes. We drilled into it."

"From where? There's no rig. There's no production facility—"

"From an installation on the seafloor." Victoria stood up, crossed the room as if her body couldn't stop itself from moving. A moment later, she got a grip on herself and came to a stop, then leaned against the wall near Lucy's desk.

Sam noticed that as calm as she appeared, her hands were folded into white-knuckled fists and her disconcertingly blue eyes were tense and shadowed with dark circles.

"Dr. Briscoe, I remember meeting you several years ago when you visited Taino. Dr. Collins, I know you were expected to arrive next week," she said coolly. "You are both experts with regard to the topic of methane and are highly regarded in your respective fields of research. You know of President Cavendish's interest in methane hydrate. It shouldn't be much of a surprise to you that the Climate Research Institute developed a mining system. But what happened today on the seafloor has happened in defiance of every statistical risk we studied, and the extent of the damage has overwhelmed our ability to contain or repair it. We need some answers and we need some help."

Well, that explains why they let us in here.

Sam met Marty's eyes, which were on fire with anger.

"I appreciate the information, Ms. Clark," Marty said, his voice not nearly as even as it had been a few minutes ago. "But that deposit you opened up is only the tip of the problem. I won't even get into how environmentally reckless it was to drill in such a seismic area but, after this morning's landslide, the effects of that drilling are indisputable. After just a few hours, we saw the subsidence of one nearby area of seafloor that caused a small pockmark to open up. You can be sure that that pockmark implosion won't be the only one. The real risk is precipitating a catastrophic underwater landslide—one much bigger than the last—and that risk is growing as we speak."

"It wasn't a pockmark implosion, Dr. Collins. The place where the methane is breaking the surface is directly over the spot where the pipeline enters the seafloor," Victoria replied quietly. Marty's eyes widened. "As for another landslide doing more damage, I think that risk can be ruled out. There was only one pipeline laid. We were planning to do some testing before we opened up the rest of the bed. In that respect, I suppose we're lucky."

"You're joking, right?" Marty said, then paused. "According to what that wildman's been saying on the Internet—and I haven't heard anybody in this room contradict him—that first event was a planned detonation. And now you're admitting that whatever it did apparently led to the pipe getting ripped out of the way. Well, here's some breaking news for you: because of all the unnatural seismic activity in the area combined with the fault-ridden structure of the seafloor there, whatever happens next—and something *will* happen—is going to be *natural,* which means *unpredictable.*"

"Dr. Collins—"

"Let me finish," Marty interrupted, looking directly at Victoria. "Lady, that methane bed you poked into is *huge.* And judging by what's coming up, I'd guess that pipe you shoved into it isn't small. I'll tell you right now that if another underwater landslide happens in the right spot, it could rip open a fissure that could result in the release of one gigaton, maybe more, of methane *all at once.* That would be a thirty-three percent increase in the concentration of atmospheric methane over an incredibly short period of time. I'm talking *days* here, or weeks at the most. And, like Sam just said, atmospheric methane is bad news—" He stopped abruptly and shrugged, then sat back in his chair. "But I guess it really doesn't matter much at this point, does it?"

"Get back on point, Dr. Collins. You've just stopped making sense," Lucy snapped.

"Director Denton," Sam said quickly, knowing Marty was about to blow. "Marty's makin' perfect sense. What he means is that none of it will matter because none of us would likely be around to care. As I was sayin', the thing that made the Permian event so remarkable was the suddenness of the release. We're not even sure how 'sudden' it was, but nearly all oxygen-dependent life on earth died because of it, and very quickly, long before the release itself ended. And there were no people around then."

He pointed toward the window and the Capitol dome visible through it. "There were no megacities huggin' coastlines fifty miles from the release point, no populated islands, no boaters, no cruise ships, no fleets of submarines, no airplanes zippin' around at thirty thousand feet. What's happenin' right now, this minute, is that, thanks to Dennis Cavendish and that crazy GAIA guy, the earth is *pumpin'* methane through highly traveled waters and into the air supply of highly populated areas. When those crystals start to melt into gas, ma'am, their volume expands one hundred and sixty times. Do you have any idea what that means?" He stopped and shook his head. "But what's really concernin' me is that the gas comin' up isn't pure, and nobody—NASA, NOAA, nobody—knows what's in it. Or if they do, they're keepin' it real quiet. So that mixture of methane-and-whatever comin' out of President Cavendish's big ol', badass pipeline is huggin' the surface." He stopped and pushed a hand through his hair, then returned to his seat, his energy suddenly gone. "Don't any of y'all get it?"

"You're saying this is the apocalypse."

Sam looked up at Tom's impassive face. "Call it whatever the hell you want to, Mr. Taylor. Call it the Dance of the Methane Fairies and set it to music," he snapped. "All that methane will kill off living things much faster than any models have ever predicted, even the doomsday ones. If that storm brewin' off the Bahamas changes course and moves toward Taino, you could see a hurricane form that would make Katrina and Rita and Simone look as scary as a Beastie Boys reunion tour."

Finally, Victoria Clark seemed a little alarmed. "A hurricane? Wouldn't the high winds disperse the methane?" she demanded.

Sam shook his head. "Nope. It would get sucked into the spin and concentrated, and the temperature in the convection tower would shoot way up."

"Why is that bad?" she asked.

Sam looked at her. "The methane will drive up the temperature inside the storm, which increases the speed and drives down the air pressure, which lets the circulation get bigger. And it keeps on goin' that way. Like I said, it's a feedback leap. Before you know it, that hurricane's winds could be movin' at five hundred miles an hour and spannin' the Atlantic. Okay? *That's* what I'm talkin' about."

Looking around, Sam was satisfied. The so-called intelligence experts were finally looking a bit green around the gills. He smiled coldly at Lucy Denton. "Of course, that's a worst-case scenario. What's more likely is that the methane gas will collect in some places, like urban areas, for instance. And if the concentration gets high enough in those places, and I wouldn't rule that out, that gas could ignite. Then, literally, you'll see fire in the sky and all Hell will have broken loose."

"Dr. Briscoe, let's keep this in the realm of the believable."

Sam couldn't help himself. He rolled his eyes against the condescension in Lucy Denton's voice. "Unfortunately, Ms. Denton, I'm serious. Marty and me—we're not makin' this up. It's a simple fact of basic chemistry that air containing less than about five and a half percent of methane won't explode. If it gets higher than that and there's a big spark, say a lightning strike or a fire nearby, exothermic combustion—that means an explosion—is a distinct possibility. And I'm talkin' about one *hell* of a big bang, ma'am."

"If the methane replaces the oxygen and doesn't ignite—"

Sam turned to look directly into Victoria Clark's exotic blue eyes. She stopped talking.

"Okay, there's a good set of choices: asphyxiation or combustion," Sam said. "They'll be either cold and blue or charred and smokin', but either way, there will be a lot of dead people around, Ms. Clark."

"Dr. Briscoe—"

Sam swiveled his head to look at Lucy. "With all due respect, Director Denton, we need to get this show on the road," he said, getting to his feet again. "The gas is movin' in a fairly compact plume but it will soon begin to disperse. Given the steady supply, it will blanket large areas of land, killin' a lot of people and a lot of critters."

He dropped back into his chair as if he were one of his students, legs spread wide and hands folded over his waist, and looked from face to expressionless face. "I know I've been goin' on like I've got a battleship mouth and a rowboat ass, so I'll shut up, but just let me say one more time that it's not like there's any lead time involved. People are probably already dyin', and that's not goin' to stop unless we do something about it."

You arrogant hillbilly.

The acute nausea billowing through Lucy's stomach was momentarily forgotten as she held Sam Briscoe's gaze for a few heartbeats. Despite her annoyance at his condescension, she had to admit she respected him. He'd come storming to Washington, demanding to see her, and had shouted down an entire shift of armed military police at the entrance to the base. Then he'd sat in custody for half an hour while they debated whether to bother her with his story. And he'd just given her a semester's worth of earth science lectures.

He might be a loose cannon, but the man had balls.

"Thanks for the overview, Dr. Briscoe. I don't suppose you have any idea what we should do about it?" she asked conversationally, as she rose to her feet. As she'd known he would, he immediately stood. He was a Southern boy, after all.

"I'm thinkin' hard on that one, ma'am."

"Good. Let me know when you come up with something." Lucy let her eyes sweep across every face in the room and settled her gaze on Marty Collins, who had gone silent and was looking alternately angry and scared as he sat there, unshaven and wearing a truly tasteless Hawaiian shirt. "Dr. Collins, do you have anything to add?"

He nodded, then shrugged. "Everything Sam said is true, but I think it has to be noted that there are several moving parts to the situation and they're independent of each other. First, there is the pipeline, which has to be sealed, and then there's the problem of the released methane, which is now present in extraordinary volumes in both the water and the atmosphere. If we don't get rid of it, we're going to face a runaway greenhouse effect."

"First things first. How do we plug the pipeline?" she asked.

Marty shrugged again. "Beats me. Call Red Adair back from the dead. This problem is just as nasty as plugging those oil well fires. Except we're dealing with water currents instead of wind, not to mention depth and pressure, and the pressure differentials in the water column directly over the leak."

Not bad. Lucy pressed a button on the console of her desk phone. "I need some hydrogeologists, marine chemists, and some underwater demolition guys in here." Moving her hand away from the phone, she met Tom's wary frown.

"You want to use explosives to close a methane leak?" he asked, his incredulity poorly hidden.

She lifted an eyebrow. "It's just an idea. If the sea-floor can be blown open, maybe it can be blown closed."

"Sending explosives into a column of methane would turn the Caribbean Sea into the Cuyahoga River circa 1969," Tom pointed out, frowning at her. "Remember the headlines? RIVER ON FIRE. Only this would be a bit more spectacular."

"Hardly, Mr. Taylor," she replied coolly. "The Cuyahoga River was never actually on fire. But as for the matter at hand, if small, uncontrolled explosions caused so much damage, perhaps controlled explosions could be used to repair some of it."

"That's ludicrous."

"Perhaps," she snapped, "but that pipeline has to be sealed before anything realistic can be done to counteract the atmospheric release. I'm willing to consider all options, and mine is only the first one to be brought up. All of you are welcome to add your thoughts at any time."

Tom shook his head and resumed his position leaning one shoulder against the wall.

"Excuse me, Director Denton, but were you listening to anything I just said? The atmosphere. Can't. Be. Repaired." Sam Briscoe paused, staring at her as if she had sprouted a second head. "There's *nothing* that will change the amount of methane already in the atmosphere until it oxidizes, and after that happens, there's nothing viable that's going to pull the CO_2 out of the atmosphere in any significant quantity."

"Nothing viable? Would you care to define that?"

"Oh, hell, Ms. Denton," he exploded. "You've heard all the ideas about creatin' artificial carbon sinks. Plantin' more trees, seedin' the ocean with iron pellets—any one of 'em might have worked up 'til yesterday, but this is a whole different scenario. We—"

"Excuse me."

All heads turned to Marty, who sat in his chair looking a little surprised at the sudden attention.

Lucy nodded at him before any of the others could speak. "Yes?"

Marty looked at Sam. "What about that paper you wrote for that independent study your first year in the doc program? The one on microbes."

Sam Briscoe blinked once, then shook his head. "Oh, hell, Marty. That was a controlled experiment in a lab. It's not real-world. Besides, there's no precedent, and there were no follow-up studies."

"But it worked," Marty said flatly. "And there have been follow-up studies. I've read them."

Lucy flicked her eyes between them, not wanting to miss any clues. "What experiment?"

"It was microbiology—" Sam began, shaking his head dismissively.

"Sam cultured colonies of organisms that consumed four hundred times their weight in atmospheric methane," Marty said over Sam's voice as he rose to his feet.

"You *what*?" Lucy demanded in unison with Tom. It was the first time they'd done anything simultaneously in more than a decade. Even Victoria Clark had straightened and was staring at Sam Briscoe.

Sam let out a heavy breath. "I developed a mutation of a methanotrophic microbe and cultured a colony of them. It was no—"

"Is this for real?" Lucy interrupted, pleased to see the cocky son of a bitch flinch from the question.

"Well, yeah, but it was in a lab—"

"You said that already. You're the one who just finished giving us the doomsday version of things, Dr. Briscoe. How dare you hold back information that might present a solution?" she snapped. "Why wouldn't it work outside of a lab?"

Lucy watched Sam's eyes widen. "You can't release millions of unknown microbes into the atmosphere."

Her anger showing, Lucy dismissed his reply with an abrupt flick of her hand. "Of course we can. It's been done for centuries. Mold spores, germs, cross-pollination, anthrax bombs—whether through biological warfare or burning leaves in the fall, microbes get released into the air all the time. And 'unknown' doesn't necessarily mean 'deadly.' Can you get me that paper, Dr. Briscoe?"

"Oh, hell—" Sam began.

"I can," Marty said, deliberately not looking at Sam. "I can get it now, and the follow-up studies, if you have a computer with PC Anywhere on it."

"No need. The paper is on my laptop. Somewhere," Sam said grudgingly, reaching into the computer bag at his feet.

Lucy walked around her desk and half sat on the front of it. "Good. I want to see it. And the follow-ups, Dr. Collins. Dr. Briscoe, what quantities of microbes would be needed to get the process under way, and where would they be released?"

"Lady, with all due respect, you are some kind of crazy," Sam muttered.

Lucy bit the inside of her lip to keep from smiling at his words. "No. Quite the opposite. As you've pointed out, we are facing imminent and ugly changes to a planet I happen to like the way it is. I need a viable proposal to take to the president in—" She glanced at her watch. "About twenty minutes."

"You're going to tell the president about this?" Sam sputtered while tapping furiously on his keyboard, which was now humming and propped open on his lap. "Ma'am, this isn't a viable solution. It's old research done by a grad student. I did it for a grade, not to advance science."

"Oh, shut the hell up, Sam. You were head-over-freaking-heels when it worked. And you were a grad student who already had a master's in microbiology and another one in chemistry, and you were pursuing a doctorate in atmospheric science," Marty pointed out.

Sam shook his head in disgust and muttered something under his breath. A moment later he looked up at

Lucy. "Can I get Wi-Fi here? What's your e-mail address, Ms. Denton?"

He typed it in as she recited it, then he sat back with an air of resignation. "Can I say one more time, Ms. Denton, that you can't just release clouds of microbes into the air. It's . . . it's so far beyond irresponsible that I don't even know the word for it."

"Bold?" she offered lightly.

"With all due respect, ma'am, I was thinkin' more along the lines of 'stupid.'"

Lucy didn't so much as bat an eyelash at the word. After all, he could be right.

Sam shoved a hand through his hair and shook his head, exhaling his frustration loudly. "It might be something to consider later—"

"You've made it very clear that there is no 'later,' Dr. Briscoe," Lucy pointed out.

"—but right now we don't have a firm read on the methane that's coming up. We know it's not pure and we don't know why, but we know for damn sure that microbes can mutate very quickly and in unpredictable ways. A release could spawn a whole slew of problems, or runaway reactions. If the Russians or the Iraqis suggested doing this, you'd call it germ warfare."

"True, but if they did it on their own sovereign territory to save their own people, we wouldn't be able to stop them." Lucy raised an eyebrow. "Is the microbe you used considered a germ?"

"No. I used a strain of a tiny single-celled organism called 'archaea.'"

"And this organism exists in nature?"

"Well, yes, but so does anthrax—" Sam sputtered.

"Tell me about it," Lucy ordered calmly.

Sam let out a heavy breath. "Archaea are all over the

place. They were originally thought to live only in hostile environments, but they don't. The type I worked with is anaerobic, which means it thrives in oxygen-deficient environments."

"How can releasing that into the atmosphere work? Won't they die?" Tom Taylor interrupted.

Sam looked at him. "I've been trying to make it clear that that methane plume *is* oxygen deficient. The organism I worked with absorbs the methane and almost completely oxidizes it, and doesn't take eight years to do it."

"How fast?" Lucy asked crisply.

"Oh, hell. Director Denton, don't pursue this," Sam pleaded. "It amounts to atmospheric engineering. It's Frankenstein stuff. We don't know the risks."

"But we do know the risks of not pursuing it, Dr. Briscoe. *How fast?*"

"I don't have any idea how fast the breakdown would happen in the atmosphere. I can only tell you what I observed in a setting controlled for temperature, humidity, and pressure. The mutation I worked with was what you'd now call a 'designer bug.' It doesn't have a natural environment, unless you consider a petri dish a natural environment." He spread his hands to indicate that he was finished. "It's all detailed in my paper."

"What is it called?"

"Methyljonesium."

Lucy nodded. "Excellent. I'll need you to compile a list of every researcher in the country who might have colonies available."

Sam blinked at her. "I have no idea who's working on it. This paper is nearly ten years old."

"Did you destroy the colony when you finished the paper?" Lucy demanded.

"No, I handed it off to—"

"Well, track down whoever has the original colony and get it back," she said simply, and watched Sam's face change from incredulity to outright disbelief.

"You're serious."

"Yes, I am," she replied.

Victoria Clark stood up and crossed the room, then turned to look at Sam. "How long would it take to culture enough of them to deploy?"

"*Deploy?* Can we just hold on a God-damned minute here?" Sam burst out and flung himself to his feet, holding on to his laptop with one hand. "Ms. Clark, Director Denton, and whatever the hell your name is—" Sam gestured wildly toward Tom Taylor, and Lucy had to bite back an inappropriate laugh. "You just heard about this a few minutes ago and don't know anything but what I've told you. You can't 'deploy' these critters into the atmosphere—"

"Dr. Briscoe," Lucy interrupted, giving him a look intended to freeze the blood in his veins. "You've made your position on this matter perfectly clear. Obviously, this scenario is subject to further review and, while I appreciate your input, the decision about what to do is not yours to make. I need more facts before I mention anything to the president."

"Okay, here's a fact. Dropping a bomb into a methane cloud will—"

"You're getting ahead of me, Dr. Briscoe. I never said anything about a bomb," Lucy replied calmly. "Given what you said earlier about pressure differentials and aircraft, I inferred that the reduced density of the methane-filled air column would cause a rocket's casing to disintegrate. The sudden change in pressure would just sort of pop the rivets, so to speak. Wouldn't it?"

Sam stared back at her. "It might."

"So we could feasibly deploy rockets carrying payloads of microbes rather than warheads, couldn't we? With some sort of nonreactive propellant to help disperse the microbes if needed."

He nodded slowly.

"Excellent." Lucy turned to Marty. "Pull together that list of researchers, Dr. Collins. And, by the way, thank you very much for bringing the subject to our attention." She scanned the faces in the room. "Now, unfortunately, I have to close this meeting and head to the White House to meet with the president. Ms. Clark, I'd like you to continue trying to get through to Taino. Let me know instantly if you do. Dr. Briscoe, I need you to continue monitoring that plume and figuring out how best to eliminate it."

Everyone nodded silently, with the exception of Sam, who glared at her with something close to loathing. Lucy pressed a button on her phone console and instantly her office door opened and her assistant stepped in with a smile and began to usher everyone out.

CHAPTER

6:30 P.M., Sunday, October 26, Bolling Air Force Base, Washington, D.C.

As they were being led down the hushed corridor, a still righteously pissed-off Sam ended up walking by himself, a few feet behind Marty and Victoria Clark, who were following Lucy Denton's aide. As furious as Sam was at Marty and what that so-called best friend had just done, Sam knew he had to get over it. And it was probably a good thing that they weren't somewhere private, or they'd most likely both have black eyes about now. There was no mistaking that Marty was mad as hell that he'd had to be the one to bring up that old research paper—and that everyone but the paper's author was jumping on it.

Well, damn, shouldn't that say something to you, Methane Man? If I don't buy in to the idea that the microbes are the solution, how the hell can anyone else?

Sam shook his head. It was just like Marty to pull shit like this. For all his rigorous research and geeky habits, Marty Collins had always had the soul of a tree hugger, whereas Sam had always considered himself a reality-based scientist—and had told Marty so on many occasions. While Sam's choice of terms had been intended to annoy the hell out of his friend, the terminology hadn't been entirely facetious. The conversation that had just taken place was proof of it.

"Whatever the microbes might do, it probably won't

be as bad as what the methane will most certainly do if left unchecked."

Sam jerked his head up to see that Victoria Clark was walking beside him. "Excuse me, Ms. Clark. Was I thinking out loud?" he asked, surprised.

She was probably one of the quietest people he'd ever met, and undeniably striking, even when she was obviously exhausted as she was now. He'd had a hard time looking away from those eyes of hers every time he'd glanced at her.

Victoria gave him a tired smile and shook her head. "No. You didn't say anything. I just thought that there was probably only one thing on your mind at the moment."

"Dozens, actually, but they're all related," he admitted.

"I know you're not in favor of releasing the microbes, but is that because you think it won't work?" she asked softly.

"Mostly." He shrugged and let out an exasperated breath. "I have no idea if it will work. That question—this scenario—this wasn't anywhere near what I was thinking when I did the research and wrote that paper. I mean, there was no thought of those bugs ever havin' any practical, large-scale application." He shook his head. "Even discussin' the microbes further is goin' to get Lucy Denton's or the president's hopes up, and that's a huge mistake. We're not talkin' about a small thing here. We're talking about a major release into the atmosphere—Ms. Clark, it's too much of a long shot to work."

"Releasing the microbes is the only solution on the table, Dr. Briscoe."

"Call me Sam," he said absently, and held the door

open for her as they entered the conference room a few steps behind Marty and the aide.

"Thank you." She waited for him as he closed the door behind himself. "The microbes are natural; they're not a manufactured organism, and you said all they do is eat methane. What damage could they do, other than to die without consuming the methane?"

"I don't know. Mutate. Replicate. Infiltrate other systems or organisms. Even if it works, there *will* be negative side effects, Ms. Clark. It's just impossible to know how bad they'll be."

"They could be negligible."

"They could be."

"Sounds like there's no reason not to give it a try then." Victoria looked him straight in the eyes and he found it hard to look away or even blink. "I've never been accused of being an optimist, Sam. I've spent my career studying the dark side of things and preventing worst-case scenarios from happening. But I think this is a chance we have to take. Work with us. There isn't any alternative."

"For me, or for the methane?"

"Either."

He was quiet for a minute. "Any chance you know what's in that methane?"

Victoria's expression zeroed back to neutrality before she answered. "What do you mean?"

"We all know it's not pure. You would have done analyses on it before going into a full-scale drilling operation. What's corrupting it?"

"What I know won't help you," she said after a brief pause. She set her briefcase on the table.

"Try me."

She hesitated again, then met his eyes. "We injected

a chemical into the deposit to stabilize the methane hydrate and keep it in a solid state as we removed it. That's all I can tell you. It was developed in-house and I don't know what's in it. Only a few people do—" She stopped and Sam could see a muscle move in her cheek as she clenched her jaw.

"And in all likelihood, all of those people are dead," she finished. "All I can tell you is that the compound was named dennisium. I don't know its chemical composition or properties."

Fucking great. "That's all the more reason we shouldn't mess around with microbes, Ms. Clark," he muttered. "The strain I used was very fast-growin'. How it might interact with that dennisium is a total crap shoot. Microbes are fussy in some ways but, on a microbial scale, there will be lots of variation in environmental parameters within that plume and there's no way of tellin' which ones will be hospitable. The organisms could form new mutations faster than you can blink. And not just one mutation. Could be lots of different ones. Nasty ones."

"We have to hope for the best," she said weakly and looked away.

Hell, yeah, lady, you should *be damned embarrassed to have just said that.*

"I'll do that, Ms. Clark," Sam replied sarcastically, then turned away from her and slapped his laptop on the conference table. "I got a question for you, Ms. Clark. Doesn't have anything to do with microbes or methane."

"All right."

"I was talkin' to someone over at your embassy earlier today and got hung up on."

The look she gave him left Sam in no doubt of her opinion of his brain power.

"I'm sorry to hear it. As you can imagine, it's been rather hectic—" she began quietly.

He shook his head. "Thank you, but I'm not lookin' for an apology. I called over there to try to find out some information about a boat that might have been taken into custody."

Victoria's expression didn't change but everything about her seemed to go still. "Taken into custody? By Taino security?"

A spider of panic raced up his spine and disappeared. He shuddered before nodding at her question. "My girlfriend and a few of her girlfriends were on a clipper cruise and got permission to go divin' somewhere inside your waters. After the crash happened, they were told they couldn't go divin', but they decided to go nosin' around anyway. My girlfriend is a TV news producer and an all-around bad influence," he finished, his attempt at humor falling flat.

Victoria gave him a tight smile, any recent softness he might have imagined in her eyes gone. "My orders were that all vessels not our own were to be kept outside the boundary waters, Dr. Briscoe. Any boat that did cross over would have been escorted back to the territorial coordinates. We don't take anyone into custody."

"That doesn't surprise me, but Cyn—that's her name, Cynthia Davison—she told me they were goin' to sneak in from around the other side of the island," he said, looking down as he clicked his mouse to open an application. "And if you knew her, you'd know why I'm concerned. To say she's a loose cannon is like sayin' a rattlesnake isn't the ideal pet. Is there any way you could check if a boat—" A glance at her face made him stop. "Ma'am?"

She swallowed and immediately replaced her look of alarm with one of relative composure, which did nothing for his gut.

Oh, hell, Cyn, what did you do?

"There was a report of a boat that had strayed into our waters near the southwestern end of the island," she replied slowly. "What sort of boat did you say it was?"

"A clipper. One of those big old-fashioned sailboats where the passengers pay through the nose to be a crew member for a week."

"And when did she say they were going to try to make this attempt?"

"Last time I talked to her was yesterday. They were goin' to try it today, I'm pretty sure."

"Do you know the name of the boat?"

He frowned. "Something Dutch. They took off from Miami, but the boat was registered in the Bahamas. The *Flying Dutchman*?"

"The *Floating Dutchman*, perhaps?" Victoria asked slowly.

"That sounds more like it. Yeah, I'm pretty sure that's the name," Sam replied, the knot in the pit of his gut tightening painfully.

After a split second of hesitation, Victoria gestured that they should move toward the corner of the room. Sam glanced over his shoulder to see Marty seated at the far end of the table, where a laptop had been set up for him.

Sam and Victoria came to a stop near one of the tall windows and when she didn't start talking right away, Sam shoved his hands into his jeans pockets and looked her straight in the eyes.

"I appreciate you tryin' to think of a way to soften whatever news it is you have for me, Ms. Clark, but it's not necessary. Just tell me where she is. I'm guessin' she's in jail."

"No, she's not in jail," Victoria began slowly. "As I said, we don't take anyone into custody. But—Dr. Briscoe, I'm not sure how to explain this, and it pains me to be the one to have to tell you, but my security personnel did have an encounter with the *Floating Dutchman* earlier today. The clipper had crossed into our territorial waters and was coming around the southern headland when our officers made visual contact. The timing—"

"Ms. Clark, please just get to the point," he said, trying to keep his impatience out of his voice. "I haven't been able to contact her since yesterday, and I'm gonna wring her neck when I finally do. Just tell me where she is. Please."

"She may be on one of our ships that is taking part in the search-and-recovery operation. There was a passenger from the *Dutchman* who came aboard after—" She stopped. "I don't know her name."

"Came aboard after what, Ms. Clark?" Sam demanded, a sick jitter in his gut.

Victoria paused and took a deep breath and, to her credit, kept her eyes on his. "The clipper was in the area where the landslide occurred at the time it was occurring. Going by what we know of the landslide and the initial reports from our security officers who encountered the boat, the clipper appeared to be almost directly above the . . . the pipeline. The point at which the methane is erupting into the atmosphere," she said slowly, her words softening as her voice became hoarse. "Nobody knew exactly what was happening, but the officers reported that the sea surface became unstable. They described it as turning foamy."

Sam stared at her with mounting horror. "Ms. Clark, did you say 'foamy'?"

She nodded, her face tight with suppressed emotion. "Our officers reported seeing the boat sink, Sam. With all hands on board. No one on the boat was able to escape. No survivors were found. My officers were too far away to offer assistance, and the nature of the situation precluded any rescue attempts."

Her words couldn't have had a bigger effect on him if they'd been delivered with a brass-knuckled blow to his solar plexus. His breath was just as hard to come by, and his brain was just as foggy.

As Sam stared at Victoria Clark, her face, her eerie blue eyes, seemed to fill his entire field of vision. Her voice was low and indistinct, and coming at him as if from a great distance.

After a minute of what he thought might be silence, he felt a hand grip his arm lightly and then felt his body move forward until it dropped into a chair.

"The only person from the clipper to survive was a female passenger the boat's captain had dispatched to meet our security officers. The male crew member with her became hysterical and drove the inflatable they were in back toward the boat. She threw herself overboard. The inflatable—" She stopped talking and looked down at her hands.

A small, silent movement at the blurred periphery of his vision caught his attention and it took him a minute to realize it was a tear splashing on to the back of her hand, which was clasped over its mate and hugged to her chest.

Marty had joined them and was crouched near Sam's chair, looking concerned. Sam nodded at him, then blinked and refocused on Victoria Clark's face. She looked hollow. About as hollow as Sam felt.

Sam shook his head as if to dislodge the information, and then tried to swallow. It was nearly impossible to do, his mouth was that dry.

"What I said back there, what I said would happen— the Bermuda Triangle—" he said, his voice so hoarse that it didn't sound like his own. "It happened to Cyn? She just . . . disappeared?"

"I'm so very sorry to have had to tell you, Sam. Let me try to find out the name of the survivor," Victoria whispered in a voice that wasn't steady, and picked up his hand and clasped it between her own. "Let's hope for the best. Let's hope it was Cyn who survived."

7:10 P.M., Sunday, October 26, off the coast of Islamorada, Florida Keys

Sixteen-year-old Glory Bennett sat in her ocean kayak rocking in the light chop. Her paddle was out of the water and resting in her hands against the bright red fiberglass of the hull. The rest of the girls from her group had already headed into shore. She could see them climbing out of their kayaks and pulling them onto the beach, or pulling on their sweats for the drive home.

Such obedient girls. Glory could hear her mother's voice as if she were sitting out here next to her. She could also hear the comment her mother would never say out loud: *You should try to be more like them.*

"Right. As if you know a thing about any of them. As if you know what they do when adults aren't around," she muttered.

Glory knew she should have followed the others— they'd had a full day on the water and it was a long drive home—but she just wanted one last look at the sunset, one last, quiet, solitary moment on water that had turned to molten gold. So they'd leave ten minutes later. Maybe fifteen. It was no big deal. Her mouth turned down into a pout and she stared defiantly straight into the last glare of the melting sun.

It doesn't matter anyway. It's not like there will be consequences when I finally do *get back to shore.*

Her father—Pastor Ted to everyone else—wouldn't do anything more than frown at her. He frowned at her most of the time regardless of what she did anyway, so what difference would this make? He'd frowned at her when she'd told him she didn't want to join the all-girl teen Bible study group that he led, and then he'd frowned again when she'd grudgingly changed her mind and said she would. There was no pleasing the man.

She heard her name shouted from the beach and deliberately didn't turn to acknowledge it. It wouldn't kill them to wait another few minutes for her.

She took a deep breath and tilted her face to the last of the rainbow hues painting the sky. "Only two more years and then I'm free. I don't care what they say. I am so outta here," she whispered into the breeze.

The promise, made to herself and the warm, darkening wind, made her smile, and then the thought of what she'd be like once out from under the microscope of her parents' nosiness turned the smile into a laugh.

Another shout from the shore wiped it from her face.

The whiff of a rancid odor, like something rotting, blew toward her on the breeze.

No doubt Dad would call it a Sign. Or a punishment.

Rolling her eyes, Glory lifted her paddle and took a deep breath to brace herself for the exertion of getting back to shore. But the breath didn't help her get going.

An invisible sheet of fire seemed to coat the back of her throat, making her cough, and she dragged in another huge breath. That only made it worse, and Glory bent forward, dropping her paddle in the water as her hands rose to claw at the neck of the wet suit she wore.

With the next inhalation, the fire in her lungs burned hotter and she flung herself into the water to get away from the searing pain. Nothing helped, and Glory wasn't sure if the darkness that settled over her was the water or something else.

It didn't matter anyway.

1:40 A.M., Monday, October 27, Annaba, Algeria

Arms folded across his chest, Garner rested his ass against the edge of the wide, stone windowsill and looked at the young woman standing a few feet in front of him. Her name was Bridget Malloy, and she was young enough, beautiful enough, and smart enough to do anything she wanted in the world of business. A degree in computer science from the Massachusetts Institute of Technology had been followed by a master's from the London School of Economics. And then, one fine day, two years ago she'd blown off an interview at British Telecom to spontaneously participate in a peaceful demonstration outside an animal research lab.

It hadn't taken his staff too much time or too much effort to persuade her to join the ranks of GAIA. Since that day, she had proven her loyalty to the cause over and over again. That steadfastness was one of the reasons Garner had brought Bridget into his inner circle and to this villa. He was sure it was also why she wasn't complaining about the many inconveniences North Africa had to offer someone used to a high-end, thoroughly Western lifestyle.

Despite being an American, Bridget Malloy was amazingly adaptable and wonderfully easygoing. She didn't complain about working around his schedule as he recovered from jet lag. She didn't complain about the food, or the heat, or having to hide herself beneath traditional Muslim clothing.

Though Garner had no patience for religion of any sort, he'd nevertheless instructed his women to wear the region's long robes and head scarves, even on the villa grounds, to avoid drawing undue attention to themselves. The household employees were locals, and the last thing he needed were rumors drifting through the city about any goings-on at the villa, real or imagined. He needed GAIA's next project to stay under the radar and on schedule.

Garner shifted position and felt sweat trickle down the side of his face and from underneath his arms. It was the middle of the night, but the air was still hot and the wind was still dry and gritty with the fine sand that found its way everywhere. Neither seemed to bother Bridget. She'd arrived in his suite a few minutes ago, covered from shoulder to foot in a loose-fitting dark blue abaya, her head and neck draped in a lavender hijab.

But even though she followed his rules without argument, she found ways to make herself comfortable. The moment the guards who had let her into his private office had closed the door behind them, she'd casually let her face veil drop and slipped the lightweight scarf from her head. And as she'd begun debriefing him on the imminent deployment of his latest project, Bridget had slowly been opening the trail of buttons down the front of her long, dark tunic. Stopping after undoing the button just below her waist, Bridget shrugged off the garment designed to protect her modesty and presented Garner with a vision that couldn't be more Western or more decadent. Every curve, every shadow was visible through compellingly sheer lingerie.

"Your interpretation of my dress code is as unique as your execution of it is provocative," Garner said quietly, lifting an eyebrow and letting his gaze drift appreciatively over her body before meeting her eyes again.

She put her hands on her hips and executed a quick twirl. "I had to show *someone*. This is the first summer in my life that I haven't had tan lines."

"So I see."

"These getups aren't as uncomfortable as I thought they'd be, even in this heat, but swishing around in all that shapeless fabric makes a girl want to get a little . . . dirty," she said softly, her voice extending an invitation.

"In a moment. Business first, unfortunately," Garner replied lightly. "When will you deploy the malware?"

Bridget pushed her bottom lip out in a false pout and then laughed immediately, the blinding-white wholesomeness of her smile at odds with her sexiness. "I have already."

"Really."

"Yes, really, Garner. While I've been pining for your return, your dirty girl has also been a busy girl." She pushed her long, loose blond hair over her shoulder, away from her face in a motion imbued with both youthful triumph and the knowing sensuality of a high-priced call girl. "The failure code has already been embedded on corporate e-mail servers all over the world. At a preset time, just a few hours from now, it will insert itself into every attachment that passes through an infected hub and begin to do its business of changing strategic numbers, deleting key files." She shrugged and sent him another smile. "It's so nasty, it's lovely. And completely undetectable."

"You're sure?" Garner asked, getting to his feet and walking toward her slowly.

"Absolutely. It will bypass every means of detection. We've tested it against every piece of antivirus software and antispyware that's out there, and every known firewall. It's a randomly self-mutating code, so every generation is different from the last and all are different from one another." She offered him a subtle, rich laugh. "Pardon my pride, Garner, but it is truly the most superior code ever written. It will drive cyber cops and IT people crazy. There is no pattern to be discovered, it leaves no trail, and it will die off and disappear in twenty-four hours, and no one will even know where to begin looking to see what it has destroyed. And it can never be traced, which means there is no cure for it."

"So we can use it again." It wasn't a question.

"Yes." She brushed away a fly that had landed on her face.

"And it's in every organization on the list?"

Bridget nodded, swatting at another fly.

"Stop doing that," Garner said mildly. "Just let them be."

With an affectionate roll of her eyes, she complied and then began moving forward to meet him in the center of the airy room, her dark eyes sparkling with a fiendish playfulness.

"Every petroleum company, every major bank, every shipping and telecom company, agribusiness concern, every company that even dabbles in the pharma sector—*everyone,* Garner. By the time Western civilization is up and running, our code will be replicating millions of times every minute, burrowing into every level of every one of the companies. By the time the Stock Exchange opens in New York, conservatively fifty million servers will have gone AWOL and will stay that way for at least twenty-four hours."

"What about the other code?" he asked.

"The code that Cyril was working on will take over a few more million systems and launch massive, simultaneous denial-of-service attacks on all the government, corporate, and academic Web sites you listed. The networks will crash, and in the ensuing panic, people will—" She shrugged with a smile, which turned into another laugh. "Do whatever it is you want them to do, I guess."

Coming to a stop in front of him, Bridget reached out and unfolded Garner's arms, then slid into the freed-up space against his chest.

"I will, too," she whispered. "But you already know that."

"Indeed I do. You don't give me much of a chance to forget it." He smiled at her, lowered his mouth to hers and kissed her just long enough, just deeply enough to get a full taste of her. Raising his head, he met her eyes.

"Hey, I've been working hard for you. I deserve more," she whispered in a soft pout against his lips. "That was a great kiss, but one kiss isn't enough for me."

He slid his hands upward from her waist, lingered over her breasts, then brought his palms up to rest on her shoulders, his thumbs lightly stroking her throat.

"But one kiss was enough for me. I'd forgotten that the flavor of treachery can be so sweet. Too bad it's one I've never acquired a taste for," Garner replied and snapped her head back, applying deadly force to the fragile tissue surrounding her windpipe.

Her fingernails dug into his forearms and her eyes widened with panic as she tried to suck air past his stranglehold.

"Don't bother struggling, Bridget. You're dead," he said calmly, maintaining the pressure on her throat.

"Garner—" Her garbled scream was cut off and, even as her hands pulled at his and her long, lithe legs connected with his body in a painful, powerful kick, he could tell by the look in her eyes that she knew he was right. She was dead.

"Don't worry, love. We'll let your Washington friends know you died. And why."

With a cold smile, Garner added just a bit more pressure and felt her whole body go limp. He held on for a few more seconds, then let go.

She hit the floor with a heavy thud, a crumpled and ungainly heap of femininity. As he watched, the faint bluish cast quickly faded from her skin.

Stepping over her, Garner went to the door of the room and opened it. Beckoning to the two armed men who leaned against the courtyard wall a few yards away, Garner pointed at Bridget's limp, nearly naked form. The men's eyes followed the gesture, then flicked back to Garner's face with expressions that were both prurient and wary.

"She's an American spy," he snapped at them in French. "I need her gotten rid of. She's unconscious. I don't care what you do with her. Enjoy her. Just make sure she's very dead when you're done, and put her somewhere she'll be found."

Slinging the straps of their semiautomatic weapons onto their shoulders, the stock of the weapons resting against their backs, they moved into the room and picked up the woman by the armpits and ankles. As an afterthought, Garner flung her discarded clothing across her stomach. He had no need of it.

Not that she does, either.

Garner smiled when he heard her dull moan, and was a little disappointed she didn't open her eyes before she was out of the room. It would have been interesting to see how she reacted when she realized what was going to happen to her.

Stupid whore. Whatever they do to you, it will be less than you deserve.

Closing the door behind the trio, Garner crossed the room and pulled open the heavy door on the opposite wall.

Although the ceiling fan in the room was spinning and the shutters on the window were open, the room stank of sweat and spicy food and fermenting oranges. Flies buzzed loudly as they feasted undisturbed on a pile of discarded rinds.

At least some things are proceeding as they're meant to.

"Cyril," Garner said, his voice clipped with annoyance at being ignored, however briefly.

A tall, gangly Englishman looked up as if startled and unfolded himself from a seat at a table strewn with paper and two laptops.

"Oh, hello." The man looked at his watch. "Must have lost track of time. Buggery bollocks, it's late. Where's Bridget?" he said, rubbing eyes that were bleary behind dark-rimmed glasses.

"She's been working so hard, I thought she could use a little R and R. Sent her off straightaway. Bloody hard to get Americans to take a holiday, isn't it? It's all work, work, work with them," Garner replied smoothly. "How was her code, Cyril? She said she'd already deployed it. Did you have a chance to look at it? Did it need a scrubbing?"

"Jolly right it did. Some things in there didn't make

much sense." Cyril shrugged. "Just a few small things, really. Nothing terribly amiss. Works better now, though."

I'll bet it does. Miserable whore. Garner kept his anger hidden. "What was wrong with it?"

Cyril scratched his scruffy, sweaty cheek absently. "Hard to tell, really. She writes very dense code, bloody hard to read. I'd have expected more elegance from her. Anyway, there seemed to be some negations buried in some of the longer strings."

"Negations?"

"Commands that would undo other commands," Cyril explained, adjusting his glasses again. "It's not so unusual to find them in code. Sometimes I do it myself. Put things in just to remind myself how I got them in there and working." The man gave a small laugh. "Just a geek thing, I suppose. Nothing worse than getting to the end of some code and forgetting what you've done halfway through."

"Right. Did you take them out?"

"Certainly. I wouldn't mind asking her why she'd forgotten to remark them as comments, though. They quite undid things. Bloody careless." He shook his head in a mild scold. "Unlike her."

Garner forced a smile. "That conversation will have to wait, I'm afraid. Is it all set then?"

"Oh, yes. Quite. I've re-sent what's already gone out. You know, the new code without the negations. We may not get exactly quite the same bang as we might have originally, but we'll make a proper showing."

"Excellent, Cyril. Excellent."

CHAPTER

7:15 P.M., Sunday, October 26, the White House, Washington, D.C.

Lucy stepped into the Oval Office and did a quick count of the people looking back at her. Ken Proust, the president's campaign manager, Katy Wirth, secretary of defense, a few others—the usual suspects. All the faces were famous, and all of them were drawn, ashen, and angry.

"Good evening, Mr. President," she said.

The president nodded. "Lucy. Have a seat."

She sank into the nearest chair.

"As I was saying, sir, every Caribbean nation is completely freaked out over this—"

Lucy bit the inside of her cheek as the president, sleek, silvered, and as self-important as the office required, dropped the temperature in the room by a few degrees with the look he leveled at the person who had just spoken. Lucy's private opinion was that the youngest-ever assistant secretary of state might well be a wunderkind on policy, but he was in a state of arrested development when it came to presentation.

" 'Freaked out'? For Christ's sake, Grover, can't you come up with a better term than that?" President Benson snapped.

Grover Hartfield adjusted his glasses but there was no air of apology about him. "Not really, sir. It's an apt description. They're, like, totally worried about the earthquakes and the methane release and the idea that these smaller ruptures could continue to happen all over the region."

The president shot a look at Lucy. "Could they?"

"Yes, sir, they could. But they weren't earthquakes. We've confirmed that they were detonations."

"Oh, hell." The president shook his head and looked at his campaign manager, then back to Lucy. "Bring us up to date."

His tone—annoyed, condescending, and impatient— lit a flame of anger in her.

Why don't you try to give a damn, Mr. President? Or at least pretend to, instead of worrying about what this is going to do to you at the polls.

Keeping her face neutral, Lucy folded her hands in her lap and met his eyes. "GAIA has claimed responsibility for the detonations and for the landslide they precipitated. The target seems to have been a methane-hydrate mining operation that Dennis Cavendish was about to bring online. That facility has been destroyed, as far as we know, and the pipeline into the methane bed has been severely damaged. Methane is coming out of the opening and filtering through the water column into the air. There are serious long-term climate implications, but the immediate problem is that the methane is not pure and is displacing the air at the surface, creating a plume of unbreathable air that is migrating to the Keys."

"The Keys? The *Florida* Keys?" Ken asked.

"Yes, the Florida Keys," Lucy replied, and continued as if he hadn't interrupted her. "I have it from Taino's secretary of national security that in the process of mining the methane hydrate, they injected a proprietary additive to stabilize the crystals. This additive makes the methane heavy, so it is remaining much closer to the sea surface than it normally would. As I said, the gas has formed a plume and is moving toward the Keys. According to our expert on atmospheric methane, a stable air current that typically moves through the area will most likely begin to disperse the gas in a northerly direction."

"Toward Miami," the president said bluntly.

Lucy gritted her teeth against the cold fear that sliced through her without warning. "Yes, sir, that's a distinct possibility."

"What's the worst case?"

Lucy hesitated only for a second. "If the wind stays as calm as it is, pockets of mass asphyxiation could continue to occur. For instance, on beaches or on the water in the path of the gas. Anywhere a—"

Staring at her in disbelief, the president held up his hand and she immediately stopped talking.

"Lucy, did you just say 'mass asphyxiation could *continue* to occur'?"

"Yes, sir, I did."

He leaned toward her. "People are starting to die on the beach just from *breathing*?"

"From breathing methane, sir. The density of this plume is displacing the air at sea level," she repeated as neutrally as she could. "There have been some odd reports filtering in from Coast Guard patrols. A few unexplained deaths. A pod of whales, a few dozen dolphins here and there. Whole flocks of sea birds."

"Christ, Lucy, what are you, a reporter for *Animal Planet*? Like we give a fuck about animals," Ken Proust sneered. "I thought you were talking about human deaths. Give me something we can use."

Lucy didn't even look at him. The urge to drive the

heel of her pump deep into his eye socket was nearly overpowering.

"Some of the dead creatures were people, Ken. Rich people, judging by the boats they were on. Does that make you happy?" she replied.

"No, Lucy, it doesn't," he snapped. "This isn't good."

She knew he was thinking of all the voters—and all the electoral votes—in South Florida. It made her want to vomit.

"How very astute of you, Ken," she replied coolly.

"Cut it out, you two. What are we doing about it?" President Benson demanded, his eyes boring into hers.

"We've brought in experts on Caribbean methane beds and the effects of atmospheric methane releases—"

"I'm sure that's charming, Director Denton, but can we focus on, as you called it, the 'immediate problem'?" Katy Wirth spoke with her customary sarcasm. Lucy ignored it.

"Thank you, Secretary Wirth. That's precisely what I am focusing on. With your permission . . . ?" Lucy directed her attention once more to the president. "We've brought in Dr. Sam Briscoe. He's well respected in his field and his explanations are fairly easy to understand. The atmosphere itself is the vector. The adulterated methane is displacing the air along the trajectory of the air current, forming plumes of oxygen-deficient gas. Anyone or anything trying to breathe in such an area will suffocate in less than a minute." Lucy paused. "We believe this was the cause of death of the people and animals that I previously mentioned. They come up for air, or fly, or otherwise move through the plume, and die."

"Jesus H. Christ." The words burst out of Ken Proust's thin-lipped mouth as he launched himself out of his chair.

Drama queen. Lucy resisted the urge to roll her eyes at him.

"Wait a minute. Who is this so-called expert? And where the hell is he getting this stuff?" the president demanded. "Sounds crazy to me."

Lucy shook her head. "I wish such a scenario were crazy, sir, but unfortunately, it's happening. Dr. Briscoe is with the University of Florida. He has a background in chemistry and microbiology in addition to his atmospheric research."

"How long is this going to last?" Ken demanded, still on his feet and pacing to the door and back. "When is it going to stop?"

"The time that the concentration will remain lethal depends on its rate of diffusion, which depends on wind speed and direction, but the gas won't stop coming up until we plug that leak. There are additional concerns besides deaths at the surface, sir," she said, her voice rising as Ken tried to interrupt her again.

"There's *more*? For God's sake, Lucy," President Benson snapped.

"Dr. Briscoe indicated that the methane is essentially being pumped out of the cavity. That was his word. 'Pumped.' As the gas rises through the water, it decreases the density of the water column, and as it rises through the air, it could do the same thing to the air column. So even if the rate of diffusion renders the air breathable at the surface, the atmosphere may not be able to support aircraft, or it may become combustible."

Ken came to an abrupt stop in front of her chair. "Lucy, are you *sure* this guy is sane? This all sounds like a James Cameron flick."

Only Katy Wirth had the nerve to give a snort of

laughter and Lucy ignored her. Stiffening her spine against an especially withering presidential glare and the wary disbelief of everyone else in the room, Lucy met the president's eyes.

"I know it sounds bad—dire, even, Mr. President—but we did check him out. He's published quite a bit on the subject in peer-reviewed journals. And Dennis Cavendish tried to hire him a few years ago."

President Benson shoved his hands into his trouser pockets and pursed his lips as silence fell over the room.

"So we have to issue some sort of alert for South Florida so people stay indoors?" he asked after a few minutes.

Too damned little, too damned late, you soulless prick.

Lucy took a deep breath, and wondered why she'd ever taken this job. She hated politics almost as much as she hated politicians. "Sir, that could be a solution if the weather helps us, but if the wind stays calm, the methane won't diffuse and people could be trapped in their houses. I think the only real option is an evacuation."

Katy let out an incredulous gasp. "Evacuate *Miami*? Tell two million people they have to leave home to avoid a threat they can't see? Are you insane, Lucy? That's political suicide."

Lucy shot her a sharp look. "The alternative is mass murder, Secretary Wirth. Not suicide, *murder*. Because with suicide the victim has a choice," she snapped, then looked back to the president. "Sir, if people wait, it will be too late to save them. One good lungful with no oxygen in it and you're dead where you fall," she replied bluntly. "Everything and everyone present when the gas plume comes through will be dead. Cops on their beats, executives in limos, babies in strollers. Everyone, sir."

"An evacuation isn't necessary, sir. We're prepared for this," Ken Proust said quickly. "Our first responders are trained to handle biological warfare—"

"No," Lucy interrupted, getting to her feet and facing him. Ken actually took a stumbling step backward.

You should *be afraid of me, you stupid little shit.*

"This isn't biological warfare. Forget about first responders," she snapped. "It won't be like what happened after Katrina or Simone. No one will have to go house to house looking for survivors, Ken. There won't *be* any survivors, and the bodies will be everywhere. And until that gas cloud moves or disperses sufficiently, we won't be able to get any personnel on the ground there anyway, unless they're wearing full hazmat suits and self-contained breathing units. And if the plume is stationary, every person going into the danger zone will have to be on foot or use battery-powered vehicles because combustion engines need oxygen." She paused and took a breath, adrenaline still burning through her bloodstream. "I could go on but I won't, because I think I've made my point. We are *not* prepared for this, Mr. President. It's not sarin in a subway or an airplane flying into a building. It's a blanket of invisible poison miles long and potentially miles wide and *it's moving.* And there's an unlimited supply of it."

Lucy let out a hard breath and sat down, staring at her hands. "Unless we cut off the supply of methane at the source, it will just keep coming straight up, sir."

The room was so quiet that the faint ticking of the antique carriage clock on the president's desk seemed loud.

"Well, yes, obviously we need to seal the rupture. There are technologies for capping—"

Lucy looked at Katy. "Yes, there are conventional

technologies for capping things like burning oil wells and the reactor at Chernobyl. Is that what you're talking about?"

"Yes, along those lines."

Lucy shook her head and reined in her fraying temper with difficulty. "Don't you get it? *There is nothing conventional about this situation.*"

Instantly regretting her display of anger and frustration, Lucy leaned back and took a deep breath. "We can't get any equipment near the site of the rupture. It's *four thousand feet* underwater. That's nearly a mile, straight down. When you dive, one atmosphere of pressure is added for about every thirty-three vertical feet of water. You do the math—that's a lot of pressure. And anything we sent down there would have to withstand moving from the pressure at sea level to that intense pressure, and then possibly to a dramatically reduced pressure the instant it crosses into the degraded water column. There is nothing we know of that can withstand such rapid, catastrophic changes in pressure. That means anything entering that water column will be destroyed instantly."

When she looked up at President Benson, Lucy noticed that his face had paled beneath his tan. Scanning the room, she noted with satisfaction that Ken, who was still standing near her chair, looked like he'd just been kicked in the balls. Katy Wirth and the others looked like scared little rabbits.

"How fast would this gas cloud get big enough to reach Miami?" the president asked, his customary abruptness somewhat subdued.

Lucy frowned. "I don't know if there's any real way of knowing exactly—"

"Before the election or after?" Ken interrupted.

Lucy had to work hard to keep her disgust off her face. "The election is more than a week away. If we're still talking about this in a week, there may not be any voters left in South Florida to worry about, Ken."

"That's enough," the president snapped. "I want to hear what we're going to do about it. I need timelines and scenarios. Get whoever you need on it immediately. Joint Chiefs, FEMA, NOAA, everybody. I don't give a damn."

As if the president had poked them with live wires, everyone in the room began to move and a buzz of low conversation erupted.

It stopped when Ken asked, "What about the press? What do we tell them?"

The president glared at him. "We don't tell them a fucking thing until it's over. And I mean *not a fucking thing*, Ken. *No leaks*."

"There is one possible solution that we're already pursuing, sir," Lucy said, cutting through the murmurs and bringing the group back to silence. "I think it has to be fast-tracked. Dr. Briscoe has done extensive research on, to put it bluntly, methane-eating microbes. They occur naturally all over the globe. I've put him in touch with people at NOAA, GISS, Homeland Security, and the National Geospatial-Intelligence Agency to see if they can come up with a workable rapid-response plan to enlist the microbes in lessening the impact of the methane release," she said carefully. "At this point, I'd like to include the Joint Chiefs, too, sir."

"Let me get this straight. You want to deploy biological weapons *off the coast of Florida*?" Katy Wirth said stridently. Lucy shot her an icy look.

"It's the only solution on the table at the moment," Lucy snapped. "Bombs won't work, robots won't be able to do anything, and we can't send in any land, sea, or airborne divisions, so I don't really see what options we have other than to explore this."

"Are we going to get any return on this, Lucy?" the president asked.

She turned to face him. "I'm not sure what you mean, sir. What sort of return?"

She watched him frown at the floor for a moment.

Don't say votes. Please God, don't say votes.

He raised his eyes to hers. "All that methane hydrate. It's still going to be down there, and Cavendish is the only one who knows how to get it out. I think that learning how he does it would be a reasonable payback for all the lives he's ended and the damage he's causing."

Lucy couldn't remember any other time in her life when she'd been speechless.

"We're going to bail out his sorry ass on the world stage. I think sharing that technology with us—exclusively—would be an appropriate thank you." The president shrugged one shoulder, then met her eyes with his trademark steely gaze.

Just some routine industrial espionage—you've done it before, he seemed to say.

Yes, I have, but in those days I knew I was working for the good guys. Now I'm not so sure.

"See what you can do about that, will you, Lucy?" The president gave her a tight grin. "As for the rest of it, do what you need to do. Keep me apprised."

"Yes, sir. Thank you, sir." She had to force the words out.

The president issued a casual gesture of dismissal to Lucy and turned back to the young assistant secretary of state, who had gone very quiet and rather green.

Commit industrial espionage. And keep the press out of it.

Lucy fumed as she exited the Oval Office. She knew the president wanted to operate in the dark, keeping the people ignorant and dying until Ken could determine where to lay the blame. Obviously, it would be Cuba. New leader or not, if something was affecting Miami, Cuba was the best scapegoat. Even in an election year, demonizing Dennis Cavendish wouldn't be enough to secure the proper result. She had no doubt this would be spun into a Cuban Missile Crisis, updated for the new millennium.

Ken, you are a son of a bitch, and it will be a good thing to see you taken down.

Stepping into the sunshine, Lucy took a deep breath, then climbed into the waiting limo.

CHAPTER

7:15 P.M., Sunday, October 26, Key Largo, Florida
Millicent—Miley—Cody sat in the Back Bay rocker she favored and looked out over the beach that gleamed like half-polished pewter in the light of a rising quarter moon. Even though her house was a block away from that stretch of talcum-soft Key Largo sand, she had an unencumbered view of it and had long since considered it *her* beach. She'd been here long enough, and was wealthy enough, to enjoy the conceit.

A brief, impulsive marriage to a washed-up bad-boy rocker years ago had been both the means and the incentive for her move to the Keys. Miley hadn't been young and she hadn't been stupid, but she'd married him anyway, and it turned out to be the only positive return-on-investment she'd enjoyed in her entire life. She'd had to endure only a few months of his incoherent rages. Being stoned most of the time had helped. Then, before they'd reached their first anniversary, she woke up one hot L.A. afternoon next to a cold, stiff body.

Dealing with the cops had been a hassle; so had dealing with the press. Her old friends had been the worst, though, with their hushed statements about cautionary tales. She'd ignored the commentary and stayed in L.A. as if she'd had something to prove. Then she'd hit her forties and couldn't face middle age among the trite suburbanites so many of her old friends had become.

That's when she'd fucked off for the Keys where she could lie in the sun naked without sunscreen and without censure, and could, with impunity, inject, smoke, snort, and sleep with anything she wanted to.

The way she looked at it, the many decades' worth of recreational pharmaceuticals she'd taken had prepared her for what she was undergoing now. Of course, what she was doing now was legal, and they called it chemotherapy. Once a week she was pumped full of toxins and the rest of the time she spent puking, or toking to get her mind off it.

Without even thinking about it, she took another hit from the neatly rolled spliff in her hand and held the hot smoke in her lungs.

Hell of a way to go, with half your organs missing and the other half slowly falling to shit.

She closed her eyes and exhaled, then breathed in the easy, peaceful night scents that surrounded her. Night had always been her time, and it was still her best time, even now. Maybe especially now. The nature of her days had changed, though. They were no longer just the means to another night. She had to endure the daylight hours now, and they had their own identity: harsh, bright, hot, too full of promise, too reminiscent of what she was going to lose all too soon. Miley preferred the darkness, the magic, bone-deep island darkness that wrapped itself around her like a wizard's cloak and made reality reinvent itself. It's why she spent so much time out here on her widow's walk with nothing but the sea in front of her. At night she had soft air, soft light, and, except for when the tourists arrived, the nights were usually full of soft sounds.

And her beach. She loved her hidden slice of beach for many reasons, but one of the best was its entertainment value. Her beach was a perennial favorite for unsuspecting tourists. Couples, always couples, would park their cars near the dunes and jump and skid down the rocks or, if the tides were right, walk around the broken old seawall that jutted out from the sand. Thinking they were unseen, they would usually get right to it. No messing around, just togs off and—*Action!*

After years of it, most of the action was pretty fucking boring—*pretty boring fucking,* she thought with a grin—but that didn't stop her from watching. Hell, if they wanted privacy, they should pay for a motel.

She didn't think of her behavior as voyeuristic; it just was what it was. Life went on, and she had a seat in the bleachers.

She heard the door to the widow's walk open.

"Miley?"

Her new nurse's voice was too gentle, too sweet, but what else could she expect from a blond, blue-eyed angel? Miley preferred the last nurse, Barbara. She'd been big, strong, and loud, strident almost. Barbara had been compassionate but unsympathetic, and had made Miley laugh too hard. But the big house tucked away on a quiet edge of the Keys hadn't been to her liking. Barbara needed people around her, and all the dirt and noise that came with them, so she'd headed back to Detroit. The aptly named Angela had taken her place just this week and now Miley had to put up with the tender touch of an angel. Obviously, she was nearing the end or the universe would never play such a cruel joke on her.

"Yes?" Miley rasped.

"I just wanted to check on you. Are you okay? Do you need anything?"

Angela wouldn't come into the small space unless Miley asked her to. It wasn't the three-story open height that bothered her, it was the couples on the beach. Angela had made it demurely clear that she thought watching them was perverted, even if it was from a block away.

Miley shifted to look at the nurse's young, unlined face. "I'm fine. But I think I'll go downstairs, since you're here. That way I won't have to call you in a few minutes."

"I don't mind coming back for you."

"I know. But I'll be nice to you for a change."

She carefully tamped out her joint until it wasn't glowing any longer, gently slid the nasal tubes back onto the perpetually sore skin of her septum and turned on the small flow of oxygen, then stood up. Grabbing the frame of her walker, Miley felt its legs meet the ground sturdily as she began to put her weight on it. Angela's arms were around her then, lifting, guiding. When Miley was on her feet and steady, she lingered for a minute, trying to detect a last hint of the night's scents past the faintly antiseptic odor of her manufactured oxygen.

Vague human commotion down on the beach brought forth a delicate sound of disapproval from Angela, and Miley glanced at her with a grin. Then other muffled noises, strange and ominous, pulled the women's attention from each other.

"What is that?" Angela asked suddenly as a soft shape plummeted to the ground from the top of a tree a few yards away. "A bird?"

"I've never seen one fall out of a tree," Miley replied dryly. "Maybe it ate some pot seeds I left lying around this afternoon. It wouldn't be the first stoned seagull in the Keys."

"One fell over there, too." Angela was pointing toward the other end of the widow's walk and, as Miley turned to look at her, a look of surprised panic filled the nurse's face.

"I . . . I can't breathe." She let go of Miley and sucked in a huge lungful of air, her hands wrapping around the base of her throat. Then she bent from the waist and dropped to the floor, writhing and making choking, squealing sounds as Miley watched the young woman's eyes roll back in her head, their whites glowing horrifically in the shadows of the night.

"Angela," Miley cried and dropped to her knees, smoothing back the soft blond hair from the distorted, darkening face. The oxygen tank was too heavy and the tubes had little give, so Miley reached up and pulled them out of her nose, seconds later realizing they were the only reason she was still alive.

As she breathed in, her lungs filled with a heavy, burning emptiness. Groping weakly for the tubes that lay near to her on the floor, she felt the suffocating pressure of death swelling inside her head, pushing on her eyes, and then she fell forward. She felt the cool stream of air on her weakening fingers as her hand curled around the thin tubes—

CHAPTER

8:45 P.M., Sunday, October 26, Bolling Air Force Base, Washington, D.C.

When Tom walked into to Lucy's office after a quick knock on the door, she looked up from her computer screen, then leaned back in her chair. She was exhausted. It showed on her face, in her eyes, in the way she held herself.

"What's up?" she asked.

"I was just thinking of a term I used to use a lot. I haven't used it lately, but it just came to mind. Can't imagine why."

"You came over here to tell me that?"

"I thought you'd enjoy it."

She put down the pen she held in her hand and folded her arms across her chest. "Let me guess. Is it FUBAR?"

"Hell, no. I mean, it fits—this situation *is* fucked up beyond all recognition—but I use that one all the time. Do you remember what BOHICA means?"

She didn't crack a smile, didn't even blink. "Bend over, here it comes again."

He acknowledged her memory with a nod. "Very good. It's an expression that might come in handy in the next few hours or days," he replied, seating himself in one of the chairs in front of her desk. "The winds near Taino are holding steady. The plume is maintaining a fast and firm course toward Miami."

"Is there any good news?"

"Yes, actually. A small system from the Gulf brought some rain to parts of Miami tonight, so that will help keep things under control."

"So if we cloud-seed—"

Tom shook his head. "Briscoe doesn't think that will do much."

"So we're screwed," she said dryly.

"I've come around to the idea of the microbes."

"Somehow, I knew you would." She stifled a yawn. "Any more reports of deaths?"

"The coast guard has found a few more boats adrift off the Keys. Some of the bodies showed signs of being cyanotic, but they'd also been roasting in the sun for several hours. We probably won't know any more for a while. Anyone looking for dead people would be dead soon themselves, right? Unless the wind changes direction." He sighed. "God, I just love election years in South Florida."

Lucy stood up abruptly, as if he'd poked her with a lit match. "I'm not in the mood for your black humor, so just shut the fuck up if you can't say anything constructive."

For the first time in a long time, Tom felt undisguised shock course through him and he rose to his feet, concerned more at her actions than her words. "I'm sorry. What's wrong?"

"What the hell is going *right*?" she snapped.

"Lucy." It came out so softly, he barely realized he'd said it.

She brushed it away and took a harsh breath. "I have family in Miami, okay? They can't be moved," she said tightly. "Subject closed. Have any of those bomb doctors come up with any ideas?"

Knowing she would resent and likely never forgive any show of sympathy, he simply shook his head. "They're still in a huddle with Briscoe."

"Well, I need some answers. Fast."

He narrowed his eyes at her. Her color was high and her body was so tense she was practically throwing off sparks. "What are you going to do?"

"I'm going back to the president. We need gas masks and we need evacuations."

"It might already be too late. Even if it isn't, he'll never go for it."

"The hell he won't—"

Tom leaned across the desk and grasped her wrist, jerking her toward him and forcing her to meet his eyes. "Lucy, think about it. *There's nowhere for anyone to go.*"

9:50 P.M., Sunday, October 26, Bolling Air Force Base, Washington, D.C.

"Dr. Briscoe, Director Denton said you should see this."

Sam looked up to see a young woman standing at his elbow with a manila folder in her hands. He'd been so absorbed by the chaos on his screen that he hadn't even heard her come in.

"Thanks," he said, taking the folder as he sat back and rubbed his burning eyes. The hours spent in the glare of the computer screen were taking their toll. Taking a breath to clear his head, he glanced down at the folder. The top was covered with thick blue stripes, with the words TOP SECRET stamped in large letters in the center.

Oh, hell. What now?

He flipped open the folder and began reading an e-mail sent from some department in NOAA that he'd never even heard of. Seconds later he jumped to his feet, cursing, as a bad excitement flooded his brain.

"What is it?" Marty asked, already on his way to Sam's side.

"God-damn son of a bitch," Sam roared, shoving the paper at Marty, who took it and scanned it as quickly as Sam had.

Sam barely had time to shove a hand through his hair and tug on the roots before Marty raised his eyes, wide with disbelief, to Sam's face.

"This has to be wrong, Sam. It has to be," he said quietly.

"No, Marty," Sam said, his voice full of loathing at the results on the paper, at Dennis Cavendish. "Between the satellites doin' gas spectrometry and the devices they've been droppin' into the plumes for the last few hours, I gotta believe this."

"Sam, that methane can't be converting to phyrru-luxine. It . . . it can't. It's got to be—"

Sam looked at his oldest friend, who seemed to have aged a lot in the last few hours. Even the dancing hula girls on his shirt were starting to sag. "Forget 'can't,' Marty. It *is,* and all bets are off. What's comin' out of the water is adulterated methane. What's blowin' ashore is phyrruluxine. You do the math."

Marty stared at him. "The dennisium."

Sam shook his head. "Whatever is in that dennisium is causing one helluva transformation."

Both men looked up as Victoria Clark and Lucy Denton entered the room. Victoria walked directly to Sam, who was trying to ignore the clawing nausea in his stomach. What fresh Hell was she bringing him?

"The woman our people picked up from the clipper is Cynthia Davison," she said quietly, searching his eyes.

Thank God. Sam's legs nearly went out from under him as relief and emotion threatened to choke him.

"Excuse me," he muttered as he sank into a chair. He buried his face in his hands, his breath hard and choppy as it fought its way past the aching lump that had suddenly formed in his throat.

A light hand came to rest on his shoulder. "I'm so glad for you, Sam. She's got a dislocated shoulder and a broken wrist, and is pretty bruised and shaken up, but she's otherwise okay. We'll get her back to you soon," Victoria said softly.

Sam nodded, then stood up, wiping his hands across his wet face. "Thank you, Ms. Clark. Thank you." Taking a deep breath, he shook his head and looked around the room. "Now back to our regularly scheduled programmin'. Ms. Denton, we got trouble. There's phyrruluxine in the plume."

She frowned. "What is that?"

"It's a highly toxic, highly flammable gas. It's not something that methane typically converts to. Make that *never* converts to. Not without help." Sam shook his head.

"Phyrruluxine is bad, Ms. Denton. Worse than methane. It's even worse than hydrogen sulfide, but stinks just as bad. Seriously nasty stuff. You don't want it blowin' around," he said.

"Do we have a solution?" she asked quietly.

His heart rate still coming down, Sam shoved his hands in his pockets and shrugged. "Marty found some researchers with live methanotrophic colonies. Some have agreed to begin building the colonies and to give them to us."

"You don't sound pleased."

"I've told you before, this is dangerous, Ms. Denton. We'll be gettin' all different bugs, and we'll be sendin' 'em into an unknown and unpredictable environment." Sam shrugged as he watched Lucy's intelligent, expressionless face. "Microbes can mutate just as fast as their environments do. We've gotten an idea of some of what was in that dennisium, but not its original molecular structure, which can make a difference. What we do know is that the interaction between methane and dennisium is supposed to take place under extreme pressure at low temperatures, and the interaction is supposed to be with methane *hydrate,* not methane *gas.* So that's three parameters that have changed already. The new mixture has been exposed to air, sunlight, heat, and surface pressure for about twelve hours, and bad things are happenin'. The steady and, frankly, ma'am, alarmin' production of phyrruluxine may be just the beginnin'. At this point, I don't think it's an exaggeration to say anything is possible, includin' some sort of chain reaction."

"What sort of chain reaction?" Lucy asked cautiously.

Sam shrugged and picked up the top secret file folder, then smacked it with the back of his other hand.

"Could be a spontaneous air burst. Or another change in the chemical composition. Hard to say. There's no way of knowing what to expect or when to expect it. But there's goin' to be a lot more dead people on the ground soon."

Without commenting, Lucy turned to Marty. "Do you have a list of the colonies that will be made available to us and their locations?"

He nodded.

"Good. E-mail it to me." She paused. "Just out of curiosity, how big are these colonies?"

Marty adjusted his glasses. "They range from a few thousand microbes to a few million. Lab sized."

She frowned. "How long will it take to get more if we need them?"

"Some of the bugs replicate in as few as six hours, some take longer."

"Oh." She looked slightly confused. "What size containers will we need to transport them?"

Sam coughed to cover up a choking laugh, and Marty looked at him.

"A few shoeboxes ought to do it. All the colonies are, Ms. Denton, are petri dishes or lab beakers containing some agar that's been smeared with a few microbes. You make sure they're held in an environment at the right temperature with the right amount of light, and let 'em replicate," Sam replied. "No matter how many microbes you have in one spot, they're too small to see with the naked eye."

Lucy's face didn't change color but the way she tightened her lips and straightened her shoulders made it clear that she realized she should have known the answer to her own questions.

"Thank you, Dr. Briscoe, Dr. Collins. Please continue

what you were doing," she said stiffly, then turned to leave the room.

2:15 A.M., Monday, October 27, Bolling Air Force Base, Washington, D.C.

Victoria had been delivered to her hotel at midnight. Now, waiting with her security detail in the lobby for a driver to pick her up to take her back to the bland building housing Lucy's office, she was glad she had taken a shower before crawling into bed for a brief nap.

No matter how long this meeting lasted, she knew this was just the beginning of her day.

The driver was unexceptional: clean-cut, silent, and too highly trained to be ferrying even the most high-value guests around the city. Before too long she found herself back in Director Denton's office, with Lucy's assistant offering her a cup of coffee.

"Thanks." Taking the mug from her, Victoria sat. Lucy was behind her desk, a phone pressed to her ear. How she managed to look so fresh when she obviously hadn't slept was a mystery.

With an abrupt word, Lucy hung up the phone and looked straight at her. "Thanks for coming. We believe phase three of Blaylock's plan has been put into effect."

Victoria set her mug on the table next to her with suddenly shaking hands. "There's nothing left on Taino to blow up."

The barest hint of a cold smile crossed Lucy's face. "Not Taino. Everywhere else. A computer virus has hit every major bank, heading west from Tokyo. We've got the North American banks on alert, but based on how it's been spreading, the virus is already embedded and is just awaiting a timed activation." She took a sip of her coffee. "You're a computer security expert, aren't you, Ms. Clark?"

"Yes."

"Will you help us?"

"Of course."

"Good. We want you to contact Blaylock."

Victoria recoiled. "I thought you meant with the virus."

Now Lucy smiled for real. "Thank you, but that's not necessary. We know who wrote it and what it looks like. It's been altered somewhat from what we were told it would be, but we've got people on it. It—"

Lucy's voice faded as the meaning of her words sank in, and Victoria interrupted her, blood surging in anger. "You know who wrote it? You have people inside GAIA? Why didn't you stop this?" she demanded. "How could you have let this—any of this—happen?"

Lucy recoiled in surprise for just a second, then met Victoria's eyes with a cool expression. "Yes, we know who wrote the virus code. Yes, we have contacts inside GAIA. As far as preventing what has happened, Ms. Clark, you know as well as I do that no intelligence or security operation is airtight."

"But you've let people die—"

"Ms. Clark," Lucy replied, her words slicing through the air like a razor through flesh, "let me remind you that it was *your* government that made this possible, not mine. Obviously, had we known specifically what Blaylock was going to do, we would have prevented it. Had we known what Dennis Cavendish was doing, we would have been able to anticipate trouble. As it happens, we didn't learn about either in time. So might I suggest that you forget about pointing fingers and focus on the issues at hand."

Knowing Lucy was right and hating her for it, Victoria reined in her anger and gave her a brief nod.

"Thank you. As I was saying, the virus won't melt down the world markets the way Blaylock intended it to. He's a narcissist and a control freak, so this failure should send him closer to the edge. He may even want to vent. What I'd like you to do is find out what Blaylock wants. I'm fairly certain we can arrange a linkup. Would you talk with him?"

Her composure nearly back in place, Victoria tried not to react. "Why me?"

"First of all, he knows you, or of you." Lucy shrugged. "He's penetrated your very thorough and very impressive security perimeter at least twice. Once with Lieutenant Colonel Watson and once with whomever is the insider still on Taino, presumably Micki Crenshaw. Secondly, you're a smart, attractive woman, and we know he likes smart, attractive women. And he likes to be blunt and to shock people. My impression is that you don't shock easily, and that alone may rattle his cage a bit. He also doesn't know you're working with us. Are you willing?"

Before Victoria could formulate an answer, there was a quiet knock on the door and a young woman with a serious expression on her face entered the room. Without a word, she crossed to Lucy and handed her a sheet of paper, then turned and left.

As Lucy read, Victoria saw an ominous expression ripple over her face. A muscle in her cheek flexed rapidly.

Setting the paper face down on her desk, Lucy got to her feet abruptly. "Circumstances have changed. I won't need to put you in contact with Garner Blaylock. Please excuse me, Ms. Clark."

It took a few seconds for Victoria to register that she was being dismissed.

"Of course. I'll be in the conference room," Victoria said hurriedly as she rose to her feet and left the room.

That son of a bitch. If he were in front of me now, I'd kill him. Slowly. Viciously. With pleasure.

Livid, Lucy watched the door close behind a wary Victoria Clark. The instant she was alone, she picked up her phone with shaking hands and called Tom.

"Where are you?" she demanded when he answered.

Typically, he displayed no surprise. "In my office."

"I need some air," she said. "Meet me at the elevators."

She hung up without waiting for his reply.

Tom arrived at the elevator lobby at the same time she did and they rode in silence to the ground floor. Under the watchful gaze of the MP at the security desk, they swiped their smart cards and exited the rear of the building at street level.

The night was beautiful, chilly and clear with a breeze strong enough to blow the cobwebs out of her head. But it still took ten minutes of walking briskly along the frosty, artificially bright streets of the base until Lucy considered her thoughts coherent enough to try to put them into words.

Slipping her hand around Tom's arm, she tugged him in the direction of the razor-wire-topped fence that ran along the bank of the Potomac. Lucy stopped near the fence, right at the edge of the parking lot, and stared at the dark water.

Reagan National Airport lay on the opposite bank and the runway lights and ground traffic sent red, white, and blue light strobing into the night, sparkling off the water. It was a sight she'd always enjoyed, but tonight that patriotic glitter seemed to taunt her with a bitter irony as she considered what she was about to do.

Lucy let go of Tom's arm and wrapped her arms around herself, glad and not at all surprised that Tom remained silent while her rationality wrestled with her gut instinct. After a long silence, so long that she was shivering in the damp wind and her teeth were chattering, she turned to him and met his eyes.

"How long have we known each other?" she asked.

"I believe that's classified," he replied lightly.

She couldn't help but flash a rare, genuine smile before she glanced away. "We've been through a lot."

"That we have."

"Are we friends?"

"Hardly."

She gave a silent laugh, then took a deep breath. "This job, the DNI—it should have been yours."

"I wouldn't have taken it. You're the warm, fuzzy, people person, not me," Tom said, pushing his hands into his trouser pockets and glancing out over the water.

Lucy stared at the water, letting another silence grow before she continued speaking.

"So in your esteemed opinion, have I lost my edge? Am I getting weak?" she whispered, her voice brittle and quavering with real emotion for the first time in decades.

"No."

The speed and force of his reply bolstered her confidence and she brought her gaze back to his. Tom's eyes were cool, his expression neutral. His hands hung loosely at his sides, fingers half curled, as if he were bracing for a fight.

It was exactly what she needed from him.

"Your report said Blaylock was holed up in a villa in Algeria. Outside Annaba. Didn't it?" Lucy asked.

"Yes."

She nodded and took a measured breath. "I just received word that the body of one of our covert officers was found about two hours ago propped against an outside wall of the police headquarters in Annaba. She hadn't been dead long. Less than an hour, they figure." She swallowed hard and heard Tom swear under his breath. "She'd been raped, beaten, and severely mutilated. Among other things, GAIA's logo was carved into her face." She stopped again and took a deep breath. "Her cover was Bridget Malloy. Was she one of the—"

"She was the one who was the closest to Blaylock," Tom said, interrupting her. "She wrote the code for the virus."

"How long was she with us?"

"Five years. She was very good."

Lucy nodded once, swallowed hard again, and waited until she felt a familiar coldness that had nothing to do with the weather sweep through her. She straightened her back and met Tom's eyes.

"I understand the full consequences of what I'm about to say, and I want to assure you that you are in no way obligated to carry out this mission or assist in its execution in any way." She paused. "I want Garner Blaylock dead," she said in a voice that was barely audible but powerful despite that. She watched Tom's eyes, aching at the knowledge that the order she'd just given had changed their relationship—as close and as strange as it was—forever.

Tom said nothing for the space of several heartbeats.

"Lucy," he began.

"Save your breath," she said, stopping him with a look. "I know the arguments. I know the consequences. It could cost me my job. It probably just cost me what's left of my soul, if I ever had one. I don't care. That kid didn't deserve what happened to her. Neither has anyone else he's hurt or killed. He's evil and he's been around too long. He needs to be gone."

After a short pause, Tom nodded.

"I don't want it painless and I don't want it pretty, but I want it done fast," she added.

"Understood."

He wouldn't meet her eyes and Lucy knew that they both understood that she had cracked under pressure. She'd crossed the line that a true professional never crossed: She'd made a decision based on emotion rather than circumstances.

She'd made it personal.

3:30 A.M., Monday, October 27, Taino

Dennis had sat for hours throughout the night, pinging the night sky in what he'd known from the start was probably a vain hope of establishing a link with the satellite Micki had targeted. The battery on the ground unit had eventually died and, with it, his last hope of contacting the outside world to let someone know what was happening on Taino. He was sure the world was already aware of a lot of it.

There were experts who would put two and two together. And Victoria was out there—who knew how much loyalty she could be expected to maintain if things were getting bad. She'd never given up her U.S. citizenship; they could have her in custody and he knew her well enough to know that she wouldn't take a bullet for anyone. Especially him, after he'd called her a traitor.

Before he'd made the decision to go ahead with the mining operation, he'd had environmental impact studies done for every possible scenario, even this one. Dennis had read them all, assessed the risks, and then went ahead and took some of those risks. And now he was facing the greatest one of all, the one that he'd always thought had the lowest chance of happening.

He knew that the dennisium would make the methane gas hug the surface of the water and the land, and that it would travel as far as the wind would take it, dissipating slowly. The wind had picked up over the last few hours. With any luck, the rising wind would diffuse the gas to the point where it wouldn't kill people, but that wouldn't take it out of the atmosphere, and that's where the real problem lay for the future.

Dennis knew that the destruction of his dream had sent a huge amount of methane into an anthropogenically altered atmosphere that was already in flux. When the methane bubbling out of his pipeline eventually began to pool at the poles, the gas would start to function as a giant two-way mirror. The sun's ultraviolet rays would pass through the layer of gas and warm the earth's atmosphere. At the same time, the gas would trap the heat rising from the earth's surface the way a window traps heat in a house. Heat would continue to collect, measurably diminishing the planet's ability to cool itself. In real time.

The oceans would warm and become diluted with the increasing fresh-water runoff from melting glaciers and sea ice. Global circulation patterns, which relied on both temperature and salinity differentials to keep going, would slow.

The Southern Hemisphere's summer would be hot; the Northern Hemisphere's winter would be warmer than any other in recorded history. What Arctic sea ice formed would be thin and patchy. The vast Greenland and Antarctic ice sheets would continue to melt, and do so at a rate faster than anyone could have predicted.

A few months from now, the northern spring would arrive weeks sooner than anticipated. What glaciers and snowpack remained would melt faster and earlier, causing catastrophic avalanches. Rivers would run wilder, tides would be higher than expected, and the rains would be harder, each bringing more flooding to places unprepared for it.

After the rain, the temperature would begin to soar in the northern part of the planet. Droughts would threaten harvests and livestock, heat would claim the lives of those not able to tolerate it, and severe weather would destroy property at random. Civil society would recede as water shortages everywhere primed local, regional, and national tempers for harsh and even violent resolutions. Vain and wasteful cities would learn how precarious their existence is, and idyllic suburbs and rural areas would grow desperate to protect and maintain their ways of life. Coastal areas would learn the futility of trying to hold back inevitably rising waters.

The next winter would never arrive.

Eventually, within a matter of years, there would be no change of seasons anywhere on the globe; there would be no autumn, no rainy or cool season to bring relief, no growing season. Deserts would evolve on once verdant land. Lake beds and reservoirs would shrink, revealing their macabre histories. Islands would disappear beneath waves the world over. Wars would begin and have no end.

Eventually the oceans would achieve a critical warmth. Then the tens, perhaps hundreds of gigatons of methane hydrate beneath the ocean floors would begin to melt, releasing catastrophic amounts of lethal gas into the atmosphere.

And then life, *all* life, would end.

These thoughts had repeated endlessly in Dennis's mind during the long wakeful hours he'd spent under a night sky irreparably altered at his hands. The experience had made one thing become unutterably clear to Dennis.

It was his responsibility to rectify what had gone wrong. The fate of the earth had to come before the agonizing fate of few thousand, or even a few million, people.

There was only one way, one ancient way, he could do it.

He had to burn off the methane before it could leave the vicinity.

He had to build a fire in the sky.

CHAPTER

"You *think* it will work, or you *know* it will work, Dr. Briscoe?"

Lucy Denton had been bristly and abrupt ever since the "Hole in the Water Gang," as Sam had started calling them, had come together in the conference room half an hour ago to discuss options. Right now, he was the one under the microscope. He'd have been more comfortable with it if he'd gotten some sleep.

"Well, ma'am, considering nothing like this has ever been attempted as far as I know, or as far as Lieutenant Commander Cartwright over there knows," he said, pointing to the demolitions expert he'd been working with for the last twelve hours, "we're pretty sure it will work but we're not going to know for sure until it either does or doesn't."

"Walk us through it again. Without all the math, this time. Just the action."

Hiding his exasperation, Sam turned to the whiteboard behind him and started diagramming as he spoke. "The underwater phase will happen in two stages. We launch torpedoes—what did you call them? Deadheads?—anyway, ones with no explosives in them toward the area where the rupture is. They'll come in from three angles and strike the seafloor near the pipeline but outside of the degraded water column. When they hit the sediment, which is a few hundred feet thick in that region, they'll cause minilandslides, creating significant dislodgement of the surrounding substrate. We hope they'll dislodge enough to plug the fissure, at least temporarily. Then we'll send in the torpedoes carrying the anaerobic methanotrophs. The tubes will explode and release the microbes. At least some ought to survive to set up shop near the point of the methane release." He stopped writing on the whiteboard and turned back to face the group. "If we can stop the majority of the flow, or even diminish it, we'll be in good shape. The downside is that we don't know how damaged the subsurface structure is down there."

"Is that correct, Dr. Collins?"

Sam looked at Marty, who was looking back at him with naked fear in his eyes. Sam sent him a tight smile, which Marty didn't return.

"Yes, Director Denton, it is," Marty replied. "The last set of pictures from the satellites with ground-penetrating radar and magnetic imaging indicated some changes had occurred in the substrate, but the images were inconclusive as to determining the extent of the damage."

"What are the risks?"

"We could end up widening the gap or even opening a new fissure. There's also the possibility of triggering another landslide—not the small ones Sam mentioned, but a big one—or even an earthquake. With all the instability that's been introduced in the immediate region, I wouldn't rule out a tsunami if either of the latter scenarios occurred. The damage to the Keys and other Caribbean islands would be catastrophic. We're very close to the edge of the continental shelf and there would be no time to issue warnings."

Lucy looked grim.

"Dr. Collins, I appreciate your candor, but what are the odds that attempting to block the pipeline will make the situation worse?" Victoria asked.

"About ten to one, Ms. Clark," he said flatly. "Maybe worse."

Victoria turned to Lucy. "Perhaps—"

"No. If there were a better idea, it would have been brought up before now," Lucy replied. "We're committed to this. Dr. Briscoe, please continue with your briefing."

Sam hesitated, and considered making one last pitch for not releasing the microbes, but realized immediately that Lucy would probably have him thrown in jail if he did that. She was on the edge.

Hell, I'm *on the edge. This had damned well better work.*

He took a breath and continued. "Irrespective of whether the attempt to block the flow is successful, we'll immediately shift our focus to the atmosphere." He paused. "Actually, if the underwater attempt doesn't work, it will be even more important to deploy the atmospheric microbes. We'll do that by shooting missiles into the plume. Their payloads will contain several varieties of microbes instead of warheads."

"Several varieties?" Victoria asked.

"I'd like to say that that decision is based on careful thought, Ms. Clark, but the truth is, we're goin' with the spaghetti theory. You know how you throw a piece of spaghetti at the wall and if it sticks, it's done? Well, we're goin' to throw everything we've got at that gas and see what sticks. We're doin' the same thing down below. It's very likely that a lot of the bugs won't embrace the environment. We're just hopin' some will."

He turned back to the whiteboard.

"With regard to the missiles, we've got the degraded air column and the plume to consider. The plan is to deploy the missiles so they enter the tainted airspace at staggered intervals of several minutes and about nine miles from each other. Lieutenant Commander Cartwright suggested a total of five missiles, with the one nearest to the coast bursting a few miles offshore." He shook his head and pointed to the other edge of the whiteboard. "The missile tubes will start to break up as soon as they pass through the plume due to the change in air pressure. We'll have backup devices in them, too. The explosions will release the microbes and they'll scatter. If they survive, they'll start munching on methane."

The room was silent when Sam finished. He put the markers he'd been using in the tray and sat down, looking expectantly at Lucy.

"I just need to remind you, ma'am, that if this all works, we'll only be taking care of the methane. We've got phyrruluxine forming inside that plume, and that is a whole other big-ass world of hurt. It's highly explosive, and it's toxic."

"So is the methane," Lucy replied. "Why is this a problem?"

"The methane isn't toxic, ma'am. Too much of it just pushes the oxygen out of the way so there's none left to breathe until the concentration returns to normal. The phyrruluxine is highly toxic, and it doesn't behave like methane. Very small amounts can be lethal." He paused. "I don't know what gets rid of that. We may just have to pray that stuff disperses."

"Thank you for the update, Dr. Briscoe." Clearly furious, Lucy held his gaze briefly, then looked down the table to the cluster of navy officers at the other end. "Well?"

"Director Denton, we'll give it a shot," the highest-ranking one replied.

"Good." She glanced down at her watch and then back at Sam. "The cruiser *Eutaw Springs* is anchored off Taino and the secretary of the navy has ID'd that ship as the base of this operation. The personnel transporting the microbes should be arriving there in a few hours. There will be an assembly and staging area set up when you get there."

It took Sam's sleep-deprived brain a few seconds to register what she'd just said.

"When *I* get there?" he asked, not enjoying the unexpected blood pressure spike her words had provoked.

"You'll be on board for the duration of the operation, Dr. Briscoe. Dr. Collins and Ms. Clark will be there, too."

"Wait a damned minute, Ms. Denton. I'm not—" Her look stopped him mid-sentence.

"You won't see this through?" she asked quietly.

The look in her eyes, in the eyes of the four navy officers at the end of the table, in Marty's and Victoria Clark's eyes shamed him, made him feel like the skunk at a garden party. No, worse than that. They made him feel like a traitor.

He shook his head and looked down, rubbing a hand over the back of his stiff neck. "Just surprised me, is all. Of course I'll go," he muttered. *And spend every minute on that boat pukin' my guts up. Damn it.*

"Thank you, Dr. Briscoe." Lucy was about to continue when Sam saw her look down at the open laptop in front of her, and immediately touch a few keys. The occupants of the room remained silent as she read something on the screen, then looked up.

"Something's happening on Taino," she explained. "We've been monitoring the island via satellite since before the crash occurred. Its communications went dark approximately twenty-four hours ago, but there was an encrypted signal sent from it yesterday afternoon. There's been indiscriminate pinging going on for the last eight or so hours, but no contact has been made with any transponder."

"You didn't tell me—" Victoria blurted, and Lucy gave her a look.

"I'm telling you now. Three persons made it onto the island yesterday afternoon at a small beach on the north end. They disappeared into the brush almost immediately and have not been seen again. However, someone emerged from a higher point on the island's north end approximately twenty minutes after the three figures landed on the beach. That person, presumably one of the group, sent an encrypted message that was picked up by a leased transponder on a low-earth orbit satellite owned by a European telecommunications consortium. So it appears that at least one person is alive and active on the northeastern end of the island."

Sam looked at Victoria, who had gone very still, anger etched onto her face.

"Ms. Clark," Lucy continued, "do you have any idea who is on that island? Where did the people who landed on the beach go?"

"They would have been heading for the bunker." Victoria's voice was cold and quiet.

"What bunker?" Lucy asked sharply.

Sam could have sworn he saw the hint of a smile on Victoria's face as she turned to face Lucy. "President

Cavendish had an emergency shelter built into the side of Mount Taino. It was completed several years ago."

Lucy was clearly not pleased at just learning this. "How many people could be in there?"

"The bunker was constructed to house the entire population of Taino, around seventy people, or even more if it had to," Victoria replied. "It wouldn't be comfortable, though."

"Ms. Clark, please stay on point," Lucy replied with an edge to her voice. "How many people do you think could have survived and might be in that bunker?"

"Realistically, there can't be more than a few people in there. Everyone in the *Atlantis* habitat was presumed dead within minutes of the first detonation. Based on the earlier footage you showed me, a dozen or so bodies were scattered near the beachside compound. Captain Broadhurst was directing the sea-based recovery operation. Once he learned about the clipper and deaths on the beach, he ordered all land-based security personnel offshore," Victoria explained.

"Why?" Lucy demanded, interrupting.

"If the people outside the bungalows were dead, the people inside them would be, too," Victoria said simply. "They weren't airtight. None of the windows even had screens, just shutters. So anyone who is still alive on the island is in that bunker. There can't be many. There weren't many people on the island to begin with, and all the security personnel have been accounted for. So I can only surmise that President Cavendish and Deputy Secretary Crenshaw and perhaps a very few others made it to the bunker."

"Do you think it's likely that President Cavendish survived?"

"If Micki Crenshaw is Garner Blaylock's mole, then

I think it's likely both Micki and Dennis survived," Victoria said flatly. "Micki doesn't have all of the information needed to make things run. Dennis liked to keep some things secret."

"Well, Ms. Clark, if President Cavendish and Micki Crenshaw are still alive, why haven't they tried to contact anyone? The only communications coming off that island in the last twenty-four hours are the ones I just described."

"Micki would be trying to evade detection, Ms. Denton. As for Dennis, I think he would want to be found. So I would imagine that he is her hostage, if he's still alive."

"Thank you, Secretary Clark." Lucy gave everyone in the room a tight smile. "You'll all be leaving for Andrews Air Force Base shortly. You should be aboard the *Eutaw Springs* by eight. Good luck."

She left the room, leaving an uncomfortable silence in her wake.

5:45 A.M., Monday, October 27, Taino

Just before dawn, as the horizon was finally turning the palest shade of pink, Dennis emerged from the bunker. He had his plan; now there was enough light to begin executing it.

With a grimace of distaste, he began to wrestle the set of air tanks from the stiff body of one of the three security officers Micki had killed. Although rigor mortis rendered it unable to flex the way he needed it to, the soft tissue had already begun to decompose in the tropical heat and humidity. The too-soft flesh was clammy and disgusting and the stench kept bile surging high in his throat. Fighting nausea, he wrenched the tanks from all three bodies. He stacked two sets of tanks near the bunker door, and donned the other, although he didn't need the air supply right away.

Dennis began making his way down the familiar, well-marked path that led from the bunker to the dock at the southern tip of the island. He walked slowly, careful to watch and listen to the wildlife. After he'd been walking for about twenty minutes, he noticed that both the noise and movement around him had diminished. A few paces later it seemed to stop. He put the regulator in his mouth, opened the valve on one of the tanks, and continued his cautious descent. Seconds later, he rounded a curve. A burst of color on the path ten yards ahead of him brought him to an abrupt halt.

The brilliantly colored body of a Cuban parrot looked as if it had been thrown to the ground. One wing rested awkwardly, twisted upward against the lower branches of a shrub; the other lay crumpled beneath the corpse. A quick look into the scrub revealed more dead birds splayed on and under shrubbery. Looking higher into the canopy, he saw some leaning drunkenly against whatever supported them and others still clinging to branches.

Yea, though I walk through the valley of the shadow of death, I will fear no evil. He gritted his teeth, grinding them against the hard plastic of the regulator. *I don't have to fear it. It's been here and gone.*

The thought occurred to him that he might need to kill Micki all over again, just because she deserved it.

Between his exhaustion, the rising heat, and the dead weight of the air tanks, Dennis's progress was slow and he was sweating heavily, tripping frequently. Once he lost his balance completely. He kept walking through the now eerily silent tropical forest, trying to avoid stepping on the carcasses of birds, lizards, rodents, and insects that littered the path ahead of him.

Eventually, he reached the treacherous, unmarked side path that led to a hidden vantage point overlooking the island's western shore. The small path hadn't been used in months, which, in the tropics, meant the jungle had reclaimed it. Pushing aside the vines that begged to trip him, the leaves that yearned to cut him, Dennis finally stepped into the small clear area that had been his target. He stood atop a jagged, table-topped rock that jutted baldly from the wall of vegetation into the air and hung over the beach like a bad omen.

He lowered himself heavily onto a rotting stump that had rolled to the edge of the outcropping and, breathing hard, took the opportunity to look at the sea. The sun, behind him, was just beginning to edge above the horizon, but the shadow of the volcano refused to let any of that early light illuminate the water below him. That water had cradled his dreams four thousand feet beneath its dark, ruffled surface—dreams now smashed beyond utility or repair.

Turning on the low-light binoculars he'd brought with him, Dennis scanned the terrain around and below him. Unrecognizable shapes glowed faintly green against the shadowy darker green backdrop.

Carcasses.

Alive, they would have been brighter, the brightest objects in his field of vision, but the luminescence of life had drained from them, leaving only whatever bacteria could thrive in this dead and airless place.

This was Micki's doing. Traitorous bitch.

Justified rage gathered, and Dennis released its primal scream within the confines of his mind, slamming his fist into the log beside him again and again until the urge subsided.

He turned his focus to the sea, speckled with infinite

small bioluminescent life-forms that sparkled almost painfully bright, like the stars against the night sky. Scanning far to the left, his vision was arrested by the huge, pale, foaming patch of ocean that marked the rupture. Shifting to its own rhythm as it rose slightly above the sea around it, the water surged and bubbled madly, like a witch's cauldron left too long on the boil.

The sight of it shook him and, suddenly trembling, he leaned clumsily forward to rest his head in his hands, the specialized binocs dangling from their strap.

His paradise had gone silent; indeed, it had gone mad.

He sat up then, and spent several moments watching the high, dark clouds lighten to become a pale shade of purple against a pinkening sky.

I allowed this madness to happen.

I made it happen.

With death and an alien, overwhelming sense of helplessness pressing upon him, Dennis pulled himself to his feet, feeling ancient. Then he turned and fought his way back to the path he'd just descended, and began to retrace his steps.

Whatever else the new day had in store for the planet, Dennis was going to try to bring his world salvation.

35
CHAPTER

Garner Blaylock was pacing in the large, airy room he used as his brain center, infuriated that somehow, something had gone disastrously wrong with his plan to attack the world through cyber channels. As daylight had moved west across the world, stock exchanges and other financial markets had been opening late and the bloggers and talking heads were all blathering about the problems with their usual tone of high-pitched hysteria.

But in the streets, in the banks, and on "the wire" there was no panic, no chatter about paralyzed trading floors, no talk of shutdowns and crashes. In soothing tones, industry spokesmen were using terms like "mischief" and making allusions to "a few hackers" when they should have been half-crazed at the incursion of the self-replicating, self-mutating virus that he'd unleashed. He'd meant to bring the world's financial markets to their knees, and all he'd given them was a case of mild indigestion.

The more he thought about it, the more his fury increased, and the more he wished he hadn't been so hasty to disavail himself of the dubious charms of Bridget Malloy.

That bitch had to be behind it. And whatever she'd done, even that idiot Cyril hadn't been able to fix.

She'd been too clever and too attractive by half, that

one. Those desert buffoons he'd given her to might have had their fun but, at this point, Garner wasn't so sure she'd gotten what she deserved. If he'd kept her around a bit longer, he could have made sure she paid in full for her treachery.

He walked to the door that led to the corridor and flung it open, about to roar for somebody to bring that bloody idiot Cyril to him. He stopped short, however, at the sight of the startled and bowing figure of one of the household's servants, who was making murmured apologies for the interruption caused by the arrival of Garner's midday meal.

Disconcerted, he stood aside to let the short parade of silent servants into the room. Then he called to one of the bodyguards lolling against the far wall of the wide, shadowy corridor.

"Bring Cyril to me," he barked in French. "Immediately."

The servants bowed their way out of the room and Garner resumed pacing as the lush, spicy aroma of a vegetable tagine filled the air. Several long minutes passed before Cyril, out of breath and more disheveled than usual, burst into the room.

"About bloody time, you fucking wanker," Garner snarled. "Where were you?"

Cyril took a startled step backward. "What? Right. Sorry. There were some problems with—"

"I'm not interested in anyone else's fucking problems," Garner snapped. "I'm only concerned with mine. And I've got a bloody big one, thanks to you and your former colleague. Where the fuck are all the system crashes? Where's the panic? Why haven't all the networks gone dark?"

Cyril just blinked at him. "I've been trying to—"

"Well, quit fucking *trying* and just fucking *do* something," Garner ordered. He closed his eyes and took two deep breaths, trying to calm himself. Then he moved to the low table holding the food and sat down in front of it carefully, so as not to disturb the several flies that had landed on his meal.

Cyril stood there awkwardly until Garner glanced up at him, the first scoop of his lunch dripping through his fingers as he paused with it halfway to his mouth. "Do you want some?"

"Er, no, no, thanks. Thank you, no," Cyril stammered. "Had a bit of loo trouble this morning. North Africa's version of Delhi belly or some such. I'll stick to tea, thanks."

Garner rolled his eyes at the man's vulgarity and shoved the food into his mouth. The tagine was rich and well spiced but, after he'd swallowed it, a strangely harsh taste filled his mouth.

God-damned peasants. Can't cook worth a fuck.

He dipped into a different part of the dish, avoiding the bitter eggplant. But the second bite was no better, and he pushed aside the low bowl of roasted vegetables in favor of the carrot salad ubiquitous to North Africa. He usually despised its honeyed sweetness, but right now anything would be better than the tagine's aftertaste.

The salad was as bad and he reached for the glass of beer to wash the flavor out of his mouth. It wasn't until he'd swallowed nearly half the beer in a large gulp that he noticed a few grains of white powder swirling in the bottom of the glass.

With a shout, Garner flung the glass against the wall and rose to his feet, rage pumping through him. "I've been poisoned. Get the guards. Get those fucking servants back in here," he screamed.

Cyril seemed frozen in place. "Good Lord. What did you say? I'm sorry, Garner, I don't seem to—"

"Get the fuck out of the way, you bloody fucking moron. I've been poisoned. There was something in the food," Garner roared as he lunged for the door.

Suddenly, oddly agile, Cyril stepped into his path, effectively blocking him from the exit. "Garner, you must calm down. There couldn't possibly be anything in the food. I think the heat is making you mad. Sit down there for a minute and I'll call for the guards."

"I don't need to fucking sit down. I need a doctor. I need to have my stomach pumped," Garner said, trying to shove the taller, skinnier man out of his way.

"I said I'd take care of it," Cyril snapped, and it took Garner a few seconds for him to realize that his body, his muscles weren't responding as they should. He didn't—couldn't—resist as Cyril settled him firmly onto one of the low divans that were scattered about the room.

Cyril took several steps toward the door of the room, then stopped and turned around. Garner stared at him, knowing something wasn't right. He didn't look the same. Cyril looked . . . sure of himself.

I'm going mad.

"I have to get out of here," Garner muttered, his voice sounding oddly thick as he tried to push himself off the cushions. His legs were heavy, as unwieldy as if they were made of wood. "Cyril, help me up. Cyril."

The man just stood there, watching him. Smirking.

The first spasm wracked his body, sending his legs straight out from under him in an excruciating snap. His scream came out muffled and he saw a smile cross Cyril's face. Garner watched in terror as, with a decided lack of concern for the situation, Cyril reached up and took off his glasses, folded them, and hung them over the neck of his faded, sweat-stained T-shirt.

"How are you feeling, Garner?" he asked quietly, his thick English Midlands accent gone, replaced by one that was unmistakably American. "It's amazing, isn't it, what a very small amount of strychnine can do to a human body. It's going to get better, don't worry. You'll enjoy every bit of it as much as Bridget enjoyed what your boys did to her. It won't last as long, unfortunately, but I'm going to sit here and watch just to make sure you die the way you deserve to."

The second muscle spasm sent Garner's back into a whiplashed arch. The pain was severe, and seemed to pierce his very brain. Every muscle in his body was straining past its limit. He was on fire inside.

"You're a man who likes symbolism, aren't you, Garner?" the American asked, settling himself comfortably on one of the other couches. "You ought to get a kick out of this, then. I mean, here you are, the guy who hates people, who wants to make the world a better place for all the rats and cockroaches and flies, and you're dying of an overdose of something most people use to kill those very rats. Clever, isn't it?"

The third seizure sent his body over the edge of the sofa and onto the unforgiving hardness of the polished tile floor. He cracked his head along the brass edge of a table as he fell. A follow-up tremor edged him backward and, as his vision cleared, Garner could see a smear of blood on the table. His blood.

His torturer got up and helpfully moved the table out of the way, then resumed his seat, his view now unencumbered.

"It's a bitch that, with strychnine, the voice is the

first thing to go and the brain is the last, isn't it? Aw, look at that, Garner, you've wet yourself," the American said with a grin. "Too bad all your devoted lady friends can't see you now. Where's that damned iPhone when I need it?"

Horrified, humiliated, Garner tried to scream, to curse. He felt his mouth opening, his vocal cords straining, but he made no sound. He watched in spastic, involuntary silence as the smirking American folded his arms across his chest and continued to observe his descent into Hell.

The spasms became more frequent, more violent, and more painful until Garner would have been screaming for mercy if he'd had a voice. And though every single muscle in his body was convulsing madly and continuously, he remained conscious, aware of every unbearably horrific motion, every agonizing twitch.

Slightly less than an hour after he'd taken that fatal mouthful of food, Garner's body arced in one last, massive, shaking paroxysm and then went completely still, locked into instant, convoluted rigor mortis.

The American case officer waited for a minute or two to see if there would be any more movement, then went over and poked the tip of his shoe into Garner's groin with no small force. The body moved the way a fallen log would—stiffly and as a whole. Satisfied, the agent put on his fake glasses, resumed the slouched, tentative posture of his geeky British alter ego, Cyril Ponsonby, and slunk out of the room.

Closing the door carefully behind him, he gave the incurious guards an exasperated look, complete with a roll of his eyes, and walked down the corridor. He had forty minutes to meet his contact and get the hell out of Dodge.

8:10 A.M., Monday, October 27, the White House, Washington, D.C.

The man needs to take a course in how to make friends and influence people.

Lucy blinked at Ken Proust, the president's campaign manager and unchallenged political powerhouse. His face was dark red and entirely too close to her own as he loomed over her as she sat in a chair in his West Wing office. His ranting at Lucy was accompanied by a jabbing index finger and stagnant, coffee-laced breath.

She'd stopped listening to him several minutes ago, and was thinking that if he fell over from a heart attack right now, she might have to forget she'd ever learned CPR.

"Did you hear me?" he bellowed.

She looked up and calmly met his eyes. "Yes, I heard you, Ken. Now would you please step back and get your finger out of my face before I rip it off and hand it back to you?"

Startled, he followed her advice immediately and, from the look of it, instinctively.

Before he could resume his place inside her personal space, Lucy rose to her feet, moved away from the chair, and assessed him coolly. "Thank you. Now, Ken, yes, I did hear everything you said. I'm wondering, however, if you've heard anything I've been saying. Let me recap: There are bodies being discovered all along the Upper Keys—in homes, on the beaches, in boats out on the water. Dead marine life is washing up on the beaches, and dead wildlife is being found everywhere else. First responders are in full hazmat gear, moving slowly through affected areas on foot and in golf carts. It's the scenario I described to you last night."

She paused. "An unexpected change of wind speed and direction has dispersed the methane to a still-high but no longer lethal concentration. It is still, however, at a concentration that will support exothermic combustion." She stopped and looked at him. "That means fire, Ken. Very, very hot fire that starts with a big boom."

His face turned a darker shade of red but she continued before he could get a word out.

"Overnight, the mixture of the methane and the dennisium has encouraged the production of phyrruluxine, which is both highly toxic and highly combustible. So people are still dying. That's the story with the Upper Keys. Reports are coming in of people getting sick in areas between the Keys and Miami, Ken, places like Leisure City and the area around the former Homestead Air Force Base. Sound familiar? The same people who got flattened by Hurricane Andrew, what, fifteen years ago?" she snapped. "They're not rich voters, Ken, but they're the ones who make great headlines. Think babies, Ken," she said, taking a step closer to him. "Think trailer parks and elementary schools and senior centers."

He took another abrupt step backward.

"They're not dying, thankfully, not yet, just experiencing varying degrees of respiratory distress. There've been reports of large, spontaneous fires here and there, Ken. Have you seen the morning news shows? The talking heads are falling over themselves, not knowing what to rant about first."

Lucy took another step toward him and Ken actually stumbled as he moved away from her. "I told the president last night in unambiguous terms that this is what we would be facing. You were in the room when I did. He gave me carte blanche, Ken. You heard that, too. So tell me why you're blocking me at every move?"

"The media are crawling up my ass, Lucy," he snarled. "The governor of Florida has called out the National Guard. The tourism industry is already screaming about lawsuits. There's talk of opening a Senate investigation."

"There's no need for one. We know exactly what happened and who did it. And who did what about it," she added pointedly.

"Listen, Lucy, this is your problem. You're a key member of the cabinet. There's a national election in a little over a week."

"I've got news for you, Ken: That's not your biggest problem," she snapped. "Your inability to see daylight when you look out through your own asshole is the problem. People are dying, Ken. *And you're not letting the president save them.*"

He made a visible effort to calm himself, swiping a chubby hand over his shiny, sweaty face. "Germ warfare is not the answer."

Her hands itched to grab the Montblanc pen he always kept in his breast pocket and jab it through his heart.

She took a breath. "Then what *is* the answer? People are getting sick and dying, and it looks like we're not doing anything. Like the *president* isn't doing anything."

He stared at her. It was like being watched by the devil.

"I've got the microbes and the people who know what to do with them on their way to the region," she said quietly. "All I need now is the president's okay to go ahead."

"We need—"

"I need the president's approval, Ken," she repeated slowly, returning his glare with a far more effective one of her own. "If I don't get it—and get it right now—I'm resigning, effective immediately. And I'll go public. I'll hold a press conference on Pennsylvania Avenue with the White House as a backdrop. Does that help your decision-making process, Ken?"

Lucy watched the color in his face increase to an almost muddy hue.

"You bitch. I'm going to make sure you regret this," he snarled.

"You do that, Ken," she said coldly as she turned to leave the room. "In the meantime, I'll make sure you still have an electorate to lie to in South Florida."

CHAPTER

8:40 A.M., Monday, October 27, Taino

Dennis pulled the regulator out of his mouth, shut off the air tank's valve, and dropped to the ground. Not even bothering to slide the tanks off his back, he leaned against the curved trunk of a coconut palm and took a few deep breaths of the sweet, heavy, island air. With a justified grin, he acknowledged that he'd completed his task just as the last of the air tanks was running low, and that was in spite of his efforts to keep his pace relaxed and his breathing easy as he'd made his way back and forth from the bunker into the dead zone.

He was proud of what he'd accomplished in three hours. The hundreds of books and other papers he'd carried out of the bunker's library and down into the poisoned part of the forest would be enough dry fuel to get things started. He'd laid them open on their spines in a long path that snaked from the edge of the death zone to well into it. Then, just in case the concentration of methane wasn't high enough to trigger or sustain combustion, he'd doused the books with the liquid propane that had been stored in the bunker to keep the emergency generators running.

The exertion, even the loss of his books, would be worth it. The methane flowing into the atmosphere would be burned off, breaking down into carbon dioxide and water. And it would continue to burn off until the source was removed—until the broken pipeline was sealed.

That task he would likely have to leave to others. No doubt there would be plenty of governments willing to attempt it if for no other reason than to gain access to the site of *Atlantis* and harvest his technology, if not his crystals.

After allowing himself a few more moments of self-congratulatory relaxation after his grueling workout, Dennis gave a huge yawn and shut his eyes, just for a moment. But more than forty-eight high-stress hours with little rest took their toll and he fell asleep in a matter of seconds.

8:37 A.M., Monday, October 27, approaching the USS *Eutaw Springs*, off the coast of Taino

"What the hell am I doing here?"

Victoria heard Sam's muttering over the roar of the engines and rotors only because she was seated right next to him. They and Marty Collins were the only civilian passengers on the large navy helicopter that was ferrying them out to the ship stationed off Taino. They had just received official word that the microbes had arrived on the ship and were being secured.

"Saving the world as we know it?" she replied with a tense smile and received a quick glance in response.

"Kinda hard to do when you're about to toss your cookies."

She shrugged and refrained from patting his knee. She wasn't feeling too well herself. The chopper wasn't built for comfort.

"Is that Taino?" he asked, pointing out the small window.

Victoria turned, then nodded, a hard lump forming in her throat. She hadn't anticipated the emotion that rushed through her at the sight of the small slash of green edged by beaches of dark gray volcanic sand and frills of white breakers, by the miles of water that was green and translucent as sea glass, then rapidly turned to the darkest blue.

That blue marked the trenches that held the object of Dennis's dark desire.

Victoria closed her eyes briefly. Somewhere on the other side of the island lay the murderous patch of foaming sea.

"Then that must be the ship we're headin' to. Looks too damned small from up here."

She opened them at Sam's words and craned her neck to see a large military ship set slightly apart from the flotilla of boats of every description, which hugged the invisible boundary line of Taino's national waters.

They began to descend, closing in on the ship rapidly, and Victoria could see several other military ships flying other flags, as well as yachts, sailboats, fishing boats—

Moments later they came to a rocking stop on the *Eutaw Springs*'s helipad. They had barely stepped out of the chopper before being hustled on a winding journey through a maze of narrow gray corridors and shallow doorways and down two sets of steep, compact iron stairs. They eventually reached a reasonably large conference room filled with banks of computers and flat-screen monitors, and a lot of busy, silent people. No one looked up when they walked in.

Another surprisingly strong wave of emotion swept over Victoria as the memory of her last trip to the operations center of *Atlantis* crashed into the front of her mind. That had been just over forty-eight hours ago. Since then, everyone who had been there with her had died. And she'd been branded a traitor by Dennis and, less directly, by Tom Taylor and Lucy Denton.

Damn them all.

She clenched her fists and started a slow count. By the time she reached five, she had unclenched her hands. By the time she reached twelve, Victoria felt calm. She looked up to see Sam watching her with a concerned look on his face.

"How's your stomach?" she asked quickly.

"Better than expected. You okay?"

"I'm fine," she whispered with a smile and looked away.

The commander of the ship, a tight-jawed, white-haired man who obviously hadn't taken any shit from anyone in a very long time, stood up from his place at the center table. The civilians' escorts snapped to attention and saluted him. He nodded in acknowledgment and they relaxed.

"Ms. Clark, Dr. Briscoe, Dr. Collins, welcome aboard the USS *Eutaw Springs*. I'm Commander Duffy," he said, shaking their hands.

He invited them to sit down and immediately turned to Sam. "Dr. Briscoe, I understand you're the one who came up with this plan."

"Yes, sir, I am."

"Is it going to work?"

Sam nodded. "The last time I checked the data, everything was behaving just as we modeled it, sir. The temperature, the currents. We've triple-checked the crustal structure using the most recent images that we have access to, and Marty here was studying reports of drilled cores for a good part of the night. I believe it will work, sir. I believe it will."

The commander nodded. "Good. The payloads are being installed on the torpedoes and the missiles. I'll get the current water and air data for you so that you can make sure all the conditions are still within acceptable parameters." He turned away to speak to a uniformed woman.

Moments later, the woman came forward and turned on the monitors on the table in front of them. She briefly explained the layers of windows that appeared, each of which displayed different data that updated itself in real time. Sam and Marty both went a little slack-jawed with admiration as they flicked through the screens.

Victoria looked around the room, too tense to be bored, but knowing she was just extra weight until the operation was over and they could safely gain access to Taino. In a brief, private conversation, Lucy had made it clear to Victoria that she was only there to be the liaison with Taino, should one be needed—in other words, if there was anyone left alive on the island to give orders to. Whether anyone was alive or not, Victoria was to be the one to let the fox into the henhouse, the one who would let the American military in to see and steal pretty much whatever they wanted from Dennis's files and those of the Climate Research Institute. Apparently what she'd already given them wasn't nearly enough. They wanted everything. And she had to help them.

If she didn't, she'd be vilified, investigated, and most likely indicted for crimes yet to be determined.

If she did, she might be granted immunity, but the press would still brand her as untrustworthy and a traitor to two countries. She'd never work on this planet again.

Brilliant set of options.

Victoria took a deep breath and looked up to find a senior officer walking toward her looking less than happy. Sam was by his side.

"Ms. Clark, you're with the Taino government, aren't you?" the officer asked.

Depends on who you talk to, but there's no need to bore you with the details. "Yes, sir, I am," she replied.

"Ma'am, would you be willing to speak to a Captain Maggy Patterson, who appears to be the senior officer on site? She's failing to cooperate with our team. We need to get sensors in the water. We're behind schedule."

She blinked and looked at Sam. "I'm sorry. What sensors?"

"We need to place some sensors at various points around the rupture zone. We'll fire beams of light through the degraded water column to receptors on the far side of it. The data will provide reasonably good estimates of the volume of methane passing through, as well as information on the density of the water column, among a lot of other things. We need that data in order to figure out if what we're about to do will work."

Despite all her familiarity with electronics and surveillance equipment, this still seemed a little bit like voodoo to her. Things done at those depths always had. Victoria nodded, then paused. "Did you say Maggy Patterson is the senior officer on the site?"

The officer nodded.

Maggy was a good captain, but not nearly experienced enough to be running an operation like this. Victoria had left Simon Broadhurst in command, and he would never have relinquished that duty. Not voluntarily.

"I'm glad to assist however I can," she said.

Moments later Victoria was on the phone with a very distraught and understandably exhausted Maggy Patterson. The woman sounded like she had little patience and little rationality left.

"Ambassador Deen told me not to speak with you. He said you're not working for Taino any more." Maggy's voice was higher than usual and shaky.

"Maggy," Victoria said in as calm and soothing a tone as she could manage. "A lot of things have happened since I last spoke with Charlie Deen. I'm not working against Taino, but I am working with the Americans to resolve this situation. Maggy, things are very bad. What's bubbling up on the other side of the island is methane. It's drifting toward the Florida coast and killing everything in its path, just like it did on the south tip of the island. It doesn't matter any more who stops it, Maggy, it just needs to be stopped. The Americans are the only ones who can do it." She paused, but the other woman said nothing. "They need to place some sensors around the rupture."

"I can't let them in, Ms. Clark." The young woman's voice was breaking.

Well trained. By me. Victoria took a breath. "I'm on the *Eutaw Springs* with the scientists who are going to get this situation under control, Maggy. Will you allow me and one member of the American team to come aboard the *Marjory* to explain what we're trying to do? Would that ease your mind?"

Another small silence, then, "Yes, ma'am. I'll allow you on board. You and one other person. No weapons."

"Of course, Maggy. I—" Victoria stopped as she glanced at a wall clock. "Is there anything you need? Any supplies? You haven't been able to get back to shore, have you?"

The next sound Victoria heard sounded enough like a sob to make a chill skitter down her spine.

"I'm low on everything, Ms. Clark. We came out here expecting to do a ten-hour shift. We've been here for more than forty-eight hours and between the three boats, we've got every member of the security staff aboard and as many of the topside personnel as we could save. And the survivor from the clipper. We can't get back onto the island." She hiccuped a breath. "We're out of food and drinking water and we're low on fuel. Simon led a team onto the north end of the island yesterday afternoon and we haven't had any contact from them since they radioed that they'd arrived and could breathe without their tanks. Until I hear from him again, I won't let anyone else try going onto the island," the young woman finished, her voice breaking.

"We'll bring some supplies with us, Maggy. I'll be there shortly," Victoria replied briskly. She ended the call, then looked at the man standing a few feet away from her. "Commander Duffy, that survivor that Captain Patterson mentioned is an injured American citizen, a tourist. I'd like permission to have her brought aboard this ship when we return. She might be able to give us some information about what happened out there."

The man nodded once and gave an order. Twenty minutes later, Victoria, an American officer, and several cases of food and bottled water were on a small launch heading inside the boundaries of Taino's waters.

When Victoria laid eyes on Maggy Patterson, she could hardly believe the difference two days could make. Ordinarily brisk and businesslike but with an air of ease about her, the young woman was clearly stressed to her limits. Her uniform was wrinkled, obviously slept in, but the dark circles under her eyes and her pallor showed that she had gotten little rest. Lines had etched themselves into her forehead and around her mouth, and her movements were rapid and abrupt. She might be in command of the operation, but she was barely in command of herself.

She greeted Victoria and the U.S. naval officer stiffly, then directed her equally exhausted-looking crew to unload and distribute the supplies. Then she led her guests into the small space she was using as her command center and burst into tears.

Not knowing quite what to do, Victoria gave a quick glance at the American who'd accompanied her. He was standing by impassively, staring at the wall and trying very hard to keep his contempt from showing. Victoria sighed. She stepped closer to Maggy and gave the woman a brief, awkward hug, and was rewarded with a surprisingly fierce, tight embrace.

Slowly, she eased away from the sobbing woman and suggested they all sit down at the small table. Maggy seemed to be gathering some of her wits already, but Victoria knew there was no time to let her indulge in hysterics.

"So Simon is presumed dead, then?" Victoria said calmly and was pleased by the sharp intake of breath from Maggy, who instantly stopped sobbing and looked at her with wide, outraged eyes.

"I didn't say that. I said we haven't had any contact with him."

"Or with anyone in his party," Victoria added.

"Yes, ma'am."

"Is there any reason the radios wouldn't work?"

"No, ma'am."

"Were they armed?"

"Yes, ma'am."

"Then we'll presume they're incapacitated at the very least," Victoria replied tautly. "But we'll discuss that in a moment." She turned to her companion. "This is Lieutenant Gray. He'll explain what his team needs to do."

As the lieutenant spoke, Victoria carefully watched Maggy. She seemed to be regaining some of her usual good sense, but not all of it. Which could come in handy.

By the time they were shaking hands and saying their goodbyes, Victoria's mind was made up.

"Maggy, would you have the survivor of the clipper brought to us?" she asked, then turned to the lieutenant. "Did Commander Duffy tell you that you'd be bringing back an injured—"

He nodded and Victoria smiled. "Excellent. If you would let Dr. Briscoe know when she's aboard, I would appreciate it. We have reason to believe the woman is his fiancée."

The lieutenant's brows drew together in a frown. "I'm happy to, ma'am, but wouldn't it be just as easy for you—"

"I'm not returning to the *Eutaw Springs,* Lieutenant. At least not immediately. I have work to do here with my staff. Thank you so much for escorting me. Please tell Commander Duffy that I'll be in contact with him shortly," she replied, and turned to face a surprised Maggy Patterson.

"Ma'am—" the officer began.

"But—Ambassador Deen—" Maggy sputtered.

Victoria cut off both of them with a cool smile. "Lieutenant, as I said, I'll be in touch with Commander Duffy soon. As for Ambassador Deen, he isn't here, Maggy, and I am. And I will take full responsibility for everything that happens while I am. Ah, there's the passenger," she said, turning to look at a bedraggled and somewhat stoned young woman with a makeshift sling cradling one arm.

"Ms. Davison? I'm Victoria Clark. I'm so sorry for all of your troubles," she said gently. "This is Lieutenant Gray. He will take you to the U.S. Navy ship over there." She waved toward the horizon, which the *Eutaw Springs* dominated like a disapproving giant. "You will get better medical treatment there."

The woman gave her a wan smile. "Thanks."

"Ma'am, Ms. Clark, I really—"

"Lieutenant," Victoria interrupted with a glare, "I'm staying aboard the *Marjory,* which is part of the Taino security force, which I command. Please tell Commander Duffy that I will return to his ship after the operation has been executed. Until then, I must remain here if for no other reason than to be certain no one and nothing interferes with the operation from this end. Do I make myself clear, Lieutenant?"

Obviously furious, the officer nodded. Maggy looked from one to the other, then directed two of her crew to assist Cynthia into the navy boat tied up to the side of the *Marjory*.

Less than twenty minutes later, Victoria and a grim, silent Taino security officer cautiously berthed the *Marjory*'s inflatable above the high-water mark on the island's southern beach. Wearing face masks and air tanks, they made their way carefully along the sand. There was no life, no sound but the pounding of the waves against the shore.

Bodies of gulls and other seabirds lay strewn across the black beach. The odd angles of their crumpled wings and necks told of their fast, plummeting deaths. Crabs and insects were frozen in their places. Not even flies had landed on any of the carcasses.

It didn't take long for Victoria and her companion to reach the first human corpse. Forty-eight hours in the tropical heat had caused it to burst and now it lay simultaneously rotting and desiccating in the sun. Victoria was glad she couldn't smell anything through her mask. The sight was more than enough to make the bile rise dangerously in her throat. The only thing that kept her from vomiting was the sure knowledge that removing the regulator from her mouth would guarantee she would rapidly end up in the same condition as the corpse.

Willing her mind to ignore the horrors surrounding her, Victoria stepped past the bodies as she continued making her way up the path and finally pushed open the door to the communications center.

More of her fellow islanders lay sprawled in chairs and slumped over keyboards. She went directly to the workstation of her network guru. Pulling on one of the sets of latex gloves she'd brought with her, Victoria pushed the chair, with the dead man still in it, away from the desk. Body fluids had leaked into the upholstery and the liquefaction of the soft tissue had made the chair as gruesome as the body it held.

Solar panels had kept the generator, located on the other side of the island, alive. The computer was still humming, seeming as loud as a jet engine in this otherwise silent tomb, and the monitors, although dark, were only in sleep mode. She reached out a hand, then hesitated. Her fingers hovered over the keyboard.

A methane-enriched atmosphere was highly combustible. One spark—

The humidity in here is too high to allow static. Get moving.

Gritting her teeth, Victoria let her fingers touch the edge of the keyboard, half expecting to see a flash.

Nothing.

Letting out a measured breath, Victoria tapped a key and brought one of the screens in front of her to life. The bright blue glow of the background and the flashing cursor were eerily cheerful in this stinking place of death.

Her eyes focused on the screen as her fingers began to fly over the keys. Her surroundings seemed to fade as she quickly lost herself in the maze of commands and code that she knew so intimately. In just a few minutes, she reached the root of the system and carefully tapped in her emergency password.

The system began to rapidly delete directories.

God damn you, Micki. I'll personally put you in Hell if you're not already there.

She slammed a fist onto the desk and spun around, racing to the far side of the room and the door that led to the room housing the backup system. Running into the room, she began yanking plugs out of the walls, knowing that would probably not do much. The commands had been sent and received and all the machines were on battery backups. All the data for the island, for the systems, the research, everything she'd worked to protect for years, would be gone in minutes, if not sooner.

Sliding to a kneeling stop in front of the tower that held all the backup hard drives, she began tearing out cables and power cords, bringing the buzzing drives to a chaotic stop.

As she dropped the last cable, she rocked back on her heels, aware that she was breathing too fast and would run out of air too soon if she didn't calm down. She turned to motion to the guard she'd brought with her, then reached for the set of tools that was always kept near the rack. Together, they began loosening the clamps and screws holding the hard drives in place. They carefully placed the units in the empty backpacks they carried. The drives might or might not contain any salvageable data, but whatever was there, she was going to be the one to decide what happened to it, not the Americans, who were undoubtedly furious that she hadn't returned to their ship. She had no doubt that Commander Duffy had a reconnaissance team on the way to the island right now.

When the last hard drive had been harvested, Victoria went into the room housing the command encoder and decoder units and placed them in her backpack. The balpeen hammer lay in wait on the table near the units. She turned away from it abruptly and left the building, then she and the guard headed inland on the rugged path that led to the bunker.

They had been on Taino for nearly an hour when they rounded a curve and saw piles of books lying open on their spines in a haphazard trail leading in the direction they were going. The pages she could see were stained with something.

She knew there would be only one reason to douse books with anything, and that was if you intended to burn them. Setting them on fire in this methane-enriched environment would turn the island into an inferno.

Hot, sweaty, and already exhausted, Victoria continued up the trail at as fast a pace as she could manage. She was in good shape, but running up a mountain with fifty or sixty extra pounds on her back was a strain, and she couldn't keep up the pace for too long. She came to a stop, sucking hard against the regulator. Too hard, she knew. Especially considering that she was already into her second tank.

Tough.

She stood against a tree as she caught her breath and realized that she was hearing things.

Live things.

The silence of the southern end of the island had been replaced by the normal sounds of the jungle. A bird careened past. Victoria looked at the ground. Insects were thriving on the shadowed path.

She signaled to the security agent that they should continue their trek, and after moving forward several more yards, Victoria slowly removed the regulator from her mouth and took a shallow, cautious breath.

With a relieved grin, she dropped the regulator and reached behind her to shut the valve on her tank. Pulling off her mask, she felt like laughing out loud. She was still alive.

That could change any minute.

The thought sobered her and, dropping to a crouch, she carefully lifted one of the sodden books and gave it a cautious sniff, then looked up at her companion.

"Tommy, what is this? It smells familiar but I can't place it," she said and handed it to him.

Tommy Friedman didn't even need to bring it close to his face. "It's propane."

She dropped the book and sprang to her feet. "Good God."

As if all that methane isn't enough? What madman is doing this?

"We gotta keep moving. If this stuff goes up, we're toast," he said.

The adrenaline burst that followed his words was what Victoria needed and, now able to breathe more easily, they resumed hiking.

The unmistakable stink of rotting meat began to assail them when they were about one hundred yards from the bunker's entrance, and Victoria's sense of elation disappeared. Without a word passing between them, each unholstered the sidearm they wore and then eased into the clearing.

The presence of dead bodies up here would not be due to the methane, and she braced herself for more death. For murder.

"Let me go first," the officer behind her whispered fiercely, and Victoria looked back at him with a tight smile.

"It's all right. I know how to use this thing," she replied and kept moving forward, listening carefully for any human sounds as they drew closer to their target. It was probably futile. The cacophony of the jungle would have masked any low conversations as efficiently as it masked the sound of their own movement.

They slowed as they approached the curve in the trail that would lead them into the clearing near the bunker's entrance. The stench was nearly unbearable, and holding up her hand, Victoria counted down from three. Then they both rounded the bend, arms extended and hammers cocked.

Ignoring the hissed "no" of her companion, Victoria uncocked her gun and holstered it as she rushed to Dennis's still form.

She was about to feel for the pulse in his neck when he shifted and let out a soft . . . *snore*.

Rocking back on her heels, Victoria didn't know whether to laugh or cry. Or strangle him while she had the opportunity. She settled for grabbing him by the shoulders and giving him a hard shake. And then another, until his eyes finally blinked open.

When he focused on her, she saw him start as if he were seeing a ghost. She stood up and took a step away from him.

"What are you doing with all those books?" she demanded, jerking her thumb in the direction of the trail.

Clumsy and still disoriented with sleep, he rose to his feet. "What are you doing here? Vic—how did you get here?"

"We came up from the south end."

"But that's—"

"Yes," she snapped. "Toxic. I know. Who else is here?"

"Just me. Alive, I mean. Micki is in there." He motioned toward the bunker. "Simon Broadhurst and two other security officers are over there. Micki killed them."

"And you killed her?" she asked dispassionately.

"Yes."

Before she could respond, the first of a series of small, distant explosions shattered the eerie tranquillity and Victoria felt the blood drain from her head.

The missiles.

The microbes were out there.

CHAPTER

11:08 A.M., Monday, October 27, aboard the USS *Eutaw Springs,* off the coast of Taino

"All systems are go, sir."

Sam's head snapped up as the words came from the mouth of the sailor at one of the terminals across the room from where Sam and Marty were sitting.

"This is it," Marty whispered harshly. "I hope to fuck you know what you're doing."

We're only here because of your big mouth. Sam didn't spare him a glance but kept his eyes on Commander Duffy as his crew answered the staccato questions he fired at them. The commander had been righteously pissed off when his lieutenant had arrived back on board without Victoria. And with Cyn.

They'd only let him see her for a few minutes and he'd nearly fallen over at the sight because, Jesus, she looked bad, like she had been rode hard and put away wet. Dopey on drugs and hugging him with one arm, half crying and half moaning all sorts of nonsense about boats and foam and seagulls. It had been tough to leave her like that, but he had to get back to the command and control center. Since then she'd had X-rays taken and had gone into surgery. She wouldn't be conscious until the excitement was over.

That was probably a good thing or she'd want to be in the middle of it.

Sam could feel the tension in the room rising until it finally spiked when Commander Duffy gave the order to release the first torpedo.

The sonar images showed the tube racing through the water, then its abrupt disappearance. It was as if everyone in the room held their breath and waited in suspended animation until the first report came back seconds later.

"Strike."

Other calm voices from around the room called out their results.

Sam was really only concerned with one result, and his eyes were glued to the monitor in front of him. When the numbers on the screen began to change, he felt himself go limp.

"There's no spike in the methane readings," he murmured and looked at Marty, who seemed about ready to pass out.

"What does that mean?" the commander barked.

"It means we haven't opened a new fissure. It's the best news we could have at the moment, sir."

Several more minutes passed with hardly a word being said in the room. At one point, Sam felt his hand begin to tingle and looked down to see it curled so tightly that his knuckles were white. Unclenching it, he returned his attention to the screens.

The order was given to fire the second torpedo, and then the third, and Sam didn't think it was possible that the room could have gotten any quieter than it had the first time, but it did. Even the equipment seemed to stop making noise.

The strength of the second concussion knocked out one of the sensors, and the sudden extreme turbidity in the water confused a few of the others. Overall, it took longer this time for meaningful readings to register and, to Sam, the wait seemed endless. When solid information finally started to become available, it was announced in hushed voices.

"We scored a hat trick, sir."

"The abyssal floor has been penetrated."

"Seismic readings indicate there's slight lateral movement."

"Dr. Briscoe? Do you have anything?" the commander asked.

"Yes, sir." Sam took in a hard breath and pointed at the screen. "The volume of methane in the water column is decreasing," he said in a voice gone hoarse with emotion. "And the water density is increasing."

As Sam watched the monitor, the numbers next to the notation for methane were dropping rapidly.

"What does that mean? Did we seal the rupture?" Commander Duffy demanded.

He shook his head. "It's too early to tell. But something closed part of it, anyway."

"Then let's deploy the microbes."

There wasn't much excitement in the room when that first microbe-filled torpedo burst, because there was nothing to watch blow up. *No flash and no bang,* as he'd been warned, but Sam thought he would nearly lose his cookies anyway at the thought of it.

"Dr. Briscoe."

Sam had to give his head a little shake before he could focus on the man in front of him, who was watching him curiously through half-squinted eyes. "Yes, Commander?"

"We're going to deploy the missiles now. Would you like to watch from the bridge or would you like to remain here?"

The sight of all that water was a sight Sam was willing to forgo, especially in his current condition. "I'll stay here, sir. Thank you."

The commander nodded and then the hum in the room resumed immediately. Sam's attention was torn between watching the slowly changing numbers on his monitor and the real-time images on the monitors across the room. The day was sunny and clear, with a nearly cloudless sky. It was a perfect day in a tropical paradise.

Except for the deadly plume of methane and phyrruluxine that was killing everything in its widening path.

"Systems ready, sir."

"Dr. Briscoe, do you have anything to say?"

Oh, hell. Sam looked at the commander, wondering if he meant something like a prayer. *As if I could think of one now.*

"Uh, bombs away. Sir."

The commander and a few of the officers surrounding him smiled. "That's what the flyboys say, son. Air force."

Sam mumbled his apologies as low laughter erupted from a few corners, and the tension in the room dropped for a moment until the countdown to firing the first microbe-laden missile began. The missile was gone in a blink, the stream of smoke behind it the only evidence it had been fired. Seconds later one of the monitors captured the visual of it shattering in mid-air.

"Take that, you son of a bitch." Marty's muttered words seemed almost a shout in the heady quietude of the room.

The firing sequence was repeated four more times, with the missiles streaking along different trajectories so as to disperse their payloads at different places and levels in the toxic plume.

When the last one had fired and its shrapnel had been lost from view, the commander turned back to look at Sam. "Not bad figuring for a landlubber."

Sam's smile was a bit shaky, but broad and genuine. "Thank you, sir."

"What now? How long before we know anything?"

"At least an hour, sir. Probably a lot longer. Even with the diminished rate of methane coming up through the water column and the dispersal of millions of microbes, it's going to take a while before the atmospheric readings start showing any changes."

The commander nodded and then left the room, as if his presence had been just a routine visit. Sam, on the other hand, couldn't have stood up if he'd wanted to. His kneecaps were shaking like they had a mind of their own, and his heart was fit to give out.

He slumped back in his chair and closed his eyes. And hoped like hell that this madness worked.

11:15 A.M., Monday, October 27, Taino

"What the hell is that?" Dennis demanded, looking, as Victoria was, at the slim lines of white smoke streaking across his sky.

"The Americans devised a plan to close the rupture

on the seafloor and launch missiles into the methane plume."

"How dare they— Who gave them permission—"

"I did," Victoria said bluntly, so bluntly that he swung his head to look at her, his eyes full of outrage.

"You had no right—"

"Yes I did. Somebody had to fix what you did."

"What I—"

"Shut up, Dennis," she snapped and spun away from him. She wasn't a violent person, but she knew if she remained within reach of him, she'd end up slugging him. And she'd enjoy it.

Victoria stalked a few yards away and then turned back to face him. "Your precious dennisium made the methane dense. It's changing into phyrruluxine, Dennis. It's turned into a murderous cloud of gas that's killing people and animals everywhere it goes. Those missiles are full of microbes that eat methane."

"That's insane. They have no right to do that to the atmosphere," he shouted.

"Whether that's insane remains to be seen. And you had no right to do what you did, either."

"Victoria, how can you say that? You were part of—"

"Yes, I was, Dennis. I fell for your very convincing madness. And I'm going to be paying for it for a long time," she muttered. "Now stand up. Are those tanks full? You'll need full ones. We're going back to the boat. We can continue talking there."

"What boat? I'm not going anywhere," he snarled. "And you shouldn't be here, you disloyal bitch. I know it was Micki who sold me out, but apparently you have, too. You go back to the Americans and tell Winslow Benson he can shove those missiles up his presidential ass. This is *my* island and that's *my* sky. And *I'm* going to fix what I started."

"You can't fix anything, Dennis," Victoria said tiredly, the strain of the last few days and the exertion of the hike to the bunker suddenly weighing her down. "The atmosphere is irrevocably altered. The microbes are the only thing that can possibly help the situation, and even that's an incredible long shot."

"That's what you think," he said. Before either she or Tommy, who'd holstered his weapon but remained on alert, could move to stop him, Dennis sprinted to a point near the edge of his trail of combustibles. Pulling a Taser from a holster on his thigh, he fired at the first propane-soaked book.

Victoria and the officer were knocked backward as the jungle exploded with an unearthly roar and a blinding flash. Flames raced along the line of books and burst into the dry undergrowth.

Landing hard on her tailbone, the heavy tanks slamming into her back, Victoria let out an ungodly bellow of pain and fell onto her side to catch her breath. Opening her streaming eyes a split second later, she blinked and saw Dennis spin to face her from across the clearing. His eyes were wide with excitement, his face was split with a grin full of victory. His fists pumped the air as if he'd won a prize.

"This is *my* island, Victoria. *Mine*. I told you I'd fix it," he shouted above the roar of the inferno. "You should have believed me."

He's insane.

Her entire torso was screaming in pain at the slightest movement, but she made herself ignore it as she inched her hand toward the gun at her hip.

She'd stop him. Whatever she had to do, she was going to stop his madness.

Before Victoria could slide the weapon from its holster, the fire licked out at the empty propane tanks Dennis had carelessly tossed too near the beginning of his trail. The trace fumes leaking from the tanks ignited with a concussive force that knocked him off his feet.

Victoria watched in horror as Dennis flew into the air and landed in a heap on his back—on top of the air tanks he still wore. She could hear his labored gasps.

He was still alive.

"Tommy, we—" She looked across the clearing to where he'd been standing. A smear of blood trailed downward along the wall of volcanic rock. Tommy lay slumped at the base of it, his head tilted forward onto his chest. Blood was gushing from the back of his skull. He wasn't dead already, but he would be soon.

It's just me.

Fighting against the driving pain, Victoria pulled herself to her knees. She crawled to the backpack Tommy had dropped and grabbed it, then moved as quickly as she could toward the entrance of the bunker. She was reaching for the door handle when, from the corner of her eye, she saw the flames lick out in the light breeze, sending a shower of sparks into the air near Dennis. One landed too near the broken valve on one of the air tanks still strapped to his back. Less than a second later, the tanks that had kept him alive while he worked exploded in a ball of fire, and Dennis truly became one with his island.

Shaking and sick to her stomach, Victoria pulled open the bunker door and crawled inside.

11:19 A.M., Monday, October 27, aboard the USS *Eutaw Springs*, off the coast of Taino

"Holy Mother of God." The words burst out of the otherwise silent sailor seated next to Sam near the head of the table and all heads turned to look at him. A split second later, following the sailor's gaze, everyone in the room swiveled to look at the large screen at the end of the room.

The jungle on the northern end of Taino had exploded into a fireball. Fire raced through the jungle in a snaking path, then leaped outward from the cliffs and bowed to the ocean's surface like some sort of hellish rainbow. Flames were shooting into the sky and the wind was whipping the line of fire toward the open sea like breath from an angry dragon. The forested area was slowly, completely becoming a conflagration as the flames spread outward from its initial line into the heavy vegetation.

Sam knew that every uniformed person in the room was combat-hardened, so it didn't surprise him to note that they were watching the footage with the same degree of interest that he would watch a football game. It was obvious they'd seen plenty of large-scale destruction in their time. This might not be much more than a bit of unexpected excitement for them.

Marty, the only other civilian there besides himself, wore an expression of utter shock. Sam forgot his nausea as he watched the wildfire burn with a sense of something close to wonder.

The phone on the table rang instantly, jarring everyone from their silent awe. Sam had a feeling he knew who it was.

After a brief, monosyllabic conversation, the commander put the call on the speakerphone.

"Dr. Briscoe, this is Lucy Denton. I assume you're watching the footage of Taino. What's that fire going to do to our microbes?"

"Ma'am, I don't know. It's going to get some of them. Depends on how far from it they are," he replied, still feeling slightly dazed from everything that had happened in the last few minutes.

"Is there any benefit to keeping this fire burning? Is it a short-term solution? Will it burn off the methane as it comes out of the water?"

"Well, yes, but—" he said haltingly.

"That's all I need to know. When do we put it out?"

"That plume rising from the water will burn out on its own when the concentration of methane goes below the combustible level. But if it reaches the part of the plume where the phyrruluxine is forming—"

The tongue of fire was arcing outward in some places and licking higher in others, but all the while it kept snaking steadily through the sky toward the shore, following the invisible flow of methane. Without warning, a huge, magnificent fireball burst in midair, with flames in every shade of red and orange rushing in all directions, like an exploding star.

Seconds later, a line of the blaze surged outward from the still-burning center. As if it were the devil's own comet heading toward the west, its tail a glorious banner of thrashing fire, the streak of fire ruptured the holy blue of the sky.

It seemed to Sam as if the world had split open and Hell was making itself welcome.

"Never mind," he said faintly, light-headed with disbelief as he watched the screen.

He heard Lucy mutter something, then she said, "Was that the phyrruluxine?"

"Yes, ma'am."

"Now what, Dr. Briscoe?"

Sam shook himself but couldn't tear his gaze from what was happening on the screen. "The good news is that between the microbes and what we did underwater, there should be less methane in the atmosphere, which means the formation of phyrruluxine should stop. The other good news is that phyrruluxine burns hot but fast. Unfortunately, it's goin' to ignite everything in its path 'til it burns out, Ms. Denton. If I was you, I'd start prayin' it doesn't reach the Keys."

"Thank you, Dr. Briscoe. Commander Duffy, please liaise with other ships in the region to get that fire on the island under control."

The line went dead and the room burst into a flurry of activity.

Sam remained in his chair, dazed, watching the fire.

11:42 P.M., Monday, October 27, aboard the USS *Eutaw Springs*, off the coast of Taino

The rest of the day passed in a blur. Cyn came out of surgery and Sam was told she would be kept pretty doped up until the morning. The fire on the island had been put out by early evening and Victoria and her cache of hard drives had been rescued shortly thereafter. Lucy Denton had arrived some time around eight-thirty. Sam and Marty had been in debriefing sessions with teams of naval investigators and other feds since after lunch.

Now it was nearing midnight and, craving whatever peace could be found aboard a ship built for war, Sam found himself up on deck standing next to Victoria. She was in a wheelchair and on some strong pain meds for the cracked tailbone and broken ribs she'd suffered, but she was still fairly lucid, if not downright loose compared to the other times he'd been in her company.

Both of them were beyond exhausted but too wired to sleep.

"That has got to be the strangest thing I'm ever going

to see in this lifetime," Sam murmured, knowing it was an understatement.

The phyrruluxine had burned itself out before it reached land, and the methane drift had diffused to below a combustible concentration. The only evidence that the pipeline was still open and the methane was still rising to the surface was an eerie plume of flames that rose from the sea and reached into the sky like a torch from the underworld. It was beautiful and terrifying. A funnel of fire, it rose straight out of the water, then bent gently to undulate in the sky, changing direction with every eddy of air and flaring occasionally.

"I wouldn't count on it," Victoria said dryly, her words ever so slightly slurred. "It's a strange world out there, Sam. And it's going to get more strange."

He gave a silent laugh. "I suppose it will."

A long silence ensued.

"How long did you live down here?" he asked.

"Eleven years," Victoria replied. "It's going to take a while to absorb the fact that it's all gone. I mean, for the last ten years—everything we did was about the habitat or the mining. The people I knew. And now everyone and everything is just . . . gone."

"What's going to happen now?"

"I'm not sure. I had access to everything except Dennis's long-term plan of succession," she said with a shrug. "He kept that to himself. Probably to avoid giving anyone ideas. But I'm sure he also expected to live forever."

Sam rubbed a hand over his chin, idly wondering if he should just grow a beard. He'd developed a good head start on one. "Who do you suppose is going to take over?"

Victoria smiled sleepily. "I'd be very surprised if it was anyone other than Charlie Deen. He's known Dennis for ages, and Dennis trusted him."

"Dennis trusted you, too, didn't he? Maybe you're it. Just like playing tag."

"That's cute, Sam, but it wouldn't be me. Dennis put people into categories, and I wasn't in that category."

"Because you're a girl?" he asked lightly.

"Because he thought I could sell him out," she replied bitterly. "For all his genius, he didn't know people very well."

He leaned down to rest his forearms on the railing in front of him, then turned to look at her. "You wouldn't have? You were that loyal?"

She had a sad smile on her face. "Yes, I was. Until he accused me of betraying him. That's when I realized how stupid I'd been."

"So will you stay here if Charlie takes over?"

"He might order me to, or put me under house arrest again if I say no," she replied wryly. "After all, I'm still a citizen of The Paradise of Taino. And it was a paradise. Then again, Lucy might decide to throw me in prison after she picks my brain. I'd get ten years of hard labor, and spend all of it decrypting Dennis's files."

"Seriously, what will you do now?"

Victoria took in a deep breath that obviously hurt, and met his eyes. "I don't know. I haven't considered doing anything else in a long time. I thought I'd be here for a few more decades." She paused. "Between you and me, I only accepted Dennis's offer in the first place because of the commute. It's a well-kept secret, but I'm really lazy at heart."

He laughed and she replied with a smile.

"Seriously, as long as I have my computers nearby,

I'm fine. I like my little cocoon. I suppose I'll have to find another one. If anyone will hire me."

Sam paused for a minute. "Computers and cocoons, huh? Sounds a lot like academia. Maybe you should become a professor."

"Of paranoia? I didn't know they offered that as a major these days."

He glanced away. "You'd be surprised. Hey—" He stopped talking and pointed, speechless, toward the plume of fire. Or where it had been a few moments ago.

"It's gone," he whispered, his eyes going wide. "Tell me if I'm hallucinatin', Vic. Is it still there and I'm just not seein' it?"

"If you're hallucinating, Sam, then I am, too."

He grabbed her wheelchair by the handles and practically ran all the way to the elevator that would take them both up to the bridge. He was pressing buttons before the doors closed, and rushed off it as soon as the doors opened.

With admirable restraint, Sam stood outside the door of the ship's command center and asked for permission to enter. The commanding officer on the shift, a lieutenant they hadn't met earlier, introduced himself and invited them in.

"I'm real sorry, sir," Sam said. "I know you're busy, but I had to see it from here to make sure I wasn't seein' things. It's gone, isn't it?"

The officer nodded, grinning. "Looks like it. That's pretty impressive, Dr. Briscoe. We're getting the satellite data now. The readings started dropping about half an hour ago, and now this."

"What's 'this'?"

The lieutenant shrugged. "Our sonar array picked

up some shifting still going on down on the seafloor. There's still a lot of turbidity, which is causing some background noise, but the analyst thinks it might be shifting sediment. The fire going out seems to support that."

A sailor turned from her place at a workstation. "Sir, the sensors are showing a rapid rise in the water density."

The lieutenant walked over to her area and looked at the numbers on her monitor, then turned to look over his shoulder at Sam with a grin. "Looks like you just became a hero, Dr. Briscoe."

CHAPTER

11:42 A.M., Monday, October 26, one year later, Miami, Florida

Victoria Clark turned away from the stunning view of downtown Miami's skyline. Urban settings would never be her first choice for a work environment but this one wasn't so bad. The late morning autumn sun was lending the heavy city air an otherworldly shimmer and beyond that the Atlantic sparkled just as beautifully as it had through the window in her office on Taino.

None of it mattered, though. She wasn't going to work here.

She turned back to face the three people in the room. None of them were seated, which didn't surprise her, and only one of them was smiling, which also didn't surprise her.

"You haven't told me yet why you chose me," she said coolly. "I pled guilty to three federal offenses and was pardoned. That still makes me a convicted felon. Hardly the reputation you want lurking on your letterhead. And such nice letterhead," she finished, running a finger over the letter that lay on the desk in front of her.

"Do you like the office?" one of the men asked.

"Of course I like the office. I even like the décor."

"And the job description?"

"I like that, too," she conceded. "And the money, and the benefits. Don't trouble yourself itemizing it. I like it all." She shrugged. "I want to know why me."

"We need you, Victoria." The woman folded her arms in a way that was too familiar and leveled a look at her. "Do you want us to beg?"

Victoria cocked her head. "You know, I think I do. More than a little. In fact, I'd like to see you grovel, Lucy."

Lucy Denton didn't lose her cool, didn't even roll her eyes. She just started to laugh.

"You talk to her, Sam. She always liked you best," she said and crossed the room to the low sofa and sat down.

"Come on, Vic. It will be like old times," Sam said hopefully.

Victoria looked at him, not hiding her incredulity. "Old times? Are you *insane*? Those old times weren't good ones, Sam. I nearly got killed. Lots of other people did get killed. I saw people get killed *in front of me.*

That does not qualify as the good old days in my book, Sam."

"But we saved the world, Vic. That was a good time. Maybe we can do it again." He shrugged and spread his hands. "Terrorism is a growth industry. We're part of the antidote."

There was nothing for Victoria to do but laugh. "You're all nuts. Thank you for the offer, but no. I don't like high-rises. I like sitting in a dark room looking at a bright screen, preferably at sea level."

"You can do that for us. And work from wherever you want to."

She bent to pick up her briefcase from the floor and winced as a hot needle of pain shot through her lower back, then straightened. Putting a note of finality in her voice, she addressed all of them. "No, Sam. Lucy, Tom, thanks for the—"

"Victoria, I wasn't kidding. We do need you. Not just any computer wizard. We need *you*." Lucy stood up and walked back to the desk, where she flipped open a manila folder that Victoria hadn't even noticed.

Lucy slid out a slim stack of papers marked TOP SE-CRET and pushed it across the smooth mahogany surface. On top was a full-color aerial photo of an island with a familiar outline and topography.

Victoria went still, her heart flipping in her chest. She looked up, her gaze moving from Sam to Tom and coming to a stop when she met Lucy's eyes. "That's Taino."

"No, actually, that's Ellen Island, home to the Atmospheric Research Center, which is the United States' newest, most secret installation for weather-based weaponry research and development," Lucy replied silkily.

"This is what you need me for?"

"We've been contracted to design and implement security—physical, digital, chemical, the whole she-bang," Tom responded. "Much of what was there when Dennis Cavendish died is still in place. We get access to all of it."

"But Charlie—" Victoria shook her head as if to clear it. "Charlie Deen is president of Taino now. He succeeded Dennis. No one disputes it. He's recognized internationally. I've spoken with him."

"That's old news, Vic. Charlie resigned and retired," Lucy said.

"What do you mean he resigned? He was president of a country," Victoria sputtered, looking from one to the next.

"Charlie Deen has been a CIA case officer since he graduated from college some time in the early seventies and Dennis Cavendish was the first and only asset he handled. Did a hell of a good job at it, too. It's made Charlie somewhat of a legend in the agency," Lucy said. "So after all the dust settled, Charlie quietly handed Taino over to the USG and here we are. Ellen Island. What more do we have to throw at you, Victoria?"

"You'll have your old commute back," Sam said with a grin.

Her brain reeling, Victoria felt herself settle slowly into the chair behind her, heard her briefcase hit the floor with a thump. After a few moments, she looked up at Lucy. "Full partner?"

"On the letterhead."

"And I can live on Ta—on the island?"

"In your old cottage, if that's what you want. Although the new condos they're building are pretty nice," Lucy admitted.

"No more secrets?"

"Don't push your luck."

Victoria shook her head and smiled at the three of them. "I hope I don't regret this. When do I start?"

The hurricane is a killer: Category 7

BILL EVANS
AND MARIANNA JAMESON

CATEGORY 7

A huge disaster is brewing: the biggest, strongest storm in recorded history is headed right for New York City. But this hurricane isn't natural—and only two people have a chance to stop the storm before it devastates the entire population.

978-0-7653-5671-0

tor-forge.com